36

A Novel

D1526303

DIRK
PATTON

Dirk Patton

Published by Voodoo Dog Publishing, LLC

2824 N Power Road

Suite #113-256

Mesa, AZ 85215

Printed in the United States of America

First Printing, 2016

ISBN-13: 978-1523865093

ISBN-10: 1523865091

Table of Contents

Also by Dirk Patton 7

Author's Note 9

1 11

2 29

3 35

4 43

5 53

6 62

7 74

8 83

9 95

10 104

11 112

12 120

13 132

14 141

15 150

16 158

17 176

18 186

19 199

20 209

21 223

22 240

23 245

24 255

25 268

26 281

27 291

28 308

29 323

30 336

31 349

32 367

33 381

34 393

35 401

36 411

37 422

38 431

39 439

40 453

41 461

42 468

43 481

44 495

45 507

46 522

47 534

48 543

49 555

50 567

51 573

52 586

53 602

54 616

55 624

56 635

57 642

58 649

59 671

Also by Dirk Patton

The V Plague Series:

Unleashed: V Plague Book 1

Crucifixion: V Plague Book 2

Rolling Thunder: V Plague Book 3

Red Hammer: V Plague Book 4

Transmission: V Plague Book 5

Rules Of Engagement: A John Chase Short Story

Days Of Perdition: V Plague Book 6

Indestructible: V Plague Book 7

Recovery: V Plague Book 8

Precipice: V Plague Book 9

Anvil: V Plague Book 10

Merciless: V Plague Book 11

Dirk Patton
Other Titles by Dirk Patton:

36: A Novel

Author's Note

Thank you for purchasing 36.

I know, you're probably thinking "Oh crap, not another time travel book." Can't say that I blame you. That's why I hope you'll find that what I've created is something a little different and unique. Is there time travel? Yes, there is. But I believe I have achieved a good balance where the reader's enjoyment of the story isn't dependent upon their ignoring the theories posited by Einstein that prove movement through time is impossible.

At its heart, 36 is the story of a lost soul who is miraculously given a second chance at life. He's not a bad man, but he's made some bad choices and very nearly paid the ultimate price. Now, he gets to start over. Just like most of us wish we could at some point in our lives.

So sit back, tighten your seatbelt, and enjoy the ride.

You can always correspond with me via email at dirk@dirkpatton.com and find me on the internet at www.dirkpatton.com and follow me on Twitter @DirkPatton and if you're on

Facebook, please like my page at
<u>www.facebook.com/FearThePlague</u> .

Thanks for reading!

Dirk Patton

February 2016

2

1

Trevor Solverson sat watching the massive white and green ferry slowly approaching Pier 52 on Seattle's waterfront. The sun was shining brightly, gleaming off the boat's bridge windows. It was another glorious, summer day in the Pacific Northwest, the waters of Puget Sound almost impossibly blue under a clear sky.

All around, cars and trucks were lined up, waiting to board the ferry which would transport them across the open waters of the Sound to Bainbridge Island. It was a short trip, taking no more than 35 minutes from dock to dock, and was one of the busiest routes served by the Washington State Ferry System.

Trevor lit a cigarette with nervous hands, his stomach threatening to rebel. He was only 17 years old, and this would be the first time he had ever driven a vehicle onto one of the giant ferry boats. For that matter, it was the first time he had driven beyond the confines of his well-heeled, suburban neighborhood other than a few practice runs with the truck. Navigating the maze of freeways and surface streets had been nerve-wracking for the young driver. Doing it in choking traffic had nearly caused him to abandon his quest.

But he had persevered. Pushed on. Reminded himself that he was doing God's work. That thought had given him the strength to calm his racing heart and keep pushing the large GMC truck to the docks. Now he sat, waiting as vehicles began streaming off, sweating as he puffed on the cigarette.

He jumped when his cell phone rang. Snatching it out of a cup holder between the seats, he sent the call to voicemail after checking the caller ID. His mother. Checking the time, he realized why she was calling.

Trevor was on probation with the King County Juvenile Court, and she had probably tried calling him on their home phone. He wasn't supposed to be anywhere other than at his residence. No school. He'd been expelled after what his father had taken to calling "the incident".

He hated that term. Somehow it trivialized not only what he'd done, but everything he believed. It made light of not only him, but the global cause in which he'd eagerly become a soldier. A holy warrior.

Four months ago, halfway through his Junior year of high school, Trevor had slipped out of the house late one night. Sneaking through his quiet neighborhood, he had arrived at his school in the early morning hours. Getting in had been simple. A window in one of the classrooms had broken easily, and he was able to reach through and unlock it.

Trevor well knew the consequences of what he was doing. Both of his parents were attorneys. His father practiced criminal defense law, and his mother was part of Microsoft's legal team. He'd heard enough stories at the dinner table about his father's clients to understand the gravity of the crimes he was committing.

However, he was only 17 and knew that if he were caught, he'd only have to face the authority of the juvenile court system. Short of a violent felony, he was confident he'd receive nothing more than a slap on the wrist and could look forward to his record being sealed when he turned 18. If he was caught.

So, he'd moved through the dark hallways, heading for a large vestibule where visitors first entered the school. There, in a glass display case, was a well worn, leather bound bible. It had belonged to Luke McRedmond, the founder of the small city of Redmond in which Trevor lived. The bible, and several other historical artifacts, were on loan to the School District from the Historical

Society as part of an effort to foster interest in local history among the younger generations.

The presence of the bible, and several writings that prominently featured bible verses, were offensive to Trevor. He had been raised in a Catholic home, but his parents were far from devout Christians. Mass on Easter and Christmas Eve had been enough for them. As he'd grown into his teens, Trevor began searching for something more than what his parents professed to believe.

Like most middle and high school aged children, he turned to the internet. Surfed the plethora of websites devoted to different religious beliefs around the world. For a time, he had identified with Shinto, then quickly moved on to Buddhism. But neither sparked his interest the way Judaism did.

For several months, he devoured everything he could find about the history of the Jewish race and faith. Accounts of the holocaust fascinated him, and as he learned about the formation and struggles of the nation of Israel, he decided he wanted to emigrate and become a Jew.

During his searches for information on how to accomplish this, he began to encounter sites and chat rooms with posts calling for the destruction of Israel and the annihilation of all Jews. At first, he was horrified and incensed, but for some inexplicable reason, he continued reading the hate-filled comments.

He didn't understand the hostility being directed at such a small group of people and continued reading led to posting questions. Many of the regular visitors of the forums responded vehemently, calling him a Jew-lover and an infidel. He was taken aback at the level of animosity directed at him for simply asking questions.

Dismayed, he had decided he would no longer visit the antagonistic websites, but there was one man who responded articulately and with extreme courtesy. Who answered his questions with articulate responses. Who made a compelling case for the injustices perpetrated on the Muslim faith by the nations of Israel and the United States.

They began chatting each night. Abdul, Trevor's new online friend, patiently explained the plight of the Palestinian people. He slowly and meticulously drew the impressionable teen into his dialogue before carefully branching out into examples of how the United States and its Western Allies were keeping their boot firmly on the throat of the Arab world. Within a month, they were having profound discussions about Allah and his prophet Mohammed.

Trevor withdrew from his friends and family as he learned the *truth* of what Christianity and Judaism were really all about. He soon came to believe that all of the death and despair in the world that he saw on the internet was coming directly from US foreign policy. A policy intended to hold down any non-Judeo-Christian nation.

Two months after meeting Abdul in the chat room, the man suggested they move their conversations to a more secure forum. Trevor had a Play Station and happily began using it to communicate. They would both login to an online game at the same time each evening, speaking directly over headsets connected to the gaming consoles.

Trevor was surprised the first time he heard Abdul's voice. With nothing more than movies and caricatures to draw from, he'd expected a voice with a thick, Middle Eastern accent, direct from central casting. The last thing he'd been prepared for was a man with a quiet, cultured tone who spoke with an upper-class English accent.

They talked for hours at a time, Abdul telling him about the struggle against the Great

Satan. Trevor reveled in the stories, envious of the soldiers fighting in the global jihad. Soon, with Abdul's help, he was praying multiple times a day, prostrating himself before Allah as he faced Mecca.

Desperate to belong to a cause, any cause, and wanting to impress his new friend, Trevor had decided to take action when the McRedmond bible went on display at his school. If he had told Abdul what his plans were ahead of time, he would have been talked down, but he had wanted it to be a surprise.

As he entered the vestibule, he noted with disgust that a small spotlight was on, illuminating the bible in its display case. Prepared for the moment, he'd brought along a hammer, a homemade stencil and a can of fluorescent red spray paint. Smashing the glass, he put the cardboard cutout in place and carefully began working. He sprayed the words "Allahu Akbar", first on the cracked leather binding, then on dozens of the internal pages of the antique book.

Finished, he looked around and smiled when he saw the large American flag standing in the corner. Pulling it down, he spread it across the floor. Using the stencil, he defaced it with the same words across the white stars on the blue field. He was standing over his work, mumbling a Muslim prayer under his breath when a brilliant flashlight spotlighted him. He hadn't known the school had a silent alarm system.

Several court appearances later, and the calling in of multiple favors by his father, Trevor was placed on supervised probation until his 18th birthday. He was expelled from school, and his parents had taken away his computer and Play Station. Most 17-year-olds would have been lost without the conveniences of modern technology, but he retreated into his newly acquired faith.

With approval from his parents and his probation officer, Trevor had enrolled in an online high school. While they thought he was showing promise, he had no intention of wasting another moment on education. He simply wanted to regain access to the internet so he could talk to his friend.

Abdul had praised Trevor's jihadist's zeal but cautioned him to do nothing more without first discussing it. For several weeks he continued the young man's indoctrination, finally steering the conversation to the rewards given to the faithful in the afterlife. Never having had a girlfriend, Trevor was enthralled with the thought of a small army of virgins, waiting just for him.

The discussions were carefully steered until Abdul felt Trevor was ready. When he began talking about an opportunity to strike at the heart of the infidels, Trevor's heart had beaten faster. His breath had grown short in excitement. Abdul elegantly painted a detailed portrait of what the young man's life would be in Paradise. When Trevor asked how to make it happen, the hook was set.

Events accelerated rapidly from that point. Abdul, a top recruiter for the Islamic State, was in Turkey. On his alert, one of numerous teams spread across North America were quickly moved to the Seattle area. Trevor was given a method to contact them upon their arrival.

Late at night, he climbed out a window and slipped into the dark forest that backed to his parents' property. Five minutes later he reached a quiet residential street where he was picked up by a man no more than a year older than him. The driver didn't speak. Staying below the speed limit, and carefully obeying every traffic law, he drove from the quiet enclave of Redmond to a commercial area of nearby Kirkland.

There, in a rented warehouse, Trevor was introduced to the team leader and got his first look at the white GMC box truck. It was only a couple of years old and adorned with signage for a plumbing company that he'd never heard of, complete with a local phone number and website.

"The number works and will be answered if anyone checks and the website is good, too," the team leader assured him.

They spent the next two hours driving around the Kirkland area, getting on and off the freeway. Trevor was behind the wheel, getting the feel for the vehicle. The team leader sat in the passenger seat, giving him occasional tips and repeatedly cautioning him to hold his speed slightly under the legal limit.

He was driven home and was back in his room before the sun came up. As he had been leaving the warehouse, each of the members of the team had hugged and kissed him on the cheek. His heart swelled with pride as he realized they were showing him great respect.

"Be ready in two days," the team leader had said in parting. "Allahu Akbar!"

Trevor responded in kind, smiling all the way home.

Time had passed slowly. The hardest thing for Trevor had been containing his excitement. But he was an only child, and both of his parents were busy. They didn't notice anything different about him. Daydreaming to pass the time while he waited, he briefly considered killing them before he left.

It would have been simple. Take one of the large, razor sharp knives from the kitchen and creep into their room while they were sleeping. He knew his mother would be out from her nightly Ambien. His father would be sleeping soundly from the five Scotches he consumed after dinner each evening.

They wouldn't even know he was there until the blade slipped home. But he had taken Abdul's warning to heart. No further actions without discussing them first and Abdul had gone dark leading up to the strike. He had explained it was necessary to maintain operational security, which was something Trevor thought he understood from watching spy movies.

He had let them live, but still experienced a visceral thrill in the knowledge that he could have ended their lives so easily. On the day of the strike, they left for work early. Each was already on their cell phones before they were out the door. As soon as it closed, he texted the number given to him by the team leader. Even though he was assured they hadn't drawn the attention of the infidels' law enforcement, he had been instructed to only send a simple, generic message of "whassup."

If he had received any response, it would have alerted him that the operation was compromised, and he should do nothing further until contacted by Abdul. He didn't get a response. Three minutes later, the same car and driver from before pulled to a stop in front of his house.

When they arrived at the warehouse in Kirkland, the team leader met Trevor at the door and greeted him warmly with hugs and a kiss. Leading him inside, he steered the young man past the truck's cargo area to the driver side door.

"Drive carefully, just like we practiced. The GPS is already programmed and will take you to the dock. Here is money for the ferry toll."

Trevor accepted the cash and shoved it into his pocket. He was nervous and excited, his heart threatening to beat out of his chest. The leader recognized this and with a smile, placed his hand on Trevor's shoulder.

"You are a young lion, and I am very proud of you. Abdul sends his love and respect. Would you like to pray before you depart?"

"But it's not the right time," Trevor said after glancing at his watch.

"It is permitted for lions going to battle," the team leader said, nodding his head. "Allah will be pleased."

Trevor nodded, and together they spread prayer rugs on the concrete floor and faced to the east. As they prayed, Trevor felt his mind begin to calm. His resolve harden. By the time they were done, he was steady and prepared to go.

"Turn the headlights on high beam to activate the trigger," the team leader said, making sure Trevor understood the instructions.

With additional praise, and reminders to drive carefully and not draw attention, the young Lion of Redmond had been sent on his way.

Trevor's phone rang again, his mother still trying to reach him. He declined the call and powered the device down. There was nothing he had to say to her, and nothing she had to say that he wanted to hear.

All around, people had returned to their vehicles and started the engines in anticipation of loading onto the ferry. The last arriving car drove down the ramp and onto the dock, turning sharply and heading for the exit from the terminal. Traffic control cones were repositioned, and a worker waved the first two lines of waiting vehicles forward.

They moved, each line being sent to opposite sides of the cavernous car deck. Most of the passengers were locals and drove quickly to the locations indicated by crew onboard the ferry. There were tourists who didn't know the routine, slowing the process. They were quickly identified by the men and women overseeing the loading and given assistance in getting their vehicles to the correct location.

Trevor glanced in the mirror at the sounds of a commotion. A person on a motorcycle was driving between two rows of waiting cars, and the drivers were shouting and honking their horns at the severe breach in etiquette. He watched long enough to satisfy himself it wasn't a cop on the bike, then the line ahead began moving.

The truck was already in gear, Trevor holding it in place with the brake. As soon as the Toyota sedan in front of him moved, he lifted his foot and followed. The GMC's tires thumped as he drove onto the ferry. The Toyota was directed towards a ramp that swept up to a second car deck, but the crewman pointed at Trevor and waved him to continue straight forward into an area at the center of the large boat.

He pulled to a stop behind another box truck and shut off the engine. The nerves from earlier had turned to steely resolve. He had the power of life and death over everyone on the ferry. He was in complete control. He was a Lion!

The loading continued for several minutes. Vans and medium sized trucks filled the empty spots around the GMC. Soon, the vessel was fully loaded. Trevor jumped slightly when the Captain sounded the horn in preparation for sailing. Moments later, the diesel engines roared, and he could feel their power vibrating the floor and seat of the truck.

Checking his watch, Trevor noted the time. He had been instructed to turn the high beams on three minutes after the ferry left the dock. The huge boat would still be within Eliot Bay, and close enough to the Seattle docks for the disaster to be clearly visible from shore. Maximum exposure, the team leader had called it.

Looking around, Trevor noted a crewman working his way through the parked vehicles. He was looking inside each one, pausing to speak with the driver of a truck parked two hundred feet in front of the GMC. After a moment, the crewman stepped back, and the driver climbed down.

"They're making drivers leave their cars," Trevor thought to himself, panic threatening to take over.

He checked the clock again. One minute gone, two to go. The crewman said something else to the truck driver, who headed for a stairwell that led to the passenger decks above. Trevor's eyes flicked to the clock as the crewman continued his inspection, approaching quickly.

Two minutes gone. Trevor's eyes were glued to the crewman now, watching as the man drew closer. He knew when he was spotted, knew it was only moments before he would be told to get out of the vehicle.

Reaching out, he moved the turn signal lever forward until it clicked, setting the headlights to high. On the dash was a small switch that rotated left to right with three stops. Off, Parking, and Head Lights. He placed his hand on it and checked the clock, prepared to turn the knob the instant the clock showed three minutes had passed.

The crewman paused at the window of the box truck directly in front of his, speaking with another driver who had stayed with his vehicle. Trevor checked the clock. It wasn't time.

He jumped and turned to his right when the passenger window suddenly exploded in a shower of glittering safety glass. A woman with long, red hair met his eyes. She was wearing a black leather jacket and black helmet with a clear face shield. The motorcycle rider that had been cutting in line on the dock!

She thrust something into the cab. A gun! Her eyes were locked on his. He saw the weapon come in line with his face, the round hole in the muzzle appearing huge. Her finger was on the trigger. All Trevor could think to do was turn the switch. So he did. His brain registered a flash from the muzzle of the weapon, then nothing else.

When the GMC's light switch was turned on, electricity from the battery flowed through the vehicle's wiring harness, but was diverted before reaching the bulbs behind the lens covers in the front grill. Newly installed wires carried the current to a series of blasting caps embedded in sixteen, 55-gallon drums riding in the back of the truck.

Each drum contained the same explosive that had been used by Timothy McVeigh to bomb the federal building in Oklahoma City in 1995. In total, the bomb driven by Trevor was the same size, weighing in at slightly over 7,000 pounds.

The resulting explosion tore the ferry boat in half and shattered windows all along the Seattle waterfront. In less than five minutes, the two halves of the devastated vessel sank beneath the calm waters of Puget Sound. Over two thousand passengers and crew lost their lives.

2

"She failed," Ian Patterson said when the large clock reached zero.

The clock was mounted high on a wall, above a set of thick windows that looked into a small chamber. A round dais was in the middle of the room, surrounded by curved glass panels. A powerful, low-frequency hum came from beneath the floor.

Turning, Patterson studied a muted TV screen. It was tuned to CNN and playing a live image of multiple Coast Guard ships spread across Seattle's Eliot Bay.

"Run the security footage from the docks," he said to another technician. "If she got close, we should be able to see it now."

The TV screen went dark for a moment, then the image of Pier 52 in Seattle appeared.

"There's the truck," FBI agent William Johnson said.

Patterson nodded, intently watching the display. He watched as more cars arrived and took their place in the queue to board the ferry.

Soon the arrivals had completed driving off the boat and boarding began.

"There!"

Agent Johnson pointed at a slight figure on a motorcycle, slowly driving along the back of each row of waiting cars. The rider was dressed all in black with a matching helmet, pausing at each space between the rows and looking for something.

"How are you sure?" Patterson asked without turning his attention away from the screen.

"She loves bikes, and I recognize her hair."

Patterson didn't say anything, looking closer at the thick mane of red hair that spilled from under the helmet and down the rider's back.

"She sees the target," Johnson said softly.

On the screen, the rider cranked the big bike to the side and accelerated down a gap between two lines of vehicles. Arms were being waved by the waiting drivers and both men cursed softly when they saw the door of a pickup open suddenly, directly in the motorcycle's path. The rider barely stopped in time, a large man wearing jeans, work boots and a flannel shirt stepping out and yelling at her.

By the time she had backed up and squeezed through a gap between two cars, the white GMC had disappeared onto the ferry. Weaving through moving vehicles, the rider chased the truck. Had to stop when a Port of Seattle police officer stepped in her path and waved a minivan onto the boat ahead of her. He held her there until all of the vehicles were loaded, then motioned that she could proceed. She gunned the engine and shot forward, going out of sight aboard the ferry.

The two men stood watching the footage as the ramp was retracted. Moments later, the large vessel began moving away from the dock. Patterson started a stopwatch function on his phone and looked at the timestamp on the screen. It was departing two seconds later than the last ten times he'd watched the same video.

"She caused a two-second variation," he said.

"How?" Johnson asked.

"Maybe the commotion during the loading. No way to know," Patterson said.

The two men continued watching as the boat sailed out of the visual frame of the security camera. Workers adjusted the traffic cones and cars began to queue up, preparing for the arrival of the next ferry. When the stopwatch reached 2:54:38, the camera violently shook, the image blurring when the lens shattered from the pressure wave of an explosion.

"Almost six seconds early," he said, turning to look at Agent Johnson.

"She affected it."

"Yes, it appears so. But, she didn't stop it. And the window has closed."

"Don't forget she just died," Johnson said, anger creeping into his voice.

"So did more than 2,000 other people," Patterson said, turning fully to face the FBI agent. "And frankly, I'm a little concerned that you may have grown too close to the asset. Should I be worried?"

The two men stood staring at each other for a long pause. Patterson noted a light sheen of sweat forming on Johnson's forehead. His ebony skin gleamed brightly under the fluorescent lights.

36

"She was a person, not an asset. If you'd ever had a conversation with her, you'd know that," Johnson said.

"It's not my job to have conversations with assets," Patterson said sternly. "It's my job to make sure this project does *its* job. Perhaps you are having too many conversations with them."

"You know better than that," Johnson said.

"Very well. Just make sure you keep your relationship with the next asset strictly professional. What is his status, by the way?"

Johnson took a deep breath, calming himself before answering.

"My team is in place to interdict. They should have him in hand within twenty-four hours and will bring him directly here."

"I'm not happy about this one," Patterson said.

"We don't have a choice. He's all that's available," Johnson replied, earning a curt nod of agreement.

"Get started on him the moment he arrives. We're non-operational until he's ready.

The way things are going in the world, I'm afraid it won't be long before we need him."

Agent Johnson nodded, turned and left the room.

3

It was hot. Not the kind of heat you find in Georgia or Alabama in the summertime, where the air is so thick with humidity you feel like you could cut it with a knife. This was desert heat. Everything was baking under a relentless sun, directly overhead in a perfectly cloudless sky.

Randy Palmer removed his sunglasses long enough to mop the sweat off his face, keeping his eyes averted from the harsh glare. With them back in place, he turned a slow circle to survey the area. He was not surprised when he didn't see anyone moving. When it was this hot, people didn't venture outdoors if they didn't have to.

"Car coming," Jim Olsen, the man on duty with Randy, commented.

Randy turned and looked in the direction Jim was facing. From the glass-walled guard tower, he had an unobstructed view of a four-year-old Buick. It was slowly approaching on a narrow strip of asphalt, bordered on each side by twenty-foot-high, security fencing.

The access road ended at the first of two gates that controlled entry into Arizona's maximum security prison in Florence. At the other end was state highway 79. The highway had broad, gravel shoulders where it passed the penitentiary.

On the near side, a dozen news vans were haphazardly parked. All of them had their antenna masts high in the air. Reporters smiled for the cameras in between dashing into the air conditioned interior of the vehicles to cool off.

On the far side, close to twenty cars were parked nose to tail, sunlight glinting off their windshields. The people who had arrived in them stood on the blistering ground, waving signs at passing motorists and shouting slogans. They were protesting the impending execution of a death row inmate. Five state police cruisers sat idling, keeping watch, the troopers inside not leaving the air conditioning unless there was a problem.

Randy glanced down to make sure the guards at ground level had spotted the approaching vehicle. They had, one of them already standing in the sun to meet the driver.

"It's his attorney," Jim said, leaning close to the glass for a better view. "Looks like he's got some others with him, too."

"Probably family," Randy said, returning his attention to scanning the area for anything out of place.

"Family? What do you mean?"

Jim was new, hired only a few months ago. The State of Arizona hadn't put an inmate to death since he had begun working at the prison.

"The inmate's family," Randy sighed. He knew this had been covered during Jim's initial orientation. "They have the right to witness the execution. Not sure why they'd want to, but some show up."

"Right," Jim said. "Now I remember. That's some fucked up shit. Why would you want to see someone you care about die?"

Randy shrugged his shoulders and made another scan of the barren prison yard. All of the inmates were on lockdown, which was normal in the hours leading up to an execution. There shouldn't be anyone moving that wasn't wearing a guard uniform. He didn't see a soul, just dun grey buildings and glittering, silver fences.

Below, the guard had finished checking the IDs of the people in the Buick. He motioned to his partner and the outer gate trundled open. The attorney pulled through, stopping with his front bumper several feet from the next portal. As the outer gate rolled shut, another guard with a dog on a short leash appeared.

The man walked the dog around the perimeter of the vehicle. Randy didn't know if this was the team that sniffed for firearms and explosives or the drug K9. They were randomly rotated, so visitors never knew what to expect.

The dog finished without alerting, the guard walking him away as a second man appeared with a pole mounted mirror. He stuck it under the Buick and quickly checked for contraband, then briefly spoke to the driver. The hood and trunk both popped open a moment later, and he thoroughly inspected each area of the car.

Search complete, he slammed the lids closed and nodded to an unseen guard who controlled the inner gate. With a loud buzz, it began opening. The attorney waited until its motion had stopped before slowly driving through to a parking spot near the visitor's entrance.

The attorney stepped out, opening the rear door on his side of the Buick. An attractive Hispanic woman in her early-30s got out and followed him to the passenger side. Together, they assisted an elderly couple out of the car.

Once everyone was standing, and the ladies had adjusted their clothing and hair, they moved slowly across the pavement to a heavy steel door.

Inside, they were met by the assistant warden. He expedited another check of their IDs and the issuance of visitor badges. He didn't speak to the family, and only to the attorney when necessary. Accompanied by two guards, the group moved through three security checkpoints before arriving at the viewing room.

The assistant warden escorted them inside. The room was small and terraced downwards, like a movie theatre. Every seat had an unobstructed view of the large window at the front that was currently covered by a heavy curtain. When it was open, the execution chamber would be revealed.

The viewing room was full to capacity, but four seats in the front row had been reserved for the new arrivals. As the group slowly made their way down an aisle, all eyes watched them in silence. Family members of the victims occupied over two-thirds of the available chairs and had been warned ahead of time that any disturbance would result in their removal and arrest.

Several women cried softly, the only other sounds coming from the pens of a handful of reporters as they documented the event in their notebooks. No recording devices were allowed in the viewing room. The small contingent of press scribbled furiously as they attempted to describe the feel in the room as the inmate's family entered and took their seats.

After several minutes, a muted tone sounded. There was a hum of electric motors and the swish of fabric as the curtain opened. The lights were low in the viewing room. The stark execution chamber on the other side of the window was brightly lit.

Robert Tracy, convicted murderer, lay strapped to a gurney. His eyes were closed, and he was barely conscious, the result of a sedative he had requested. A display that monitored his vital signs was connected, his heart rate and blood pressure clearly visible. IVs were in place in each arm, the tubing snaking up to bags of saline. Each was also connected to a large red tube that disappeared into the wall, out of sight of the witnesses. The red line would introduce the lethal combination of drugs that would end Tracy's life.

Two guards and a doctor stood behind the gurney, the warden to the side, near the glass. A member of the clergy was noticeably absent, having been refused by the inmate. After nearly a minute of silence, the warden reached out and pushed a button that activated a speaker in the viewing room. The speaker was connected to a microphone in the execution chamber.

"Robert Hammond Tracy," he intoned. "Having been found guilty of the crime of capital murder, you have been sentenced to death by lethal injection."

The younger woman who had accompanied the attorney sobbed loudly as the words were spoken. The elderly woman slowly put her arm around her shoulders and pulled her close. The warden continued.

"Before your sentence is carried out, you may say a few brief words."

The crying woman caught her breath and looked up. Everyone's attention was riveted onto the restrained prisoner. There was a long pause before Tracy opened his eyes and lifted his head off the gurney. The window was clear glass, but due to the difference in lighting between the two rooms, all he could see was his own reflection.

"I'm innocent," he said in a drug-slurred voice.

He lay his head back and closed his eyes. The woman began sobbing again. After a brief pause, the warden spoke.

"Robert Hammond Tracy, by order of the Supreme Court of Arizona, your sentence shall now be carried out."

The warden turned off the intercom and nodded to someone that could not be seen from the viewing room. At first, it seemed as if nothing was happening. Then, the heart rate displayed on the monitor began to drop. Slowly at first, just a few beats per minute, then it quickly declined. Robert Hammond Tracy never moved, never indicated he felt anything amiss. Ten minutes later, the attending physician pronounced him dead.

4

Six Weeks Later

I woke up with a splitting headache. The kind that feels like a splinter of molten steel is being driven into your temple. What the hell was going on? Was I in the infirmary? Then it came flooding back.

The final meal. The uncomfortable visit by the Catholic Priest, who I had sent on his way. Then the small pill that had made me relax before being wheeled to the execution chamber. The pinch on first one arm, then the other, as IVs were started. The warden saying something, to which I think I responded, then darkness. I was dead!

With a sharp intake of breath, I tried to sit up. Something was restricting my movement. I couldn't see, either. Was this death? But if I was dead, why could I feel my body and the restraints that were holding me down? Why was I thirsty? Why did my face itch? And what the hell was that beeping sound? Was I just not dead yet? Was I still on the table in the execution chamber? Oh, fuck me! Please just let it be over with.

Dirk Patton

There was a sucking sound, like a door with a tight seal being opened, then a set of footsteps approached. I jumped when someone lightly touched my shoulder.

"What's happening? Where am I?" I croaked, feeling my upper lip split open as it moved.

"You're safe," a female voice said. "Just lay still. I'm going to put some balm on your lips. They're very dry."

The sound of a metal lid being twisted off a glass jar. A moment later she lightly rubbed something that felt oily onto my lips. The burning from where the upper one had cracked immediately eased.

"Who are you? What's happening?"

"You're being taken care of," she said. "Don't try to talk. Just rest. The Doctor will be in to see you in a moment."

I heard the lid twist back onto the jar. Then her footsteps began to retreat.

"Wait," I wailed. "What the hell is going on? Where am I? What happened to me?"

She didn't respond, and by the sound, I could tell her steps didn't falter. The door closed with a pneumatic hiss, and I was left alone with my thoughts and the goddamn infernal beeping. I didn't know what it was, but it was driving me nuts.

It wasn't long before the door opened again. This time, two people entered. Both were wearing harder soled shoes than what I assumed had been a nurse. And by the sound, I was guessing both were male. I didn't know how I could tell this by ear, but I was pretty sure.

"Who are you? Where am I? What the fuck is going on?"

I was shouting in a hoarse voice. Fear was leading to panic. I yanked against the soft restraints that kept my arms at my side.

"You're fine," a gentle male voice said. "My name is Doctor Freeman. You're in the hospital. You're alive and well. I'm going to touch your face now. Don't be frightened."

Despite the warning, I sucked in a breath and flinched when his fingers came into contact with my head. I didn't *feel* the touch, rather only the pressure. There was the sound of tape being pulled free. Then something that I hadn't realized was wrapped around me began being unwound.

It seemed like it took him forever to finish removing what I now thought was a bandage. Cool air caressed my skin as the last turn came off, but I still couldn't see.

"Get the lights," he said.

The other person walked away a few steps. Then I heard a faint hum from overhead. I recognized the sound light bulbs make when they are dimmed.

"There is a shield over each of your eyes," the Doctor said. "I'm going to slowly remove one at a time. Close your eyes until I tell you to open them. OK?"

"OK," I said, tightly squeezing my eyes closed.

He carefully removed something covering my right eye, reminding me to keep my lids shut. Next came the left, then a damp cloth was gently rubbed around each orbit.

"These are artificial tears," the Doctor said a moment before I felt several drops on the inside corner of each eye.

"OK, I want you to slowly open your eyes," he finally said.

Even though I was pretty sure the lights were dimmed to their lowest setting, my eyes hurt when I opened them. Blinking rapidly, I reflexively tried to raise a hand to shield them, but my restraints hadn't been removed. As I kept blinking, the drops spread out and eased the feeling of gritty sand beneath my lids.

After almost half a minute I was able to keep them open, but everything was blurry. Like looking through a fogged windshield. The Doctor leaned over me, and I could see the shape of his head but not make out his features. He held a hand up, and there was a soft click preceding a brilliant light shining in my left eye.

"I'm just checking to make sure you're healing properly," he said as he leaned closer and held the instrument only inches from my face.

"What happened?" I asked, noting the smell of garlic and cigarettes on his breath.

"Excellent," he said, ignoring my question. "Let's look at the other one."

The light moved, and when it did, the vision in the eye he had just been examining was improved. I could make out some of his features, noting a jagged scar that ran horizontally across his forehead.

"Also coming along very nicely," he declared after a long moment of peering through the instrument. "You're almost fully healed."

"Healed? What the fuck happened, doc?"

"I'll leave that to my colleague," he smiled, then quickly left the room.

The door hissed as he pulled it closed behind him. A shadow moved to my right. I turned to look at an imposing figure standing a few feet away.

"I'm going to turn the lights up a bit," a baritone voice said as the figure stepped to the wall next to the door. "Let me know if they're too bright."

A moment later, panels set in the ceiling flared. I had to squint and blink as pain stabbed into my skull. The discomfort passed quickly, and I looked up at the man as he dragged a chair across the floor and sat down next to me.

I was lying in a bed. Looking down, I saw that each wrist and ankle was locked in a leather band that was secured to the metal frame. A broad strap was across my chest, preventing me from sitting up.

"How are you feeling?" He asked.

I turned and stared at him, realizing for the first time that he was a black man. Even seated, he was a huge presence in the room. He wore a nicely tailored suit and had highly polished wingtips on his feet. Despite the clothing, I could tell that his size was muscle, not fat. I suspected that underneath the expensive finery, he looked like he'd been carved from a slab of obsidian. He smiled when our eyes met, perfect teeth flashing brightly in contrast to his skin.

"I'm FBI Special Agent William Johnson," he said.

"Feds? What the fuck is going on and where am I?"

"You're in a very special government facility."

He leaned back and crossed his legs, taking a moment to ensure the crease in his trouser leg was straight. A microscopic piece of lint was flicked off the sleeve of his suit coat. Then he looked back up at me.

"I'm supposed to be dead," I said, fear and anger causing me to raise my voice. "What the hell have you done to me?"

"Done to you? I haven't personally done anything to you. But if you mean all this? You're alive and receiving the best medical care available. Isn't that enough for now? If it wasn't for me, you'd be rotting in the grave."

"Why?"

"I'm not ready to tell you everything. Yet. You're alive because I intervened. A powerful cocktail was substituted for the lethal dose of chemicals you were supposed to receive. Synthetic poisons based on the chemical composition of the venom of the puffer fish. They suppressed your heart rate and respiration to the point that you appeared dead, even to the medical equipment and the prison medical staff.

"My team intercepted you at the mortuary after you were released to your family for burial. You were retrieved. Another body was placed in your casket. As far as the world knows, Mr. Tracy, you are dead and buried."

I stared at him in shock for a long moment. Maybe I really was dead, and he was the devil, just fucking with me. Or maybe my brain was reacting to the lethal injection, and I was hallucinating this whole thing in my final moments on Earth.

I didn't want to believe him. I had accepted my impending demise. Prepared for it emotionally. Whatever game was being played, either by him or my drug addled mind, was just plain cruel.

"I assure you, this is all quite real," he said, as if he could read my thoughts. "You're not dead. I'm not playing some sick game."

"Where did you get another body to replace me?"

I asked the first thing that popped into my head.

"That's not important," he said. "All you need to know is that your funeral has already happened, and you are officially no longer among the living."

We both turned when the door opened. It was a nurse, probably the same one from earlier, but I had no way of knowing. She carried a small, white plastic tray with two filled syringes resting on its surface. Stepping into the room, she paused and looked at Agent Johnson as if asking permission.

He stood and scraped the chair across the floor back to its original position. Then spent a moment adjusting his jacket, so it hung perfectly on his powerful frame.

"We will talk further. You have some healing to do."

"Tell me now!" I shouted, panic at all the unanswered questions coursing through me.

"All in good time," he said, already heading for the door.

The nurse stepped forward and placed the tray on a small table next to my bed. Cranking my head around I could see her reaching for an IV bag and noticed the tube connecting it to my arm for the first time. Beyond, a small machine monitored my vital signs. It was where the damn beeping was coming from.

She removed the cap from the first syringe. After cleaning a port on the IV tubing with an alcohol swab, she inserted the needle and depressed the plunger. A feeling of warmth began to spread through my body and by the time she inserted the second needle my eyes were closed, and I was rapidly drifting towards unconsciousness.

5

I woke up feeling better than I did the last time I could remember being conscious. My head didn't hurt and my face only itched a little. The worst thing was my fingers. They were burning like I'd grabbed something out of the oven without using mitts to protect myself. I started to raise my right hand to examine it, but it came up short against the restraints.

Fuck! I'd forgotten about that little detail. Looking around in frustration, I noticed that the IV was gone as well as the electronic equipment monitoring my vital signs. That left exactly two objects in the stark hospital room. The bed I was strapped to and the chair the Fed had sat in when he'd talked to me.

And just exactly what the fuck was he talking about? I was dead and buried? The FBI had cooked the execution, so I survived, then spirited my unconscious body out of the mortuary? Why? What the hell did they want with me? I'd been in prison for ten years, three of those on death row. I didn't know anyone or anything, so what the hell did they want?

The door opened with its sucking sound, and the nurse walked in carrying a small tray.

She saw me looking at her and smiled. I smiled back. She was a good looking woman. At least, I think she was. I hadn't seen a lot of women in the past decade. Right now they all looked good to me.

"Hi," I said.

"Good to see you awake," she said, pulling the sheet off my body and placing the tray on the bed next to my hip. "It's time to remove your catheter."

She opened a package and withdrew a pair of latex gloves.

"My what?"

"Catheter," she said, snapping the wrist of one of the gloves into place. "It's a tube in your bladder, so you don't have to get up to urinate."

"I know what the fuck it is," I said. "Just didn't know I had one."

She raised the hem of the hospital gown until my privates were exposed and I could see the large, white tube protruding from the end of my cock. I stared in surprise for several moments. I'd had no idea.

"This will be uncomfortable," she said, attaching an empty syringe to part of the tubing and drawing what looked like water into it.

"What the hell is that?" I asked, starting to freak out a little.

"The catheter has a small bulb inflated with sterile water that keeps it in place. OK, now hold still and this will be over in a second."

She grasped me with one hand, the tube in the other, and smoothly pulled it out of my body. It didn't hurt, just felt really odd and left me with the sensation that I needed to take a piss. Quickly and efficiently she bundled everything up and stuffed it in a plastic bag.

"While you're down there," I said, grinning at her.

She just smiled, patting my leg before pulling the gown down and covering me with the sheet. Gathering everything, she opened the door and nodded at someone I couldn't see before disappearing down the corridor outside my room. A moment later the Fed walked in and closed the door.

He was dressed similarly to the last time I'd seen him. Immaculate suit and tie, shoes gleaming in the overhead lighting. He carried a round mirror in his right hand, holding it up as he approached.

"Take a look," he said, holding it so I could see my reflection.

Only it wasn't my reflection. It was someone I didn't recognize. I was stunned into silence, staring at the man I didn't know.

"What the fuck?" I was finally able to mumble. Then, "what the fuck did you do to me?"

I shouted the last but was unable to take my eyes off the mirror. Everything was completely different. My brow, my cheekbones, nose, chin. Fuck me but even my eyes were a different color. The only thing they didn't change was my hair, which I'd let grow in prison. It was full and thick, hanging well below my shoulders. At the moment, it was in a tight ponytail.

"Your new face, Mr. Whitman," the Fed said.

He took the mirror away and dragged the chair across the floor until it was next to my bed. He sat, crossing his legs at the knees. After he adjusted the creases on his pants, he looked up and smiled at me.

I was in shock. Mind whirling, but unable to comprehend what I'd just seen. What I'd just heard.

"What?" I sputtered.

"Your new face and name," he said calmly. "Whitman, Joseph Ryan. Born in Germany on Ramstein Air Base to an Air Force Captain named Gloria Whitman. Unknown father. You moved around, growing up, as your mother's career advanced. You attended school at various Air Force Bases around the world until graduating from high school. Your mother retired soon after you graduated, then passed away three years later. You have no siblings. Your mother having been an only child, you have no living family."

"What the fuck are you talking about?" I shouted, yanking my arms against my restraints.

"Relax, Mr. Whitman. If you get too agitated, I'll have to call the nurse to administer a sedative."

"Fuck you, relax! What the hell have you done to me?"

My blood was pounding in my ears, and if I could have gotten free, I would have attacked the FBI agent. He most assuredly knew that and just sat there smiling at me. I wanted to wipe that fucking smile off his face for him.

"Shall I continue, or should I call the nurse?" He asked after nearly a minute of watching me struggle against my restraints.

"Why don't you just get to the point, you fucking..." I paused. "Asshole!"

"Going to say nigger, weren't you?" He asked as easily as if he'd inquired about the time of day.

"Fuck you!" I said, after a beat.

"That's quite all right, Mr. Whitman. Human nature in fact. You can't hurt me with words. Worse men than you have tried. If it helps you accept what I have to tell you, by all means, call me whatever names you like."

I lay there panting from exertion and anger. He remained completely composed, watching me as if he didn't have a care in the world. For the first time since waking, I began to feel in control of my emotions. Perhaps I was starting to process what was being said to me, or maybe it was just the drugs they'd used to keep me unconscious were wearing off.

"Very good," he smiled. "I'll continue, then. Now, where was I?"

He tilted his head back and looked at the ceiling as if trying to remember what he had been talking about. I recognized it as an affectation. This guy was sharp. He remembered precisely what he had been saying.

"Ah, yes. No living family. So after high school, you took a job working in the oil fields in west Texas. You stayed there for nine years before relocating to Dallas where you began driving a truck for a freight company. Traveled all over the US, but mostly in the southeastern portion of the country. That's what you are now. A long haul truck driver."

"Are you going to get to the point anytime soon? I'm not a fucking moron. You pulled me out of an execution chamber, changed my face, and now you're sitting here telling me all about a life I never had. You're creating a new identity so I can do something. What? You want someone killed? Is that it?"

"We'll get to all that in due time," he said. "First, let's talk more about you. The other you. The one who was on death row."

"What the fuck is there to talk about? If you could pull enough strings to get me out, then you must have my record."

I had forced myself to calm. To start thinking. Planning. All I needed was to get free of my restraints. He might be a big, strong fucker, but I'd had the best fighting education in the world. A maximum security prison. You either fought and won, became a bitch, or died. I had avoided options two and three for ten years.

"Records are so impersonal, but yes. Let's start there."

He reached into his jacket for a folded sheaf of papers. Plucking a pair of wire-framed reading glasses from another pocket, he placed them on his face and peered at the file.

"Up until eleven years ago you'd never had a run-in with the authorities. Then you decided to smuggle drugs across the border from Mexico. Twelve kilos of heroin, to be exact. You must have thought you were going to make it, too. Made it almost all the way to Casa Grande, Arizona before a sheriff's patrol spotted you crossing the desert.

"They intercepted you. Chased you for a couple of miles across some pretty rough country until you broke an axle. But you didn't give up. You fought when they tried to arrest you. Killed both deputies and kept running. They arrested you that evening, outside your apartment. Everything correct so far?"

He cut his eyes up and looked over the top rim of his glasses. With a sigh, I nodded.

"You were tried and convicted of drug smuggling and the murder of two police officers.

Your trial lasted three years, then the penalty phase another four. It's not in your file, but as I recall, your defense attorney found some irregularities with the prosecutor's evidence and the trial kept getting delayed as the lawyers filed motion after motion.

"Eventually, your conviction was upheld, and you were sentenced to death for the murders. But here's what I find fascinating. Your claim of innocence. That you were coerced and only defending yourself. That was never presented to the jury. I was in the viewing room for your execution. Do you remember your last words?"

"I'm innocent," I said, staring hard at him.

"Tell me about it," he said, folding the file and removing his glasses.

6

Eleven Years Ago

It was hotter than hell. Just as hot as I remembered it being in Iraq. At least here you didn't have to worry about being shot just for walking down the street. Well, at least not too much. But it was fucking hot.

Late afternoon. June in Phoenix, Arizona, 118 Fahrenheit in the shade. The sidewalk had been baking in the sun since five in the morning. I could feel the heat even through my thick-soled work boots. The bus I'd just stepped off of pulled away from the curb, a thick cloud of stinking diesel fumes swirling around me and sticking to my sweat soaked clothes.

Another day of roofing rich peoples' houses was done, and all I wanted was to go to my shit hole apartment and take a cold shower. But I knew that wouldn't happen. When the weather was this hot, the water coming out of the tap was warmer than the ancient water heater could get it in the winter.

I trudged the six blocks home, thankful for the long sleeves and hat that protected my skin from the blistering sun. Reaching the run-down complex that was the best I could afford, I gave a wide berth to the two buildings where a minor street gang lived.

Los Locos was what they called themselves. They were minor thug wannabes, but that didn't make them any less dangerous. They ranged in age from barely thirteen to their jefe, who was no more than 25. I was pretty sure there weren't any of them that hadn't done time either in juvenile detention, county jail or state prison. And they always traveled in packs of at least five.

I'd never had a problem with them as I made a concerted effort to mind my own business and keep to myself. Somehow, I'd managed to stay off their radar. Still, I always made sure the Russian pistol I'd taken off a dead insurgent in Iraq and smuggled back into the country was loaded and easily accessible in my pack. Not that I wanted a fight, but sometimes assholes don't give you a choice.

One advantage of the summer heat was that none of them were outside as I entered the apartment complex grounds. They would be holed up inside, most likely still sleeping. Just like vampires, they would start emerging when the sun went down, and the temperature changed from fucking hot to just hot. By then, I planned to be showered, have had dinner and be settled in for the night.

Keep my head down and don't draw attention. That's how I'd survived two tours as an infantry soldier in Sandland, and that's how I was surviving now. Do my job, earn my paycheck and maintain a low profile. I was scheduled to start school in the fall, attending a local community college as part of my benefits for four years of service. Nothing was going to fuck that up.

Unlocking the two deadbolts that secured my front door, I stepped into what felt like a furnace. Air conditioning was expensive, and I couldn't afford to leave it running while I was at work. Stepping over to the undersized unit that had been cut into an exterior wall, I turned it to maximum cool, and the ancient thing wheezed to life.

Sometime around midnight, it might drop the temperature in my small place to the low 80s. If I was lucky. I turned on a couple of thrift store fans to get the hot air moving and dropped my pack on the cracked and peeling kitchen floor. Taking a barely cool beer from a fridge that was probably older than I am, I looked around my castle while taking a deep pull on the bottle.

Water stained ceilings. Old, single pane windows, that did little to keep the heat out. Lots of cracks and a few holes in the drywall and a ratty carpet on the living room floor that was some indeterminate shade of shit brown. All things considered, it was a palace compared to some of the hovels I'd seen in Iraq.

Finishing my beer, I dropped the bottle in a waste can and headed for the shower. Even hot water would feel good as it washed the sweat, dirt and grime of the day off my body. Turning the faucet on, I stripped while the pipes in the wall banged as water began flowing.

For several minutes it ran brown, giving off a stink I'd never been able to identify. Slowly it cleared, and after nearly five minutes it was good enough that I was willing to step under the sputtering stream. My head was shaved for the summer, so it didn't take long to lather everything up and get clean.

Stepping out of the shower, naked and dripping, I thought about Monica. She lived two doors down and was the only person I knew in the complex. A couple of years younger than me, she was a single mom who worked at the local Walmart.

Dirk Patton

With her looks, she could have made a lot more money doing any number of things. But she was a good girl. Until we got in bed, then she was a freak. Smiling, and still naked, I opened the bathroom door, intending to call her and see if she wanted to roll around in the sheets for a couple of hours.

My place is small, and the bathroom is close to the kitchen where I'd left my pack with a cheap prepaid cell phone inside. I was focused on thoughts of Monica's naked, brown body and reached the kitchen in two quick strides. Looking down, I froze when I realized my bag wasn't where I'd left it.

Looking into the living room, I saw two large men standing between me and the door. My pack was resting on the floor next to one of them. He was holding my Makarov pistol in his hand.

"What the fuck?" I said, eyes locked on the weapon.

There was an illegally short shotgun under the kitchen sink, and if he started to raise the pistol in my direction, I was going to dive for it. Then I spotted the shotgun, unloaded, lying on my threadbare carpet by the far wall.

"Hi, Bob!" The man holding my pistol said in a bright, friendly voice. "Come on in and take a seat. We need to talk."

I was frozen in place. Naked. Caught completely off guard in my own home. The old anger swelled in my chest, but I tamped it down. At the moment, I didn't have a play.

"C'mon, Bobby. We just want to talk to you. Have a seat."

The two men took a step away from each other. The one who hadn't spoken moved his hand until it was resting on a holstered pistol. I took a closer look, seeing the OD Green cargo pants and tan desert boots. The web belts with identical holstered pistols. Coyote tan t-shirts. Cops. What the fuck? I hadn't done a goddamn thing.

"What do you want?" I asked without moving.

"I told you, Bob-O. We want to talk to you. Now quit standing there with your dick waving in the breeze and sit down. Please. That monster is making me nervous!"

He laughed, his partner smiling. I looked at them for a few more beats and not coming up with any bright ideas, decided to do as they asked. Maybe I'd be able to get close enough to make a grab for one of their weapons.

As I moved into the cramped living room, the talker took a couple of steps back to keep space between us. His partner did the same, putting his back against the front door and keeping his hand on the pistol butt. I sat on the couch, tucking my very flaccid cock between my legs and pressing them together.

"Now, you may not like what we have to say, Bobberino. But you'd better behave. We can just as easily shoot you as not, and with this illegal shotgun, no one's going to give a shit about you. So, you keep your ass glued to that couch and listen. Understand?"

He smiled, reminding me of a shark. After a moment, I nodded. My mind was swirling. Wondering what they wanted. Trying to come up with a plan to get to a weapon. But for the moment, at least, I was fucked.

"So here's the deal. Your little brother was working for us, and he really and truly screwed the pooch. That's why we're here."

"I haven't seen him in months," I said.

Internally, I groaned. Tim, my little brother by five years, had always been into shortcuts. Easy money. Any way he could get it.

He'd work harder to pull off some harebrained scheme than I would roofing mansions in Scottsdale in the summer heat. But it was on his terms, which seemed to be all about not punching a clock or answering to a boss.

My parents had spent a small fortune on lawyers for him over the years. They finally cut him off while I was on my second leisure cruise in Iraq. I'd seen him a couple of times since I'd been home.

The first, he had been flush with cash, driving an Escalade and playing the big shot. Eight months later he'd shown up at my door in the middle of the night. He begged for money to pay a loan shark who was threatening to ventilate his kneecaps with a power drill.

Against my better judgment, I'd cleaned out a savings account I'd had since junior high. He'd taken the money with promises of repaying me every penny, with interest. That was almost a year ago, and I hadn't seen or heard from him since. But he was still my little brother.

"What the fuck did he do?" I asked.

"Well, Roberto. Let me tell you. He was working for us. Was supposed to bring some merchandise from old Mexico to us. But he was stupid. Instead of just picking it up and making the delivery, he took a side trip after collecting our property. Stopped at this little whorehouse in Nogales. Got his rocks off, then got in an argument with the proprietor who wanted more dinero. Seems little brother has some rather unconventional tastes. They accommodated him, but he didn't have the cash to pay for the premium add-ons.

"An argument turned into a fight, and he wound up as a guest of the Mexican government. Real shit hole prisons they got down there, too. Hot and cold running syphilis. Guys that don't care what the hole they're fucking is attached to. Gangs. Rats as big as dogs. Last I heard, little Timmy had become a bitch, being pimped out by a real nasty piece of work that runs the prison from the inside."

"Why are you telling me this?" I asked with a sinking feeling.

"Well, I was just getting to that, Booby Boy! You see, we were able to get in and have a little chat with the Timster. He stashed our stuff before going to get laid, and he won't tell us where it is unless we get him out and back home to the good ole US of A. Now ain't that a bitch?"

"So why don't you get him out? What are you guys? Cops? Feds? Maybe Border Patrol?"

"See, I told you this one was smart!"

The talker turned to his partner and grinned. His partner nodded. He looked back at me and smiled even broader.

"Well, to answer your question, Robby my man, nothing happens south of the border unless there's cash changing hands. The prison warden wants a lot of American greenbacks to spring your baby bro. More than we've got."

"I ain't got no fucking money," I said. "Maybe ten bucks in my wallet 'till payday next week. What the fuck do you want with me?"

"We got to thinking," he said. "What we need is for little Timmy to tell someone where he stashed our shit. Then that someone could retrieve it and bring it to us. Once that happens, we'll have the cash to pay off the warden.

"But he won't tell just anyone. No, he doesn't trust us. What we need is someone he will trust. That's where you come in. You go see your little brother and convince him to tell you where he hid our property. Then you get it and bring it to us. You do that, we give you the cash to get him out."

He stood there watching me, smiling like a TV preacher who's just revealed the secret to guarantee your place in heaven.

Dirk Patton

"You think I was fuckin' born yesterday? Why the hell would you give me money to get my brother out once you've got your drugs?"

"Whoa, Bobster! Who said anything about drugs?"

"That's the only thing that gets smuggled *in* from Mexico that's worth anything, asshole. Quit fucking talking around it and just call it what it is. You guys are cops of some kind, and you're dirty. You're drug dealers or working for drug dealers. I think I'll pass, but thanks for letting me know where Tim is."

"Now, that's not exactly going to work," he said. "You see, there's more than one thing we can pay the warden down there to make happen. One is to release little Timbo. The other is to have one of the gangs slit his throat. And guess which is cheaper? Enough cash to get him a new smile carved into his neck? Hell, son. That's cheap in Mexico. We've got that much squirreled away for a rainy day.

"So, the choice is yours. You can do this, or you can tell us to fuck off, and we'll leave. But. If we leave, tomorrow morning we pay a visit to the warden and hand him a nice, fat envelope. Tim-Tim will be a corpse before lunch."

I wanted to come off the couch and beat these two guys to death. Part of me thought I was fast enough to pull it off. The thought must have shown on my face as the quiet one suddenly drew his weapon and held it in front of him in both hands. It wasn't pointed directly at me, but he could have it on target and fire before my bare ass made it off the couch.

7

Nogales, Mexico reminded me of Iraq. Too much so. No one spoke the same language I did, and everyone looked at me with distrust in their eyes. That didn't bother me. What did were the openly hostile looks I was receiving as I made my way through a dust-choked neighborhood.

Several times, young men who were sitting in the shade stood up and flashed guns. Challenging the gringo. Daring me. I studiously avoided making eye contact with them, keeping my gaze on the dirt road I was walking on.

The pair of cops had given me two grand in cash before they left my apartment. That and a slip of paper with a handwritten phone number. I was supposed to go to Nogales and talk to my estranged brother. Convince him that he had no choice other than telling me where the drugs were. And promise him I'd be back to get him out.

They had been gone for less than five minutes, and I was still sitting on the couch thinking when there was a knock. Expecting they had come back for some reason, I didn't bother making any attempt to cover my nudity before answering the door.

I was surprised to see Monica Torres standing there, as beautiful as ever in a lightweight sundress. She looked me up and down and smiled.

"Expecting me?" She asked playfully in thickly accented English.

Stepping across the threshold, she kissed me lightly on the lips and gently raked her long, red nails across my bare upper thigh. I tingled from head to toe, little Bob instantly responding to her presence. She came to an abrupt stop when she spotted the pistol and shotgun on the floor where the cops had left them. I closed the door, shot both the dead bolts home and moved behind her to circle my arms around her narrow waist.

"What is going on, Roberto?"

From the moment we met, she had insisted on using the Latin version of my name. I'm not sure she was even capable of uttering "Bob".

I thought about lying to her. I didn't owe her any explanations. We were nothing more than what pop culture labeled as friends with benefits. A couple of times a week we got together and satisfied each others' needs. That was it. But if that was it, why did I feel better when she was around?

"It's about my little brother."

I pulled her tight against me. Automatically she pressed her ass back against my growing erection, then paused and pushed away from me.

"What's wrong?" She asked, dark eyes full of concern.

I don't know for sure, but I think it was that exact moment when I fell in love with her. She was a good woman, and that had always been part of what attracted me to her. But the obvious concern for me, as well as someone she had never even known existed... well, it kind of melted my heart and pushed me over the edge. So I told her everything.

"Do you trust them?" She asked when I finished speaking.

By this time, we were both on the couch. Drinking the last of my beer. I was seated at an end, and she was turned sideways. Her sandals were on the floor, and her feet were on my lap, legs stretched the length of the small sofa.

"Not as far as I can throw them," I said, draining the bottle in my hand and leaning down to place it on the floor.

"What are you going to do?"

"I don't have a choice," I said, absently rubbing her smooth calves with one hand.

"We always have choices, Roberto. They may not be the choices we want, but they are there."

She turned one of her feet sideways and wiggled her toes against my limp cock. Explaining my problems had killed my desire.

"Then I guess the answer is that I'm going to Nogales. I'll get my brother to tell me where he hid the drugs, and I'll bring them across."

"You do not really believe they will give you money for your brother's release, do you?"

"No," I said. "But my parents have money. I'll talk to them when I get back. If I don't do this, Tim won't survive long enough to get sprung. They'll have him killed."

Monica looked at me for almost a minute, then drained her beer and put the bottle on the floor next to her sandals.

"Then here is what we do," she said.

"We?"

"Si. We. You need my help whether you know it or not. Manny is sleeping over at a friend's house tonight. I am going to stay here with you, and we are going to take my car and leave for Nogales in the morning. It is a four-hour drive, so we should go early tomorrow morning."

"No! Absolutely not! You are not coming with me. Way too dangerous!"

I had spoken loudly and saw her eyes immediately flash with anger. That was the other thing about her. As beautiful, smart and good-hearted as she was, she also had a classic Latin temper. She was not someone you ever wanted to try and tell what to do. Or not do. She jerked her feet out of my lap and curled them under her hips to sit forward and get in my face.

"You are a big, dumb gringo," she said, the tone in her voice warning me to keep my mouth shut. "I'm not going into Mexico with you. I have a child to think about, and no matter what I feel for you I'm not going to do something stupid and risk being taken away from him.

"But I can drive you to the border. And after you come back and deliver the drugs, you're going to need a ride home. How were you going to get there? Greyhound?"

She was right. The money the two cops had given me was enough to buy a crappy used car that would probably make the trip. Renting one wasn't an option as I didn't have a credit card. But if I did that, I wouldn't be able to pay the "fee" that would be required by the guards to let me see my brother. It would be much better if I didn't have to worry about transportation.

"Thank you," I said in a slightly meek voice.

"De nada," Monica replied, smiling once again.

"So, what exactly are those feelings for me you mentioned?" I asked, poking her a little but also hoping to hear that I was more to her than a booty call.

"Plenty of time to talk about that when you get back."

She smiled and reached behind her, pulling the sundress off over her head. She was completely nude underneath. Leaning forward, she grasped me firmly in her hand and pressed her face against mine.

"First things first, mi amor," she breathed.

I lost track of time after that. We didn't come up for air for what seemed like hours, and when I checked my watch, I wasn't surprised that it had been. It was nearly midnight. We had started in the living room, made a stop in the shower to rinse off our sweaty bodies, then had picked right back up in the bedroom.

"What time is it?" Monica asked.

I looked over at her. She was stretched out on the far side of my small bed, dark hair fanned across a pillow. Filtered light from a security lamp outside my bedroom window played off her bare skin, making it seem iridescent. Looking at her like that, I realized I could be happy lying next to her every night.

"Almost midnight."

I put my watch on the wobbly bedside table and stretched out next to her. She rolled up slightly and threw her leg across mine, resting her hand on my stomach.

"Sleep now," she said dreamily, already drifting off. "We have to leave in a few hours."

The alarm on my watch woke us at 3:45. I was groggy and thick headed from too little sleep and a marathon session of love making. Monica sprang out of bed as if she'd just had a solid eight hours of rest. It took her less than ten minutes to wash, brush her teeth and hair and slip the dress back on.

She sang something in Spanish while she got ready, low and soft. It was the first time I had heard her sing, and for a minute I stood in awe, just listening to her. Her voice was beautiful. She saw me watching her in the bathroom mirror and gave me a smile that whisked away all the cobwebs in my brain.

By four, we were in her car and pulling out of the apartment complex's parking lot. We stopped for gas at a small station just down the street. The night clerk was secure behind a thick sheet of bullet proof glass. I pushed cash through a sliding metal drawer, paying before pumping. Collecting my change, we hit the road.

We made one quick stop in Tucson to top off the tank and get coffee. The time passed quickly. We talked the whole way, each of us learning things about the other that had never come up between the sheets. The more I learned, the more I liked this strong, beautiful woman.

It took us slightly more than four hours to reach Nogales. Monica stopped in a small parking lot a hundred yards from the border crossing. I reached down between my feet and picked up the small duffel I'd brought along. Passing it over, I took her hand and looked into her eyes.

"There's a pistol and shotgun in the bag, and a thousand dollars in cash," I said. "The shotgun is illegal, so don't get caught with it. If you do, play dumb and blame it on me."

"Where are you coming back across?"

"There's a canyon about twenty miles to the east that cuts across the border. It's in the middle of nowhere. I used to go hunting in the area. No roads. Probably there. I'll call you when I'm back, maybe sooner if this shitty phone works in Mexico. What are you going to do while you're waiting?"

"Going to check into a motel so I don't get noticed just hanging around. Be careful, and come back to me."

Monica wrapped her arms around my neck and held me tight as our lips met. The kiss lasted a long time, and definitely wasn't the kind of kiss you share with someone who was just your fuck buddy. Heart lightened at the thoughts of things to come with her, I stepped out of the car and headed for the line queued up to get into Mexico.

8

It wasn't visiting hours at the prison, but that didn't deter me. Five, crisp twenty dollar bills disappeared into the guard sergeant's pudgy hand so deftly it was as if they'd never existed. He barked some orders in Spanish, and after a thorough search, I was escorted to a small room with a couple of tables and chairs.

The furniture in the visiting room was bolted to the raw concrete floor. I took a seat and looked around when the iron door I'd come through banged closed behind me. On the opposite wall was another, identical door. A window, without any glass, looked out onto a courtyard that was mostly dirt with a few struggling weeds. It was covered with heavy, iron bars set into the wall's masonry, and provided the only illumination in the room.

Overhead, a squeaking ceiling fan turned lazily, stirring the hot, dusty air. Movement caught my eye, and I looked at the window in time to see a rat poke its whiskered nose through the bars and test the air. It was the biggest fucking rat I've ever seen, and I've seen some big ones hanging around the open sewers in parts of Iraq.

Nearly an hour later, the door to my front clanged open, and a heavily mustachioed guard poked his head in and looked around. There was nothing to see other than me and the rat, which was nosing along the far wall. He withdrew, and a moment later my little brother was roughly shoved into the room.

"Cinco," the guard shouted, staring at me.

I nodded that I understood I had only bought five minutes of time with Tim. A hundred bucks doesn't go as far as it used to.

I stood as Tim walked over. He looked like hell. No, hell would have looked better than he did. He had been beaten. That much was obvious. Two black eyes. A nose so swollen it had to have been broken and not set. Bruises on his jaw and neck and one ear crusted with blood where the large hoop he liked to wear had been ripped out.

His clothes were in tatters, and he was filthy. I could smell him from ten feet away. But that didn't stop me from stepping forward and wrapping him in a hug.

"What are you doing here?" He sobbed into my shoulder.

"Trying to save your dumb ass," I whispered back. "We don't have much time.

Your cop buddies came to me. They want their shit, and if you don't cooperate they're going to pay the warden to have you killed. If I take it to them, they'll leave you alone."

"They'll never leave me alone," he said as we moved apart slightly. "I know who they are. I could testify against them. That's why I won't tell them where it is."

"Tim, listen. If I don't bring that shit across, today, you're dead. I looked in their eyes, man. They aren't fucking around. Maybe they won't have you killed at first. Maybe just peel some skin off or take your eyes. Whatever the gangs in here can do to make you talk, but these are serious guys.

"Tell me where it is. I'll deliver it. Then I'll get the money from Mom and Dad to pay off the warden and get you out of here. That's your only choice. And we've got to hurry. That guard's going to be back any minute."

I stared hard at him. Gave him the look I used when we were kids and he was being an ass about something. The look that told him he'd better do what I said or shit was going to get a lot worse. He stared back at me, bloody snot alternately appearing and disappearing in his nose as he breathed. Finally, he nodded and looked down at the floor.

"The Pink Pussy," he mumbled. "It's a whorehouse on the western edge of town. Know it?"

"No, but I can find it."

"In the back parking lot is a beat to shit Ford Ranger. Black. The shit is in a false compartment behind the seat."

His head was hanging down and he stared at the floor as he spoke. I felt for him, but at the same time, I was angry with him for having made his own mess.

"Keys?"

"Stand at the rear bumper and walk ten yards straight out into the desert. Look for a rock shaped like Texas. They're under it."

I was surprised. This was a simple, yet effective trick to not have any ties to a vehicle on you in case you were arrested. Not that it would keep some local kid from breaking out a window and hotwiring it, but it showed more cunning than I thought Tim possessed.

"Anything else I need to know?" I asked as the interior door clanged open.

"Come back for me. Please, Bob! Don't leave me here!"

The guard had walked into the room and began shouting at Tim, gesturing at the open door with his billy club.

"I'll be back for you," I said as the guard grabbed his shoulder and propelled him away from me. "I promise."

I watched him disappear through the door, the guard still yelling. When it slammed shut, I let out the breath I'd been using to contain my anger. Turning, I pounded on the exterior door. There wasn't an immediate response so after half a minute I pounded again. I was getting pretty worried, five minutes later, when I finally heard the sound of a key scrape in the lock.

The door was yanked open. The guard sergeant stood blocking my exit to freedom with his bulk. I stepped closer, wanting out of that room nearly as much as I've ever wanted anything, but he didn't budge. Just held his hand out and smiled.

With a sigh, I reached into my pocket and thumbed five more twenties off the rapidly shrinking roll of cash. I did it so he couldn't see how much I had. When I held it out, the money disappeared as neatly as the first hundred I'd given him, and he stepped to the side and made a grand sweeping gesture for me to exit.

I walked through, keeping a close watch on the club tightly gripped in his hand. If he started to swing, I was going to fight. The odds weren't good that I'd be able to overpower him and make it out of the prison's gate, but I wasn't going to willfully submit to a beat down either.

The air was hot and dusty and heavy with the stink of rotting garbage when I walked through the gate, but after being inside the prison, it tasted as sweet as a mountain meadow in spring. Behind me, I could hear the low roar of the prisoners going about their daily business within the high walls. A voice rose above the babble, screaming in pain, and it took all of my self-control to not turn and look. I just wanted the fuck away from this place.

Half a block from the prison I saw two ancient Chevy pickups parked at the curb. Their drivers were sitting on the lowered tailgate of the one in back, smoking and talking. The two trucks were as much rust as not, but all I cared about was that *Taxi* had been crudely hand-lettered in black paint on their doors.

"Pink Pussy," I said, walking up to the two men and holding a single twenty up for them to see.

One of them leapt down and dashed forward, smiling, reaching for the money. I pulled it away from his grasping fingers and shook my head.

"When we get there," I said with little doubt he understood the meaning even if he didn't understand the language.

He nodded and smiled, chattering away in Spanish as he escorted me to the lead pickup. Once I was seated, he slammed the door and ran around the hood to climb behind the wheel. The engine wheezed to life, and we were quickly rolling, a dense cloud of blue smoke hanging in the air behind us.

"Pink Pussy!" He said excitedly, smiling as he took his hands off the wheel and mimed masturbating with both of them.

"Pink Pussy."

I smiled back at him and nodded. He said something else in Spanish that I didn't have a chance in hell of understanding, then remained quiet for the remainder of the drive across Nogales.

The town isn't large and it didn't take us long. Buildings were thinning out, replaced by tar paper shacks that lined the road. Women were doing chores while children played in the dirt. I didn't see any men, and that was fine with me. If someone was going to start a problem, odds were it would be a guy, not a woman who just wanted to get her work done.

I wasn't sure what to expect, but when we rounded a curve in the dirt road I was surprised to see a relatively new building with a paved parking lot. A massive billboard fronted the street and I was amazed when I got a good look at it. It was a full-color photo of three naked women, each in a different pose that fully exposed their genitals.

Hell, not just exposed. Their genitals were the focus of the camera. Two of them were giving blowjobs; the men mostly cut out of the frame except for the important parts. The third was smiling away as she lay her back on top of a man who had his cock deep in her ass. Across the top of the billboard, in six-foot high, neon pink lettering, were the words *Pink Pussy*.

I shook my head, frankly a little shocked. Not that I'm a prude, by any stretch of the imagination. No, not even close. But my travels had been mostly limited to Arizona, then basic training in Kentucky followed by deployment to the middle east. None of these places, especially the middle east, would have ever tolerated such a public display.

Shaking my head, I pulled my eyes away from the sign and motioned for the driver to head around the side of the building. He gave me a funny look but did as I asked. At the very back was the truck. I breathed a sigh of relief that it was still there. But then looking at it, even from a distance, I could tell why no one had taken it. It made the rattletrap rust bucket I was riding in look like a shiny new Cadillac.

Telling the driver to stop, I handed him the twenty, thanked him in my clumsy Spanish and stepped out onto the hot asphalt. I stood there until he drove away, looking around to make sure no one was watching. Everything looked clear, so I walked over to the ancient Ranger and peered in the driver's window.

It was about what I expected. The seat was more duct tape than fabric and springs were poking up in several places. A battered plastic seat cover was in place for the driver, probably to keep a seat spring from doing what the guy on the billboard was doing to the girl. Half the dash was missing, exposing metal braces and wiring. The steering wheel wasn't original and appeared to be held on by only a rusty nut with some wire wrapped around it.

Stepping back, I looked over the exterior. There was not an inch of sheet metal that wasn't dented, creased, torn or rusting. The back window was shattered, nothing more than a jigsaw puzzle held together with a liberal application of duct tape. The ground was visible through several large holes in the bed where rust had eaten completely through. At least the tires were good. Not new, but still plenty of aggressive, off-road tread on them.

Moving to the back bumper, I put my butt against the tailgate. Looking straight ahead, I started pacing. Stopping at ten, I cast around until I spotted a rock that looked vaguely like Texas. If Texas didn't have a panhandle and was all smushed in from each side. But it was the right rock. When I turned it over, a small scorpion slowly crawled away, leaving a pair of silver keys embossed with the Ford oval emblem.

I walked back to the truck, looking around to make sure I still didn't have any observers. The key fit and I pulled the door open and took a step back. What the fuck was that smell? Wet, dead dog? Maybe three-week-old vomit that's been baking in the sun? Throw in a good healthy piss and let it heat up in a black vehicle in the sun and you'd have the sickening miasma that assaulted me.

Taking some deep breaths, I slid behind the wheel and started breathing through my mouth. Glancing at the gear shift, I pushed in the clutch, knocked the lever into neutral and turned the ignition. To my great surprise, the engine started easily and immediately settled into a smooth idle. I revved it a couple of times and it responded instantly.

"Smuggler's Truck," I thought to myself. "Make it look like an absolute piece of shit, but the part that counts, the drivetrain, is maintained and will get you where you need to go."

Leaving the engine running, I stepped out and was immediately grateful for the fresh air. Leaning in and holding my breath, I tilted the seat back forward and began searching for the hidden compartment Tim had said was there. It took me twenty minutes of banging around and pulling panels off with a rusty screwdriver that was in the glove box, but I found what I was looking for.

Twelve packages, neatly wrapped in plastic and thoroughly taped, were crammed into the small space. After counting, I replaced them and hammered the panels back into place.

Fishing my cell phone from my pocket, I pulled out the slip of paper with the number the cops had given me. Punching it in, I held the phone to my ear and listened to it ring.

"You'd better be calling with good news, Bob-O."

I recognized the voice as belonging to the talker from the previous evening.

"I've got it. Still down south. Where do you want it?"

"Chuichu. Few miles south of Casa Grande. South of Interstate 8. Can you find that?"

"Yes."

"Get on Indian Route 15 heading south. One mile after you pass the turn off for Indian Route 53 you'll see a pair of hills on the right, about a mile from the pavement. There's a dirt track leading to them. We'll be on the back side in four hours. Don't be late."

He hung up without saying anything else, and I shoved the paper and phone back in my pocket.

9

The truck drove as well as any vehicle I had ever driven. Not that I've had many cars, but none of them had looked as bad as this one did. The brakes were solid and quiet, and the clutch was crisp. It shifted easily as I drove out of the parking lot and onto the road back into town. I slowed for the first of hundreds of pot holes, but the suspension had apparently been worked over as I barely felt the bump.

Both windows were down, and I was seriously considering smashing out the rear glass just to get more air flow. Whatever they'd done to cause the smell was a stroke of genius. If someone did decide the battered hulk was worth stealing, they'd certainly change their mind as soon as they got the first whiff of the interior.

Glad that Monica and I hadn't stopped for breakfast, I drove slowly across Nogales. Nearer the center of town, in what passed for a commercial district, the roads were paved. At least, I think that's what they were. There was something covering the powdery desert soil that resembled asphalt, but it was so rutted and crumbled that I wouldn't have bet on it. Outside that couple of square miles, I didn't drive on anything that wasn't just a bladed track.

Dirk Patton

Fortunately, the truck handled it well. The engine was strong and other than the odor, it wasn't bad to drive. Soon I left the main area of town. Now I was on a perfectly straight and level track of dirt that was lined on both sides by shacks. Many appeared to be nothing more than heavy cardboard cobbled together around a few boards. Just like the other side of town leading to the whorehouse, women and children were everywhere. The few men I saw were old, sitting in whatever shade they could find.

As I passed, the dust kicked up by the tires hung in thick clouds in the air and slowly drifted across the residents of the area. I felt bad, knowing what it's like to get dusted by a passing vehicle, but none of them paid any attention. In fact, as I continued to pass through the area I began to realize that they were making an effort to not notice me.

To not notice the truck, I realized. They probably knew who it belonged to, or at least what it was used for, and none of them wanted to even see where it was going. That was perfectly fine with me.

I was nervous as hell. Even though I'm used to working outside in the Arizona summer, sweat was pouring off of me from the thoughts going through my head. I was carrying enough drugs to get twenty years in an American prison.

In Mexico? A gringo driving around with a load of whatever drugs were hidden behind the seat? I'd never see the light of day again if the Federales or Narcos took an interest in me.

Continuing on, I left the outermost edge of the shantytown behind. If I was remembering right from hunting trips, there was a deep canyon coming up in about ten or fifteen miles. I'd never been on the Mexican side of the border through it, but knew it did cut deeply across the line. My plan was to follow it north into the US and pick up some of the lightly traveled roads that would take me to my meeting.

I just hoped the Border Patrol was either chasing some illegals or visiting their girlfriends. Anything other than sitting there bored, waiting for some idiot to come driving along. If I was spotted, I was fucked. These guys have some serious desert vehicles, as well as helicopters. I wouldn't be slipping away if they spotted me.

The terrain remained perfectly flat for several miles, then suddenly descended sharply. I drove through a series of switchbacks and braked to a halt when I reached the bottom. Looking out the driver side window, to the north, I hoped the truck could negotiate the rugged terrain and soft sand that defined the canyon floor.

Dirk Patton

Shifting into neutral, I set the parking brake and hopped out. The Ranger had four-wheel drive, but it was old and required the driver to manually lock the system. No automatic switches here. The hubs engaged easily, again showing the care that was taken with the vehicle's mechanicals. Back behind the wheel, I shifted into gear and made a left turn.

I worked my way through soft sand that had been deposited by runoff from rain storms. This only lasted a few hundred yards, then I had to slow and carefully crawl over jumbled rocks. The Ford never missed a beat, and I made slow but steady progress.

An hour later, I reached the northern mouth of the canyon and came to a stop before exiting into the open desert of Arizona. Shutting the engine down, I stepped out and walked fifty yards to crouch behind some boulders. If I was the Border Patrol, I'd be sitting right here waiting.

On the stretches of sand I'd navigated, there had been dozens, if not hundreds, of footprints. All heading north. No tire tracks, but this was obviously a heavily traveled corridor for illegal immigrants to sneak into the country. The men and women of the Border Patrol would certainly know this, but I was hoping they weren't watching too closely in the daytime.

Most illegal crossings are done under the cover of darkness. I was counting on the day shift being lightly staffed and focusing on other border problems, leaving the cat and mouse games for the guys who worked at night. Peering around the rocks, I was relieved to not see any of them lying in wait.

I took my time, slowly scanning across the horizon. Each stand of creosote bushes and palo verde trees were carefully examined. I looked for dust plumes from vehicles in motion. Nothing. At the moment, it looked wide open.

Dashing back to the truck, I jumped in and started driving. I wanted speed but knew that the faster I went the more visible I'd be. Clouds of dust hanging in the air behind a vehicle can be seen from a very long distance.

Following one of the well-worn paths made by human feet, I was starting to congratulate myself when I remembered a news report about the Border Patrol using electronic sensors to monitor the vast open stretches of desert. If an alarm was tripped, they'd dispatch a helicopter to get eyes on what had set it off.

With a mental image of a bunch of guys hunched over monitors in a dark room, watching me drive across the sand, my right foot pressed harder on the accelerator. My stomach was in knots and my palms were sweaty on the steering wheel. As I drove, I kept leaning forward to peer at the sky through the windshield. Not that I could do anything if I spotted an aircraft, but I couldn't help myself.

Finally, I made it to pavement without incident. Checking my watch, I wasn't happy to see that it had taken me two hours to get this far. I only had two left before I was supposed to meet the cops.

The road wasn't marked and was barely wide enough for two vehicles to pass without driving onto the sandy shoulder. Turning north, I accelerated to 60, happy to be making progress. Fishing my phone out, I checked for signal, sighing when it showed *no service*. Not surprising, considering I was in the middle of fucking nowhere.

I needed to call Monica and tell her to head for Casa Grande. I debated the wisdom of calling the cops and telling them I was behind schedule. Would that piss them off and cause them to do something rash? Or would showing up late without having given them a heads up be worse?

The road wound its way through desolate countryside. Nothing but sand and cactus with the occasional palo verde tree. And it was noon and hot as hell. The wind blowing through the open windows felt like the breath from a blast furnace.

There wasn't air conditioning to turn on, and even if there had been there was no way I was going to seal myself in with Ralph. Ralph was what I had decided to call the odor. It was so vile and intense it was like a physical presence, so I'd given it a name.

The pavement changed from level to rolling as I continued to make my way north. I was checking my phone for signal as I climbed a low hill, looking up when I crested and nearly soiling myself. A few hundred yards ahead, neatly hidden in a low spot between two hills, sat a pair of green and white Border Patrol vehicles.

One was the commonly seen Chevy Tahoe, the other, one of the Ford Raptor trucks they were using. Built for high speed driving across open desert, there wasn't much they couldn't catch. I'd seen a segment on one of the local Phoenix TV stations where a reporter had gone on a ride along with one of the agents who drove a Raptor. She'd had a great time as he pushed the truck to 90, over terrain that most vehicles would be hard pressed to navigate at 20 miles an hour.

They were sitting on the sandy shoulder at a ninety-degree angle to the pavement. I could see two figures standing at the rear of the Tahoe, one of them watching me approach through a pair of binoculars. My first instinct had been to lift my right foot and slow down, but these weren't traffic cops. They didn't give a shit if I was speeding or not. All they cared about was who I was and what I might have in the truck with me.

Heart pounding and a lump in my throat, I forced myself to maintain my speed. I knew if I deviated, after having obviously seen them, it would be like waving a red flag that they made me nervous. Glancing at the speedometer, I saw I was up to 65, but didn't dare slow.

Inside a hundred yards I could see the one with the glasses lower them and turn his head to speak to the other. What the fuck was he saying? Stop this one? I had no way of knowing, and I was committed. If they wanted me, there wasn't a damn thing I could do.

At fifty yards I could see that both of them had rifles slung on the side of their bodies opposite holstered pistols. The only positive news was the rifles were hanging down and not being pointed at me.

At thirty yards the road flattened out. My heart stopped when the one with the binoculars raised his right hand. But it was just a wave. A fucking wave! Somehow, I had the presence of mind to return the wave as I flashed past where they were parked.

Immediately, as I started climbing the next hill, I focused my attention on the rearview mirror. Certain I would see the Raptor spitting sand and gravel as it pulled out to pursue, I couldn't believe my luck when neither of the vehicles moved. I watched them until I crested the rise, but they weren't coming after me.

When they were out of sight, I let out a huge breath that I hadn't even realized I was holding. Then the shakes hit so bad I wanted to pull over for fear of crashing. I was considering doing just that in another mile or two when something suddenly vibrated against my hip. I let out an involuntary shout and very nearly drove off the road.

10

It was my goddamn phone! Monica. Relief flooded through me when I saw the caller ID.

"Hi," I said, my voice shaky.

"Are you OK?" She asked, the concern clear in her question.

"I'm good," I breathed, steadying my nerves.

"Where are you?"

"I'm back," I said, wanting to be careful with what I said over the phone. "On a road that I have no fucking clue where it is or where it goes. Where are you?"

"I'm in a hotel in Nogales. On the Arizona side of the border. Everything go OK?"

"Yes. I'm on my way to meet them. Can you head for Casa Grande?"

"Is that where you're going?"

"Close to there," I said, not wanting to broadcast specifics about the location of the meet. "Close enough I can find my way into town.

There's a truck stop just east of where I-8 and I-10 meet. Can you go there and wait for me?"

She was silent for a moment before speaking again in a cautious tone.

"Listen. I've been thinking, and I'm scared. Do you really think they're going to just let you walk away once they get what they want? You've seen their faces. You can identify them."

The knot in my stomach that had loosened when I heard her voice returned with a vengeance, threatening to double me over in pain.

"What are you saying?" I asked.

"Maybe you should go to the police. Tell them everything."

"These are the police, Monica," I said, trying to hide the frustration in my tone.

"The FBI, then. Or the DEA."

"No," I said after a very long pause to think about what she was saying. "I'm already running late. If I don't show up, they're going to have Tim killed. There's no time to convince anyone I'm telling the truth. It would be a bunch of bullshit, and if I could convince them it would be days before they'd do anything. Tim would be dead by dinner."

She was quiet for a long time. I'm sure she was trying to think of an argument that would change my mind, but apparently she couldn't.

"Then you need to take a gun with you," she finally said with absolute conviction.

"I don't have one," I said. "Didn't want to risk taking one across the border."

"I have them. Remember? I'm leaving now. Meet me at the truck stop before you go see them. Get your gun."

I thought about what she was saying, liking the idea of having a weapon to defend myself. Things had been such a whirlwind that I hadn't thought through all of the potential pitfalls of meeting these guys in the middle of the desert. I wished I had the rifle I'd carried in the infantry. Hell, I wished I had my whole platoon with me. But I didn't have either of those.

"OK," I said. "Good idea. I'll meet you there as soon as I can. Be careful. Don't get pulled over because you're in a hurry. That shotgun is illegal and if your car is searched you'll be in trouble."

"I already ditched it," she said in a quiet voice.

"You did what?" I shouted. "Why the hell did you do that?"

"You told me it was illegal," she said, anger in her voice. "I already told you. I'm a mother and I'm not going to fuck that up for any man. I'm not taking that chance."

I let out a sigh, realizing she was right. I'd had no right to put her in that position.

"I'm sorry," I said. "You're right. But you still have the pistol?"

"Si. I still have the pistola."

As she came under stress, I'd noted that her accent thickened, and she fell back on the use of words in her native language. I actually thought that was kind of sexy. Maybe if I survived this, I could get her to start speaking Spanish in the bedroom.

"Are you still there?"

I'd been quiet too long, retreating into a daydream about her lying naked on my bed and talking to me in Spanish.

"I'm here," I said. "I need to go. Need to call them and let them know I'm running late. I'll see you in Casa Grande."

"Roberto?"

"Yes?"

"Be careful," she said after a very long pause, then the call was ended.

I don't know if it was just wishful thinking or not, but I was almost certain she'd wanted to say *I Love You*. Had to be just what I wanted to hear. Right? What the hell did I have to offer a woman like her? But then, why the hell was she helping me?

Dismissing thoughts of Monica, I thumbed through the phone's memory and found the number I'd dialed before leaving Nogales. The call was answered after two rings.

"Bobby Boy, where are you?"

"I'm on my way. North of the border," I said. "But I'm running late. Took longer than expected to cross."

"Not what I want to hear, Bob-O. Not what I want to hear at all. Late isn't good. Late gets the Timster a shiv for dinner. Understand what I'm saying?"

"Look, I'm coming as fast as I can, and I've got your shit. OK? Just fucking relax. I'm still south of Tucson. There's no way I can be there in," I paused to look at my watch. "Eighty minutes."

He was quiet for over a minute, probably with his hand over the phone as he consulted with his partner. When he came back on his voice was low and dangerous.

"Two hours, Bob. Two. Fucking. Hours. That's all. If you're not here in two hours, I make a call, and your baby brother is on a slab. No more extensions, no more excuses."

"If that happens, I'll drive this shit right into the closest DEA office, you motherfucker. See how you like that shit, cocksucker!"

I was taken aback when he chuckled, and his tone reverted to the overly friendly, condescending asshole I'd gotten used to.

"Bobberino, that would be the second biggest mistake of your life. Tell me if you recognize this address."

He read off a street address in Scottsdale. Before he finished speaking, I was gripping the phone so hard my hand was cramping.

"If you fucking touch them..." I started to say before he cut me off.

"Mom and Dad will be just fine as long as you do what you're told. Two hours or Timmy is toast. Fuck with me and Mommy and Daddy will join him. So you see, Booby Boy, all you have to do is get here in two hours and everyone is fine. It's all up to you."

He hung up when he finished speaking, and it took all my self-control to not smash the phone against one of the exposed metal braces where the dash used to be. My parents! Dragged into this by more of Tim's bad choices. When was the little shit ever going to grow up?

Setting my anger aside, I focused on my driving. I pushed the little truck as fast as I dared on the narrow road. Foolish, I know. I could top a rise and be surprised by a cop waiting for a speeder, just like the Border Patrol had suddenly appeared. But the stakes were higher.

I finally figured out where I was when I reached the Patagonia Highway. It ran in the wrong directions, so I continued on the small road, heading due north. The pavement wasn't smooth, but the small Ford handled it without fanfare and soon I began seeing signs of civilization.

Small homes on large tracts of land. The occasional car or truck going in the opposite direction. Soon I began seeing signs alerting drivers to the approaching intersection with the Interstate that ran from the border up to Tucson. Knowing this was prime territory for a radar trap, I reduced my speed to exactly the posted limit. The last thing I needed was for some rural Barney Fife to pull me over and decide to search the truck.

Not that he'd be that interested with Ralph along for the ride. It would just depend on how bored he was. I wasn't going to take the chance. I'd make up some time once I got on the Interstate with a legal limit of 75 miles an hour. I'd be able to safely push my speed to over 80 without worrying about drawing attention.

11

Monica was waiting for me, parked at the far edge of the massive truck stop. I checked my watch as I wheeled into the lot, grimacing when I saw I had less than 25 minutes to make the meet. Racing across the asphalt, I braked sharply and slid to a stop next to her 15-year-old Honda.

Jumping out, I wrapped my arms around her when she rushed to hold me.

"I was getting worried," she said, her voice muffled against my chest.

"Me too," I said, holding her tight. "I have to go. I'm running out of time."

She stepped away and grabbed my duffel out of her car. Handing it to me, she moved close and put her hand on the back of my head. Pulling my face down, she pressed her lips against mine for a long moment. Breaking the kiss, she looked directly into my eyes.

"I've decided something," she said.

"What's that?" I asked, antsy to get back on the road.

"I've decided you are who I want to be with. Come back to me. Maybe, someday, we can tell our grandchildren about this."

I was momentarily frozen in place. Surprised. Yes, I'd thought she wanted to say something like this on the phone earlier. Had been thinking similar thoughts myself the entire day. But I wasn't prepared for her to be so open and frank.

"Did I shock you?" She asked, smiling as she gazed into my eyes.

"Read my mind," I said, kissing her hard for a brief moment. "I have to go. I'll be back."

I kissed her again and jumped back in the truck. Seconds later I was screeching out of the parking area onto a road that headed south. A glance at my watch showed I had nineteen minutes left. I needed to cover seven miles, so I should be on time.

Pushing the truck as hard as I could without risking being noticed by a local cop, I made it south of town and turned onto Indian Route 15 with seven minutes left. Praying for luck, I pressed the accelerator to the floor and raced down the rolling ribbon of asphalt.

Roaring past several slower moving vehicles, I passed the turnoff for Indian Route 53 with three and half minutes left. Glancing at the odometer, which surprisingly worked, I started watching the right shoulder as I reached nine-tenths of a mile. I hadn't slowed, and when the cut in the desert vegetation that bordered the pavement appeared, I slammed on the brakes and skidded through a turn onto the dirt track.

Fighting for control, I floored the gas and flew across the rough terrain. The truck bottomed out twice and went completely airborne at least once. It wasn't a Raptor like the Border Patrol drives. As I started into a curve to circle the base of the twin hills, I flew over a rise and heard one of the rear shocks snap off when the truck's weight came down.

I didn't slow, keeping the gas on as I struggled with the now ungainly vehicle. There was a dip just before a sharp rise, and I hit it at full speed. The impact was brutal, the wheel tearing free from my hands and the windshield cracking from top to bottom. I still had the throttle wide open, but several somethings had been damaged, and I was losing speed.

Sounds were coming from the engine and transmission that shouldn't, but I didn't care. I was almost there and had less than a minute. Sliding around the curve, I wrenched the steering, trying to maintain control. Keeping the Ranger traveling in generally the correct direction, I let off the gas and stomped on the brakes when I saw a large Dodge pickup and the two cops standing next to it. Their truck was painted dull black with a large gold star on the doors. *Casa Grande Sheriff* was lettered along the top edge of the bed in the same paint as the star.

The Ford skidded to a stop, wobbling on its damaged suspension. The engine wheezed, stuttered and died as steam began to shoot out of the damaged radiator. I didn't care. I'd made it in time.

Looking down, I made sure the front of my shirt was covering the Makarov pistol stuffed in my waistband. *Thirteen shots*, I reminded myself. Twelve rounds in the magazine and one already in the chamber. Not nearly enough to go into a gunfight with two opponents who were almost certainly better with a pistol than me. But it's all I had.

Pulling on the handle, I had to ram my shoulder against the door to get it to open. Guess my final mad dash had tweaked the truck's frame. The door squeaked like the gates of hell as I forced it open and stepped out. The two cops were slowly approaching, plenty of distance between them.

The talker had a phone pressed to his face and I wasn't happy to see that. It could have been innocent, maybe the wife or girlfriend. It could have been good, telling whoever was watching my parents to call it a day and leave them alone. Or it could have been the absolute worst case scenario and my entire family was about to get wiped out.

"Bobby!" He called out with a smile as he disconnected the call. "You made it!"

"Who were you talking to?" I couldn't stop myself from asking.

"That? Oh, that was a personal call," he laughed. "My partner here is the one that will make the call if we need to teach you a lesson."

My eyes snapped to the other cop, who smiled. It wasn't pleasant. In fact, it was one of the most soulless, terrifying smiles I'd ever seen. But it wasn't the smile that told me bad things were about to start happening. It was his eyes.

Some people are good enough at hiding their intentions that you have no idea what's about to happen. Most aren't. I had seen this same look in the eyes of the driver of a car in Iraq. He had pulled to a stop at a checkpoint I was assigned to, along with nine other soldiers. Only then, I'd been too young and inexperienced to recognize it for what it was.

I was alive because it was my turn to be behind the up-armored Humvee that was blocking the road. Manning a radio and keeping an eye on our rear. When the bomb in the car went off, I was the only survivor. I still carried some shrapnel in my leg, and my hearing wasn't what it used to be, but compared to what happened to my buddies that day...

Now, here I was in the middle of the Arizona desert, facing two men who had threatened my entire family. And I'd just seen the same look in one of their eyes as I'd seen in the Iraqi insurgents. I reacted without thinking.

With my left hand, I yanked my shirt up, right hand already wrapping around the butt of the pistol. Time slowed as I pulled it out of my pants and brought it onto target. I saw the two cops freeze for an instant before they began to react. They had been supremely confident that I was cowed. That I wouldn't fight.

The pistol came on target, Mr. Evil Eyes, as he began to draw his holstered weapon. I pulled the trigger three times, certain one of the rounds hit him center mass but not sure where the other two went. As he was spinning away, I started to turn towards the talker, noting but not reacting to the sound of his pistol firing.

I have no idea where his shot went, but it didn't hit me. I began pulling the trigger as the Makarov was still swinging onto target. At the same time, I dove to the side, still firing and seeing the flashes from his muzzle as he returned fire. I hit the dirt and rolled towards a shallow ditch, firing a final shot before I was below the level of the road surface.

Remembering hard learned lessons from the war, I started crawling so I could pop up from a different location. As I moved, the world returned to normal speed. I was panting like I'd just run a marathon, but my hands were steady as I came to a stop and stuck my pistol over the low berm. Keeping its movement in sync with my eyes, I scanned for the two cops, spotting both of them on their backs.

Carefully, I climbed out of the ditch and approached, weapon at arms length in both hands. I wasn't sure how many rounds I'd fired but knew I couldn't have more than two or three remaining. Coming closer, I circled the area, so I was on the side of the first guy I'd shot.

He was dead. One of my rounds had torn his throat out. But I noticed for the first time that he was wearing body armor. Fuck! I snapped the pistol up to cover the talker, but he was gone. I'd been so focused on the first guy that I hadn't seen him move.

Looking around, I saw him at the driver's door of his pickup, holding a radio microphone to his mouth. Son of a bitch! He was calling for help! Running directly at him, I fired. The round punched through the windshield and he dropped out of sight. I didn't slow, diving to the ground when I was ten yards from the truck's front bumper.

He was huddled on the ground, shouting into the microphone. I saw blood on his arm and leg where some of my bullets had found their mark, then our eyes met. He stopped talking, frozen as he stared at the pistol I was aiming at his head. We stayed like that for a couple of beats; then I pulled the trigger. His head snapped back, and his lifeless fingers released the microphone, which was pulled back into the cab by its coiled cord.

12

I slowly climbed to my feet and looked around. That's when the shakes hit. Standing there in bright sunshine and over 100-degree weather, and I was cold and shaking. I'd experienced it before and knew it was just my body's reaction to the intensity of the fight. I gave it a few seconds to pass. Taking slow, deep breaths helped and soon I was thinking again.

"What the fuck did you do, Bob?" I said aloud. "What did you do?"

Two cops dead. From my gun. And one of them had gotten a radio call out. I wasn't terribly panicked about that. Yet. The desert is a big place. It was very unlikely there were any other cops in the vicinity. In the city, backup can arrive in minutes if not seconds. Out here? I've heard stories that it can take half an hour for the closest unit to arrive.

But I couldn't count on it. We weren't that far from town. Maybe one of the local police was on the way, which meant I could be hearing sirens any moment. I took a step forward, intending to hop into their truck and get the hell out of the area, pausing when a thought hit me. In this day and age, that vehicle was almost certainly equipped with a GPS tracker. Shit!

Making up my mind, I looked to the north across the open desert. Rugged terrain with a series of low hills stared back at me, but I'd been in deserts all my life. I respected them, but I wasn't intimidated by them.

Run. I could make it to Casa Grande in maybe an hour and a half on foot. Thumb a ride across town to where Monica was waiting, then disappear. No one other than the two dead men knew who I was. I seriously doubted the talker had been providing a description over the radio. He had been screaming for help. If I could get away, I was home free.

I had gone three steps before skidding to a stop on the dirt track. Fingerprints! My prints would be on all of the fired brass from my pistol and all over the Ford truck. It would take the cops about five minutes to run my prints, which had been taken by the Army when I enlisted. They wouldn't need to be Sherlock Holmes to identify me.

Turning, I dropped the magazine out of the Makarov and held it up. It was empty. Pulling the slide back, a glittering round ejected and tumbled through the air to land in the dirt. Scooping it up, I blew the dust off and inserted it back into the chamber.

That meant I had to find twelve empty shell casings. Casting around, I spotted one where I'd been prone on the ground when I shot the talker in the head. It went in my pocket and I moved to where I'd been standing when I started firing. I found eight more shells quickly. Three to go, and I wasn't seeing them.

That's the thing about brass in the desert. It's small, and the color is very close to that of the sandy ground. Plus, they have a tendency to bounce and roll, especially if they hit a rock. Moving in a small, slow circle with my head bent down, I searched. And found two more. One of them was on its end, leaning against a small rock, and I knew I was very lucky to have seen it. One to go.

It took me nearly three minutes, though it felt like an eternity, to finally find it. It was in plain sight in the very middle of the track, but until I looked from the right angle and saw the way it reflected the sunlight, it had been invisible. With a feeling of relief, I grabbed it up and turned to look at the Ranger.

Fire. That was the only way. The truck had to burn. It wasn't just prints I had to worry about. I'd driven the damn thing for several hours. My DNA would be somewhere in the cab. The only problem was; I didn't have a lighter or matches.

Rushing to the closest dead cop, I ran my hands over his pockets, hoping he was a smoker. I came up empty. Dashing to the second one, the talker, I had the same results. Straightening up and cursing I spotted a pack of Marlboros and a cheap butane lighter inside the cab of their truck. Leaning inside, I picked up the lighter, careful not to touch anything and leave another print.

Running back to the Ford, I dropped to my hands and knees and peered beneath it. Drawing the Makarov, I aimed and fired, using my last round to punch a hole in the fuel tank. Gasoline streamed out, soaking into the sand beneath the truck. As I watched it flow, the distant sound of a siren reached my ears. I was out of time.

Snatching the brass case off the ground, I began using the butt of my pistol to carve a small channel into the sand, extending it away from the rapidly growing pool of gasoline. Fuel flowed along the trench, following me as I opened some distance. The siren was growing closer, but I could tell it was still on the pavement, at least a couple of miles away.

The edge of the dirt road dropped away a couple of feet, providing a berm for me to shelter behind. When I had scraped a track all the way across its surface, I dropped into cover and held the lighter over the gas soaked sand. Flicking it, I thrust it against the fuel and watched flames spring to life and race towards the truck.

Dropping completely below the level of the road, I covered my head with my arms. It was only a matter of moments before the fuel tank exploded with a dull whoosh, a wave of heat washing over me. I gave it another couple of seconds, then leapt to my feet and began running north.

I ran like the hounds of hell were at my heels. And I knew they would be soon. I'd covered maybe a quarter of a mile when the sound of the siren changed. I could tell the police vehicle had rounded the base of the hills and had reached the site. A quarter of a mile isn't all that far, certainly close enough for me to be spotted, but I was hoping the new arrival's attention would be focused on the burning truck and the two dead bodies.

Doing my best to stick to the lowest part of the terrain, keeping bushes and the occasional tree between us, I pushed as hard as I could. More cops would be coming. Fast. Probably a helicopter, too, once the call went out that officers were down. Even dogs. I knew they'd pull out all the stops to track down a cop killer.

Half an hour later I had slowed to a jog. I was in relatively good shape from doing physical labor to earn a living, but roofing doesn't exactly improve your stamina for running. I was thirsty as hell, too. Extreme exertion in the middle of the day is generally best avoided, especially when you have no shelter from the blistering sun.

I'd been hearing the faint sounds of a helicopter for the past ten minutes, thankful that it hadn't drawn any closer. I had no idea if it was searching for me, but wasn't about to assume it wasn't. What I did know was I had to get out of this desert and into town before dark. Both the Border Patrol and state police would have Forward Looking Infrared (FLIR), and once the sun went down, I'd stand out like a sore thumb against the rapidly cooling ground.

Following a dry arroyo that was bordered by heavy growths of creosote bushes, I rounded a turn and almost fell when I skidded to a stop. A small group of people were sitting in the soft sand. Two men, three women and a child. They had dirty faces and their clothes were sweat stained. Illegals, making their way north.

They had stopped in the meager shade provided by a stunted palo verde tree. One of the women had been holding a canteen out for the child, a small girl of no more than eight or nine. She froze for a moment when she saw me, then scrambled to wrap her arms protectively around what I suspected was her daughter.

The two men leapt to their feet, placing themselves between me and the women, drawing knives. I held my hands up, palms facing them, then hooked a thumb over my shoulder in a southerly direction.

"La Migra!" I said in Spanish, meaning the Border Patrol was behind me.

Fear passed across all their faces and without a word, they turned and began running. The woman scooped the little girl in her arms and carried her. I fell in behind them, keeping some distance in case one of the men took exception with me following. But they didn't seem to care. They'd made it this far and were determined to keep going.

We stayed in the arroyo as it wound its way through the hills. The helicopter sounded like it was growing closer. Slowing, but not stopping, I looked over my shoulder. Nothing but a sun-bleached sky. I couldn't spot it.

Turning back to the front, I was surprised to see the small group had pulled well ahead of me. Nearly a hundred yards. I froze, then dove behind a scraggly stand of bushes when voices began shouting ahead of me and several figures dropped into the arroyo just in front of the fleeing illegals.

I recognized the dark green uniforms of the Border Patrol as they surrounded and captured the group. Squirming deeper into cover, and hoping I didn't encounter a rattlesnake or scorpion, I peered through the branches to see what was going on.

All of the Mexicans, well they could have been from anywhere else in Latin America for all I knew, were made to get on their knees and place their hands on their heads. They were searched, the knives taken from the men who were then restrained with flexi-cuffs.

The Border Patrol agents relaxed slightly at that point, one of them handing the women and little girl bottles of water. He stepped up to the men and since their hands were restrained behind their backs, helped each of them drink until they shook their heads that they didn't want any more.

While he did this, two more with rifles began walking down the arroyo in my direction. My pounding heart shifted into overdrive. I was hidden, but not well enough. If they came much closer, they would surely spot me. Panic nearly took control and caused me to run when a helicopter suddenly popped up over one of the hills we'd passed. It went into an orbit around the area. As it banked, I got a good look at it. State police.

The two agents walking in my direction stopped and looked up, watching the aircraft circle the area. I had no doubt the helicopter was looking for me. One of them reached to his shoulder for a radio and began speaking into the microphone as he kept his eyes on the orbiting helicopter.

He was too far away for me to hear the conversation, but it went on for several minutes. They were probably discussing the possibility of the group that had just been caught having been responsible for the murder of the two cops. That was OK with me. The agents were distracted, both looking up.

When the helicopter was pointing away from my position, I moved. Crawling, I put as much distance between me and the arroyo as possible. I scrambled as fast as I could, keeping an eye on the sky as well as the two men. Freezing under a clump of bushes as the aircraft turned back in my direction, I moved again as soon as it curved away.

Within thirty yards of the dry wash, the vegetation thinned and became too small to use for concealment. I flattened myself into a shallow depression, screened by two small bushes. Thank God I'd worn jeans and a brown T-shirt. I blended in with the ground. I could just as easily have thrown on a white or red shirt that would stand out like a flag against the muted browns and greens of the desert floor.

The helicopter finally left the area after another twenty minutes of orbiting. The Border Patrol agents had walked far down the arroyo, well past my initial hiding place. If I hadn't moved when I'd had the opportunity, they would have found me. I stayed right where I was, eyes poking up over the lip of the depression, watching them return to where the group was being held.

Once they rejoined the rest of the agents, it wasn't long before I heard doors slamming and two engines starting. The helicopter had moved out of earshot, and the desert was silent except for their vehicles. I could clearly hear them drive off to the north, the sounds of their motors and tires taking several minutes to completely fade.

I gave it another few minutes, then stood and ran to the arroyo and continued my trek north. The sun was still high in the sky, but it was sliding towards the western horizon. I checked my watch, but it was broken. It must have slammed against a rock when I dove for cover.

Pushing on, I tried to ignore my building thirst. I wasn't in danger, yet, but it was hot. Had to be at least 110, and the humidity was very low, sucking every bit of moisture out of my body as I breathed the dry air. A hot breeze had sprung up, occasionally strong enough to pepper the right side of my face with sand.

It was several minutes later when the significance of this dawned on me. This part of the state was dust storm alley. Not just some gentle breezes blowing dust around to make pretty sunsets. No. These were every bit as big and potentially damaging as the massive haboobs that would sweep across the middle east.

Visibility drops to zero, or so close as to not matter. Traffic stops. Airports shut down. Not much moves. And this was the prime time of year for the storms to kick up, gathering dust from thousands of square miles of flat, open desert. With nothing to slow or stop them, they routinely roar into the Phoenix area during the summer.

If I got caught out in one, I'd be stuck. Unable to see well enough to even try walking. Sure, it would ground the helicopter and hamper the manhunt I was certain was underway, but as soon as it passed they'd be back on my tail. And if I was still out here after dark I didn't like my odds of evading their technology advantage.

Stopping and turning, I shielded my eyes and looked to the southeast. At the very limit of my vision, I could see a brown smudge covering the horizon. Dust was coming. I had maybe an hour to get to town. Turning back to the north, I resumed my run.

13

I walked on the shoulder of the road, dividing my attention between the storm and watching for approaching vehicles. I felt more or less safe. The cops might be conducting a manhunt, but they had no idea who I was or what I looked like. I hoped. Well, at least the odds were in my favor.

I'd made sure I didn't have anything on me in the event I was stopped. The paper with the talker's phone number, my Makarov pistol, and expended brass were buried in a hole in the middle of the desert. I was confident they would never be found. Other than those incriminating items, all I had left was my phone, wallet with a few hundred bucks in it and the keys to my apartment.

The arroyo had intersected pavement about a mile and a half north of where the Border Patrol had taken the small group I'd encountered into custody. I was pretty sure I was west of where I needed to be, so after a few minutes of careful thought, I'd decided to strike out on the pavement and try to thumb a ride. But there hadn't been any traffic.

"Until now," I said to myself when the hiss of tires on asphalt reached my ears.

Turning to the west, I squinted into the late afternoon sun to see the approaching vehicle. Heat shimmers coming off the baking blacktop created an optical illusion, making it seem as if the old pickup was floating above the surface of the road. As it drew closer, the tires resolved in my vision, and I stuck my arm out and held my thumb in the air.

I knew the driver saw me. He moved slightly away from the edge, towards the centerline to give plenty of room. A few moments later he flashed past without slowing or even looking in my direction. Sighing, I turned and kept trudging east.

Looking up at the horizon I saw that the dust storm was noticeably closer than the last time I checked. Two minutes ago. And it looked like a monster. It was probably still twenty miles away, but the leading edge of the solid, roiling brown cloud completely filled the horizon and soared high into the sky. I knew powerful winds would be pushing it and estimated I had no more than twenty minutes before I was completely engulfed in its fury.

I turned at the sound of another car approaching, my breath catching when I saw the outline of a police car silhouetted against the lowering sun. Turning back east and continuing to walk, I didn't stick my thumb out, hoping the cop would drive by. But of course, he didn't.

The cruiser, belonging to the Department of Public Safety – what Arizona calls the state police - slowed as it drew closer, gliding past me at an idle. I looked over and met eyes with the officer driving. Without thinking, I raised my right hand and waved. He didn't wave back, just accelerated enough to get thirty yards past me before pulling over and turning on his overhead lights. I could see him speaking on the radio, looking at me in his mirror. I stopped where I was, waiting. Panicked. Scared out of my mind.

It didn't take long for him to finish his radio call, then the driver's door popped open, and he stepped out. He was about my age and looked as tough as old shoe leather. Thin, but the kind of whipcord thin that has a lot of strength behind it. His hand was on the butt of his holstered pistol as he stepped to the back of his car.

"Sir, please step to the side of the car and place your hands on the fender," he called, sunlight glinting off his mirrored glasses.

"Why? What did I do?" I called back, desperately trying to come up with a way out of this.

"Sir, now. Step to the side and keep your hands in sight. I'm not going to ask you again."

With a sigh of resignation, I moved my hands away from my body and slowly walked the short distance to the idling police car. He pointed where he wanted me, stepping back and keeping some part of the vehicle's sheet metal between us. I did what he told me, winding up on the passenger side with my hands resting on the burning hot rear fender.

He moved around the car, circling wide until he was coming up behind me. I started to turn my head to keep him in sight, but he barked at me to face forward. I complied, and a moment later a strong hand pushed on the back of my neck and shoved my upper body forward across the trunk.

"Do you have anything on you that I should know about?" He asked from behind me.

"No," I said. "What the hell is wrong? I didn't do anything."

"I'm going to search you. We'll talk in a minute. Do not try to raise up or take your hands off the vehicle. Do you understand?"

"I understand," I said.

He searched me thoroughly. Removed my phone, wallet, and keys and placed them next to my face on the trunk of the cruiser. When he was finished, he picked my wallet up and stepped away.

"You can stand up now," he said after having returned to the driver's side of his car.

My wallet was in his hands and he began looking through it. He rifled through the cash, then looked at a couple of slips of paper that were tucked away. One of them was my boss's cell phone in case I needed to call in sick, the other my VFW card. He put them back and extracted my driver's license from behind a clear plastic window.

His eyes flicked from the photo on my ID to my face, making sure they matched.

"Long way from Phoenix, Mr. Tracy. What are you doing out here?"

"I was hiking in Casa Grande Mountain Park," I said, having had a few moments to think up a story. "I got lost and came out a mile or so back down the road. Trying to get back to town where my wife's supposed to pick me up."

"Hiking without water or a hat? No pack?"

"I ran out of water a few hours ago and didn't feel like carrying an empty pack. Left it behind. What the hell is going on?"

I was making it up on the fly, now. Unsure what the right response was. Should I be indignant that I was being treated like a criminal, or should I be polite and cooperative? I decided to settle for a little of both.

"What am I going to find out if I run your license?" He asked.

"Nothing. Am I under arrest? I just want to get to town before that storm hits."

I hooked a thumb over my shoulder and saw him glance at the swiftly approaching wall of dust. Saw something in his eyes, he didn't want to get caught out here any more than I did.

"You're being detained at the moment," he finally said. "Go stand in front of my car."

"Seriously? I haven't done a damn thing!"

"Sir, we can wrap this up here, or I can put you in cuffs and take you to the station. Which would you prefer?"

I looked at his face and saw the sincerity and determination. With a sigh, I nodded and walked to the front of the cruiser and leaned my ass against the heavy duty push bar. I heard him open the door. Then the car shifted slightly when he got in. The door closed and the locks thunked into place.

Resisting the urge to turn and look through the windshield, I crossed my arms and looked at the horizon. Ten minutes and we'd be in zero visibility. Could I stretch things out that long? Escape under cover of the storm? Maybe. But what was the point? He was calling my name in right now. That meant there was a record of me being in the area. I was fucked.

A couple of minutes later the door opened, and the car shifted again when he stepped out.

"Mr. Tracy?"

I turned my head to look at him without moving my ass off the push bar.

"You're good to go. Thank you for your cooperation."

I shook my head, playing the role of aggrieved, upstanding citizen. Standing up, I headed for the back of the car to retrieve my belongings.

"Don't suppose you're going to tell me what that was all about," I said, shoving my property into pockets.

"There was an incident a few miles from here," he said. "We're looking for people that might have been involved."

"Un huh," I said, shaking my head and turning to continue my way into town.

"Hang on," he said before I'd taken more than a couple of steps.

Heart falling, I stopped and turned to look at him.

"Saw your VFW card. Sandland?"

"Iraq. Two tours," I said.

"Did two myself. With the Corps." he said, meaning he was a Marine.

I nodded, unsure what he wanted.

"Look," he said. "That fucking haboob is going to hit any minute. Where were you supposed to meet your wife?"

I looked at him for a long moment, trying to decide if this was a trick or not. Making my decision, and hoping it was the right one, I named a truck stop adjacent to the one Monica was waiting at.

"Hop in back," he said, nodding at the car. "I'll get you there in five minutes."

"I'm good," I said. "I was infantry. I'm used to walking."

"In that?" He asked, pointing at the front edge of the storm which was now within a couple of miles of where we stood.

"Actually, yes," I said, and couldn't help grinning.

He grinned back and gestured at the car. Nodding, I opened the rear passenger door and got in, and was immediately claustrophobic in the confines of the rear seat of a police car. He came around and shut the door, which had bars over the window and no handle on the inside. Fuck me. I hope I didn't just make the second biggest mistake of my life.

14

The storm hit a minute after we started driving. Wind buffeted the cruiser, rocking it violently. Dust and sand were driven against us so hard it sounded like the paint was being blasted off the sheet metal. Visibility was poor, but we were still in the leading edge of the cloud, and it hadn't dropped to zero. Yet.

Gunning the powerful engine, the cop navigated the empty streets of Casa Grande with ease. All the locals had already found a place to button themselves up and ride out the storm. Wind driven debris tumbled down the roads, actually passing us at one point. The older traffic lights that were only suspended from cables swung wildly, one of them twisting all the way around before snapping free and crashing to the pavement.

"Going to be a bad one," the cop said.

"Looks like," I answered, just to be saying something.

"You ever miss it?"

"Miss what?" I asked, even though I knew what he meant.

"The war."

"No," I lied.

"Me either," he said, and I couldn't tell if he was telling the truth or not.

We were silent for the rest of the drive. It didn't take long, despite the steadily diminishing visibility. He had the radio turned up, and I could already hear calls going out to units being sent to accidents on one of the two freeways in the area. Then we pulled into a massive truck stop.

"See your wife's car?" He asked, slowing to a crawl.

"No," I said, pretending to look around what I could see of the lot. "She might have heard about the storm and be waiting for it to pass before she drives down. Thanks for the ride. I'll hang out inside while I wait."

He nodded and steered for the large store-restaurant combination on the far side of the gas pumps. Pulling in to a handicapped spot, the only one not occupied, he jumped out and ran around the back of the car to open the door for me.

"Thanks for the ride," I said, reflexively sticking my hand out when I was standing.

"No worries," he said, shaking mine briefly. "Take care."

With that, he dashed around the back of the car and jumped behind the wheel. Ducking my head and squinting my eyes, I ran for the entrance. An employee was manning the doors, trying to keep the wind from ripping them off their hinges. When I appeared out of the storm, she pushed one open and moved aside.

I stepped into clean, air conditioned comfort. Turning, I could just make out the shape of the cruiser as it backed out of the spot. A moment later it disappeared into the storm. Wanting to give the cop plenty of time to clear the area before I went to find Monica, I bought two bottles of water and drained both of them in less than thirty seconds. Buying two more, I shoved them into a plastic bag and moved back to the doors.

The storm was in full swing. The wind howled. The girl that was watching the doors was struggling to keep them from being torn out of her hands. The first row of pumps, no more than twenty yards from where I stood, were invisible. All I could see was brown dust.

An idea struck me and I turned and went back into the store. I asked at the counter, the old man working the register pointing out the aisle I was looking for. A couple of minutes later I was back at the doors, brand new goggles firmly seated on my face. I helped the girl control the door as I stepped outside, then pushed as she pulled to get it closed again.

It was an adventure crossing first one, then another large parking lot in the storm. The wind was a physical force, a fierce creature trying to knock me over and carry me away. I had the collar of my shirt pulled over my mouth and nose, but was still pretty sure I was inhaling a good quantity of dirt.

Ten minutes later I reached Monica's aging Honda. It was still parked in the same spot where I'd met her earlier in the day. Stumbling up, I banged on the window and a moment later slipped inside when she reached across and unlocked the door. As soon as I was seated, she wrapped her arms around me and squeezed as tightly as she could.

"What happened," she asked after several minutes of holding each other. "A few hours ago there were sirens going off everywhere. I was starting to think I'd never see you again."

I sat back in the passenger seat and opened one of the bottles of water. The Honda was idling, the air conditioning on high. As it blew across my bare arms, I realized I had a bad sunburn. I may work outdoors in the sun all day, but I wear long sleeves to protect my skin. When

I got dressed in the wee hours of the morning, I hadn't expected to be wandering around the desert.

After I had finished half the bottle, I started talking. Told her everything. Even about the cop who'd given me a ride. As the story progressed, she began crying. Softly. Tears running down her face.

"What's wrong?" I asked when I finished.

She reached out and pulled me into a hug, burying her face against my shoulder.

"They will find you," she said, her voice muffled. "They will find you and take you away from me."

We talked as the storm raged, buffeting the small car so hard it felt like it was going to flip us over. I stated my case, arguing as much with myself as her that there was no evidence to link me to the murders. She listened, but I could tell she wasn't convinced. Finally, we were talked out. Unable to keep rehashing the events and possible outcomes.

After a few minutes, Monica dried her eyes, drank some of my water and picked up her phone. She dialed a number from memory and had a brief conversation in Spanish that I couldn't hope to follow.

"What was that about?" I asked when she ended the call.

"Making sure Manny could stay over again tonight. I don't want to sleep alone."

The storm had passed by now, moving on to the Phoenix metropolitan area. Half an inch of dust had been deposited on the exterior of the car. As we pulled out of the parking lot and accelerated onto the freeway, it was blown away. We drove in silence, frequently having to slow for traffic as the DPS worked to clear accidents from the roadway.

I was exhausted from the stress of the day and my panicked flight across the desert. Within minutes of leaving the truck stop, I was asleep. It should only have taken an hour to reach our apartments from Casa Grande, but with the snarled traffic in the aftermath of the storm, it wound up taking close to three.

Pulling in and parking near our doors, I realized I was starving. I had worked all day yesterday, with only a sandwich for lunch. There hadn't been a dinner with the events of the previous evening, and today hadn't exactly presented many opportunities for a meal.

"I'm starving," I said. "I'll get cleaned up then let's go out to dinner."

Going out to dinner was an extremely rare luxury for me. I just didn't have the money. But I still had some of the cash the dirty cops had given me, and I couldn't think of a better use for some of it at the moment. Monica nodded and told me to meet her at the car in an hour.

We each went to our own apartment. I shaved and showered, dressing in my last set of clean clothes. Only half an hour had passed, and I was ready but knew Monica wouldn't be. She was probably showering, putting on fresh makeup and I expected to see her in one of the sexy little dresses she liked to wear. As tired and hungry as I was, all I wanted was to see her.

Leaving the hot box apartment, I stepped out into the evening to wait for her. It was still hot, but the sun had gone down, so it was tolerable. Better than the furnace inside and listening to the wheezing air conditioner. Leaning my ass against the front fender of her car, I pulled out my phone and dialed my parent's number. My dad answered on the fourth ring.

He was glad to hear from me, as he always was, and I didn't let the conversation drift into discussions of the latest political news. I knew that once he got started, there would be no stopping him. Getting his attention, I told him about Tim's current predicament. I answered the questions I could but didn't tell him anything about my involvement.

"How much do you think it will take?" He asked.

"I don't know, Dad. Probably a lot. You and I should drive down there tomorrow morning. You stay on the US side, and I'll go talk to the warden. When I have a number, I'll call you, and you can go to the bank. When you've got the cash, I'll come back across and get it, then take it to the warden. And hopefully, come back with Tim."

There was silence on the other end for a long time, so long, that I thought the call had dropped. Not unusual with my shitty prepaid phone.

"Dad? You still there?"

"I'm here," he said, sounding older than I'd ever heard. "I'll pick you up in the morning. Six too early?"

"No, that's good," I said. "I'll be ready."

With nothing else to discuss, I hung up and let out a big sigh. I turned my head when I heard a door open. It was Monica, looking even better than I had predicted. Her thick hair was pulled back, spilling across her shoulders. Her makeup was fresh, applied carefully to accent her nearly perfect features. And the dress. Low in front and short in the hem, it was enough to stop traffic two streets away.

I straightened up to meet her, smiling. She saw me and started to smile, her face suddenly registering fear as she saw something behind me. I whirled in time to see a dozen cops dressed in black, wearing body armor and carrying rifles.

They were only a short distance away and immediately began screaming at me to get on the ground. My stomach dropped, and I slowly sank to my knees as they surrounded me, weapons trained on my heart. By the time I was prone on the crumbling asphalt, a helicopter was overhead. A brilliant spotlight illuminated the whole area as about a hundred cop cars screamed into the parking lot with roof lights flashing.

"It was the fucking lighter," I said to Agent Johnson.

"Yes," he said, flipping a page. "I saw that was the key piece of evidence used to convict you. Your prints were on a plastic butane lighter found in a ditch next to the truck you torched. That was a grave mistake, leaving it behind."

"Thank you, Captain Obvious," I said, with as much sarcasm as I could put into it. "So, did I tell you anything you didn't know?"

"Only the part about Monica Torres," he said. "She's not mentioned anywhere in the records. You did a good job of protecting her."

"She didn't do anything," I said, suddenly realizing the stupidity of having told the complete story. "I held a gun on her and made her drive me."

"No need to worry, Mr. Whitman," he smiled. "I'm not the least bit interested in what Ms. Torres may or may not have done. That's ancient history, as far as I'm concerned. I'm much more interested in the here and now."

"Tell me something first," I said.

"If I can."

"Those two dirty cops. I told my story to my defense attorney. At first, he said that should be enough to get me off. A clear case of self-defense. But nothing ever came of that. It didn't come out at trial, even though I told that reporter I gave the interview to. And even when I fired my lawyer and got a new one, nothing ever came of it. Why not?"

"You didn't know?" He looked surprised.

"Know what?"

He leaned back and took a moment to check the crease in his pants.

"The judge that presided over your case and sentenced you. Do you know what became of him?"

I shook my head.

"He's now the governor of Arizona. In his second term. There's talk that he's going to be a candidate for the White House in the next election. And guess who his staunchest supporters are?"

"I have no idea," I said.

"Law enforcement unions. They very nearly bankrolled his first campaign."

"Motherfucker!" I exploded. "You mean my trial was fixed?"

"I don't know that I'd use that term," he mused. "But when we began looking at you, there were several things that jumped out. Evidence that was suppressed at the prosecutor's request. A prosecutor who, by the way, is married to the Sheriff's sister. Too much evidence ruled inadmissible by the judge. Then, there are bank records that show way too much money floating around the sheriff's department and the two men you killed in particular. Money that can't be accounted for.

"Certain prisoners being released after the investigators "lost" key evidence against them. Prisoners that were facing very long sentences for everything from drug and human trafficking to murder. It's a tangled web, and there's a whole team of federal and state agents about to descend and start going through everything with a fine-toothed comb."

"That's just great," I groused. "But it doesn't help me. I'm dead. Right?"

"No, Mr. Whitman. You're alive and well. Robert Tracy is dead. No one is looking for him and no one will. That's what matters."

"OK," I said with a huff of resignation. "You've got me. I get that. Maybe I should be grateful, but I've grown cynical over the past ten years as a guest of the state. Now how about telling me what's really going on?"

"How about we get some fresh air?" He asked, standing and straightening his jacket sleeves after adjusting his tie. "Ready to get out of that bed?"

"Yes," I said, surprised, and at the same time expecting him to laugh and say he was just kidding.

But, he didn't do anything of the sort. Dragging his chair out of the way, he leaned down and released the restraints on each of my ankles. Moving up, he undid the strap across my chest before freeing my hands.

"OK, easy," he said, slipping a giant hand beneath my upper back. "You haven't been on your feet in a long time. You're going to be weak and unsteady."

He helped me sit up on the edge of the mattress. I looked down at my pale legs sticking out of the hospital gown, amazed at how skinny they were. Johnson pushed a small button on the outside frame of the bed before he helped me stand. I swayed and would have fallen backwards if not for his steadying grip on my upper arms.

The door opened a moment later, and the nurse stepped in.

"Agent Johnson? You buzzed?"

"Let's get Mr. Whitman some clothes," he said.

"Of course. Right away," she said and disappeared.

While we waited, he held on to me as I took a few tentative steps. He was right. I was weak as hell and if not for his assistance wouldn't have been able to walk a straight line. We did a couple of slow laps around the room before the nurse returned and placed a neatly folded pile of clothing on the foot of my bed. A pair of simple, white, rubber soled shoes sat on top of the stack.

Johnson eased me into the chair he'd occupied and began handing me the clothes. It took some doing, but eventually I was dressed in a set of scrubs and slipped the shoes on my feet. Standing, I swayed dangerously, holding a hand out to stop the Fed from helping me. I had to learn to do this on my own again.

Gaining my balance, I slowly followed him as he led the way out of the room. Outside was a circular nurses station, equipped with monitors to help them keep an eye on their patients. There was also apparently a live video feed, and I could see the room I'd just exited on a large screen.

Five other rooms were arranged around the central area, the nursing station at the core of the circle. All of their doors were open. Each room, other than mine, was dark. I was apparently the only patient on this ward. Still getting used to being upright, I wobbled and reached out to steady myself against the wall. When I touched it, my fingers felt like they had just contacted hot acid.

"What the hell's wrong with my hands?" I asked, looking down at them.

"New prints," Agent Johnson said. "We changed your face, but if someone fingerprinted you, the ruse would fall apart."

"What do you mean they're new?"

"A rather complicated process, actually," he answered, motioning me to walk with him. "Several layers of skin are removed. Not just your fingertips, but your palms as well. Once we've gone deep enough to ensure they're completely erased, new skin that was grown from your own cells is grafted in place.

"There's no rejection because it's your skin. It takes nicely, and at key times throughout the healing process a computer-controlled laser is used to etch new prints into the virgin flesh. It's all quite detailed, and I'm told extremely painful. That's the main reason you've been kept sedated. To spare you the pain."

I had come to a stop at a pair of doors that exited the ward. Standing there, I stared at my hands and carefully touched each fingertip with my thumbs. It hurt like hell at the slightest pressure. Lifting my hands, I peered at them and could make out the loops and whorls on the end of each finger.

"So you're telling me I could walk into a police station and have my prints run, and they wouldn't come back as Bob Tracy, convicted murderer?"

"Correct. They'd come back as JR Whitman, truck driver."

Johnson smiled and motioned again for me to keep moving. I followed him through the doors and into a stark corridor. It ended at a T intersection, and he turned right. A few steps farther and we reached a blank, steel door.

A flat key card reader with a single red light was on the wall next to it. He pulled a plain white piece of plastic, about the size of a credit card, out of an inner jacket pocket and held it against the reader. With a loud click, the lock released and he pushed the door open.

It was dark outside, which was probably a good thing as my eyes were bothering me just from the fluorescent lighting in the hallway. As the door swung open, fresh air smelling of the sea rushed in, and I immediately felt rejuvenated. Johnson stepped through, and I followed, looking all around as I emerged into the night.

We took several steps on a steel deck, and I came to a stop, turning my head in all directions, examining my surroundings. Looking up, I saw a soaring superstructure, a red light at the apex flashing regularly to warn low flying aircraft. There was a steady breeze that was warm and humid, and I breathed deeply of the clean air as I followed Johnson to a waist high rail.

Looking down, I saw the dark surface of an ocean, visible in the light of a full moon. It must have been a hundred feet, or more, below our level. Looking in every direction, I saw nothing other than a dark horizon. I was on a massive, offshore oil rig.

16

"Hello, Mr. Whitman. It's a pleasure to meet you," the thin woman said as she breezed into the conference room.

The room was small, but not cramped. A table occupied the center, half a dozen well-upholstered chairs surrounding it. Agent Johnson and I were seated on the side opposite the entrance, waiting for her arrival.

It was three days following my brief stroll around the outside of the oil rig. I still didn't know any more about what was going on, and curiosity was driving me nuts. I'd spent the past two days meeting with a psychiatrist each morning and most of the afternoons on treadmills, getting my strength back.

The conversations with the shrink had been odd. At least to me. I'd never talked to one before. Some of the questions he asked were just weird. And he seemed to be obsessed with my sex life. I had to disappoint him. I hadn't had a sex life for a very long time.

People seem to think that when you're in prison, you'll inevitably succumb to need and find a willing, or unwilling, partner of the same sex. Sure, a lot of guys do. But there are a lot that don't. I was in the second category, and he almost seemed disappointed with my answer.

We'd had a lengthy discussion about the two murders I'd committed, though I refused to acknowledge that I considered what I'd done as murder. The fuckers were going to kill my family, and I had little doubt they planned to leave my body in the desert for the vultures and coyotes. They started the chain of events that led to their deaths. All I did was finish it, and my only regret was the impact on my nice, quiet life.

He asked what I felt about Monica. I was honest when I answered that there hadn't been a single day in prison that I hadn't thought about her. Missed her. Hoped she'd found someone who was treating her right.

She had visited me regularly during the first couple of months leading up to my trial. That was when I actually had hope that the truth would come out and exonerate me. She had met with my lawyer and offered to testify, but she only knew what I'd told her. He rejected her offer, explaining why she couldn't help, and when I found out I exploded. The last thing I ever wanted was for her to get dragged into my mess.

I told her to stop coming. It was one of the hardest things that I've ever done, and I'm sure I broke her heart. But she honored my wishes. Not that I didn't cherish every second I got to see her face and hear her voice, but there was no point. At best, I could hope for life in prison. At worst? In Arizona, murder of a peace officer is a capital crime. Punishable by death if the jury unanimously arrives at that sentence.

Once I was convicted, the penalty phase began. I wasn't really sure which sentence I wanted. Would death really be that much worse than rotting in a cell until I died of old age? I'd already seen some of the lifers, a couple of them so old and decrepit that they were no longer a threat to anyone. They weren't even capable of harming a fly. But they were going to die in prison. Not a dignified way to spend your waning days.

So, despite numerous problems which caused a mistrial of the penalty phase, the court finally got its shit together and empaneled a jury of my peers that decided I deserved to die for what I'd done. By the time this was all over, seven years had passed. I'd already been in prison, and the only thing that changed for me was when I was transferred from a shared cell in the general prison population to a private cell on death row.

The shrink wanted to know about all of this. What I had been feeling. What I thought.

Even what I fantasized about. He didn't appreciate my first answer that I had fantasized about his mother. But we got past that. And I had another appointment with him this afternoon.

"Doctor," Agent Johnson said, getting to his feet when the woman entered the conference room.

He smacked my shoulder and gestured for me to get up. I hadn't had a lot of opportunities to practice my manners over the past decade or so. Feeling sheepish, I stood and looked at the new arrival.

She was not just thin, she was painfully thin. My atrophied arms were larger than the sticks she called legs, which stuck out of the bottom of what I think used to be called a pencil skirt. Today, who the hell knew what the name for the style was.

Her blonde hair was cut short, almost mannish, and she wore a white lab coat over a wildly printed blouse. A thin gold chain was around her neck, suspending a pair of battered reading glasses against her chest.

Johnson nudged me again, and I turned to look at him.

"What?"

"When someone comes in a room and tells you it's a pleasure to meet you, you respond. Don't just stand there like a dork."

"Fuck you," I said, grinning when I saw the storm cloud pass across his face.

"You've been locked away from society for a long time," he said patiently. "You've forgotten how to act around anyone other than convicts. Pay attention so when the time comes, you don't draw attention to yourself. You're going to need to be able to move in any circle. You've got the lazy, redneck asshole part down pat. Now, let's try something new."

He grinned back at me, knowing what he'd said had hit home by the sudden blush that started at my neck and went all the way up. I looked into his dark eyes for a few moments, then nodded.

"Very nice to meet you, too," I said, turning back to the woman. "But I'm afraid you have me at a disadvantage. I don't know your name."

We had TV in prison before I was put on death row. Between the manners my mother had tried to instill in me, and watching TV, I knew the words to say. They just weren't automatic.

The woman looked me in the eye and smiled. A genuine smile of surprise.

"Very well done, Mr. Whitman. My name is Doctor Johanna Anholts. I will be briefing you on our little project. And don't let Agent Johnson get under your skin. He's really just a big, soft teddy bear. Now, gentlemen, if you'll please take your seats, I'll begin."

I started to sit, but Johnson reached out and grabbed my upper arm, preventing me from lowering my ass into the chair. I looked at him, and he nodded at Dr. Anholts. I glanced over and saw that she was still standing, connecting a laptop to a projector. Once she was done, she pulled a chair back and sat down. Johnson released my arm, and I slowly lowered myself onto the upholstery.

The projector flared to life and displayed an image on a screen attached to the front wall. A stylized logo of a clock face with streaks of light swirling around it steadily sharpened as the device auto-focused with a faint whine. Arcing across the top of the logo were the words *Athena Project*. Completing the encirclement of the logo at the bottom was a Latin phrase, *Adhuc Hic Hesterna*.

"Welcome to the Athena Project, Mr. Whitman. The things of yesterday are still with us."

"What does that mean?" I asked, wondering if she wasn't just a little bit touched.

"The Latin, Mr. Whitman. Adhuc hic hesterna. That's what it means."

She pressed a button on the keyboard, and the logo was replaced with a photo of me standing in front of a large 18-wheel truck. Well, not the me my parents would recognize. The new, surgically altered me.

"This is Joseph Ryan Whitman," she said. "Long haul truck driver living in Dallas, Texas. Single. Does nothing other than drive and keep to himself. He is actually an undercover FBI agent who volunteered for this project. Your new features were modeled after his."

"I don't understand," I said.

"I have a lot to tell you. I just wanted you to see this man first. To understand the amount of effort that has been expended to get you here and looking like you do."

"I got that," I said. "But I don't understand why you want me to look exactly like an undercover Fed."

"So you have a real identity, Mr. Whitman. Robert Tracy is gone. You have to be someone if you're going to interact in the world again. And, despite popular fiction, it really isn't that easy to create an identity from scratch. Not for an adult, at least.

"A competent detective, or reporter, would be able to find holes in whatever legend we tried to concoct. There should be birth records, immunization records, school records, photos in yearbooks, bank accounts, old girlfriends... Oh, my, the list goes on and on. The agent's name is not Whitman, any more than yours is. The real Mr. Whitman passed away quietly two years ago from terminal cancer.

"He was a loner. No friends or family. It was much simpler to model the undercover agent after him. To pick up where he left off when he died, if you will."

"You're telling me the agent also had plastic surgery to go undercover?" I asked.

"Precisely, Mr. Whitman. He assumed and has maintained, the identity that is now yours. Once the surgery was complete and he was healed, we inserted him into the life the real Mr. Whitman had built. His absence and spotty memory were easily overlooked since he operated as an independent driver. This was done in preparation for the next male asset to join the project. It was done for you."

She smiled at me, giving me a moment for the information to sink in.

"Why? Why would you do all this?" I asked incredulously.

"Do you read science fiction books or watch the movies, Mr. Whitman?"

"I read some while I was in prison, but didn't have the chance for a night out at the cinema," I said sarcastically.

"Of course," Dr. Anholts smiled. "Then let's just jump into this. Project Athena is the result of a fantastic scientific discovery that came shortly after the superconducting supercollider in Texas was started up. I know, you're probably thinking about the reports that the project was killed by Congress. But that's only what we wanted the public to think. It's up and running as I speak."

I had no clue what the hell she was talking about but decided to keep my mouth shut and listen.

"I'm going to simplify this as much as I can since you don't have an advanced degree in particle physics. Once the collider achieved full power, we began detecting the presence of micro Black Holes. At first, we were terrified. Even a micro Black Hole, in theory, has a gravitational pull of sufficient force to suck the entire Earth inside and collapse it to the size of a basketball.

"But no such thing happened, obviously. Once we analyzed the data, we noticed a small, yet significant, discrepancy in several of our time keeping instruments. Instruments that are incredibly precise in the measurement of time were suddenly showing a variance depending on their proximity to the collider."

She stopped, looking at me with a glow of excitement on her face. Her eyes danced behind the reading glasses.

"So... a couple of clocks were wrong. So what? You're talking about gravity. Maybe they slowed down because the gravity was pulling on their hands," I said, not having a clue what this woman was trying to tell me.

"No!" She cried. "These weren't clocks like you're thinking of. These are extremely sophisticated devices that keep time by using the microwave signal from an atom's electrons when they change energy levels. That makes them the most accurate method known to man for measuring the passage of time."

She paused when she saw me shaking my head.

"OK. I'm sorry. I've given this briefing before, and I always struggle with getting the concept across to laymen. No offense."

She took her reading glasses off and leaned forward, resting her arms on the table.

"We affected time, Mr. Whitman! Not by much, but the steady progression of time was impacted. We turned the collider back on a few months later, and did it again! Only this time, we kept it running and created a stable, self-sustaining micro Black Hole.

"We studied it. Observed the variances in different atomic clocks. Then with that mountain of data, we shut it down for several more weeks. We learned more about the Universe and how it works in those few weeks than in all the rest of human history combined. But the one thing we couldn't see was what was on the other side."

"The other side?" Despite myself, I was being drawn into the story.

"Of the Black Hole," she said, beaming at me. "You see, nothing escapes a Black Hole. Or at least that's what we thought. We devised a test plan and restarted the collider. Once the Black Hole was stable, we inserted a probe into the event horizon.

"The event horizon is the point in spacetime, at the edge of a Black Hole, where nothing that is inside can be seen or measured because of the overwhelming pull of gravity. Even light cannot escape. That's why they're called Black Holes. Anyway, what do you think happened to that probe?"

"It was sucked in and lost?"

"Partially correct, Mr. Whitman. Sucked in? Yes. Lost? We thought so at first. We didn't expect to be able to communicate with it while the collider was running and maintaining the gravity well of the Black Hole, but we hoped to be able to track its signal and find where it went once the collider was turned off. So, we powered it down. And guess where the probe was?"

"I have no idea," I said, struggling to not say something really sarcastic like "up your ass".

"It went to the middle of the Amazon jungle! But that's not the most amazing part. It came back. And one of the instruments on board the probe recorded something truly fantastic. Something we didn't believe until we replicated the test. Multiple times. That probe was not only transported thousands of miles before being returned to us, but it also went back in time. Precisely thirty-six hours!"

I just sat there. Staring at her. She was touched! This was fantasy. I wasn't the most educated guy in the world, probably not even in the room, but I did remember seeing a PBS special about Einstein and how he had proven that time travel was impossible.

"I'm quite sincere, Mr. Whitman," she said after a long stretch of silence. "We successfully sent the probe *back* in time."

"OK," I finally said. "I'm not saying I believe the bullshit you're shoveling, but if you sent something back, how did you find it? Wouldn't it be in your past?"

"Mr. Whitman! How intuitive of you! And you are exactly correct. At first, we thought it was gone. But it returned, thirty-six hours later. We analyzed the data from the onboard instruments and realized that it had traveled backwards in time by thirty-six hours. Existed in *past time*. Then snapped back to our current reality. You see, we have always theorized, and now proven, that time is elastic. Like a rubber band.

"What happens if you stretch a rubber band to its limit without breaking it? It pulls against you. Wants to return to its normal state. Only you're stronger than a rubber band. But when it comes to time, it can be stretched, but it can't be held. At least not yet. There's a calculation I could show you to explain this, but it would take up every wall in this room.

"The instant time is stretched by an object being sent back, the fabric of spacetime begins trying to restore equilibrium. At the exact moment an object arrives in the past, force starts building. It continues to build until the object has been in the past for precisely the amount of time that it traveled backwards. At that instant, it is snapped forward to what we refer to as *real time*, or the timeline the object was in before it was sent back."

My head was spinning. I thought I followed what the crazy woman was saying, but it was so far beyond my ability to grasp that it was easier to dismiss her as a loon.

"Wait," I said, growing more confused by the moment. "You're saying that you sent something thirty-six hours into the past?"

"Yes," she cried. "The probe went back thirty-six hours. When it arrived, exiting the

Black Hole, it once again became subject to the laws of physics and began moving through time as everything does. Only this was time that to us, the observers, had already occurred. Past time! Are you following me?"

"Kind of," I said, not sure I was at all.

"Because of the way the Universe always exerts force to restore balance, when the object reached the point from *when* it was sent, it defaulted back to real time. It just reappeared, exactly where it had been the instant it crossed the Black Hole's event horizon. Thirty-six hours had passed because time is a constant.

"We continued to experiment, and our understanding of spacetime grew exponentially. Old theories were tested. Some were proven, and others were discounted. New theories were developed, and the beauty of it was, we were able to immediately test them.

"Soon, we could control *where* an object arrived when it was sent back. Precisely control, as long as the desired location was properly mapped. We could drop an object anywhere on the face of the Earth with absolute precision. We played with how far back we could go and determined the boundary. Thirty-six hours. We haven't been able to exceed that mark, but we learned how to control what we call *distance*, which is nothing more than how far back we go within that thirty-six hours. And we can now do that as precisely as the location.

"The next logical step at that point was to begin trials with living tissue. Lab rats were embedded with trackers and sent. None survived more than a few hours after arriving in the past. We theorized that the stress of being pulled through the Black Hole had killed them. Careful analysis of the data proved that was the case.

"Their mitochondria were severely damaged by the gravity well. Mitochondria are responsible for the respiration and energy production within your body at the cellular level. Without them, your body shuts down very quickly. We were stumped, but one of our team suggested bringing in the preeminent scientist in the world who specializes in cellular diseases.

"With his help, we continued tests and observed that some of the rats lived longer than others. Using that as a starting point, a genetic marker specific to the longer lived subjects was identified. A very small number of the rats had this marker. The difference was their mitochondria's ability to withstand the forces at work during transport."

She paused and rummaged through a large purse for a bottle of water. I didn't want her to stop talking. Wanted to hear more.

"To shorten the story some," she continued after drinking half the bottle. "We eventually found a rat that survived. Out of well over 100,000 rats whose DNA was reviewed, we found one. And it survived with no ill effects! Now that we knew what to look for, we moved on to other mammals. Pigs. Cats. Dogs. Again, only those with the very rare and specific genetic markers survived.

"The next phase was primates. Chimpanzees. This was a daunting task. We requested and received the DNA panels for every chimp in captivity, pretty much anywhere in the world. None of them had the marker. Expeditions were sent out to capture and take samples from populations in the wild. It took over a year, but we found one. And he survived!

"We finally felt we were ready for human trials. We had already been going through vast genetic databases. And the genetic marker in humans is just as rare as it is in Chimps. Our calculations estimate that only .000001 percent of the human population has it. Out of seven billion people on the planet, that's only seven thousand.

"Out of that seven thousand predicted, we've been able to identify eighty-three that have their DNA on file. And you, Mr. Whitman, are one of those eighty-three people we've found."

"Hold on right there," I said when her statement sank in. "I'm not about to be one of your fucking guinea pigs. No way in hell."

"Relax, Mr. Whitman. We're well beyond the "guinea pig" stage."

I was startled to realize a man was standing just inside the room. The story had so captured my attention that I'd completely missed the door opening as he entered.

"Mr. Patterson. I wasn't expecting you to join us," Dr. Anholts said, looking over her shoulder at the new arrival.

"I had some time and wanted to meet Mr. Whitman," the man said.

He was in his late 40s with a severely receding hairline and a perfectly round little belly that was almost disguised by his well-tailored suit. Everything about him looked soft until I saw his eyes. Hard as flint. There was definitely more to him than a casual first impression would reveal.

Stepping fully into the room, he settled into a chair at the head of the table.

"I'm Ian Patterson. The Director of Project Athena," he said, not holding his hand out to greet me. "Dr. Anholts, please continue your briefing."

There was an awkward moment of silence. Her body language revealed that the good Doctor was uncomfortable with Patterson's presence. She covered by taking another long drink from her bottle of water, then after a moment to compose her thoughts, continued speaking.

"As Director Patterson accurately stated, we are well beyond the testing phase. That was completed a long time ago. We've been routinely sending humans back in time for over five years."

"What?" Was all I could say, stunned at what she'd just said.

"The purpose of Project Athena," Patterson cut in. "Something bad happens. We go back in time and stop it before it happened."

"What?" I said again, looking back and forth between him and Dr. Anholts.

"Allow me to demonstrate," she said, waking her laptop and clicking the mouse several times.

Dirk Patton

I looked up at the screen when an image of a burning airport was displayed. Then a large room that looked like the interior of a government building with dozens of bodies scattered across the floor. The crash site of an airliner. An aerial shot of a shopping mall parking lot littered with bodies. The mushroom cloud of a nuclear bomb boiling into the sky, the Statue of Liberty in the foreground.

"What the fuck is this?" I breathed, staring in horror at the final image.

"These are terrorist attacks on the United States that were successfully carried out over the past five years," Patterson said, staring at the screen. "Attacks that were retroactively stopped by sending Project Athena assets back in time. Stopped them before they happened, so in effect, they didn't happen."

"I don't understand," I said, unable to take my eyes off the fireball captured in a still image as it consumed Manhattan.

"Assets are the people with the rare genetic marker that work for Project Athena," Agent Johnson spoke for the first time.

"Correct," Dr. Anholts nodded her head as if she needed to confirm what he'd just said. "Let me explain."

She turned in her chair and gestured at the screen.

"This photo was taken by a merchant seaman sailing from New York just over 18 months ago. The bomb had been purchased from a Pakistani General by a radical Islam terror group and smuggled into the US over the Mexican border. Once in the country, they just drove to Manhattan and detonated it as soon as they arrived.

"Two levels below us are over a hundred FBI and NSA analysts whose only job is to wait for an event, such as this one. As soon as something occurs, they go into action. Looking for an *event point*. An event point is what we call a point in time within our thirty-six-hour window where we have an opportunity to interdict the perpetrator or perpetrators and stop them.

"They are tapped into everything and can monitor the investigation in real time. There are also another two hundred, specially trained FBI agents in the field, spread across North America. Within minutes of an event, they are in contact with the analysts, aiding in the collection of information.

"Together, they piece together a puzzle and determine *where* and *when* to send the asset. Once we have that information, the asset is sent back."

"To stop the attack?" I asked, starting to get the picture.

"By any means necessary," Patterson chimed in.

Dr. Anholts gave him an irritated look that he didn't see before continuing.

"Once the asset successfully completes their mission, time changes. The attack doesn't occur. People, other than possibly the perpetrators, don't die. Job complete, the asset simply waits for time to expire and is brought back to *real time*, where things have been changed back to the way they were. Ready for their next assignment."

"You want me to be one of your assets."

Things had finally clicked for me. The pieces were falling into place, painting a picture I wasn't at all sure I liked.

"Correct, Mr. Whitman," Patterson said, turning his full attention on me.

"What if I decline?" I asked, not really sure what I felt.

"Well then, that would be another bad decision on your part," Patterson said, glaring at me. "You see; you don't really exist. The State of Arizona executed you for capital crimes. And Joseph Ryan Whitman is alive and well, driving a truck from Dallas to Miami at the moment. Who are you, other than a dead man?"

The room went completely silent when he spoke. Not only could you have heard a pin drop, you could have heard it whish through the air as it fell. I stared at him in shock, my mouth set in a grim, hard line. Even though it only seemed like yesterday that I had been an inmate on death row, my reprieve had made me want to live again.

Anger coursed through me, threatening to turn into full blown rage. The kind of rage that had kept me mostly safe while I was in the general population of murderers, rapists and arsonists. It was only through a supreme effort of will that I kept my ass in the chair and didn't leap across the table and throttle the son of a bitch.

"I'm sorry if that sounds harsh, Mr. Whitman," Patterson said, appearing to be anything but sorry. "But there is really no other option at this point."

"So I work for you, or you kill me. Is that it?"

"Succinctly put," he nodded as he answered.

"What's to prevent me from taking off as soon as you send me back?"

"Weren't you listening to Dr. Anholts? You can only go back for a maximum of thirty-six hours. When that time expires, you are returned to us. There's nothing you can do to stop that from happening. Nowhere you can go or hide. The Universe doesn't care. It will find you, and when you come back, we'll know if you've done your job or not."

I stared at him, seriously considering going for his throat. One hard blow, in the right spot, and his larynx would collapse. Maybe they could get him to medical care in time to prevent his death. Maybe not. But thoughts of what would happen to me tempered my desire to see him writhing on the floor as he died.

Calming my murderous impulses, I thought about what he was saying. What he was offering. What was he offering? Other than being rescued from the executioner's needle, what did I get out of this?

"What's in it for me?" I asked, slowly sitting back in my chair.

For the first time, I noticed Agent Johnson sitting next to me. His hand was balled into a fist the size of a picnic ham. I realized that he was prepared to stop me if I had tried to attack Patterson. Looking at him, I grinned and cut my eyes down to his hand. He smiled back and nodded, letting me know I'd guessed correctly.

"Life, Mr. Whitman. That's what is in it for you. And I've already delivered on my end of that bargain. Without the Athena Project, you would be six feet under at the moment."

"So... what? I just hang around and wait for something to happen, go take care of it and come back to wait for the next time I'm needed?"

"That's pretty much it," he said. "But you won't be bored. Our assets need to be able to deal with any situation that arises. Be prepared for any eventuality. That's where Agent Johnson comes in. He's not your babysitter. He's your team leader, and there's a rather large team ready to start working with you.

"You will be taught everything we can think of to make sure you are the most prepared and lethal individual in any situation. Language skills. Science and mathematics. Religion.

Combat training. Everything you need to survive and successfully complete your missions, we will give you.

"And it is Agent Johnson's job to ensure you are ready. He will oversee the team that trains you. And he reports to me. If you are unable, or unwilling, to do what needs to be done, he will let me know. You do not want to find out what will happen if that is the case."

I stared at him for a long moment. Thinking. Evaluating my options. Well, trying to evaluate my options. It's hard to evaluate something that doesn't exist. Then I flashed back to a conversation I'd had with Monica. She'd told me that we always have choices, just that some of them weren't the ones we wanted. As far as I could see, I had two. Play ball, or die. I didn't doubt Patterson's sincerity for an instant.

"I don't have much choice, do I?"

"No, Mr. Whitman. You do not. So are you ready to commit?"

"Like I said, I don't have much choice. I'm yours."

I didn't voice the second part of that, rather kept "until I find a way out", silent in my mind.

"Very good, Mr. Whitman. Welcome to Project Athena. I expect great things from you."

Patterson stood and strode out of the room without another word. I sat there staring at the door for several moments after he left.

"You OK?" Johnson asked me in his rumbling baritone.

"No," I said. "But I don't seem to have much choice about that either."

We took a break at that point. Dr. Anholts scurried out of the room ahead of us. Johnson escorted me to the open platform so we could get some fresh air. It was a partly cloudy day with a gentle breeze blowing across the deck. The sea was a beautiful shade of blue, gentle swells marching across the surface towards some distant shoreline.

Johnson pulled a cigar and butane torch from his jacket, a moment later the stogie smoldering to his satisfaction.

"Want one?" He offered, blowing out a thick plume of smoke.

I shook my head. Thankfully, I'd never picked up the disgusting habit. Moving upwind, I turned to face him.

"He's serious, isn't he? I asked, meaning Patterson.

"Very," he nodded. "And don't think I'm not on board."

I was surprised at that. Here was an FBI agent telling me that he would condone my murder if I didn't do what they wanted.

"You seem surprised," he said after watching my face.

"This is so fucking surreal. Work for us or die. What are you guys? The goddamn Nazis?"

"What we are is a nation at war," he said, unaffected by my characterization of him and his boss. "Do you have any idea how many innocent Americans died in the attacks that Dr. Anholts showed you?"

"No," I said, not liking that I knew where he was going.

"Almost two million," he said gravely, puffing on the cigar. "And if we hadn't gone back and changed what happened, probably two or three million more would have died a slow and painful death from radiation sickness.

"And we've not been successful in every attempt. A few months ago there was an attack on a ferry boat in Seattle. Our asset went back, but without much time. She perished in the attempt to save over 2,000 lives. This isn't a perfect world. If the enemy employs effective compartmentalization and maintains operational security, it's very difficult to identify an event point. In the case of the ferry, we didn't even identify the perpetrator until there was less than an hour of the thirty-six hour window remaining. Because of that, we failed.

"So, if you ask me if this is fair? Is it even legal? To force you to work for us like this? No, it isn't. But it's the best option we have. And where would you be if it wasn't for us? It's not like we plucked you out of a normal life with a good job and a loving family. Said do this or die.

"We snatched you out of death's arms. We're giving you a second chance. A chance you didn't give to Mike Eppers and Ricardo Morales."

He was referring to the two cops I'd killed. I had finally learned their names when my case went to trial.

"They didn't give me a choice," I protested, getting angry.

"Did you call the FBI when they threatened your brother? The DEA? What about the State Police?"

He knew the answer but wasn't going to continue until I responded. I shook my head and looked down at the deck.

"Why not?"

"They didn't give me…"

"I didn't ask you what your excuse was. I asked why you *chose* to not call some authorities who could help."

He stared hard at me through a cloud of smoke, his eyes boring into mine when I looked up.

"I didn't think they'd believe me. Or if they did, there wasn't time to convince them I was telling the truth before Tim would be killed."

"You didn't know that," he said, more gently. "You didn't have anything to base that decision on. So what happened? You killed two men and were sentenced to death. No, they weren't good men. But did they deserve to die? Your choice to try and handle things your way set events in motion that led to their deaths, and you standing here talking to me."

"And killed my brother," I said in a quiet voice, breaking eye contact and turning to look at the ocean.

Tim had been killed about the same time I was being arrested for murder. I'll never know if this was just random prison violence, or if the cops had an accomplice who carried out their threat to pay off the warden for the hit.

"I'm sorry," Johnson said, and I believed he sincerely was.

"So. What now?" I asked, wiping my eyes and turning to face him.

"Now we finish the briefing with Dr. Anholts. Then you have an appointment with the shrink. After that, school is in session. It's time to start teaching you how to survive in the world we're going to drop you in."

I nodded and started for the door, pausing when he gently placed his big hand on my arm.

"Look, JR," he said in a fatherly tone. "I wasn't trying to rag on you or make you feel bad. This was a lesson. The first of many. A lesson about choices, and how the ones we make have an impact on everyone else. Soon, something bad is going to happen, and you're going to be dropped in the middle of it.

"You'll be on your own, and you're going to have to make split second decisions. And they have to be the right decisions or lots of people will stay dead. You have to think things through, and you have to learn to do it quickly. It's called critical thinking.

"Evaluate a situation, develop a course of action and predict the consequences. Then you make your choice after exploring all of the possible outcomes. And you have to do it fast, often by the seat of your pants.

"Not every decision you make will have a positive outcome. You're not perfect. But you have to strive to be. To think three dimensionally. Do you understand?"

"No," I said.

"That's alright," he smiled, tossing the cigar over the rail and into the sea. "We have people that will help you with that, too."

We stopped in the restroom and five minutes later were back at the conference table. Dr. Anholts had returned and was furiously typing away on her laptop. I caught a glimpse of the screen as I walked in. Row upon row of mathematical formulas. Shaking my head in amazement that a human could actually comprehend that chicken scratch, I took my seat and waited for her to look up.

"Shall we resume?" She asked a minute later, closing the computer's lid.

Johnson and I both nodded that we were ready.

"I've been doing all the talking up until now. You must have questions, Mr. Whitman."

I hadn't consciously thought about it, but my brain had been working on the fantastic things I'd learned while Johnson and I were having our discussion.

"Those pictures you showed me. They're actual photos of terrorist attacks that were… what's the right word? Undone?"

"We use the term, *redacted*," she smiled. "Yes, they are real images."

"OK. So, if they've been redacted, as you say, how do you have pictures? You sent someone back, and they changed the past by stopping the attacks. That means the attacks never happened. If they never happened, how can you have pics? For that matter, how can you even know about something that never happened?"

I was pleased with myself, thinking I'd caught her in a lie. Suppressing a smile, I sat back in my chair and waited, expecting her to hesitate and sputter as she tried to answer.

"Excellent question, Mr. Whitman. You really are very sharp. To answer it, we cheated."

"Cheated? You mean you faked the photos and are lying to me?"

"Not at all," she said, a note of indignation creeping into her voice when I questioned her integrity. "Your assumption is spot on. Not your idea that we are lying to you, but your belief that if something never happened there would be no way for us to know about it, let alone have photographic evidence.

"This was a problem we anticipated early on, and we came up with a solution. We had to. Had to be able to demonstrate our successes. We are, after all, a government funded project. That means Congressional oversight. If we didn't have a way to show what would have happened without us, our funding would have dried up a long time ago.

"In fact, after the successful redaction of the nuclear attack on Manhattan, our funding was quadrupled, and now we get anything we ask for. You see, that bomb not only killed millions of New Yorkers, it also completely destroyed Wall Street. The Federal Reserve. The list goes on and on. Can you imagine the entire financial foundation of the country wiped out in an instant?

"But, I'm not answering your question. Each asset has a data chip implanted in their body. We put yours in while you were unconscious, healing from your plastic surgeries.

From the moment an event is identified, every single bit of information that is gathered is automatically streamed wirelessly to that chip, where it is stored in non-volatile memory.

"Up to the point where the asset is sent back. That's when the record stops because we haven't figured out how to transmit a wireless signal back in time. Perhaps if we do, it will no longer be necessary to send an asset. But that's probably a long way off.

"So, an asset is sent back with a data chip implanted in their body with all the details of the event they're assigned to redact. If they are successful, you are correct in thinking that as far as real time is concerned, the event never occurred. At the precise moment the asset changes events, all of us who are here in real time are blissfully unaware that anything has happened, or that we've even sent an asset back in time.

"Until the clock runs out and the asset suddenly returns. With a chip full of horrific images that, to us, never happened. It's actually quite disconcerting to sit down and review the data from an asset's chip after they've had a successful redaction. After the New York event, several of our staff had to be sedated. It was just too much for them to think that except for our project, millions of people would be dead."

"OK, that makes sense. I guess. Why isn't the data on the chip changed? It came from a future that no longer happens, or exists, or however you phrase it."

"It took us some time to answer that very question, and the proof of why it works is impossible to explain to someone who does not understand theoretical physics. Suffice it to say that the data chip can't be affected by whatever actions the asset takes, successful or not.

"We've tested this thoroughly, and the results are the same every time. Arrive before something that is recorded happens, and it stays exactly as it was written to the chip."

I nodded, understanding the words despite my head spinning.

"Fine. I suppose I have to take you at your word. But why are you using people? Assets? You told me that you can send an object to any point on Earth with high precision. The analysts identify a when and a where and that's the location where the asset is sent.

"Why not just send a bomb or something else that would kill the terrorists before they can pull off their attack? If you can be so accurate, why do you need people?"

Agent Johnson cleared his throat and sat forward. Dr. Anholts and I turned to look at him.

"You were in the Army," he said. "How do you make absolutely sure someone is dead? Permanently out of action without collateral damage? Do you send a bomber overhead, or does it take boots on the ground? I'm not talking about a result that's classified as a "high probability kill". I'm talking about absolute certainty. The bad guy is down and dead. He's not going to recover from wounds sustained in the bombing and continue his attack on a future date. And do that without killing a bunch of innocent bystanders?"

He looked at me expectantly, and I realized just how foolish my question had been. He was exactly right. Bombs are messy things. Don't get me wrong, they're invaluable tools, but they can't replace a pair of human eyes verifying the target is down. And making sure it stays that way. Permanently.

"Point taken," I said, another thought popping into my head. "How many of us are there? You keep saying assets, not asset."

Dr. Anholts and Johnson exchanged a glance, then he sat forward.

"You're it," he said.

"What? I'm it? What happened to the others? What about all the other people you've identified with the genetic marker? What was it, 83 of us?"

"This is a very dangerous occupation, Mr. Whitman. Assets deal with some very bad people. They don't always come back alive. To answer your second question, some are children, tagged for possible future recruitment. Some are infirm or elderly, or otherwise unsuited for the job. Still others are of an ethnic origin or political/religious belief that would preclude us from approaching them."

"How many?" I asked.

"How many, what?"

"How many assets have come and died before me?"

"Four," he said after a long pause.

"How? How did they die?"

"All of them died stopping, or trying to stop, attacks before they could happen."

"I want the details," I said, worrying they weren't being completely truthful with me about the effects of being sent backwards in time.

"I'll put in a request with Director Patterson," he said, his tone clearly indicating he was through discussing this topic.

I didn't have any further questions. Well, I had lots of questions, but nothing I was ready to ask. The biggest one was what would it take to go back more than thirty-six hours? Like, say, eleven years.

Go back and stop Tim from going to Mexico. What would my life be like when I snapped back to real time if I could pull that off? A house in the suburbs? Monica and I raising a whole parcel of noisy, obnoxious kids? Then a thought occurred to me as I was getting up to be escorted to my shrink appointment.

"Dr. Anholts. One more question. If an asset changed something in the past that caused this place to not exist, what would happen when they came back to real time?"

"That can't happen," she said, pausing in gathering her personal items. "An asset can only go back thirty-six hours. This facility has been in place much longer than that. It's already in operation, in the past, when the asset arrives."

19

The next six months went by more quickly than I would have believed. But when you're busy for sixteen hours a day, there's not much time to think about anything other than what you're doing. Daily counseling sessions with the shrink. Time with instructors who taught me practical uses for math and science. Philosophical discussions on religion with a retired professor from Harvard. What was called social engineering with a former con-man who'd been sprung from a federal prison for this gig. Etiquette with a female instructor I dubbed Miss Manners.

Then there was the physical and combat training. Mile upon mile on the fucking treadmill. Then the weight room before hand to hand fighting. Edged weapons. Firearms. Everything from Close Quarters Battle (CQB) to making thousand yard shots with a sniper rifle. I enjoyed the sniper training the most as it had to be conducted outdoors on the helipad.

I would lay prone, near the edge, with the rifle tight to my shoulder. The trainer would then send a remote controlled toy boat out into the ocean, and I'd have to hit a bobbing target the size of a cantaloupe. It didn't fail to register with me that this was also roughly the size of a human head. The instructor was a former Marine sniper and was relentless. And I learned.

And healed. My hands felt normal again, as did my face. Even if I still didn't recognize myself when I looked in the mirror to shave. I've never been a fan of shaving, usually wearing a thick stubble for several days at a time rather than scrape a razor across my chin. At least since I got out of the Army.

Now, however, that wasn't an option. The plastic surgery had messed with my facial hair follicles. If I skipped shaving, soon it was obvious something wasn't quite right. No hair grew on half of my upper lip and only in a few thick patches on my cheeks and under my chin. Should I try to grow a beard, I'd look like a poodle trimmed for a dog show. So I carefully shaved every morning.

As I progressed and grew more confident with the new skills I was learning, I found myself thinking more and more about the harebrained idea I'd had to go back and stop Tim. Hell, he was dead anyway. If I had to, I'd kill him to stop him. I felt horrible every time I had that thought, but I'd had a lot of time to think about what he had cost me.

Everything. My life hadn't been my own since the afternoon those two cops had shown up in my apartment. I didn't buy into Johnson's feelings about my choice. I knew in my heart there hadn't been another option. Besides, those guys were playing a dangerous game that didn't exactly have the best record when it came to living a long and healthy life. If I hadn't killed them, someone else almost certainly would have at some point.

Part of me worried I was a bad person for having these thoughts. That same part considered discussing it with the shrink. But I knew the doctor wasn't here for my benefit. His primary role was to evaluate my mental health and report to Patterson. Was I fit for duty, or was I going to go off the deep end the moment I was free in the past and out from under their constant attention?

Keeping my personal thoughts personal, I focused on my training and how to go about finding a way to change my situation. I'd run across Dr. Anholts a couple of times in the large cantina that fed all of the staff assigned to the project. Each time, I'd acted very happy to see her, chattering brightly and smiling at whatever she had to say.

Maybe I was barking up the wrong tree, but to me, she seemed to be the key to achieving what I wanted. I saw her again at breakfast this morning, sitting by herself, hunched over a laptop. Grabbing a bowl of oatmeal from the serving line, I walked over and stood next to her chair.

"Solving more unsolvable problems? Saving the world?" I asked in a teasing voice.

She looked up at me and smiled, quickly removing her reading glasses.

"Mr. Whitman! Good morning. No, I'm just reviewing one of my staff's calculations. Nothing so dramatic as saving the world."

She smiled brightly, seemingly happy to see me. I was about to ask if I could join her when a strident klaxon began blaring. She jumped to her feet and snatched the laptop off the table.

"What the hell's that?" I asked, worrying we were about to sink or topple over into the ocean.

"There's been an event," she said as she turned to dash away. "Find Agent Johnson. He'll tell you what to do."

Then she was gone, disappearing in the crowd of people who were all running for their assigned workstations. I let them clear out, not seeing the need to push into the mayhem. But Agent Johnson had different ideas.

I spotted him, towering over all of the people squeezing their way through the exit doors. He bulled his way in, gently but firmly moving bodies out of his path. He saw me immediately and waved for me to join him. I trotted over, the area clear of people by the time I reached him.

"What's up?" I asked when I was close enough to not have to shout to be heard.

"Event. That's what the alarm is all about. Don't know details. Come on, we're going to the operations center."

I fell in behind him and followed his broad back through several twists and turns, then up a set of metal stairs to a door I'd never been through. I'd been allowed more and more freedom of movement, but still wasn't trusted with a key card to get me through locked doors. That was OK. I wouldn't have gone exploring anyway. No reason to draw unnecessary attention.

Dirk Patton

Johnson held his card to the pad, and the door slid open automatically. Keeping the card in place, he waved me through ahead of him. The door slid shut seconds after he stepped in. I stood where I'd stopped, looking around.

The room was small, only a handful of people staffing a limited number of workstations. Patterson stood on the highest level, watching his people work in between looking at several screens. He glanced at us when we entered, but didn't acknowledge our presence in any other way.

Flat panel monitors were in abundance, displaying everything from an image of the rig's helipad to a live feed from CNN. But what caught my attention was the room on the other side of a large bank of windows. And the machine that sat in full view of everyone in the operations room.

Maybe calling it a machine wasn't accurate. It actually seemed to be nothing more than a slightly raised dais enclosed with curved glass panels. I had a pretty good idea what it was, just had been expecting something much more Sci-Fi movie looking.

"Is that it?" I asked Johnson in a low voice.

"Yes. Impressive, isn't it?" He said with a sarcastic grin.

Every now and then his façade slipped, and I got a glimpse of the real Bill Johnson. I was pretty sure he was actually an easy going guy with a quick wit that tended towards sarcasm. But like the other times I'd gotten a peek, the exterior shell slammed back into place.

"Pay attention," he said quietly, pointing at the TV playing CNN.

It was a terrorist attack on an elementary school in suburban Los Angeles. A local news station already had a helicopter over the scene, and we watched as a SWAT unit rushed towards the entrance. There were small puffs of smoke appearing around the body armor clad officers, and it took me a moment to realize it was because they were firing their assault rifles as they advanced.

Two of them fell, but the rest continued their charge. It dawned on me that these guys were running into the face of gunfire because there was a building full of children in danger. I found myself growing angry as another cop dropped to the asphalt, then the rest of them moved under an awning and out of view of the news camera.

"Audio feed from the local police, sir," a woman working a complicated array of equipment said to Patterson.

She pressed a button, and the sounds of gunfire and men screaming filled the room. After my time in the Army, and more recently all of my firearms training, I could recognize the difference between the lighter NATO caliber rifles the cops were firing, and the heavier reports of what I was pretty sure were AK-74s.

The battle raged for close to five minutes, hundreds of rounds being fired by each side. Then it began to peter out, and I was encouraged to hear only police weapons. They'd gotten the upper hand.

Then the main fight was over, and it was time to clear the building and mop up. The SWAT team's tactical radios were set to transmit, and we clearly heard every word as they moved through the school searching for additional terrorists.

"I've got video now," the same operator said. A moment later a large panel on the side wall flared to life and showed the view from the helmet cam of one of the cops as he moved down an empty hall lined with corkboards covered with crayon art.

I balled my hands into fists when I saw the image. Not long before my fateful day, Monica's young son, Manny, had drawn a picture of the three of us in crayon. It was stick figures, the smallest one standing between the two adults and holding hands with them. At the time, Monica and I were nothing more than just friends who enjoyed having great sex with each other, and it hadn't meant as much to me as maybe it should have.

The cops came to a door, pausing as they stacked up and prepared to enter a classroom. I held my breath as the door was yanked open and black clad bodies flowed into the room. Then the camera followed, and I heard a couple of the officers begin hyperventilating. Soon, someone was sobbing. At least twenty small bodies were strewn across the floor. An adult female's bullet-riddled corpse between the door and all of the dead children.

"Motherfucker," I breathed and heard Johnson begin mumbling a prayer.

The cops quickly checked the bodies, not finding any of them alive. Back in the hall, they moved to the next room and found a similar scene. Only this time their weapons were up, and they were shouting. When the camera focused, I could see a wounded man lying in the far corner.

He was wearing a kufi on his head and had a thick, dark beard. Definitely appeared to be of middle eastern descent. A rifle was across his lap, but he was in bad shape and wasn't able to lift it to keep fighting.

The camera blanked out a moment before there was the sound of fully automatic weapons fire.

"Charlie one, what the fuck was that?" A voice shouted over the radio. Had to be a commander waiting outside the school.

"Suspect was reaching for his weapon," one of the cops answered. "He's down, now."

For five minutes we listened as the cops continued to move through the school. There were the sounds of doors being opened and closed, and once more a long burst of full automatic fire. Finally, the building was declared clear, and Patterson told the operator to shut off the audio.

20

"You don't need to threaten me anymore," I said softly to Agent Johnson. "Just put me in a room with those motherfuckers. I'll redact all their asses before they can hurt one of those kids."

"I thought you'd come around," he said. "I just wish I could go with you."

His jaw was clenched, and he spoke through gritted teeth. The muscles all along his neck and the side of his face were bunched and bulging. So were mine. It's one thing to target soldiers or law enforcement. Or even adults. But to go after children? These weren't humans. They were just animals that needed to be erased from the face of the planet.

"Let's go," Johnson said a moment later. "We need to start getting you ready. The team is good, and we'll probably have an event point to target in a few hours."

"Why not just send me back now? I'll wait outside the school until they show up."

I was pissed. Incensed. Wanted to wade into this group and put my newly acquired deadly skills to the test.

"I appreciate your enthusiasm, Mr. Whitman," Patterson said.

He'd heard my comment and stepped closer to us.

"But that's not a good idea. We don't know how many terrorists you'll be facing. Did they spread out and enter the school from different points? That would mean you couldn't stop all of them. And how much attention do you think an adult male skulking around an elementary school would draw? You'd likely have the police asking you questions you couldn't answer well before the time of the attacks.

"We do things the way we do for a reason, and we're very good at what we do. Stay patient and listen to Agent Johnson. He'll guide you through what you don't understand yet."

I nodded, surprised at the man's reaction. He hadn't been scolding me. It was obvious he was shaken to the core by what we'd seen, and he'd recognized that I was too. Yet he'd taken a moment to patiently explain things to me. Maybe I needed to reevaluate him. Maybe.

Johnson tapped my arm, and I turned and followed him out of the room. We headed straight for what was called the "prep". It was a combination gym locker room and military armory. All different styles and types of clothing hung in a dozen different lockers. Each piece was in my size, and I would dress appropriately for the event point I was being sent to.

One wall was covered with just about every type of personal weapon I could imagine. Pistols, rifles, shotguns, grenades, knives, collapsible steel batons, stun guns, pepper spray... if the armorer could think of it, it was there. And none of them had a serial number or any identifying marks.

"We need to go over a few things that haven't been addressed yet," Johnson said, waving me to a seat.

"What do we need to go over? Give me a gun and point me at them!"

"Patience, Mr. Whitman. Patience. You should have learned that in the infantry. Rushing headlong into a battle when you're not properly prepared and don't have all the information is a recipe for disaster. Correct?"

I nodded my head, forcing down my impatience and desire to go dispense some good old fashioned justice.

"First and foremost, you need to remember that you are our one and only shot at redacting this event. If you don't succeed, those children will remain dead. If you get impatient and go charging in, guns blazing, and the terrorists kill you, those children remain dead. Do you understand?"

"Yes. Sorry," I mumbled, his words sobering me.

"Don't be sorry," he smiled. "I understand exactly how you feel. I feel the same way. But this has to be approached methodically and professionally. Odds are already stacked against you. You will be outnumbered, most likely significantly. But you will have the element of surprise on your side. They won't be expecting you. And you must take full advantage of that.

"Remember what all of your instructors have been teaching you. Don't telegraph what you're about to do. Remain calm until it's time for action. But when it's time, you strike with every weapon and skill we've given you. No mercy. You're not a cop. It's not your job to disable or disarm the perpetrators and leave them for law enforcement to scoop up. It is your job to take these assholes off the table. Permanently."

I nodded, meeting his eyes. He didn't need to worry about what I intended to do. These fuckers were dead the instant I had my shot. But the rest of what he was saying was something I needed to hear. To be reminded that I had to go into battle with intelligent forethought. I'd have one opportunity to stop the event, and if I fucked up, there wouldn't be another chance.

"One final thing," he said. "All of these weapons, even the brass of the ammunition, have been specially coated with a silicone based compound. What that means is that nothing will take a fingerprint. Don't worry about cleaning up brass, and if you have to leave a weapon behind, it doesn't matter.

"But that only applies to what's being sent with you. Any hard surface you encounter *after* being sent will take and hold prints. Avoid that if at all possible, but we understand it can happen."

"What about DNA?" I asked. "What if I get shot or cut and leave some blood behind?"

"Even traces of blood, or hair for that matter, are still part of you that was sent back and will be returned to real time when the clock expires. That will leave the investigators with nothing to test. Assuming they are on the ball and test a sample before you're brought back, we've already erased all records of your DNA. They'd have a panel, but nothing to match it against."

"Wait. Won't my fingerprints come forward with me, too?"

"No," he shook his head. "The body is constantly producing oils to keep our skin healthy and flexible. It will be producing those oils in the past. Anything that is produced in that time will remain in that time when you come back to real time. Understand?"

"I think so. Kind of," I said. "OK. What if something happens and I'm caught? Arrested?"

"It's really best if that can be avoided. But if you can't, do not resist the police, and do not say anything. If that happens, the *me* that is in *that* time will be immediately notified the moment you're taken into custody and printed. You'll still be brought forward when time is up, and there is a team of agents on call to clean up any record of you being detained."

"You mean I might be in an interrogation room or jail cell and will just disappear when time's up?"

"Exactly," Johnson said. "Not necessarily what we want, but it's happened before. Now, we need to get you ready to go. The analysts could identify the event point at any moment."

We stood and surveyed the clothing available to us. It was Southern California. That typically meant pleasant days and chilly nights this time of year. It also meant casual, comfortable attire. Jeans with a T-shirt, a pair of Nike running shoes and a light jacket. The reflective stripes on the Nikes had been replaced with a dull black plastic, and the shirt was navy blue with no printing. The jacket was also dark.

The outfit would look perfectly normal in the daytime, and would maximize my stealth once the sun went down. A black, knit cap with a cuffed brim went into a jacket pocket. It could be worn like a beanie, or unrolled and create a ski mask to cover my features. It would hide my identity and conceal my white face which might show up and give me away in the night.

Dressed, we stepped over to the cache of weapons. Larger items, such as an assault or sniper rifle, were dependent upon the conditions identified when an event point was determined. If I was being sent back to a shopping mall or restaurant, or any public place, it might be difficult to arrive with a long gun hanging down my back.

But pistols and knives and other goodies are easy to conceal. Soon, three guns, four knives, a stun gun and a steel baton were secreted on my person. Spare magazines for what would be my primary weapon were also added. Unused to being so heavily armed, it took a while of walking around the locker room for me to get everything adjusted so I felt I could move without giving away that I was ready to start World War III.

"What about body armor?" I asked, pointing at a locker stuffed full of different vests.

"Depends on the event point," Johnson said, looking me over and adjusting my jacket to ensure the pistol at the small of my back wasn't outlined by the fabric.

"Remember, you're going to be in California. Gun laws are strict. If a cop even thinks he detects a concealed weapon, he's going to want a closer look. Be careful to not give them a reason to take an interest in you."

"But I'm going to arrive and start fighting. Right? Isn't that what the event point is all about? A moment in time when I can put them down before they attack?"

"I thought you were paying better attention than that," Johnson sighed. "OK. Make sure you get it this time. The event point is a point in time that is determined to be your best opportunity to interdict the terrorists. That doesn't mean you go hot and start shooting the instant you arrive.

"It may be decided that you need to be there an hour ahead of the event point, so you have time to prepare. Or ten hours early. There's no correct point to arrive. Each situation is different. Right now, the analysts are looking at everything that has been learned about the perpetrators and back-tracing them from the moment they launched the attack.

"Once they identify the event point, they will begin running simulations and make a recommendation on *when* and *where* you should be sent. Once that is ready, Director Patterson will review the results and make the final call. But in five years, I've never seen him not take the team's recommendation."

"Got it," I said. "Sorry. I was paying attention and I do remember that."

"Slow your roll, grasshopper," Johnson grinned briefly then realized he'd slipped again, and the smile disappeared from his face.

"You'll do fine," he said in his officious voice. "Just remember your training and focus on making sure you get it right the first time."

"Hey. What do I do once the terrorists are dead? If you send me back really early, it could be a whole day and night before I return. Right?"

Johnson sighed deeply and glared at me for a moment.

"You weren't paying attention," he grumbled. "When you get back, you've got some remedial training to go through."

I grinned sheepishly. I kind of remembered the briefing I had received on the subject. But there had been one small problem. The woman who'd delivered it. She was smokin' hot, and it had been a very long time for me. I'd probably been more interested in staring at her tits and ass than paying attention to what she had to say.

"I kind of remember, but tell me again," I said.

"Jesus H," he began, then took a deep breath. "You know what? You need a blow job worse than any white man I've ever met."

For a moment, I was stunned this had come out of Agent Johnson's mouth. Sure, he'd shown glimmers of being more than an uptight FBI agent, but this was as much as he'd ever shown of the real person behind the mask.

"I really hope that's not an offer," I grinned.

36

"Fuck off," he chuckled, then wiped the smile off his face and glared at me again. "Once the mission is complete, you are to find a private location and stay out of sight for the duration of your time in the past. You are to avoid contact with any person that is not absolutely necessary for a successful redaction.

"You will be in the past, Mr. Whitman. There is the potential for a significant impact to time as a result. A chance encounter can set a chain of unpredictable events into motion that were never intended to happen. And as was explained to you, the smallest change to the past can ripple forward through time, growing exponentially. We might not see the results for years or decades to come, but that doesn't mean the potential for disaster isn't there.

"What if, while you're in the past, you are tired of waiting and decide to go to... I don't know. Let's say a bar, to get a drink. While you're in the bar, you witness a man slap a woman and choose to intervene. You save her from a few slaps, but what else did you just set in motion?

"Maybe that slap was the only time he ever lays a hand on her, and if you hadn't stepped in they wound up working things out. And have a child. And that child grows up to be an influential businessman or woman. Or maybe even President of the United States. But because of your interference, that child is never born because the parents didn't have the chance to work out whatever caused him to slap her.

"Or what if you inspire her to stand up to an abusive husband, and she decides to kill him, rather than pack up and leave in the middle of the night. And she winds up in prison for the rest of her life. He's dead, and she's ruined. But what would either of those people have done in the future to influence the world? Because of you, they never had the opportunity to do it."

"But those are just *what ifs*," I protested.

"Exactly. And if you can't answer the question, you can't interfere. Because there's no way for you to know the impact of your actions. Sending an asset back in time is a tremendous risk. The potential for unintended consequences is almost assured. Why do you think we don't go back and prevent smaller events? Like, say the murder of one or two people. Or a suicide.

"We've gone round and round about this since the project began. The best minds in the country have argued and are still arguing, the wisdom of risking a change to time. But what everyone agreed on is that there are some events so heinous that we have a moral responsibility to redact them."

"Not everyone," I said.

"Ahh, that's right. You've spent time with Professor Riley."

He was referring to one of the theological experts I had worked with, learning about the religious beliefs of the primary threat to the safety and security of the US. We'd had several discussions about history and human nature.

The Professor's position had been that humans needed horrific events to bring us together and keep us moving forward as a society. Without those, he claimed, man would grow more and more self-centered and unwilling to make the hard choices necessary to preserve the species.

His favorite argument was that without the Holocaust, there would be one less nation on the planet. That the murder of millions of Jews was the impetus that brought about Israel. He laid out a scenario in which we were able to go far enough back in time to kill Hitler and all of his henchmen before they seized power in Germany.

Then, based on what was happening in the world at the end of the 1930s, he projected what he claimed would have been the probable events that shaped our modern world. According to his theories, without World War II, the US would not have developed atomic weapons. Would not have mobilized every single citizen to a war footing.

It would have been Germany, who was scientifically far ahead of America at the time, who created the first nuclear bomb. And facing the threat posed by Stalin, Germany used them on Russia. And didn't stop there. America was next. Then Japan and the UK. Germany, without the mentally unbalanced Hitler making grievous errors with its military, became the world's sole superpower and ruled the planet with an iron fist.

I had no idea if he was right, nor could I argue that he was wrong. But remembering the discussions with him reinforced what Johnson was saying. Every individual has a role to play, no matter how insignificant. Nudging time, by changing the path of even one person, could have devastating long term effects.

"Got it," I said. "I'll be very careful."

Johnson nodded, then looked down when his phone beeped.

"They've identified an event point," he said, turning and heading for the door.

21

We met in the same conference room where Dr. Anholts had first told me what Project Athena was all about. Johnson and I sat on one side of the table, Patterson at the head, and a studious looking man named Carpenter opposite me. The projector was on, displaying a frozen image of a large building that I assumed was in Southern California because of the palm trees surrounding it. And that's where the event had occurred.

Carpenter was the head of the analyst team that had traced the terrorists and decided upon an event point. He wrapped up a cryptic phone call, and based on Patterson's patience with him, I suspected it was directly related to the event.

"I'm Jim Carpenter. We haven't met," he stuck his hand across the table after putting his phone away.

I shook his hand and introduced myself. Well, introduced JR Whitman. At least I didn't make a mistake and use my birth name. Johnson would have never let me hear the end of that.

"What's the final count?" Patterson asked.

"97 children, eleven teachers and staff, and four police officers," he answered without having to consult his notes.

"Dead?" I asked, horrified all over again.

He nodded and after a moment Patterson told him to proceed with the briefing. He cleared his throat and looked around the table as he began speaking.

"Gentlemen. We have found an event point with an eighty-three percent chance of success. The next closest point falls below a fifty percent probability of success. The preferred point is the apartment building currently displayed on the screen.

"We successfully back-traced the perpetrators to this location, fifteen hours pre-event. I will detail the specifics of the event point, but first I have details on the subjects."

He pressed a key on his laptop and the screen changed to a collage of photos of eight men. All were swarthy and bearded with closely cropped hair. He quickly ran through a list, providing some of their names.

"These are the eight bodies identified at the scene of the event. Five are in the country legally, from Yemen, on student visas. Two at

USC and three at UCLA. The other three have yet to be identified and appear to be here illegally.

"There are two possible event points where they are all together in the same location. Once, for a brief time in a parking lot adjacent to the school. Prior to that possibility, within the distance window that can be reached, there is only one other opportunity where they come together. We are recommending the earlier time as our event point, and it is what my briefing will focus on. I can expand on the other option if there are questions or concerns.

"The apartment building is located in the city of Downey, California, twenty-one kilometers southeast of downtown Los Angeles. City population is 115,000 as of the most recent census. Our event point is in apartment number 2C and occurs from seventeen twenty-three until nineteen twenty-nine, local time. The end of the event point is precisely fifteen hours and eleven minutes before the beginning of the event."

"Do we know what they're doing in the apartment?" Patterson interrupted.

"No, sir. They appear to have gone operationally silent well before our thirty-six-hour window. No calls, emails, texts, social media posts. Nothing. They seem to be well trained and disciplined."

Patterson nodded for him to continue.

"The apartment is leased to a woman by the name of Janice Bass."

He pressed a key, and the displayed image changed to one of a poorly framed shot, probably from a cell phone, of an overweight blonde woman in her late 20s or early 30s. She was standing next to a beach, grimacing at the camera with the blue Pacific in the background.

"Is she involved?" I asked, wanting to know her status when I arrived.

"Uncertain," Carpenter answered. "One of our teams has already been through the apartment. She wasn't there when they arrived. Phone records and social media have been checked, and there is no indication so far that she is an accomplice. But there is also no evidence that she is not."

Johnson cleared his throat to interrupt the briefing. I turned to see him looking at me.

"Without evidence to the contrary, if she is in the apartment when you arrive, she is to be considered hostile," he said.

I nodded slowly, understanding the instruction but not liking it. After a moment, I turned my attention back to Carpenter, and he continued.

"Additional weapons and ammunition, as well as explosives, were discovered in the apartment. Detailed documents on the school, its staff, and surveillance notes from observing the local police patrol sectors were also found. The attack was meticulously planned.

"Our recommendation is the following. The team in California has identified that apartment number 3F is vacant. It is at the opposite end of the building and one floor above the event point target.

"We can deliver the asset into the vacant apartment ahead of the arrival of the targets. Unseen."

"So, what? I get there a little early, then break into their apartment and wait for them to arrive? Take them out as they come through the door?" I asked.

"Probably not a good idea," Johnson said, then turned to Carpenter. "Do they all arrive at the same time?"

"Negative," he shook his head. "They arrive individually over a forty-seven-minute span."

"That's why not," Johnson said to me. "You might get the first one through the door, and maybe even the second. But what if there's some code they're using. A special knock. Maybe the first one in turns on a specific light to let the rest know it's clear.

"We have no way of knowing this, and if you get some of them, there's a very real possibility the remainder are prepared to continue with the attack on their own. Or will pop up somewhere else in the future. You need to be sure you get all of them."

I nodded, glad I'd asked and appreciating his experience.

"Weapons I'll be facing?" I asked Carpenter.

"AK-74s. Full auto. This one and this one," he put up a new image with only two of the terrorists' photos. "Are both carrying pistols. Browning Hi-Powers in nine millimeters. Other than spare rifles in the apartment and explosives, that's all they have."

I stared at the screen for several long moments, burning the two faces into my memory. When I was sure I'd recognize them, I looked back at Carpenter.

"What about the explosives? What do they have?"

"Semtex, plastic explosive," he said, referring to a small notepad. "One point three seven pounds. But there were no blasting caps or detonators found in the apartment, in their vehicles or on their bodies."

"Do I need to be worried about a bullet hitting the stuff and setting it off?"

"No," Johnson answered. "It's very stable. A bullet can't cause it to go off."

I nodded, hoping like hell he really knew what he was talking about.

"How early are you proposing we send the asset?" Patterson asked.

"The scenarios we've run show that an hour would be optimal. But that's with an asset who is experienced. In Mr. Whitman's case, since this is his first time being transported, we are recommending two hours."

"Agreed," Patterson said.

Dirk Patton

I listened and kept my mouth shut. I clearly remembered the briefing I'd received about what it's like to go back in time. They had shown me a video of three former assets, now deceased, who graphically described the disorientation associated with time travel. Two of them described it as debilitating, rendering them unable to function for at least fifteen minutes.

But the third, a young woman with long, red hair, described it as like being spun on a playground whirly-gig so fast that she fell on her face and couldn't get up for nearly an hour. Since it seemed to not be consistent from person to person, no one could tell me what to expect.

I'd suggested that they send me back ten minutes, as a test, so I would know what to expect. They told me that was a good suggestion, and they'd tested it in the past. Unfortunately, it didn't tell them anything. Any distance less than twelve hours didn't cause disorientation or vertigo for any of the assets. Only when that mark was exceeded. And the farther back they went, the worse it was.

I tried to talk them into sending me back fifteen hours as I was very concerned about what condition I'd be in when I arrived. The briefer had considered my idea and taken it to Director Patterson who had rejected it immediately. It was explained to me that an asset couldn't be unavailable for that much time. There was no way to predict when the next event would occur, nor how much time within the event window would be needed.

I asked if the disorientation happened when they returned to real time, not looking forward to getting hammered by vertigo on both ends of a trip. Surprisingly, I was told it only happened when going backwards. Then Dr. Anholts had launched into a recitation of the theories and calculations to explain this.

It all came down to the difference between going back and returning to real time. Going back, you were transported through a Black Hole. Subjected to unimaginable gravitational forces. But returning was different. The machine was turned off. There was no Black Hole. Just the Universe restoring balance.

"So, if I understand this correctly, the problem with going back that kills anyone without my specific genetic marker wouldn't apply coming forward," I'd said to Dr. Anholts one afternoon.

She'd thought about my question for a moment, appearing perplexed. Then she confessed that they'd never thought about it in those terms. They'd never needed to. She had gone off and put her head together with several other egg heads. A few days later, she reminded me of my question and praised my logical thinking for having come up with a concept they hadn't considered.

When she had delivered the praise, she had given me an odd look. I got it. I'm not exactly the type that you expect to have something going on between his ears. I've kind of always been the brawny type. But there hadn't been much to do in prison other than lift weights unless one wanted to socialize. I've never been a terribly social person, so I filled the time by becoming a voracious reader.

I read everything in the prison library. Literally. Before I was sent to death row, I was even allowed to attend some community college level classes within the prison walls. They were basic math, science and English, but that was OK. I hadn't exactly paid attention in high school. Girls and football had been much more interesting.

One of the teachers, a moonlighting college professor from Arizona State University, had taken notice of me. Brought me textbooks that weren't in the library. History mostly, but there had been some physics and psychology thrown in for good measure. I'd devoured every page. And despite myself, and the circumstances, I'd learned a few things.

So, my question had created quite a stir amongst the physicists. They'd worked on it, taking it very seriously. Run tests by sending back tissue samples that contained my genetic material. They sent them back to themselves, with detailed instructions, and had piggybacked additional tissue without the genetic marker onto the test, sending it back to real time along with my sample.

They learned that only when organic matter moved through a Black Hole was there damage caused at the cellular level. Coming forward, pulled back to real time by the Universe, there was no harm caused. The other interesting thing that came of this was the possibility for an asset to return to real time and bring another person with them. I was sternly cautioned against ever attempting to do so, for any reason, and risk compromising the project's security.

"Tell me about the other possible event point you mentioned," I said. "The one in the parking lot right before the attack."

"From six minutes and eleven seconds until two minutes and thirty-eight seconds, pre-attack, all eight are gathered in the parking lot of a large strip mall adjacent to the school."

He changed the image on the screen. A shot of the eight men, gathered next to three vans parked nose to tail appeared. It looked like a shot from an elevated security camera. When he pressed a button, the image jumped backwards thirty seconds and began playing as a video.

Two vans were in the lot already, the drivers of each still behind the wheel. One of them had his arm hanging out the window, a smoldering cigarette in his hand. A curl of bluish smoke rose above the roof of the van to be whisked away by a breeze.

Within a few seconds, the third van pulled to a stop with its bumper touching the one in front of it. The men got out quickly and gathered around the new arrival, who appeared to be their leader. He took a minute to embrace each of them, kissing them on the cheeks.

When he was done, he slid the side door of his van open, and each of the men stepped forward and picked up a rifle and a bulging bag that I now knew was full of spare magazines. They spent a few moments checking their weapons, listened attentively as the leader said something to them, then they broke into two groups and headed in directions I assumed were the front and back of the school.

"No audio?" I asked.

"No. We tried to enhance the images and have an Arabic speaking lip reader tell us what he's saying, but the angle is too steep, and he can't get a good look."

"Can you rewind and blow up the leader's face?" I asked, wanting to see which of the men was in charge.

Carpenter did just that. He played with the video briefly, then stopped it at a spot where the leader was turning his head and happened to be directly facing the camera. Image frozen, a rectangle was drawn around the target's head, and the software zoomed in tightly. It was one of the two faces I'd memorized because they also had pistols.

"I need to know how to get to the school if something goes wrong at the apartment," I said after staring at the image for a brief time.

Carpenter slid what I had learned was an iPad across the table. The damn things had been a science fiction pipe dream when I went to prison. Now, it seemed every person working at Project Athena had one.

Picking it up, I tapped the screen and looked at enlarged head shots of each of the targets. There was also a photo of Janice Bass. A floor plan of the target apartment and a map of the apartment complex with units 3F and 2C clearly identified and three separate routes between them clearly highlighted.

I tapped an icon, and a mapping application opened, detailing the route from the apartment to the school. The name and address of the school were in a small balloon that hovered over its location. Looking at the map, thinking about what I was about to do, an idea came to me.

"This may be a dumb question," I said, looking around at each of the three men in the room with me. "But when I get back, why not just call the FBI and tell them about the threat? They could evacuate the school and have a whole building full of cops waiting for these assholes."

"Remember our discussion about treading lightly in the past?" Johnson asked.

I nodded that I did, but I didn't understand where he was going.

"If you were to do that, rather than take the terrorists out, you'd have a potentially greater impact on events. Sure, it would stop the attack, but think about what would happen.

"You kill the targets, and it's an apartment full of dead terrorists. Nice and private, and we have plans in place to keep it that way. No media coverage. No politicians screaming that if we do what they say, they'll keep us safe. The event will be undone, and the targets will be quietly disposed of with no one the wiser.

"But, if you were to alert the authorities and the attack was successfully stopped, someone involved will get a tip out to a reporter. The next thing you know, there will be a media circus. Police and FBI commanders will scramble to get in front of a camera and take credit. Politicians from coast to coast will try and capitalize on a thwarted terrorist attack.

"Radio and TV talk show hosts from every end of the political spectrum will milk every drop of ratings they can. And careers will be made and broken in the aftermath. Good people who work their asses off to protect us will be blamed for not having foreseen the attack. They'll be scapegoated, most likely for some politician's gain.

"Your job, the entire Athena Project's job, is to undo especially tragic events with as little impact on things that will shape the future as possible. Remember that no change is a small change."

"OK, I understand and accept that," I said. "But what if something goes wrong at the apartment and I don't stop them. The attack is going to proceed, but I can stop it with a single phone call. Save those children. What do I do?"

"Nothing," Patterson answered for Johnson. "Absolutely nothing."

"Let those children be slaughtered?" I asked in shock.

"Mr. Whitman, those children are already dead," he said bluntly. "It is only through this amazing technological breakthrough that we can even consider the possibility of preventing them from having been murdered in the first place. Time has played out, exactly as intended.

"In our supreme arrogance as a species, we are now playing God and changing past events that for all of human history could not have been changed. This has been discussed with you and explained to you. I understand it is hard to reconcile, allowing the massacre to take place, but you must remember that it has already occurred.

"Even though when you are in the past it will feel like it hasn't happened, it has. You're just a visitor when you go back. And a visitor must be very careful to not start a new direction for our timeline. It may feel that's what you're doing by stopping the attack, but in actuality, you're just maintaining the status quo."

I nodded my head, not because I was convinced or fully buying in to what he was saying, but because there was no reason to continue discussing this. I'd do what I felt was right when I got back there. Then I'd deal with whatever the fallout was when I returned.

22

I was nervous as hell. After the briefing, and a few more questions, Johnson and I had returned to prep. Now, I was outfitted with body armor and had a rifle and shotgun slung over my shoulders with plenty of spare magazines and ammunition. Both the rifle and shottie had suppressors attached, and I'd also added one to my primary pistol.

With Johnson escorting me, I waddled out of prep under the weight of all the weapons. Six months ago I'd have thought this was extreme overkill. I didn't need this many weapons. But after the intensive training, I'd undergone, I understood the need to be as heavily armed as possible.

Weapons malfunction. Ammunition can fail to fire or jam. Environments can change in a heartbeat during a battle, and the pistol that was the perfect choice in a confined room is suddenly almost useless when the enemy is more than thirty yards away. Or taking cover behind a wall.

I had one job. Hit these fuckers so hard and so fast that I was able to contain the carnage within their apartment. That would make it possible for the special FBI team to slip in and clean things up, erasing the final traces of an event that never happened. Having an adequate supply of various weapons on hand would increase my odds of completing the job successfully.

Before we'd left prep, Agent Johnson handed me two items. A specially encrypted iPhone and a leather wallet.

"The phone will only call one number," he said, holding it up in front of my face. "Mine."

"But the you back then won't know I'm there," I said, not understanding.

"No, but if he, I, get a call from you, I'll know why as soon as I hear your voice. You call when it's done. I'll dispatch the clean up team."

I nodded and opened the wallet, stunned to find a thick stack of hundred dollar bills folded inside.

"Five thousand in cash," Johnson said. "A driver's license in your new name and a black American Express card which has no limit."

"Maybe I don't want to come back," I grinned.

"It's not fun money, Mr. Whitman. It is so you are prepared to deal with any circumstances that might arise. Cash can open many doors that would otherwise remain closed."

I nodded and slipped the wallet into a pocket, the iPhone into another. Pulling on a thin pair of leather gloves that fit like a second skin, I was ready. Following Johnson out of prep, we'd gone in the direction of the operations center but had made a turn at the last moment. This was another hall I hadn't seen before, and I shouldn't have been surprised when we came to a stop facing two heavily armed Marines.

While one of them maintained close watch on us, his weapon at the ready, the other placed a call on a wall mounted phone. I could hear his conversation as he spoke in clipped phrases. He was verifying that I was authorized to enter the transport chamber.

It didn't take long for him to finish, then he stepped to a steel door. On either side was a glass panel about twelve inches square. He placed his hand on the one on the right and nodded at Johnson, who stepped forward and rested his hand on the opposite panel. The two screens didn't seem to be doing anything, but a moment later there was a loud buzzer, and the door slid open.

Johnson waved at me to enter first, following on my heels. I looked through a set of windows into the operations center, seeing Patterson, Dr. Anholts and a handful of technicians watching me. Ahead was the dais I'd seen earlier, and as I approached, a section of the curved glass that surrounded it slid open with a faint whine of electric motors.

"What do I do? Get in?"

"Yes," Johnson said. "Stand in the center of the dais. The other assets have said you feel nothing other than the disorientation upon arrival. They described it as being like blinking your eyes and you're suddenly somewhere else."

I nodded, breathing rapidly as my heart rate shot up. What the fuck was I about to do? Was I sure the whole attack thing wasn't a ruse to get me to willingly be a guinea pig? Hell, the whole attack on the school that had gotten me fully onboard could have been a Hollywood production, and I wouldn't have been able to tell. Some voices and a crappy helmet cam that cut out after only a few minutes. And faking a CNN broadcast could probably be done by a few high school kids with too much time on their hands. Fuck it. In for a penny...

"You OK?" Johnson asked.

I nodded and took a few deep breaths before forcing myself to march forward and step onto the dais. A thrum of power was noticeable, vibrations coming through the floor and up through my shoes. Turning, I faced the windows and looked at the people watching me.

"See you in a few hours," Johnson said.

I turned my head as he left the chamber, the door sliding shut with a solid boom. There was another whine as the glass enclosure slid into place, completely encasing me. I saw Dr. Anholts lean over a console and a moment later heard her voice in the chamber.

"Are you ready, Mr. Whitman?"

I nodded, wishing I had something brave or witty to say. But I didn't. I was scared shitless, sweating through my shirt under the heavy body armor. Needed to take a piss worse than I could ever remember. Opening my mouth to tell them to wait so I could go to the bathroom, the words didn't have a chance to come out before there was a sudden blink and everything went dark.

23

Well, not completely dark. I was suddenly in a musty smelling room, no lights on and the blinds closed tightly. The chamber I'd just left had been brightly lit with banks of high intensity lamps mounted in the ceiling. I guess the instant change of environments would take a moment for my eyes to adjust to the gloom.

There was a slight sensation of falling, like stepping onto a thickly cushioned surface, and I realized I'd appeared or materialized, or whatever the correct term is, about an inch above the floor. Then gravity had taken over. But looking down, I was able to make out a thick carpet, so perhaps I'd just shown up, and my weight had compressed it and the padding beneath.

It was only another moment before my body reminded me how badly I needed to pee. Looking around frantically, I spotted a narrow hall that ran past a cramped kitchen. Snatching a flashlight out of a pocket on the vest I was wearing over my body armor, I clicked it on as I dashed across the small room.

I'd guessed right. The hall led to a bedroom, passing a bathroom which I hurried into and nearly wet myself as I tried to get my pants open. The gloves I was wearing to prevent leaving fingerprints hampered my efforts slightly, but thankfully I made it. That wonderful feeling of relief passed over me as urine began splashing into the toilet. Then it hit me. I wasn't disoriented.

In fact, I felt energized. Certainly nothing like I'd seen described by the other assets who'd come before me. Finished relieving myself, I zipped and buttoned up and reached out to flush the toilet, pausing with my hand hovering over the handle. This was a vacant apartment. The neighbors almost certainly knew that. Would they hear the sound of the water rushing in the pipes? Call the office and alert the manager that someone was in an apartment that shouldn't be? Not worth taking the chance.

Leaving the bathroom, I quickly toured the apartment. It came with cheap, well worn furniture, so at least I'd have somewhere to sit while I waited. Using my small light, I checked all the closets, under the bed and sofa and opened and gently closed every cabinet door in the kitchen. The place was empty, and other than the musty smell I'd noticed when I first arrived, it was actually pretty clean.

An old landline phone rested on top of a well used phone book on the kitchen counter, plugged into a phone jack that was designed for wall mounting. I quietly lifted the handset and held it to my ear, more than a little surprised when I heard a dial tone. Why would a vacant apartment have a working phone? Realizing that was a question I couldn't answer, I replaced the handset and remembered I was supposed to start a series of timers.

Taking a seat on the sagging sofa, I brought out the iPad. It had already locked onto a cell network signal and adjusted its clock to the current, local time. Opening an app that I'd been taught to use, I pressed a couple of icons, and multiple countdown clocks appeared.

The first one showed I had just under two hours to the start of the event point. The second displayed the time to the end of the event point. Three and four kept track of what I thought of as my fall back. The secondary event point in the parking lot adjacent to the school.

Then there was the one with the second most time on it, which would zero out at the moment the first terrorist walked through the doors at the school. Finally, the countdown to my return to real time. Twenty-three hours, forty-one minutes and some odd seconds.

I sat staring at the tablet for almost a minute, watching the seconds tick off. Trying to figure out why I hadn't experienced the vertigo and disorientation the others had. Not that I was complaining, but it would have been nice to know. I was sure when I got back and reported the results, I'd spend a couple of days being subjected to a whole battery of tests.

Leaving the tablet on the scarred coffee table, I stood and took a slower tour of the apartment. I stopped in each room, listening carefully for the sounds of any neighbors. It was a weekday afternoon, and this didn't seem to be the type of place people lived if they didn't have to go to work, so other than muted traffic noise from outside the building, it was quiet.

Pausing at the front door, which was the only entrance or exit, I pressed my ear against the cool metal surface. Just more traffic noise. Putting my eye to the peephole, I looked outside the door. Other than able to tell it was a sunny day, I couldn't see anything except the walkway railing directly in front of the door.

Moving back to the sofa, I pulled up the diagram of the complex and ensured I was remembering the path I'd take when it was time to move. And I'd need to move fast. I was going to be dressed like GI Joe with weapons bristling. If any of the residents were outside or happened

248

to look out a window, it was a good bet they'd be dialing 9-1-1 as soon as they got a glimpse of me.

Closing the diagram, I opened the floor plan of the target apartment. Unlike the unit I was in, it had three bedrooms and two bathrooms. Several small rooms and two hallways. A fucking maze for one man to clear, and all potential hiding spots for the terrorists.

Part of my training on the oil rig had been CQB or Close Quarters Battle. Much of that involved how to move quickly, yet safely, through an unsecured building or residence. A former Army Delta Force operator had been my instructor, and he had been brutal. Mistakes had been cause to stop each session immediately so he could scream in my face and tell me what an idiot I was.

I'd finally graduated to the phase where he didn't stop me. He just popped up from around a corner and shot me with a rubber bullet. If anyone ever tells you those little things don't hurt, they are full of shit. Take my word for it. I've got the bruises on my body as evidence.

But, I learned and improved steadily. There was still a lot of training for me to go through when I got back, but at least I had a few months of working in the "kill house" under my belt. Maybe he'd cut me some slack if I pulled this off. Yeah, and maybe I was going to get wildly screwed by a busload of NFL cheerleaders. Hey, there's always hope!

I checked the iPad's timers. One hour to go. Pulling weapons off my body, I stacked them on the table and spent half of that time making sure they were ready. Checked the loads in every magazine, tapping them against the sole of my shoe to ensure the rounds were fully seated and would feed properly. Then put everything back on.

The sound of running feet outside the door made me catch my breath, but as quickly as my heart rate had increased, I recognized the short, fast steps of a child. Two more quickly followed, and I cursed when I realized there would be families coming home from school and work. Parents trying to prepare dinner and sending the kids out to play until it was on the table.

I worried about the possibility of a stray round, either mine or the target's, finding one of those children. It's not possible to fire a weapon in an urban environment without some risk to innocent bystanders. How would I feel if that happened? Were the dead at the school more important than one child who might die here if I made a mistake?

With a shake of my head, I shut down that line of thinking. It wasn't helping. If I didn't do my job, it was certain that well over 100 people were going to die tomorrow morning. It wasn't a certainty that anyone other than the terrorists would die tonight.

Glancing at the clock, I stood and began to pace as the timer approached ten minutes. Ten more minutes and all eight of the fuckers would be in the same place. All I had to do was walk in and start shooting. Acquire my target and pull the trigger. Over and over until they were all down.

But what were they doing in there? Going over their master plan? Praying to their God for success? Maybe they'd brought a goat along and were taking turns getting their rocks off. Who the hell knew? Then I remembered something.

In the video of the leader arriving in the parking lot, he'd had all of their weapons in his van. They had each walked over and picked up a rifle *after* he arrived. Did that mean they didn't keep the AKs with them? Perhaps not. Maybe the boss had decided there was too great of a risk of being exposed.

Eight men who fit the profile of a terrorist. Male, middle eastern appearance, military age.

Was that it? Worry over a cop seeing one of them and deciding to check them out? Sure, the police aren't supposed to racially profile the general public. And the President isn't supposed to get a blow job in the oval office from an intern, then lie about it on national television. People will do what they do.

Things were starting to become clearer in my inexperienced mind. The apartment wasn't just where they met to make plans, it was their armory. A nice, discreet location to store their weapons until it was time to use them. Eliminate the chance of one of them being caught with an illegal firearm and putting the authorities on high alert.

It made sense to me, and it changed my plan. If I was right, and the more I thought about things I was pretty sure I was, then as they arrived they were probably picking up a rifle and doing what I'd just done with mine. That meant all eight of them would have a weapon in their hands if I busted through the door in... six and a half minutes, I confirmed from the iPad.

Wheels turning, I looked at the second timer. It would reach zero when the first one walked out of the door. At that point, I couldn't get the whole group in one location until the following morning outside the school. There had been a discussion about finding where each of them went, and me moving from location to location and taking them out individually.

Agent Johnson had vetoed that. He felt there was too great a chance that they might have a method of sending an alert out to the others. That meant if I didn't take each one down instantly before he even had an idea of what was happening, the rest could melt away to continue their plotting at a later date.

But I had a better idea. Hit them at the last moment before their little group hug broke up. It would be later, after dark, and there should be fewer people out and moving. Less potential for unintended casualties. And the rifles should have been put away for the night. Safely stored, waiting for the leader to load them into the van the next day.

And that meant they'd probably be in crates or boxed and more difficult to get to when the shooting started! Yes! He couldn't just openly carry eight AK-74s out the front door and across the parking lot. They had to be concealed, which meant the terrorists wouldn't be holding them when I walked in.

Smiling, proud of myself, I moved back to the sofa and sat down after removing the rifle and shotgun. The iPad began beeping to tell me the first timer had ended. Silencing it, I looked at the second one and leaned back to wait for the right moment.

24

It was approaching six pm, local time, when the sound of a woman's high heels caught my attention. She was walking fast, taking short steps. And they were coming closer, loud on the poured concrete walkway that ran in front of the apartment door. When they stopped directly in front, I leapt up, snatched the iPad and my weapons off the coffee table and dashed for the bedroom.

As I was running down the hall, I heard the faint jingle of keys then the scrape of the lock as she turned the deadbolt. The door creaked open as I disappeared into the bedroom. What the hell? This place was supposed to be vacant. Who the hell was this? Please don't be the manager showing the apartment.

Quietly, I tucked the iPad away and carefully slung the shotgun and rifle. Then I remembered the stocking cap in my pocket. Grabbing it, I pulled it on my head and unfolded the cuff and stretched the mask over my face. Everything was concealed other than my eyes, nose and mouth. Making sure the shotgun was tight against my back, I pulled the rifle around and raised it to my shoulder.

I didn't want to shoot an innocent person. In fact, I wouldn't shoot an innocent person. But a rifle pointed at her face would be a great intimidator if I needed it. Hoping I didn't, I pressed my back against the wall next to the bedroom door and listened, trying to figure out what was going on.

The front door hadn't been closed. I could easily hear the voices of children playing from outside the apartment. Then I heard the muted thud of feet walking across the carpet. Barefoot? She'd taken her shoes off? A moment later there was a rattle of plastic grocery bags being placed on the kitchen counter.

More rapid thuds as she walked back across the carpeted floor, then bumps and scrapes as she dragged something through the open door. Now it closed with a solid bang, followed by the click of the deadbolt being engaged. A rubbing sound started up that I couldn't identify. A weak light in the hall was flipped on, and the steps approached my hiding place.

I slid away from the door, placing myself into a corner of the room. I'd be to her right when she stepped in, and hopefully, she wouldn't see me early enough to make a break for the front door and start screaming for help. My rifle was up, trained on the point where I expected her head to be when she crossed the threshold.

An instant later, a young woman dragging a large suitcase walked into the bedroom. She was moving fast, looking to her left to find a light switch. This brought her another step in, but the switch was to her right, and when she turned she saw me and froze. Her mouth was open in a large, silent "O".

"Don't make a sound," I said softly, moving a step closer to her. "I will not hurt you if you stay quiet and do what I say."

The rifle's muzzle was only feet from her face, and there was just enough light for me to tell her eyes were focused on the round hole that probably looked as large as anything she'd ever seen. I had her. Caught completely unprepared for a large, scary man with a gun waiting in her bedroom. But now that I had her, what the hell did I do with her?

I wasn't going to shoot her. I'd already decided that. She hadn't done anything to anyone, at least that I knew of. But if I wasn't going to shoot her, what the hell did I do? I didn't have any way to keep her quiet other than pointing a gun at her, and that wasn't a practical solution for more than a few minutes.

What did I do with her when it was time to go take out the terrorists? Leave her to call the police and tell them a crazy man was running around with a whole arsenal on his back? The cops would show up before I was able to complete my mission and get away. Sure, all that would happen would be I'd get arrested, then a short time later I'd just disappear back to real time.

But what if the cops got here too early and interrupted me? Stopped me from completing my job? That wouldn't be good. The attack tomorrow morning would be stopped, but the timeline would be screwed up. And there was a chance some of the terrorists would escape and live to fight another day. No. I wasn't going to allow that to happen.

"What do you want?" The woman asked quietly.

She had raised her eyes and stared into mine. I was surprised to see more than fear reflected in her face. There was also anger. She was pissed off in addition to being scared. Did that make her more or less of a problem?

"Right now, I want you to be quiet and get on the bed," I said, gesturing with my head.

"Fuck you," she breathed, eyes hardening. "You're not getting me on the bed. Kill me if you want, but that's not going to happen!"

She slowly released the handle for the suitcase and turned until she was squared off with me. Her eyes flashed, but she remained perfectly still once she had repositioned herself.

"Lady, that's the last thing I want from you," I said in exasperation.

"Why? What's wrong with me?"

I was stunned at the question. This was either one very strong and brave woman, or she was certifiable. At the moment, I wasn't quite sure which to think. My bewilderment must have been apparent even with my face covered. After watching my reaction for a few seconds, she actually laughed. Actually, fucking laughed at a masked man pointing a rifle at her head.

"OK," she said after a pause. "I'm going to take a seat. Then you're going to tell me what you want."

Cautiously, she moved the few steps to the bed and sat on the edge. She was barefoot like I had suspected. She was wearing a tight skirt that ended a couple of inches above her knees, and lots of tanned leg was exposed when she crossed them. A small tattoo on the outside of her left ankle caught my eye, probably because of the slender, gold chain she wore. I didn't know exactly what it was but had seen it on a few combat medics in Iraq.

"Army?" I asked, nodding at the tattoo.

She looked down, probably having forgotten it was there, then met my eyes and nodded. Long, blonde hair swished softly against a silk blouse when she moved her head, and I had to force myself to not get lost in her big, blue eyes.

"You're not going to shoot me," she said. "That much is obvious. You would have by now if that was what you had in mind. And you don't want to rape me. And since I haven't even moved in yet, just rented this place this morning, there's nothing here for you to steal. You don't seem like you're crazy. So what's your deal?"

I stared at her for a long beat, weighing my options. Finally, I made a decision. Lowering the rifle, I moved to stand in front of the open bedroom door to prevent her from making a break for freedom. For some reason, I didn't think she was going to, but maybe she was a really good actress.

"I'm sorry," I began. "The apartment was supposed to be empty. I wasn't expecting anyone to be here."

She looked at me and made a "get on with it" gesture by rolling the fingers on her right hand in the air, miming a wheel turning.

"There's an apartment in the building where a group of terrorists are meeting. They're planning an attack on an elementary school tomorrow morning. Want to kill as many children as they can. I'm here to stop them, and I was using this place to wait for the right moment to start my assault."

"Bullshit!" She said immediately. "If that was true, the cops and FBI would have about two hundred men ready to go in and take them down. They wouldn't send one guy. I'm not stupid. Don't insult me."

"I'm not a cop or with the FBI," I said, shaking my head. "I do work for the government, and I'm telling you the truth. As far as why I'm here by myself... well, it's kind of complicated. All I can say is that there's a reason for keeping this quiet."

"So you're by yourself, going to go after an apartment full of what I assume are armed terrorists. What are you? A SEAL or something?

Johnny Badass, going to take out all the bad guys single handed?"

"Something like that," I mumbled, blushing under the mask at her comments.

"Say I believe you," she said. "When is all of this supposed to happen?"

I held up a finger for her to wait and reached into a small pack for the iPad. She tensed slightly when my hand disappeared from sight, but she hid it well.

"Seventy-three minutes from now," I answered after checking the timer.

"So, seventy-three minutes from now you're leaving? Going to go play Rambo? That presents you with a problem. What's to stop me from calling 9-1-1 the second you walk out the door?"

"Jesus, lady," I blurted. "What the hell's wrong with you? Are you *trying* to convince me to kill you?"

"No. I'm just trying to figure out what you're going to do with me. The way I see it, you don't have a lot of options, and I'm not ready to die tonight. Maybe I can help you come up with a solution to your little problem."

I just stood there, staring at her. She wasn't crazy. She was an incredibly brave and practical woman. But if that tattoo meant what I was almost certain it did, she had already proven herself under fire. Combat medics don't have an easy job. People talk about how brave firemen are. Let me tell you, they've got nothing on someone who runs *onto* a battlefield to help wounded soldiers.

"Give me a reason to believe you," she said, eyes boring into mine again.

I looked back at her, not knowing what to do. This scenario was so far removed from all of the training situations I'd gone through, I was on my own. Had to trust my own judgment and hope I was making the right choice.

Choices. Johnson and I had talked about choices until I was sick of the topic. But it had helped. He'd gotten me to start thinking beyond the immediate consequences of a course of action. Taught me to look at the long term impacts, weigh them against each other. Critical thinking, he'd called it. And that's what I did. Or at least thought I did. Maybe I was doing it all wrong, but after almost a minute of silence, I reached up and removed the mask, exposing my face.

"You've served your country. You've seen combat, and I'm willing to bet you've lost just as many wounded men as you've saved. You understand the threats we're facing. And you understand there's only one way to combat it. Head on. No mercy, because none will be given. All they want is to kill us. Wipe us out. Am I wrong?"

It was quiet in the bedroom for a long pause. In that interim, she didn't break eye contact with me. Just stared as if she could look into my soul.

"You're not wrong," she said in a much less aggressive voice.

"Then help me," I said. "I'll be out of your hair in just over an hour. All I'm asking is that you stay quiet and don't call the police after I leave. That's all."

"How do I know you're who you say you are? What if you're a mafia hit man, here to kill some witness? Or an enforcer for a drug cartel, hunting a dealer who crossed your bosses. Maybe just a jilted ex-boyfriend out for a little revenge."

I sighed in frustration. She was right. I couldn't prove I was who I said I was. Couldn't prove I wasn't any of the things she had just listed. Glancing at the iPad in my hand, I noted the timer. Less than an hour. I was running out of time, and this conversation didn't seem to be going anywhere.

"What will it take? How do I convince you?"

"Got a badge?"

She smiled, knowing I wouldn't. I shook my head.

"Then we've got a problem," she said. "I'd like to believe you. But your story is too fantastic. And if I don't do something, that means I could wind up being an accomplice. That doesn't fit in with my plans for the future."

I shrugged, not having any idea what else I could say to convince her.

"So how about this," she continued. "You walk your ass out my door and get the hell out of the area. I'll wait five minutes before I call the cops. That should give you more than enough time to get safely away. That's the best I can do."

I shook my head.

"That's not an option," I said. "I'm telling you the truth, and I'm not going to walk away and let those terrorists kill a bunch of kids. How about I knock you out? I'm sure there's something in this suitcase I can use to tie you up. You might get free, but I'll be done and gone before then."

I tapped the hard sided rolling bag with the heel of my left shoe. It was heavy, probably stuffed full of clothing.

"You can try," she said, eyes flashing again.

This wasn't getting us anywhere. I'd already told her more than I should have. And it wasn't working. She didn't believe me. I needed to move this along and get refocused on the mission.

Ready to step forward and slam the rifle butt into the side of her head, I stopped myself before revealing what I was thinking. There was another option. Not a good one, but better than hurting this woman. Unlike the movies, a blow to the head isn't very safe. Sure, you can knock someone out if you hit them just right and just hard enough, but what if you hit them too hard? I didn't want to risk severely injuring her.

"OK, here's what we're going to do," I said. "I'm fast running out of time. Out on the kitchen counter is a phone book and a land line phone. We're going to walk out to the kitchen, and you're going to look up the number for the FBI. You're going to call it and ask for Special Agent William Johnson. You should probably tell them it's an emergency, a matter of life and death, so they put you through to him rather than wanting to take a message. Once you have him on the line, he can verify I'm telling you the truth. Fair enough?"

She looked at me in surprise, tilting her head to the side as she inspected the expression on my face.

"I must say, you are convincing," she said, pausing and thinking before continuing. "OK. If the FBI confirms you're telling the truth, I'll stay out of your way. Won't call the cops or do anything to interfere."

"Let's go then," I said, moving the suitcase out of the way and taking a step back into the hall as she stood and straightened her skirt.

"But if you try anything... try to call 9-1-1 instead of the FBI's number, or anything else foolish, you won't leave me a choice. I'll have to hit you and restrain you. Please don't make me do that. I wouldn't like it."

"I'll be good," she said, walking slowly towards me.

25

I walked backwards down the hall, not taking my eyes off the woman. Coming to a stop, I placed myself between her and the front door, waving her into the kitchen. After the training I'd received, a kitchen is the last place in a residence I'd want a potential adversary to be. Too many things for them to grab and use as a weapon. But I'd already searched this one and knew it was empty. Except for the half dozen bulging grocery bags sitting on the counter next to a large purse.

"Don't reach for the purse or any of the bags," I cautioned her.

She ignored me and gently moved the phone off the book and flipped it open without picking it up. It didn't take her long, and I made her step away so I could see the number she'd found. I wanted to make sure I knew she was actually calling who she was supposed to be calling.

Nodding, I stepped a few feet away and watched as she punched the digits in and lifted the handset to her ear. After what couldn't have been more than two rings, she began talking, asking to speak to Special Agent William Johnson. Just as I'd instructed, she told the operator that it was an emergency and lives were in the balance.

"I'm on hold," she said, pulling the phone away from her ear so I could hear the sappy music that was playing.

It took most of five minutes, neither of us saying anything, but the other end was finally picked up. She listened closely to what was said before speaking.

"Agent Johnson, I have a man in my apartment, holding me at gunpoint. He claims that you know who he is."

"Give it to me," I said, extending my left hand.

She stepped away and turned so the handset was on the opposite side of her body.

"He hasn't told me his name. All he's said is that he's here to stop a terrorist attack on a school."

She listened for almost a minute, turning and looking me up and down. I suspected he was describing me to her. There was a brief discussion, then she held the phone out towards me.

"He wants to talk to you," she said.

I took it from her and held it to my ear, saying "Hi".

"What the fuck do you think you're doing?"

Johnson yelled so loud I involuntarily held the handset away from my head. The woman clearly heard his shout and a smile spread across her face as she leaned her ass against the counter and crossed her arms.

"No choice," I said, instantly regretting my use of that word. Choice. "If the apartment had been empty like I was told, this wouldn't have happened."

"I don't know what the hell you're talking about, but I'm sure I will soon," he said, the anger in his voice barely controlled. "And, you're in Downey, California according to the phone records. How long have you been back?"

"A few hours," I said, watching the woman watch me.

"When's your event point?"

"Less than forty-five minutes," I said, checking the iPad.

"Good luck," he said. "We'll discuss your choice to have a civilian contact me when you get back. You can rest assured I'll remember this!"

There was a loud click as he slammed the phone down on his end. I breathed out a sigh and gently placed the handset back in the cradle. Looking up, I saw she was still smiling.

"Believe me now? And what the hell's so funny?" I asked.

"Yes, I do. And it's always funny when a big, tough guy gets chewed out," she said, still smiling.

"So you're going to help me?"

"If by help, you mean keep my mouth shut, then the answer is yes. My house is your house. At least for the next forty-five minutes. Now, if you don't mind, get out of my kitchen so I can put these groceries away before they spoil. And if my rocky road has melted, I'm going to kick your ass!"

I stepped back into the hall and watched as she unloaded the bags. Most of what she'd bought went into the fridge or freezer, but there were a few items that she stored in a cabinet.

"You're in luck," she said, gently squeezing the outside of a large container of ice cream. "It's still firm."

I almost made a sarcastic remark about anything that was in her hand being firm but stopped myself before the words came out. She might appreciate my juvenile humor, or she might get pissed off and make things hard for me. When I thought the word *hard*, right after the thought I'd just had, I tried and failed to suppress a snort of laughter.

"What?" She asked, looking over her shoulder at me, the ice cream still in her hand.

"Nothing," I said. "Just something I was thinking about."

I was trying to wipe a grin off my face, but after all the tension since she'd walked into the apartment, I was ready for some relief, and it wouldn't go away. She was apparently as sharp as I'd thought, for it didn't take long for things to click. With a roll of her eyes, she put the container in the freezer and turned to face me.

"Don't be a child," she chastised me, sounding only half serious. "Now, will you trust me to go to the bathroom by myself?"

I stepped back and made a grand gesture for her to walk down the narrow hall. She shook her head, probably thinking I was an immature child in an adult's body as she pushed past me.

While she took care of her personal business, I sat on the sofa and checked the iPad. Forty minutes and eleven seconds. Switching views to the building layout, I reviewed the path I would take to apartment 2C. The diagram included measurements and I did some quick math. It should take me between thirty and forty seconds to reach the target once I walked out this door.

I wanted to be standing outside 2C's door when it opened for the first asshole to walk out. That meant I needed to leave when the timer showed one-minute remaining. That would give me about a twenty-second margin of error. Any earlier, and I risked being seen by another resident who would probably call in a report to the cops. Any later and I might not be in place on time.

Sitting there, I played out what I was going to do in my head. Mentally pictured how I would enter the residence. Recalled the two faces of the men that carried pistols. They were potentially the greatest threats, assuming I was correct, and the rifles would have been packed away already. Reminded myself that if the woman the apartment was leased to was present in any state other than bound and gagged, I had to treat her as a hostile.

"That's really gross."

The woman's voice interrupted my thoughts, and I turned to see her standing in the hall outside the bathroom door.

"What?"

"Flush the damn toilet and put the seat down after you use it. Jesus!"

"Sorry. Thought I was alone," I said.

"If you go again before you leave, just try to remember. OK?"

I nodded, watching her grasp the suitcase handle and drag it into the bedroom. Standing, I walked down the hall and looked in as she struggled to lift it onto the bed. It wasn't that I didn't trust her after her conversation with Johnson, but trusting and keeping an eye on what someone is doing aren't necessarily mutually exclusive.

"Want some help?" I asked, leaning a shoulder against the door jam.

"Got it," she grunted, swinging it up and letting it flop onto the mattress.

"What's your name?" I asked as she opened the latches and raised the lid.

"Why? Going to ask me out?"

She was facing away from me as she spoke, looking down into the bag. I could hear the sarcasm loud and clear and suspected there was an impish grin on her face.

"No. You're too high maintenance," I said, deliberately sending a jab in her direction.

"You have no idea," she said, refusing to take the bait.

I stood there for a few more minutes, watching her unpack. Several of the items she pulled out intrigued me, and I couldn't help but imagine what she'd look like wearing them. Realizing I was getting distracted, I pushed away from the door and returned to the living room.

Resuming my seat on the sofa, I checked the time then made another study of the target apartment's floor plan. The front door opened into a living room that was about half again as large as the one I was sitting in. A kitchen abutted it, a bar height counter separating the two spaces.

Just like this apartment, a short hall led to a bedroom, but this one would be considered a master and had its own bathroom instead of one in the hall. A small, walk-in closet was to the right of the door into the bath, and sliding glass doors let out onto a tiny balcony that overlooked the parking lot.

Another hall, opposite the kitchen, led to a bathroom and two bedrooms. The bath was on the right, back wall matched up against the back wall of the master bath. The two bedrooms were both on the left, their doors bracketing the entrance to the bathroom so that there was a left door, right door then left door as one progressed down the hall. It ended at a wall of cabinets, probably shallow and only good for storing linens. Or weapons, I reminded myself.

"What are you looking at?"

I jumped when she spoke from right next to me. She'd walked up, silent in her bare feet, and was peering over my shoulder at the iPad. After I'd left her alone, she had changed clothes, trading the skirt and blouse for a pair of shorts and a stained T-shirt that could only have been Army issue. It didn't flatter her figure but looked very comfortable and well worn. Her hair was up in a tight ponytail, and her face was scrubbed clean of makeup. I thought she looked beautiful.

"Floor plan of the apartment where the terrorists are," I said, not seeing any reason to lie or refuse to answer.

"That's a lot of blind corners and rooms," she observed. "How many of them are in there?"

"Eight," I answered. "Plus one unknown."

"You're going up against nine on your own? That's nuts," she said, moving around and sitting in a chair with her legs tucked underneath her ass.

"Probably," I said, nodding. "But that's the job."

"You know how many times I heard that in Iraq? From guys who were about to go out and get their legs blown off or a bullet through the head?"

"A lot," I said, remembering that it was a well-worn phrase in my infantry platoon.

"Too much," she said, a far off look in her eyes as she remembered the war.

I didn't have anything to say to that, so resumed studying the floor plan to ensure it was clearly embedded in my memory. Over and over, I pictured myself walking through the apartment. Visualized the lanes of fire that would be available to me as well as the terrorists. Worried about the hall with the two bedrooms. Hoped all of them would be gathered in the living room, but didn't count on that being the case.

A final review of the path to the target location, and I closed the diagrams and placed the iPad on the table. All that was showing was the timer app. Eight minutes, eleven seconds. That meant I was walking out the door in seven minutes, eleven seconds. There was nothing to do other than wait.

Fishing the stocking cap out of my pocket, I put it on my head. Before I walked out into the open, I'd pull the mask over my face. Another check of my weapons under her watchful eye, and I still had five minutes to go.

"You were over there, weren't you," she said after I'd made sure my rifle was ready to go.

"Two tours in Iraq," I said.

I probably shouldn't have told her that. But what did it matter? Who could she tell? In less than five minutes I'd walk out her door and never see her again.

"Didn't get enough death while you were there?"

I looked at her, not sure where she was heading with the question.

"Too much," I said.

"Then why? I'm just curious. How did you wind up hunting tangos?"

"It just kind of happened," I said. "I didn't go looking for the job. It found me."

"That's a nice, cryptic non-answer," she said, a smile softening her blue eyes.

"And it's the truth."

I stood and performed a quick check of all my weapons. Made sure none of them were snagged or wouldn't draw smoothly when needed. Glancing down at the iPad, I saw two minutes remaining on the timer. One minute to walking out the door. Checking my watch, I noted the time and shut the iPad down and put it in my pack.

"Thank you," I said to the woman as I moved to stand next to the door.

"Good luck," she responded, standing and unlocking the deadbolt.

She placed her hand on the knob, ready to open the door for me. I looked into her eyes and saw something that hadn't been there before. Sadness. Loss. And a big dose of weariness. She was tired of seeing men going off to war. More than anyone, she probably had the right to feel that way. I wondered how many soldiers she'd scooped off the battlefield.

I glanced at my watch. Ten seconds. She was watching me closely as I stood there waiting for the second hand to reach its mark. At five seconds I pulled the mask down to cover my features. At two seconds I took a deep breath and nodded.

"Julie Broussard."

She told me her name as she pulled the door open.

26

The sun had set, and it was dark, low wattage lights spaced along the wall providing the only illumination on the walkway. I was on the third floor, at the opposite end of the building from the target. Turning to my left, I headed for a set of exterior stairs, striding quietly.

As soon as I'd stepped out of Julie's apartment, I began counting off the seconds in my head. I reached the landing at the top of the stairs in ten seconds. I paused long enough to scan the area and didn't see anyone out and about. There was the sound of TVs playing, and somewhere close by a man and woman were arguing loudly in a language I didn't recognize, but no one was outside their apartment at the moment.

Thirteen seconds. I went down the stairs to the second level, turning right. Eighteen seconds. A long walkway in front of me, turning ninety degrees to the right when it reached the far corner of the rectangular structure. I walked at a fast pace, rifle in front of my body and gripped tightly, ready to be brought to my shoulder in an instant.

Twenty-seven seconds. I reached the turn and swung to the right. Walked past apartment 2E. Thirty seconds and I was passing 2D. At thirty-three seconds, I came to a stop directly in front of 2C, glad to note the blinds covering the windows next to the door were tightly drawn. I hadn't thought about what I'd do if they hadn't been but didn't dwell on the topic.

Preparing myself, I raised the rifle and aimed at the seam where the door met the jam, two feet above the knob. The instant that door opened, I was going to fire, and follow the bullet into the apartment. My heart was pounding in my ears, and I was thankful for the gloves. Sweat was popping out all over, and I could feel it trickling out from beneath them and running down my raised arms.

Forty-four seconds. Sixteen to go. My heart leapt when there was a gasp of shock from my left. Without moving the rifle, I snapped my head around and saw a woman standing in the open door to 2D. Frozen in place, she held a bulging plastic garbage bag in her hand as she stared at me in shock. Shit!

"Get inside!"

I hissed the words and a moment later she jumped back and slammed her door. Fuck! She was probably running for the phone to call the cops. And I'd lost count because of the distraction.

Focusing my racing mind, I maintained aim and waited. And waited. It felt like hours but was actually less than ten seconds before I heard the deadbolt turn. Leaning forward, I pulled the rifle tight against my shoulder and moved my finger onto the trigger. One second later the knob rattled as it turned, then the door opened.

As a gap appeared, I saw a form standing in the opening. I didn't look any higher than the center of the chest. In an instant, I verified there wasn't body armor protecting the target's vital organs. Then my finger pulled the trigger twice in quick succession and the sound-suppressed rifle spat out two quiet rounds.

The figure fell back, and I paused to check the target behind him. Seeing the next man, I went into motion. Hitting the door with my shoulder, I bulled into the room, putting three rounds into the man who had been following the one who'd opened the door. Absently noting both of them falling to the floor, I kicked the door shut behind me and swiveled the rifle, keeping it in perfect sync with my eyes.

Four more rounds and two more bodies hit the floor. Halfway done. Still turning, I fired as one of the faces I'd memorized as a pistol carrier came into view. He was tearing at his shirt, trying to draw his weapon as a single round punched through his forehead. Five down.

A man was in the kitchen, yanking open a cabinet. Trying to reach a weapon? I didn't wait to find out. He was turned away from me, and I shot him in the back of the head. Six.

I was out of targets. Where were the other two? Moving fast, I headed down the hall for the master bedroom. The rifle was up, and I quickly swiveled it to the side before I passed the kitchen to make sure someone wasn't on the floor, waiting for me to show myself. Only the body I'd put there.

Refocused on the hall, I moved quickly to the master bedroom door, which was closed. Shifting, I put my back against the opposite wall and paused a beat. Listening. Loud music was coming from the other side of the cheap, hollow core slab. So far I'd been the only one firing a weapon, and the suppressor had done a good job of keeping things quiet.

Not that the rifle was completely silent, but as I stood there listening, I doubted anyone in the room could have heard the muted report over the thumping stereo. That surprised me, but maybe it was my own cultural bias. I hadn't expected radical jihadists to be listening to American music. But what the hell do I know?

Raising my leg, I lashed out with my foot, striking the flimsy door next to the knob. The thin layers of fake wood shattered as it sprang open and I lunged forward, rifle up, seeking a target. And immediately spotted two of them. The woman I'd seen in my briefing, Janice Bass, was scrambling across the bed, trying to conceal her nudity with a thin sheet.

I assessed and dismissed her as a threat in a heartbeat, turning to track a bare, brown ass as the terrorist who had apparently been screwing her dove for the closet. I fired twice, putting a round into a hairy butt cheek and his lower back. He flopped to the floor, paralyzed by the second shot. I adjusted aim and drilled a bullet through his skull.

Whipping back around I aimed at the obese woman cowering in the bed and paused. I clearly remembered being instructed to consider her a threat if she was in the apartment, but it was hard to send a round into her pasty white, terrified face. Until she pulled harder on the covers and a pistol slipped into view.

She froze for an instant, eyes darting between me and the weapon. I could see her thinking. Calculating. Deciding if she could make it.

"Don't do it," I said.

My voice galvanized her into action, and she made a clumsy grab for the gun. I fired a single round that ended her life.

As I'd moved into the room, I stepped away from the open door, so there wasn't as great a risk of someone coming in behind me. Now, I had a good view of the bathroom and closet, both doors standing wide open. The closet was clear and unless someone was in the tub, the bath was clear, too. But I had to check before I moved on. The leader of this merry little band was still unaccounted for.

I was halfway across the room when a metallic clatter caused me to spin around. It had come from the tiny balcony, right outside a sliding glass door which was wide open, filmy curtains blowing gently in an evening breeze. The noise came again, and I rushed to the open door and peeked around the edge.

A portable, emergency escape ladder hung from the metal railing surrounding the balcony. It was bouncing against the top rail, creating the noise, as someone climbed down. Stepping out, I looked over as a man reached the ground and raced away along the length of the building.

Raising my rifle, I tried to get a shot, but there were too many trees that quickly blocked my sight line. Cursing, I slung the rifle and swung over the railing, scampering down the narrow, folding ladder. I dropped the final few feet and immediately began running after the escaping terrorist.

Pulling the rifle around, so it was in my hands and ready, I pushed hard, thankful for all the mind-numbingly boring hours I'd spent on the treadmill. Without them, I would have been moving slower and knew I'd be tiring quickly.

Ahead, I saw a running figure dash out from behind some bushes and into the parking lot. Seeing where he was heading, I angled away from the building and cut between two parked cars. Within a few seconds, I closed half the lead he had gained. I had the angle on him, and when he passed under a streetlight, I got a good enough look to recognize the leader.

Running a few more paces, I skidded to a stop against the trunk of an aging Chevy and threw my upper body across it. The rifle came down, and I stretched forward, putting myself into a stabilized shooting stance. It only took a second to find the runner in the scope. Tracking him, I gave it a couple more seconds to adjust my lead and compensate for his speed.

He was naked and barefoot, running with long strides across the flat asphalt. For a beat, I thought about the significance of the two terrorists in the bedroom with the girl, all of them in a state of undress. Not liking the mental image, I exhaled and pulled the trigger.

A heartbeat later the man went loose-limbed and tumbled to the pavement, rolling to a halt against the front tire of a Nissan pickup. Keeping the rifle aimed, I stood and ran forward, firing two more rounds into his body as I approached. I walked the rest of the way and looked down.

With the toe of my shoe, I hooked under his shoulder and rolled him over. The rifle was aimed, my finger on the trigger, but I didn't need to fire. Lifeless eyes stared at the dark sky above.

Lowering the rifle, I looked around. Didn't see anyone, but did spot a couple of security cameras mounted high up on light poles. So much for keeping this quiet. Even if I moved the body, there was a recording of what had happened in the parking lot.

But, if there was no reason for anyone to look, maybe I could still pull it off. Slinging the rifle, I bent to gather the corpse into my arms. I intended to haul it back into the apartment, but stopped and looked around when I heard a faint siren. I listened for a couple of seconds, and it was definitely getting closer, coming at a fast clip.

With no time to clean up, I ignored the body at my feet and stood. Was it too late to make a clean getaway? With all these weapons, yes. Cops were probably about to flood into the area. Remembering what I'd been told, that the weapons would come with me when I snapped back to real time, I began pulling them off and dumping them on the ground next to the dead man.

I debated keeping a pistol, but there were now multiple sirens closing quickly. The cops were going to want to search anyone out and moving, and I didn't want them to find a weapon on me. Dropping the pistols and all of my knives, stun gun and baton, I quickly shrugged out of the vest and body armor, pulled off my gloves and tossed everything onto the corpse.

Weaponless, I turned to run for the sidewalk, pausing when I remembered the mask. Ripping it off my head, I threw it to the ground and headed away from the scene with my face lowered away from the view of the cameras. All I had left was the small pack that held the phone and iPad.

Stepping onto the sidewalk, I saw two police cruisers roar around a corner, lights flashing and sirens blaring. Three more appeared from a side street a moment later. One of them saw me and a spotlight lanced out and lit me up, blinding me. I jumped when a hand slipped into mine, nearly hitting Julie before I recognized her.

"You'd better tell me your name before they start asking who we are," she said as the first police car screeched to a stop in the street next to us.

"JR Whitman," I said, wondering why the hell she was putting herself at risk to help me.

27

"Officer, we heard gun shots! And there's someone on the ground, right over there!"

Julie moved towards the patrol car, dragging me along by the hand as a cop that looked too young to have even started shaving stepped onto the street. He already had his weapon out, and I was glad to see it was pointed at the ground and not us. With his free hand, he reached up and pressed the transmit button on the radio clipped to his shoulder, tilting his head sideways to speak into it.

"Where?" He asked when he finished talking into the microphone.

"Right over there, on the other side of that truck. We were walking by and saw him and some guns and were running inside to call you."

While she was speaking, two more cruisers screamed up and pulled to a stop, completely blocking the street. The drivers jumped out, one of them with a pistol in his hand, the other a rifle. The first cop to arrive spoke to them briefly, pointing in the direction Julie had indicated.

Dirk Patton

"Get behind my car and stay put," he said to us.

We moved forward as the three cops spread out and began walking towards the body of the man I'd killed. It was only about fifty yards away and wouldn't take them long to find. It, and the pile of weapons, and they would quickly realize we weren't what we seemed.

I looked up and down the street. More cop cars were arriving, blocking intersections. I could see darkly dressed figures running, converging on the parking lot. At the moment, no one was paying any attention to us, but that wouldn't last long.

The three cops were halfway there, weapons up and trained ahead. Their full attention was focused on what was ahead of them, and I had no doubt the others were racing to back them up. I took another quick look around. No one was watching us.

"Let's go," I hissed, tugging Julie's hand as I headed across the street for a darker residential area.

She didn't resist. Maintaining her grip on my hand, she ran next to me. We made it across the main street without any of the cops shouting for us to stop. The new road ran a short distance then branched out as it fed into the neighborhood. Twenty seconds later we were around the closest turn and concealed from the main area of activity.

But there was no time to relax. A helicopter would be on the way. And more cops. Probably K9 units that could track us by scent. And my scent was all over the gear I'd left behind. We needed a vehicle, and we needed one fast. Had to get out of the area before it was completely shut down.

I didn't want to get caught, but it wasn't the end of the world if I was. The Universe would solve that problem by sending me back to real time in a few hours. But for some unfathomable reason, Julie had stuck her neck out for me and gotten involved. If she was caught, she didn't have a get out of jail free card.

We were walking fast, moving down the sidewalk through the quiet neighborhood. Most of the front windows of the small, working-class houses were lit with the blue light of a television screen. Everyone was inside, glued to whatever program they liked to watch.

My heart skipped a beat when headlights turned out of a side street a few houses ahead of us. I expected to see a police cruiser and was ready to make a dash for a backyard. But it wasn't a cop. It was an older Kia SUV, and it pulled into a driveway two houses away.

I stopped, holding Julie back, and watched. After what seemed like a long wait, a heavyset woman stepped out and walked to the back of the vehicle. She stuck a key into the hatch gate, turned it and moved back as it slowly rose. Leaning in, she gathered several grocery bags and headed for the front door of the house. The keys were still in the hatch lock.

"Stay close," I whispered, moving forward as the woman fumbled with the front door.

She either didn't lock her house, which I highly doubted in the LA area, or there was someone home. Either way, she got the door open without her keys and stepped through. We had already covered half the distance, and as soon as she was out of sight, I sprinted forward, Julie on my heels.

Slamming the hatch, I grabbed the keys, ran around the side of the SUV and jumped behind the wheel. There were more groceries in back, and the owner would be stepping out the front door any second. Jamming the key in the ignition, I started the engine as Julie jumped in the passenger seat.

"Hey!"

I looked up to see the woman staring in surprise from the front porch. Yanking the gear selector into reverse, I stomped on the gas and screeched out of the driveway into the street. The Kia was still rolling backwards when I shifted to drive and floored the throttle. Tires screamed, then we were moving.

I took the first turn we came to, roaring down another dark, quiet street. Ahead, I could see a stop sign and the steady flow of cross traffic on a better lit thoroughfare. Searching the dash, I found the light switch and turned it on, coming to a fast stop at what seemed to be a major boulevard.

"Three minutes at best," I said to myself.

"Three minutes what?" Julie asked. I guess I'd said it aloud, too.

"Three minutes. She's probably on the phone with 9-1-1 right now. It won't take them long to connect the stolen vehicle with the scene at the apartments, then every cop in California is going to be looking for this thing. We've got to dump it quick."

There was the sound of a helicopter in the night sky as I finished speaking. Sticking my head out the open window, I looked up. It was easy to locate, a brilliant spotlight stabbing down not too far behind us. Probably lighting up the parking lot where the body was.

There was a break in traffic, and I made a left, turning to open some more distance between us and the cops. I pushed the small engine hard, not worrying about being pulled over for speeding. All the cops in the area were busy at the moment.

"Use the hem of your shirt and wipe down any place you've touched," I said to Julie. "We're going to ditch this in a minute, and I don't want them finding your prints."

She looked at me for a beat. Maybe the reality of what she'd gotten involved with was sinking in. Maybe not. Before I had to tell her again, she grabbed the edge of the baggy shirt and started wiping every surface on her side of the vehicle.

"What about you?" she asked as she worked.

Shit! I hadn't been thinking. I'd taken the gloves off, and now I was creating evidence that would be left behind.

Ahead I saw a large grocery store, probably the one the woman had just come from, and turned into the parking lot. It was big, and I drove to a point farthest from the street and the store entrance before parking. Ripping my T-shirt over my head, I frantically wiped down the wheel, gear shift and every other surface I could have possibly touched.

Jumping out, I took the keys with me and wiped each one before tossing the ring under the SUV. I cleaned the exterior door handle, then ran to the back and wiped a large area around where the keys had been hanging.

"Did you get your door handle?"

"Yes," Julie said, coming to stand next to me.

I pulled my shirt back on and took her hand, walking slowly towards the street.

"What are we doing?" She asked.

"Busy road and there's lots of pedestrian traffic. For the moment, we're blending in until I can find us a place to lay up for a few hours."

Julie didn't say anything else, just held my hand tightly and stayed right against my side as we stepped onto the sidewalk. It was early evening, and there were a lot of people moving. Shopping, going to dinner, stopping in at their favorite bar. For the moment we were OK, but there was probably a dash cam in that first patrol car that had captured our faces.

How long would it take the cops to broadcast the images to every law enforcement officer in the state? I didn't have a clue. But I was going to give them the benefit of the doubt and assume it would be fast. I'd gotten a good amount of training on the technology boom that had occurred while I was in prison. Once I got over my amazement, I realized just how much easier it was for the authorities to locate someone than it had been even a decade ago.

With that thought in mind, I knew we had to get off the streets. Fast. But where? While I tried to answer that, I kept us moving. We weren't running, but we weren't strolling either. Just walking at a reasonably fast pace that covered a lot of ground.

Sirens could still be heard on the night air, but they were all behind us. At the moment, it didn't sound like any of them were coming our way. I turned my head and blocked the view of Julie's face when a plain, black Crown Victoria raced past. It was heading towards the apartments and was either a detective or maybe even the FBI. If it had a dash cam, I didn't want our faces showing up in case someone decided to review the footage.

"What about there?" Julie asked, pointing down and across the street.

I looked, seeing a gaudy green and red neon sign advertising the Downey Motor Inn. I nodded and picked up the pace, reaching an intersection and impatiently waiting for the light to change so we could cross. It finally did, and we ran in the crosswalk, then a short distance to the motel's parking lot.

Slowing to a fast walk, I led her inside the small office that fronted the street. It was in dire need of a cleaning and airing out. Behind a chipped laminate counter, an immensely fat man sat watching a small, black and white TV. A cigarette was smoldering in an overflowing ashtray, and there was a bluish haze hanging in the air. My eyes immediately began watering when we walked in.

He looked up when a small bell jingled as the door opened, but didn't shift his bulk. Releasing Julie's hand, I stepped to the counter, glancing around and happy to not see any surveillance cameras.

"Got a room?" I asked.

"Got three," he wheezed. "Eighty-nine a night. Plus tax."

I nodded and brought out my wallet. He grunted as he moved, placing a form on the counter in front of me.

"Fill that out and I need ID and a credit card."

Opening my wallet, I pinched five, hundred dollar bills off the wad of cash and fanned them out on top of the form. His eyes immediately locked onto the money and lingered there for several moments.

"Look," I said, leaning close and lowering my voice. "I'm just looking for a place to have some fun for a while. Don't want to leave a trail that my wife could find. Five hundred for twenty-four hours. Just between us guys."

I smiled a lascivious grin and tilted my head towards Julie as I spoke. He looked at her, then looked her up and down, pausing for a longer inspection of her legs. Looking at me, he leaned back and picked up the cigarette, placing it between his lips.

"Thousand," he said, eyes narrowed, watching me.

"No," I said, scooping up the cash and starting to turn away.

I could imagine a married man shelling out a few hundred bucks for an unregistered room so he could get it on with a woman that wasn't his wife. But a grand? No way. Not from someone that was willing to come to a place like this.

That was too much, and would eventually make the clerk start thinking about who was really in one of his rooms and why they were willing to pay so much. I didn't want his mind going there, especially since the events at the apartment complex were probably about to be splashed all over the news.

"Let's go," I said to Julie, taking my time turning away, giving the man an opportunity to think about the cash that was about to walk out the door.

"OK," he said after I'd taken a couple of steps. "But I want you out by noon tomorrow. Can't hide the room any longer than that."

I turned back and looked at him like I was thinking it over. Julie must have realized what I was doing because she stepped forward and pressed herself against me, like a woman trying to convince her lover to do something.

"Fine," I said, putting the cash back on the counter.

It disappeared, a large, brass key appearing where it had been.

"108," he said. "Around back. A little more private."

I nodded, picking up the key and starting to walk away. Julie brushed past me and stepped up to the counter, pointing at his pack of cigarettes.

"That much money should also buy that," she said.

"Hundred bucks," he leered at her.

"Don't be like that," she said, pouting.

He looked at her, then sighed and tossed the pack onto the counter. She snatched them up, reached across and grabbed a pack of matches from next to the ashtray and gave him a thousand-watt smile. He smiled back, and I doubted there was a heterosexual male that wouldn't have responded to the smile she flashed.

We pushed out into the fresh air and followed a cracked sidewalk around the end of the building. The back of the property was well lit, a small parking lot running the length of the structure. Half way down I found the room, unlocking the door and hustling Julie inside after I flipped on the lights.

The room was about what I expected. A thin, queen sized mattress on an equally cheap set of box springs. It was covered with a faded comforter, several lumps beneath it at the head of the bed from well used pillows. A pair of battered tables framed the headboard, a digital clock resting on one, a beige phone on the other.

A single, upholstered chair was next to the heavy curtains that covered the front window and a tall table on the wall opposite the bed supported a small television. No closet and the bath was so tiny I'd have to turn sideways to shut the door.

Julie went to the sink, unwrapped a flimsy paper cup and ran some water into it. Carrying it back into the room, she put it on one of the nightstands and sat down on the edge of the bed. With slightly shaking hands, she fished a cigarette out of the pack and lit it.

"What the fuck do you think you're doing?" I asked in a quiet voice, not wanting to be heard through what I was almost certain would be paper thin walls.

"Having a smoke," she said after taking a deep drag. "It's been an exciting evening, and I'm a little on edge."

"That's not what I meant. What are you doing here? With me? You just made yourself an accomplice. What the hell were you thinking?"

She sat there and smoked the cigarette, looking at me through the haze that was quickly filling the small room. I wanted to open a window to vent the air but didn't like the thought of someone outside being able to hear our conversation.

"You were about to get caught," she finally said. "I didn't start out to get involved. After you left my apartment, I came outside to see what was going on. Didn't see anything at first, so I went out to the parking lot. The next thing I know, this naked guy was climbing down a ladder, then here you came. Ran him down and killed him.

"Saw you dumping all your weapons and gear when you heard the sirens. Could tell you didn't want to get caught, so I just reacted. Figured you'd draw a lot of scrutiny if you were by yourself. But a couple out for a stroll? They weren't going to look too closely at us. At least not at first."

She finished the cigarette and dropped it into the water filled cup. Her hands were still trembling, and a moment later she lit another.

"I don't get it," I said. "You don't know me. Why are you helping?

"A little gratitude would be nice," she said, sounding hurt.

"I am grateful. But I'm also worried. If they haven't already, those cops are going to figure out who you are. Then what? You want to go to jail?"

I was angry with her. Didn't understand why she'd go out on a limb like she had, and wasn't happy that I was responsible for someone ruining their life.

"OK, look," she said, exhaling a plume of smoke. "I talked to that FBI agent. I get what you are and that you don't want to get caught by the cops. My husband was a Green Beret. Most everything he did was classified, and the last thing the chain of command would have wanted was for him to be caught by civilian authorities. I get it. I also get that you'd probably have been detained on the spot if I hadn't been there."

"Then you understand that there's people higher up the food chain that would have gotten me out. Cleaned up any record of my arrest," I said.

She nodded, slowly smoking the cigarette. Reaching up, she pushed several strands of long, blonde hair behind her right ear.

"You know, I heard that from Justin over and over. And you know what else I heard?"

I shook my head.

"I heard about how much trouble guys that did get caught, or exposed, were in. You make that kind of mistake and you're out. Reassigned to a desk or training brigade if you're lucky. Forced retirement if you're not. That would have ruined him, and, well... I just reacted without thinking."

Time stretched out. Her smoking and me standing there looking at her. Finishing the cigarette, she dropped it in the cup and reached for another.

"Please," I said, staying her hand. "I already can't breathe. Can you wait a little bit?"

She nodded and put the pack and matches back on the nightstand.

"Thank you," I said, and she looked at me and nodded.

"Sorry. I smoke when I'm scared."

"I didn't mean for that. I meant for what you did. But I wish you hadn't."

"You'd just better be what I think you are," she said, watching my face as she spoke.

"You guessed mostly right," I said after a pause. "It wouldn't have been the end of the world if I'd been caught, but it's better that I wasn't. Don't yet know what's going to happen to you."

"Whatever happens, it can't be worse than what I've already been through," she said in a sad voice.

I finally calmed enough to sit, lowering myself into the chair by the windows. The room was so small I could have reached out and touched Julie without stretching, but it felt like a better option than sitting on the same bed as her.

"So what's the plan?" She asked after several minutes of silence.

"I don't have one," I said. "I'm being... extracted... in a few hours. Needed a place to lay low until then. Wasn't expecting to have company."

"I can take care of myself," she said, a slight edge to her voice that sounded like her feelings were hurt.

"Not what I was saying," I said. "I'll figure something out. I'm not going to leave you to take your chances with the cops."

She looked at me for a bit, then lit another cigarette. I almost protested, but settled for moving the chair as far away from the smoke as I could. It didn't help.

"Your husband," I said, after getting settled on the far side of the room.

"What about him?"

"The way you talked about him. What happened?"

She took a big drag and looked away, staring into space.

"We met at Fort Campbell," she said in a far off voice. "I was transiting through, on my way to Iraq. I'd just finished medic training and was scared and excited at the same time. Went into the NCO club for a drink and he knocked me off my feet. Literally. He was walking out, talking to someone behind him and just ran me over.

"He felt so bad. Picked me up off the floor and when he realized I'd twisted my ankle as I fell, carried me to a booth. Bought me dinner and wrapped my ankle while we waited for the food. He was this great big, strapping Green Beret, and here he was tending to my little booboo.

"We wound up talking half the night. Eight months later, I'm in Iraq and get this email from out of nowhere. He's going on leave for a week, in Germany, and asked if I'd meet him there. At first, I thought the idea was crazy. I didn't know this guy. Why the hell would I go to Germany with him?

"But for some reason I did. Flew into Ramstein a couple of weeks later and he was standing there waiting for me when I got off the plane. We went on a tour of beer halls for a week and had the time of our lives. Then it was back to the war, and I didn't see or hear from him for six months. I was upset but understood he didn't exactly have the kind of job that let him call or email at the end of the day.

"When I did hear from him again, he was rotating home. My tour was up, and we made plans to get together when we were both stateside. He was at Fort Campbell, and I was at Benning in Georgia. We got together for a long weekend when I first got home, then pretty soon one of us was driving to see the other whenever there was a break.

"Two months later, we got married. Three weeks after that, he headed back to Iraq for his next tour. I was a month behind him. We saw each other once in the next year, two weeks in Thailand. He told me all about what the Army had him doing. Probably much more than he should have.

"We'd been back for ten days when my CO called me into his office. The chaplain was there with him. They told me I was a widow. Justin had been killed by a suicide bomber. A fucking Iraqi that had been vetted and cleared to work inside the wire where Justin was. The tango just walked into the mess tent and blew himself up, along with forty-eight soldiers.

"So you ask why I got involved? Because of something you said back at my apartment. These fucking people aren't going to stop until they kill all of us, or we kill all of them. And after losing Justin, I promised myself that if I ever had the opportunity to help a few of them meet Allah a little early, I'd take it. I guess this is my way of helping."

She looked over at me, tears glistening in her eyes. My heart went out to her. I'd lost a lot of buddies over there too, and knew exactly what she was feeling. Well, maybe not exactly. She'd lost a husband. But I knew the sense of loss. Could understand how it motivated someone to do something. To make a choice that maybe wasn't in your best interest.

"I'm sorry," I said.

"Three years ago," she said with a sardonic laugh. "And you know what the worst part is?"

I shook my head.

"I'm having trouble remembering his face. I've never told that to anyone."

I didn't know what to say. I've never been the kind of person that's good at comforting someone in pain. Wish I was, but I knew that if I tried to say something helpful it would probably come out awkward and clumsy. So I settled for telling her I was sorry for her loss. Again.

Wiping her eyes, she lit another cigarette. Between the smoky haze and the maudlin mood, I needed fresh air. Badly. Standing, I moved to the window and carefully parted the curtains. Peering out at the parking lot, I didn't see anyone moving.

"Need some air," I said, flipping the light switch off before opening the door.

I stepped out, taking a deep breath for the first time since we'd walked into the room. A moment later, Julie joined me. I left the door open and didn't move very far away. If I saw or heard anything, I was prepared to dash back inside.

"Come up with any bright ideas?" She asked.

"I'm going to call the FBI agent you talked to," I nodded. "Tell him what's going on and ask him to help you."

"He's got that much juice?"

"Yes," I said. "At least I think so. Honestly, this is my first mission. I've been working with him for several months, but this is the first time I've been in the field and don't really know how he's going to react. Probably going to chew me a new one."

"Then maybe it's not a good idea to call him," she said.

"Not much choice," I said. "Besides. I'll have to include you in my debrief. I'd rather take my lumps now and make sure you're taken care of."

We stood there while she finished her smoke. The evening was waning. There was still the roar of traffic from the road on the other side of the building, but it felt like people were settling in for the night.

Back in the room, I opened my pack and pulled out the iPad and the secure phone. Activating the tablet, the timer window popped up. Return to real time was in fifteen hours and eleven minutes.

"What's that?" She asked, looking over my shoulder.

"Time to extraction," I said.

Dirk Patton

I may have already told her more than I should have, but I wasn't about to start talking about time travel. Besides divulging secrets that would probably land me in more hot water than I could handle, she'd immediately decide I was deranged.

Closing the iPad, I lifted the phone and powered it on. Time to call Johnson. I wasn't looking forward to this conversation. While I waited for it to finish booting and find a signal, Julie found the remote and turned on the TV. As soon as it came on, a news report was playing. Holding the handset, I stepped back and looked at the television screen.

An off-camera reporter was talking as the image slowly panned across the parking lot of the apartment complex. There were more cop cars than I'd ever seen in one place. Yellow police tape completely surrounded the entire area and it looked like all of the residents had been rousted and herded outside the perimeter of the crime scene. There was also a large contingent of men wearing suits and when one of them moved I spied the dull, gold badge on his belt that identified him as FBI.

"...the FBI is on scene, and a source who wants to remain anonymous has told me that this appears to be related to terrorism. I don't have details to substantiate that statement, but based on the significant response and presence of federal authorities, the information seems accurate.

"Recapping, a shootout between unknown subjects at this apartment building in Downey has left nine dead. The number of victims has been confirmed by the Downey Police Department. What we do know is that there are eight dead inside an apartment on the second floor," the camera zoomed to a shot of the balcony, the emergency escape ladder still hanging from the railing. "And one additional dead just behind me in the parking lot."

The camera changed perspective, zooming in on a large group of evidence collection technicians huddled around the spot where I'd killed the terrorist leader. Several of the techs were wearing blue windbreakers with FBI emblazoned across the back in large, yellow letters.

"A large quantity of military style assault weapons has been recovered from the parking lot, apparently adjacent to the body that was found. At this time, no other information has been provided by any of the agencies involved, but we're very early in the investigation."

The reporter, a young, blonde woman with a perfect smile, continued to rattle on as the camera cut to a shot of her standing next to a police cruiser with roof lights flashing. She continued to repeat what she'd just said, putting it in a slightly different order without providing any new information. Her job was to keep talking, filling the time until something new was released by the authorities.

"Well, that's good," Julie said. "At least our pictures aren't on TV yet, and they aren't mentioning the police looking for anyone."

"Yet," I said, returning my attention to the phone.

Pressing a couple of keys, I initiated a call to the only number it would dial. Agent Johnson. It rang one time before it was answered.

"You've made a mess, Mr. Whitman," he said immediately when the call was picked up.

"Not as much as there would have been," I said, a little defensively.

"I'm sure I'll learn all about that in a few hours," he said. "But right now you've kicked over a hornet's nest. I'm monitoring traffic, and every three letter agency I can think of is getting involved. Since you're calling me, I'm guessing you're in a secure location at the moment."

"Yes, we are," I said, without thinking about the *we* part of that.

There was dead silence for several beats before he spoke again.

"We? Would that be the woman that called me? Ms. Julie Broussard?" He asked in a low voice that made me cringe.

"Yes," I said, steeling myself and charging ahead with the conversation. "Without her, I'd be in the hands of the police right now. She provided some cover, and we made it out of the immediate area, but we're still too close. And she's going to have a problem after I, uh... after I'm extracted."

"She most certainly will," he said, exasperation clear in his voice. "OK, we'll discuss operational security when you get back. For now, what do I need to know that I don't?"

"Well, we're at the..."

"Downey Motor Inn," he interrupted. "Your phone gave me precise coordinates when you called."

"Right," I said, slightly disconcerted. "She stuck her neck out for me. And she needs some help."

"What does she know?" He asked.

"Enough," I said, evasively. "She was Army. Combat medic in Iraq. She's seen enough Special Ops to know what was going on. Understand?"

"I believe so. She's unaware of the project?"

"Correct," I said, noting that Julie had taken a seat on the bed and lit another cigarette as she listened intently to my conversation.

"You'd better hope so. For her sake."

"The cops have us on a dash cam," I said, ignoring his ominous statement. "And I'm probably on security video somewhere from the cameras in the parking lot."

"The parking lot footage has already been taken care of. As soon as I received Ms. Broussard's call, I identified the location and had them disabled. But the dash cam isn't good. Hang on for a moment and let me verify something."

There was a click as he muted the phone on his end. I was left watching the TV while I waited. Julie had turned the volume down when I placed the call, and I couldn't tell if there was any new information. Several minutes later, Johnson came back on the line.

"OK, here's the bad news. The Downey Police use an older dash cam system that records onto a disk housed inside the cruiser. It requires a direct download to a server when they return to the station at the end of shift. There's no way to get to it remotely until that happens.

"The system has the ability for the cops in the field to review the footage that has been recorded. And they can print a copy of any image that's on the disk. Without remote access, we have no way of knowing if they've identified you and Ms. Broussard and are already looking for you."

"Can't you call one of your buddies that's at the scene? I'm watching a news report, and there's FBI all over the place. Can't one of them take care of things?"

"This has already gone too wide, Mr. Whitman," he said with a sigh. "Homeland Security, the ATF and California State Police are already on scene in addition to FBI. The NSA and CIA are sticking their noses in behind the scenes. I can't shut this down without drawing a lot of attention, and that's exactly what we are supposed to avoid."

"Fuck me," I breathed, looking at Julie. "So what do we do to help her?"

"How secure are you?"

"Probably fine until our faces make the news. I paid off the desk clerk to give us a room without registering. But he's got a TV sitting right in front of him. If our images pop up, it'll probably take him about three seconds to start dialing 9-1-1."

"Room number?" He asked.

"108."

"Stay put. Don't stick your head out. I'm going to have an agent come pick you up and move you to a secure location. I'm texting you his photo right now so you can confirm it's him when he arrives."

"Both of us?" I asked.

"Yes, Mr. Whitman. Both of you."

There was a gentle beep in my ear, and I took the handset away from my face long enough to confirm I'd just received a photo.

"You're sure I can trust this guy?" I asked.

"He's one of the project's team on the ground," he said. "Yes. He can be trusted. Ten minutes and he'll be knocking on your door. We'll take this up when you get back."

"Hold on," I said, pausing until I was sure he hadn't already hung up. "What are you going to do with Julie?"

"She will be protected, Mr. Whitman."

With that, there was a click, and he was gone. I lowered the handset and opened the photo, staring at the face long enough to ensure I'd instantly recognize if it was someone else that knocked on the door.

"FBI is picking us up," I said, storing the phone in my pack. "Moving us to a safer location while this all shakes out."

Julie nodded and tried to light another cigarette. Her hands were shaking so badly she couldn't hold the flame steady, so I reached out and took the matches. I held one for her, absently slipping the pack into my pocket when the smoke was lit.

It was only eight minutes later when there was a soft knock. Looking through the peephole, I instantly recognized the face of the man from the photo Johnson had sent me. Opening the door, I stepped back to let him come in, but he stayed where he was.

"Ready?" He asked.

I nodded and extended my arm towards Julie, inviting her to go first. She dropped her cigarette in the water cup and stood, moving past me and through the door. The agent had stepped back, and I followed, bumping into Julie's back when she suddenly looked to her left and came to an abrupt stop.

Instantly, we were swarmed by large men in dark clothing. Before I could put up any resistance, a Taser was pressed against my back, every muscle in my body going into a painful knot. I heard another one clicking, a grunt of pain from Julie as she, too, was shocked.

Strong hands grabbed my arms, preventing me from falling to the sidewalk. There was a pinch on the side of my neck and almost immediately the world began to spin. Darkness rapidly closed in as I lost consciousness.

29

I woke up with a splitting headache and a tongue that felt about four sizes too large for my mouth. Dehydration, I realized without even having to think about it. I'd dealt with it before, and my brain recognized the symptoms the same way it would recognize the smell of frying bacon or the taste of an orange.

But, where the hell was I? The last thing I remembered was... what was it? I lay there in the darkness, confused for a moment. Then it all came back. Killing the terrorists then hiding out with Julie, waiting for the FBI agent to show up. And being ambushed when he did.

I sat straight up in alarm, putting my hands down on a soft surface. A bed? What the hell? Looking around, I could see nothing other than perfect darkness. There were some faint background sounds that were familiar, as was the taste of the air gently blowing from an unseen vent.

Reaching up, I found the light switch exactly where I expected it to be. Even before I turned it on, I knew I was in bed in my cramped quarters aboard the Project Athena oil rig.

Lights on, I saw two bottles of water on my small table and stood to retrieve them. I was wobbly at first, my legs not wanting to cooperate with the commands my head was issuing, but they finally got with the program, and I walked five feet across the steel floor.

I drained the first bottle without pausing, opening the second and drinking half of it in another long gulp. Quickly, I began feeling better, and the stabbing pain behind my eyes receded until it was only a faint, dull ache. With clarity, came anger. Boiling up from my gut until I was ready to throttle someone, and that someone was Agent Johnson.

Glancing down, I saw that I was still dressed in the same clothes. My shoes had been removed and neatly tucked under the edge of the bed. The wallet I'd been given was missing. I assumed they'd taken it back. All that was in my pockets were Julie's matches. I stared at them, surprised I'd been able to bring something forward through time with me until I remembered the conversation with Dr. Anholts.

While I was thinking about this, a muted knock came from the steel hatch that served as a door. It was only two steps away, and I spun the wheel to release the latch and yanked it open.

Agent Johnson stood there, looking immaculate in a pin-striped suit that had to have been custom made. He held a large mug of coffee in his right hand, the FBI seal boldly emblazoned on the white ceramic.

"I should kick your fucking ass," I seethed, seriously considering attacking him.

"That would be a futile effort as well as counter-productive," he said calmly, stepping across the threshold and into my room without waiting to be invited.

He moved across the small space, turned my lone chair around to face the bed and sat with his free hand folded in his lap. Meeting my eyes, he gestured at the bed, telling me to take a seat. I slammed the steel door and angrily spun the wheel to secure it.

"What the fuck was that all about?" I asked as I sat down. "There was no need for that."

"We needed control of the situation, Mr. Whitman," he said, taking a sip from the mug. "We needed both you and Ms. Broussard safely tucked away until things calmed down and could be managed by cooler heads. My agents had no idea if you were still armed, and with my approval, they took no chances with their, or your, safety."

I glared at him. Pissed. Wanting to rant and rave, but it was difficult to maintain the level of anger when he was so fucking calm and collected about the whole situation. A juvenile impulse to reach out and slap the mug, spilling coffee on his clothes passed through me. I barely resisted the urge.

"Wasn't necessary," I said. "And where are we? Back in real time?"

"Yes," he said. "About sixteen hours ago. And we've reviewed the data from your chip."

"That's nice," I said sarcastically. "What did you do with Julie?"

"Ms. Broussard is no longer your concern," he said. "She is being protected. That's all you need to know."

"Fuck need to know!" I shouted. "What did you do with her?"

"Mr. Whitman..."

"I'm not fucking around, Johnson," I said through clenched teeth. "That woman did nothing other than help. Now you can tell me what you did with her, or I'm going to shove that mug up your ass and turn it sideways."

"As pleasant as that sounds, I'm afraid I'll have to decline," he said, his eyes narrowing.

There was just a hint of tension that appeared in his shoulders and his free hand stiffened into a hard edge. He was prepared to defend himself if I tried to carry out my threat. I sat staring into his eyes, breathing hard as I struggled with the desire to go for his jugular.

"You're an asshole, Johnson," I seethed. "I thought you were someone I could trust, but now I see what you really are. You're just a cog in the machine, incapable of making a human decision."

"I have two ex-wives who would agree with you on those points," he smiled.

After a moment, despite myself, I felt the anger begin to dissipate. Just the blind rage anger. I was still upset and determined to know what had happened to Julie.

"Tell me what you did with her, or get out," I said in a calmer voice. "I don't work for people that I can't trust."

He stared at me for a long time. Nearly two full minutes. The silence stretched out until it was uncomfortable, but I wasn't going to be the first one to break it. Finally, he heaved a sigh, relaxed his shoulders and took another sip of coffee.

"Ms. Broussard was taken to an FBI safe house in Los Angeles. She was well cared for as we wrapped up a few things."

"What things?" I asked.

"We ensured that the dash cam footage containing her image has been completely erased. We also scoured the path you took escaping from the apartment to locate and delete any video evidence of the two of you in the stolen Kia. So far we've had to intercede and wipe three ATM cameras and the security systems in four different retail stores that captured the two of you abandoning the SUV and walking to the hotel.

"And equally as important, we talked with her to make sure none of what she saw or heard will be repeated. To anyone. Once we were satisfied, she was returned to her apartment".

"How do I know you're telling the truth?" I asked. "You lied to me when you sent that agent."

"I did?" He asked, eyebrows arching. "I don't seem to recall saying anything other than the agent would take both of you to a secure location. And that is precisely what occurred.

I'm sorry if it wasn't handled in a manner acceptable to you, but here you are. Safe and undetected by the authorities investigating your little mess. And so is Ms. Broussard."

"Fuck you," I mumbled, refusing to acknowledge that *technically* he was correct.

"I believe you meant to say, *thank you*," he said, frowning.

"What now?" I asked, ignoring what he'd just said. "Debrief so you know what happened?"

"We already know exactly what happened, Mr. Whitman. That data chip inside you? It doesn't just carry a record of why we sent you back. It also records everything you did.

"So, not a debrief, but we're going to have some discussions about how you handled things. And Mr. Patterson wants to speak with you, too."

"Fine," I grumbled, not looking forward to any of the conversations that were in my immediate future.

"Now," he said, getting to his feet. "I'll leave you to clean up and get some food. Be in the conference room in forty-five minutes."

With that, he left my quarters without another word. I watched him depart, still unhappy with the way things had gone. But then, I imagined he was as well. Glancing at my watch, I noted the time. Grabbing my kit and a small towel, I headed for a community shower I shared with half a dozen of the analysts.

Twenty minutes later I was cleanly shaven, showered, dressed in fresh clothes and heading for the cantina. Loading a plate with food, I looked around and spotted Dr. Anholts. She was seated by herself, as usual, typing away on her laptop as a tray of food sitting by her elbow went untouched. No wonder she was so damn skinny.

"Hi," I said, walking up.

"Mr. Whitman," she said brightly. "Welcome back!"

"Thank you. May I join you?"

She looked surprised, but quickly waved me to a seat on the opposite side of the table.

"I understand your first mission was successful, despite some unexpected consequences," she said, pushing the laptop to the side and closing the lid.

"I suppose," I said. "I'm about to go into a meeting with the Director and Agent Johnson. They don't seem too happy with me."

"Pffffttt," she made a rude noise. "Director Patterson is never happy. He seems to be incapable of recognizing and acknowledging accomplishments."

She looked around us, conspiratorially, and leaned close. Lowering her voice to almost a whisper, she smiled and said, "He's also a bit of a pompous ass."

Hmmm. Those were interesting insights. I was glad to know that I'd read her correctly. She loved her work but resented the government drone that was in charge of what should be her project.

"Can I ask you something?" I said, taking a bite of my food.

"By all means," she smiled. "Anything you like."

"The thirty-six hours. Why? What I mean is, why can't we go back farther?"

She looked at me and her eyes danced. Then she smiled.

"Perhaps we can," she said. "Especially since you didn't experience any of the disorientation the other assets reported."

I paused with a fork halfway to my mouth.

"How did you know?" I asked.

"Your data chip," she said, leaning closer as if taking me into her confidence. "It also records everything that occurs while you're back in time. One of the first things I did was to review the first couple of hours, post-arrival. It's quite exciting!"

I shoveled in a couple of bites, keeping an eye on the large clock attached to the wall. Being late for a meeting with Johnson or Patterson, as I'd learned the hard way, was a pain in the ass.

"Yeah, I was pretty happy about that, too," I said in between bites. "But, what do you mean by, "perhaps"? Have you found something?"

She looked around again before speaking, as if still afraid of being overheard. Leaning closer, she whispered so softly that I had to completely focus to understand what she was saying.

"It's all about power, Mr. Whitman. I'm working on a side project with hopes that with greater power we can generate and control larger Black Holes. In theory, with enough power and a large enough portal, we could send someone back weeks, months or possibly even years.

"That hadn't been a possibility due to the severe effect of even thirty-six hours of time travel. Until you came along. You were completely unaffected by the trip. Of course, extending farther back might produce undesired results, but it's given me hope."

"Speaking of power," I began, pausing to finish chewing and swallow a bite of my meal. "You told me this collision thing was what created the Black Hole, and said it was in Texas. We're in the middle of the ocean. How's it working here?"

"My, Mr. Whitman. You continue to surprise me," she smiled as if I was a student that had shown he wasn't as dull as the professor had thought. "The proper name is superconducting supercollider. If you like, I can loan you a book that will tell you all about it. There's one buried in the sea floor beneath us. The largest ever constructed and built just for the Athena Project.

"It is more powerful than the one in Texas. Much more, but I haven't been allowed to turn it up above the levels achieved when we first discovered that we could move through time. My team and I are working furiously on calculations to prove it will be safe."

I had kept shoveling food into my mouth while she spoke. My heart leapt when I heard what she had to say. Possibly go back years? Years was what I needed to correct the errors in my life. Travel back and correct some of the mistakes I'd made. There still wasn't a day that went by that I didn't think about Monica and what could have been. If I had a chance to fix things and have a life with her instead of ten wasted years in prison...

"You can't breathe a word of this to anyone," Dr. Anholts cautioned. "I shouldn't be saying anything, but if I can't tell an asset, who can I tell?"

She leaned back and smiled at me. I returned the smile after wiping my mouth with a paper napkin.

"Thanks for the time, Doc," I said. "I'd better be on my way before Agent Johnson comes looking for me. Anytime you want someone to talk to about the project, I'd love to listen."

She smiled and wished me good luck with my meeting. I smiled back as I stood, picked up my tray and carried it away. Glancing at a clock, I saw I had seven minutes left. Good. I'd arrive a few minutes early and not give either of them an excuse to chew on me for being tardy. Damn, but sometimes this was worse than being in the Army.

30

Even though I was early, Patterson and Agent Johnson were already in the room waiting for me. The projector was on and when I walked in Agent Johnson reached out and paused the video they were watching. I looked at the screen, seeing a frozen image of Julie sitting on the edge of the bed in the motel room when she was telling me about her husband's death.

"What the hell?" I asked. "You guys had a camera hidden on me?"

"Several," Johnson nodded, gesturing for me to take a seat in one of the empty chairs. "They continually stream to your data chip, recording everything you do."

I was pissed, but held my tongue and sat down. They hadn't told me about the cameras. Probably wanted to see what I did, and how I handled myself when I thought I was alone.

"We've reviewed the video several times," Patterson said. "We aren't here for you to tell us what happened. We already know that. What we want to know is why you made the decisions you made. Let's begin with your choice to assault the target at the end of the event point rather than earlier."

I was quiet for a moment, struggling internally to calm myself and not exacerbate my situation. They weren't happy that Julie had become involved, and I decided I'd rather not fight a battle over that decision at the moment. Pick your fights carefully and maybe you'll live to fight another day.

"I felt that, tactically, it was a better idea to attack as they were preparing to leave," I said, forcing the words to come out in a calm and reasonable tone.

For several minutes I spoke, describing my thought processes leading up to the decision. I told them about my observation of the leader arriving at the parking lot with all of the weapons, and what I believed that meant. And how it appeared to have been a correct assumption.

When I finished, Johnson pressed some keys on his laptop, and the frozen video image disappeared. It was replaced with a still photo of three hard sided crates sitting in the middle of a carpeted floor. The lids had been removed. Clearly visible in each were four AK-74s, resting in foam cutouts. Twelve rifles. Two crates went with the leader, and the third would be the spare weapons I'd been told were found in the apartment.

"This is a crime scene photo from the apartment," Johnson explained. "These were found in one of the bedrooms you didn't enter. Gun cleaning supplies were found, and traces of solvent and oil were on all but two of the perpetrators' hands. Your assumption appears to have been correct."

I nodded, unsure if this was praise. And not really caring if it was or not. I'd done my job. To me, that was all that mattered. Maybe it was a little messy, but right now, somewhere in California, a bunch of children, teachers and cops were alive because of what I'd done. I had to acknowledge to myself; that felt pretty damn good.

We went through the rest of the time I'd spent in the past. Reviewed every little turn of events. Every detail was discussed. Johnson asked questions, but Patterson remained silent. Listening to my answers. Observing me like I was some sort of curiosity. I was more than surprised when the topic shifted to my lack of disorientation and I hadn't been read the riot act about involving Julie.

"Hold on," I said, raising my hand like a traffic cop. "You still haven't explained what Julie was doing in that apartment. It was supposed to be empty."

"The advance team made an error," Johnson sighed. "The apartment building is managed by an older couple. They only spoke with the wife, who was unaware that the husband had rented the unit the previous morning. It was a mistake that shouldn't have happened, and will not happen again."

I nodded, resisting the impulse to bitch about the situation. But then maybe they weren't making a big deal out of this because it was their mistake in sending me to that particular apartment. I decided to let the topic drop.

"What's happening with Julie? What's being done to her?" I asked, not sure I trusted Johnson had given me a straight answer.

"Done *to* her, Mr. Whitman?" Patterson finally spoke up, sounding slightly indignant. "What do you think we are? She's an American citizen. Nothing is being done *to* her. She has been returned to her home. The agent in charge of her detail was satisfied after speaking with her that she will not reveal any of her little experience with you.

"Another agent has deleted both of your images from the local Police Department's data servers. In addition, her employer has received a visit from the FBI, explaining that Ms.

Broussard's absence was due to an emergency situation in which her assistance was required by the US Government. It was made clear to them that any reprisals against her due to her absence would be unwise. Good enough?"

I was surprised at the response. Thoughts of Julie being secreted away to a black site prison because she knew too much had been running through my head. If Patterson was telling the truth, she was being well cared for.

"I want to talk to her. Hear from her that she's OK," I said.

Patterson and Agent Johnson exchanged looks. I couldn't tell if they were worried about me uncovering a truth, or were not expecting this response. They were both quiet for a short moment before Patterson looked at me.

"Fine. Agent Johnson will arrange that once we're finished here."

I nodded, looking up when the door to the room suddenly burst open. A young woman, who I'd noted was usually at Patterson's side, stood in the entrance, breathing like she'd just run a sprint.

"Director," she said in a haunted voice. "The President has just been assassinated."

"I am declaring an event," Patterson said immediately, leaping to his feet and heading out the door.

Agent Johnson and I stood, following. Patterson's assistant tapped on her iPad, and a moment later the klaxon began blaring. There was an almost instant response, people dropping whatever they were doing and dashing to their assigned work stations. The organized chaos flowed around us as we hurried to the operations center. The woman raced ahead, opening the door with her keycard so Patterson could pass through without breaking stride.

"What do we have?" He barked as he walked into the room.

Johnson and I pulled to a stop and stepped to the side, so we weren't in the way. Looking up, I saw the large TV tuned to CNN. An image of a smoldering building was on the screen, a banner across the bottom scrolling a repeating message: *Washington DC attacked – President Scarsdale believed dead*.

"Nothing confirmed yet, Director. A large explosion at a restaurant where the President was dining with the Speaker of the House. We're only a few minutes in, and that's all we know at this time."

I glanced at a large screen displaying a countdown clock. It read -35:51:18. The bomb, if it was a bomb, had detonated eight minutes and forty-two seconds ago. Johnson tapped my arm, and I followed him to a small table with a pair of chairs in the back corner of the room.

"We wait here and watch," he said in a low voice when we sat down.

My seat had a clear view of the TV, and I watched as fresh images began being shown. A wide-angle shot of the whole block from a news helicopter gave a better perspective.

A four-lane street ran through the area. Along each side were single story businesses, the road lined off so there was on-street parking in front. The structure at the center of the shot was mostly demolished, nothing more than smoking debris remaining. The buildings to either side had sustained heavy damage, and one of them was on fire.

The shattered remains of four Suburban SUVs, the Secret Service's favorite transport vehicle for POTUS, were resting on their sides in the middle of the street. Spotting something, I stood and stepped closer to the screen, but the image changed back to ground level.

"Did you see that?" I turned to Johnson, but he shook his head.

"What?" He asked.

"Not sure," I said. "Anyway to get that feed on your laptop so we can see it again?"

He nodded and opened his computer's lid. I sat down and scooted my chair close, watching as he worked.

"Aerial shot. Right?"

"Yes," I said.

Patterson had taken note of our conversation and moved to stand behind our chairs, peering over our heads at the laptop screen.

"Here," Johnson said.

The same aerial image began playing, and when I told him, he froze it. I leaned close to the screen for a better look.

"Can you zoom?"

He clicked a couple of keys, and the image jumped, enlarging the devastated building.

"There!"

I pointed at a crater blasted out of the foundation. It was almost perfectly circular and penetrated all the way through the concrete, exposing the dirt beneath.

"Bomb," Patterson said.

I looked over my shoulder at him and shook my head.

"That's not a bomb," I said. "I saw plenty of these in Iraq. That's a missile strike. Bombs will shatter concrete, but not make a perfect crater like that. A missile, coming in fast, will penetrate before the warhead detonates. That initial penetration weakens the foundation and lets the blast wave inside the cement."

"You sure?" Johnson asked, not sounding convinced. "Won't a bomb do the same thing?"

"Sorry. When I say bomb, I'm thinking of the kind of bombs we faced. Suicide vest. Backpack bomb. Improvised Explosive Devices. IEDs. An air-delivered bomb will do this, too. What I'm saying is this was something launched or dropped from an aircraft. It was going fast when it struck the concrete."

Patterson stepped away and began barking orders. He wanted the radar logs from the FAA and nearby Anderson Air Force Base reviewed immediately.

"You sure about this?" Johnson asked me quietly.

"Yep," I said. "My platoon got sent in more than a few times to clean up after drone strikes. Seen this lots of times. And seen too many places where some fucker just set off a bomb he built in his basement. I'm sure."

We turned our attention back to the CNN broadcast as the people around us worked feverishly. Perhaps I should have been as shaken by this event as I had been by the slaughter of the schoolchildren, but I wasn't. Not even close.

Sure, it's a horrible thing when a President is assassinated. But, in my mind at least, it's a risk every person who has ever held the office willingly took. Then the import of what I'd noticed hit me. An aerial strike. A bomb dropped or missile fired. This wasn't uneducated jihadists. And it wasn't a foreign nation. Not operating an aircraft over Washington DC. I was willing to bet that didn't happen after 9/11.

When I thought about who could be flying an armed drone or aircraft around restricted airspace, there was only one answer. The US military.

We sat and watched the broadcast. Soon the scene was flooded with men and women wearing FBI, ATF and Secret Service windbreakers. There was no audio to go along with the images, but I didn't really want any. It would be nothing more than reporters repeating the same two or three facts. Then they would interview someone who was a retired something or other, and that would just be speculation. I knew I'd get the most factual briefing available as soon as we knew something.

Forty minutes later, Patterson walked over and looked down at me.

"You were right," he said. "Preliminary analysis at the scene has found residue consistent with the primary explosive in a Hellfire missile warhead."

I nodded, not happy that I was right. It would be bad if a terrorist had been able to get close enough to the President to take him out with a backpack or vest mounted IED. It was about a hundred times worse to think our military had decided it was time for a regime change.

"That means our military. Right?" I asked, hoping there was another explanation.

"Possibly," he said, grimacing. "The CIA has some drones that are armed, but I think the Air Force are the ones that actually operate them. Regardless, there aren't supposed to be any in operation over US soil. That's being checked. Hellfire missiles have also been sold to several of our allies, so it is possible one fell into the hands of a terror cell."

"Along with an aircraft to deliver it?" I asked.

He stared back at me for a moment before shaking his head.

"This is going to take a while," Johnson interjected. "You need some more rest, so you're ready to go when we have an event point."

Patterson nodded his agreement. But I didn't want to go. I wanted to see every bit of information the moment it came in.

"I'm good," I said.

"That wasn't a suggestion," Johnson said, his voice firm. "It will take hours, maybe even a day, before we have an idea of *when* to send you. You have to be fresh and ready, and you've not even been back in real time for twelve hours. Get some rest and I'll come get you when we know something."

I sat there staring at him for a long pause. I didn't want to be cut off, but I knew he was right. With an irritated sigh, I stood up and nodded. Taking a last look at the screen, I walked out of operations and headed for my quarters.

31

It was four hours later when Agent Johnson came and found me. I hadn't even tried to sleep. I was too keyed up. Needing to burn off some energy, I had headed for the kill house. The former Delta Operator, known only as Ray, had been more than happy to review my performance with me. We'd gotten the segment that began with me waiting outside the door to 2C and ended after I'd put the final two rounds into the terrorist leader.

He'd run it all the way through without pause or commentary, then restarted the video. It ran for all of two seconds before he stopped it. I was standing a few feet from the target door, waiting for the first tango to open it on his way out.

"You need to be to the side," he said, leaning forward and tapping a spot on the screen with a thick index finger.

I looked where he indicated and almost blushed in embarrassment. Directly in the upper middle of the door was a peephole. It was only blind luck that they hadn't checked first and seen me standing there with a rifle at the ready.

"You should have been against the wall, on the knob side. They can't see you through the peephole, and if they just crack the door open to peek out, you won't be visible because of the angle. As soon as the door starts to open, you roll around the jam and push in, leading with your weapon. Understand?"

I nodded, burning the lesson into my memory. Ray set the video in motion again, pausing after the first terrorist fell out of the way and I fired the first shot at the one behind him.

"Why did you hesitate between these two?"

"Waiting for the first guy's body to be out of my way, so I had a clear shot," I answered, not seeing what could be wrong with this.

"Mistake," he grumbled. "Fortunately for you, these guys don't seem to be that well trained. If I had been that second man, in the time you were waiting for the first one to drop, I'd have moved around behind the door, out of your sight, and put a whole ass-load of rounds through it."

"So what should I have done?"

"Let's back it up," he said, rewinding the video a few seconds. "Now, the door begins to open. You have a target, and you stand perfectly still and fire two rounds. He drops, *then* you push forward and slam the door fully open to enter the apartment."

As he talked, he started and stopped the video, so it was in sync with his narration.

"You should have charged the instant that door began moving. Come forward, put the muzzle right against the first guy's chest and use the rifle to shove him back as you're pulling the trigger. Push the body aside and bring your weapon onto the guy behind him, firing as you're moving.

"From the moment that door began to move until you put the second guy down, nearly four seconds passed. That's an eternity in this world. You can't hold back once you've committed. Movement is critical. Stay static, and someone's going to blow a hole in you. Got it?"

I nodded, realizing I'd been very lucky. We went through the rest of the clip in the same manner. Where I'd done something wrong, or could have done it better, Ray paused the playback and explained what he would have done. Once we had gone all the way through, he rewound it to the beginning and had me take control and explain errors to him just like he'd done. Highlighting my own mistakes really drove the lesson home, and I was glad I'd sought him out.

This took us a couple of hours, then we suited up and ran several different scenarios in the kill house. All of the walls, doors and even sections of the floor were motorized, and computer controlled. This meant he could reconfigure it in less than five minutes, and every time I went through it was different. Windows could be added or removed with the click of a mouse. Life-sized targets representing good and bad guys could be set to pop out at random times in unexpected locations.

I spent a couple of hours running through a variety of different scenarios. When we were done for the day, I felt like I'd learned a lot. And I only had three additional bruises from rubber bullets. That was a new low, and I was proud to have improved.

"You're showing a lot of promise," Ray said as we were cleaning up.

That was high praise from him. In fact, it was the first actual compliment he'd ever given me. I smiled like a kid who's finally gotten something right.

"But don't let it go to your head. As soon as you think you're good, you'll make a mistake that could get you killed," he said, popping my bubble.

"Gee, thanks," I grumbled.

"Look," he said, glaring into my eyes. "I know I'm a prick. I don't give a shit. My job is to make sure you can do yours. I'm not trying to run you down. I've been doing this for a long time, and I've seen a lot of guys get put in the ground because they got complacent or overconfident.

"The truly good ones, the warriors that can walk through hell and make it out the other side, are the guys that never stop training and trying to get better. They take nothing for granted. Ever. There are people out there that are smarter than you. Faster. A better shot.

"You want to know what will set you apart? Keep you alive? Training. Doing it over and over. Reviewing what you did and not letting your ego get in the way. Admitting when you could have done something better or different, even though what you did worked. This is a great start to that.

"I was going to come find you and go through an after-action debrief, but you beat me to it. And you listened to what I told you without trying to argue that it had worked. That's why I said you're showing promise. But you've still got a long way to go."

This was the most he'd ever said to me at one time in all the months we'd been working together. And I appreciated what he said because he was right. I'd been feeling pretty badass and cocky after successfully putting down eight terrorists, single handed. Now, I saw how many opportunities there had been for things to go wrong.

"Thanks," I said, nodding my head. "I get it."

He grinned, nodded and slapped me on the back hard enough to hurt. I was turning to continue cleaning when the steel door clanged, and Agent Johnson walked in.

"Briefing," he said, waving at me.

"Got an event point?" I asked.

"Not yet." He shook his head. "Come on. Let's go hear what Mr. Carpenter has to say."

"I got it," Ray said, taking my weapons.

"Thanks."

I appreciated that he would finish cleaning up. And maybe, if he was in a generous frame of mind, he'd even clean my rifle and pistol for me. Probably not, but I could hope.

I followed Johnson out of the firearms training room, which was actually a space the size of a large aircraft hangar. We climbed two flights of stairs and walked down a long hallway to the conference room. Patterson and Carpenter were already seated at the table, waiting for us.

"Gentlemen," Carpenter greeted us as we came in and sat down.

"No event point, yet?" I asked.

"No," Carpenter shook his head. "We're still working, but it is not looking promising."

"Let's start with what we know," Patterson interrupted before the analyst could continue.

"Yes, sir."

He shuffled some notes and took a deep breath before continuing.

"We have confirmation that President Scarsdale is dead. The bodies in the restaurant were destroyed beyond recognition by the blast. However, a special FBI forensics team was able to recover DNA and positively match it to POTUS. Also, we have a positive ID on the Speaker of the

House and the eight Secret Service agents that were inside the building.

"Moving on to the weapon. Chemical signatures left behind in the form of residue have positively confirmed the explosive device was a Hellfire II missile. And it was from an American inventory."

"How can you be sure of that?" I asked.

"All explosives have a specific chemical signature added to them during the manufacturing process. This signature tells us three important things about the warhead.

"First: It was manufactured in the United States for use by the US military. If it had been a missile that was sold to an ally, it would have a different signature.

"Second: It was manufactured less than two years ago, and we have been able to trace the explosive compound from when it was created and follow it to the final missile assembly point.

"And Third: Each manufacturing run of explosive has a unique signature added. This tells us that three hundred warheads were built from this batch.

"A team has already been to the contractors that build the warhead and the missile, reviewing their manufacturing and inventory records. The explosive contractor produced the correct number of warheads based on the size of the manufacturing run. Point three pounds was excess, and it was properly stored and accounted for at the contractor's facility.

"The missile contractor received the correct number of warheads. The same quantity produced by the first contractor. They assembled the correct number of missiles, delivering two hundred to the Army and one hundred to the Air Force. This is supported by documentation provided to the contractor at the time of delivery. We are still trying to gain access to the military's records to trace each missile, but are currently stalled as we wait for the Pentagon to release the information."

"We can't just hack in?" I asked, not at all happy about what I was hearing.

"That will be our Hail Mary if they don't cooperate very soon," Patterson interjected. "They'll know we broke in, and it will create an absolute shit-storm. I'm hoping some of the calls I've made will cut through the bureaucracy, but without a Presidential order, the Pentagon can refuse our request."

Patterson nodded to Carpenter to continue. The analyst cleared his throat before resuming the briefing.

"We are also confident that this was a well planned operation by experienced people. In an urban environment, the best way to ensure accurate placement of a missile is to have a ground team *painting* the target with a laser. The missile will lock on to the reflected energy and home in. This one struck precisely in the center of the front wall of the structure.

"A review of Secret Service records has revealed the following. This was a planned, public appearance by the President and the Speaker. A mending of fences, if you will. Many members of the White House press corps were also present in the restaurant."

"Wait," I said when a thought struck me. "Many? Not all? For something like this? Anyone looking at the ones that weren't there?"

The expression on Carpenter's face told me he hadn't thought about that. He glanced over at Patterson, who had a similar expression on his face.

"Very good observation, Mr. Whitman," Carpenter said. "Bear with me a moment."

He picked up his iPad and quickly tapped out a note. I assumed he was sending instructions to his team to begin accounting for the reporters that had passed on the dinner.

"OK, where was I," Carpenter said to himself in a distracted voice.

"Secret Service," I prompted.

"Right! OK, like I said, we verified that this was planned. Which means, an advance team from the Secret Service visited and locked down the whole area. Just like any other time POTUS goes into public. Immediately adjacent buildings each had an agent inside, keeping an eye on employees and customers. Parked vehicles, mailboxes, anything that could conceal a bomb were removed several hours before the President's arrival. Bomb sniffing dogs. Counter-electronic sweeps of the entire area.

"And several hours before the dinner, counter-sniper teams were put in place on three separate rooftops. They each had a commanding view of the area. Here's where we're hitting a bump. How did someone successfully paint the front wall of the restaurant with a laser and go unnoticed by the sniper teams?"

He held his hand up to stop me when I started to speak.

Dirk Patton

"This one we did think of. Each of the sniper teams are being interrogated and investigated, as well as all of the agents that were in the area. So far, we haven't found any indication that any of them were involved, but our efforts continue. At this time, the only viable explanation is that one of the teams allowed an individual to come into the area with a laser. Or painted the target themselves. But if that's the case, we haven't been able to locate the equipment they would have had to use."

"What about one of the agents that were inside with the President?" I asked, thinking about a new variation on a suicide bomber.

"Them, too," Carpenter nodded.

"Continuing, the other area of investigation has been into radar records from the FAA and Andrews Air Force Base. FAA records from Reagan and Dulles airports do not show anything amiss. Neither do the files provided by the Air Force."

"How is that possible?" I asked. "This had to be launched by an aircraft. How could they have nothing?"

"One working theory is a UAV," Carpenter replied. "A Reaper drone is very stealthy and has an operational ceiling of 50,000 feet. At that altitude, it would be well above any flight corridors around DC and would be impossible to see from the ground. It could be controlled from anywhere, and would exit the area as soon as the missile was released."

"We are trying to obtain records that would tell us what was in operation at the time of the attacks. The Pentagon is flatly refusing to turn them over, citing national security."

I sat back and took a deep breath, slowly exhaling through my mouth. My head was spinning with the implications of everything I was learning.

"A moment, if you please," Patterson spoke up. "Reapers have onboard lasers and targeting software. The operator visually identifies the target, locks on and fires. There's no need for a ground based laser."

"Correct, sir. However, in this instance, we believe there must have been someone on the ground. The airspace over Washington DC is some of the most carefully watched and defended in the world. My team's opinion is that the conspirators would not risk detection by flying directly over the area.

"We believe there is a high probability that the missile was fired from a helicopter over an unpopulated area, and was guided in by a ground-based designator. Hellfire missiles have a maximum range of five miles, and expanding out from the target location on Capitol Hill, our best guess is it was fired from somewhere over Anacostia Park, northeast of the restaurant.

"The park closes at sunset and is nearly two square miles of mostly undisturbed forest. It is 1.8 miles from the center of the park to the target, and it would be a simple matter for a drone or helicopter to be in position and launch the missile. With a ground-based designator, the aircraft could depart the area immediately upon firing."

"What kind of helicopter?" I asked.

"Technically, any," Carpenter said. "It would be easier to use a military aircraft as they are already configured to carry and launch the weapon, but for a knowledgeable and experienced team, it wouldn't be difficult to retrofit the launch platform to a civilian helicopter. Regardless, there's constantly helicopters in the sky over DC. Neither a military nor civilian bird over the park would draw the slightest bit of attention, as long as it was in a designated flight corridor."

"A military coup? Have we seen anything to indicate any attempts to seize power?" I asked.

"Nothing," Patterson answered. "The military has gone on high alert, a war footing if you will, but that's a standard response whenever there's an attack on the civilian leadership. Other than that, there's been no troop movements nor anything else that would indicate this was the opening shot of a takeover of the government."

"Alright," I said slowly. "There's no doubt this was an American owned missile. Am I right?"

"Correct," Carpenter said.

"And the military would have to know all about these chemicals in the warheads you were talking about. Right?"

Carpenter nodded.

"So why the hell would they take the chance? I can't believe it would be difficult for whoever did this to get their hands on a foreign owned missile and deflect suspicion."

"And start a war," Patterson said. "The Vice President has already been sworn into office. If there was a hint that another country was behind this, we'd be gearing up to wipe them off the face of the Earth. Instead, we're all knotted up, investigating our own."

"What you just said," I spoke slowly as the wheels were turning in my head. "We're not turning the military loose because it looks like our military did this. How hard would it be for another country to get their hands on one of our missiles? There's a hell of a lot of them out there, especially in the middle east. Is it a stretch to think that a determined adversary couldn't manage to acquire one?

"We have armed aircraft go down from time to time in Iraq and Afghanistan. Could one be recovered from a crash, before we got a clean up team on site, and still be operational? For that matter, what would one of these be worth? A few hundred thousand dollars in an offshore account might convince an Air Force or Army Sergeant to find a way to hand one over. Hell, we've had traitors before."

"One of my analysts has proposed the same theory," Carpenter said. "We are investigating, but again, without cooperation from the Pentagon, there's not much we can do. Unfortunately, with many missiles stored and moved around war zones, it could take months to positively identify that one is unaccounted for. And that depends on the accuracy of the record keeping of the Air Force and the Army."

"This is an interesting discussion," Patterson spoke up. "However, we do not have months."

He pointed at a large, digital clock mounted above the room's door. It was counting down the time remaining until we could no longer change the event.

-30:36:41.

"I have made a decision. Mr. Whitman, if we do not have a viable event point by the time the countdown reaches twenty-four hours, you will be sent back with a warning. The President is aware of the Athena Project and will take it seriously.

"This will thwart the assassination. The record from your data chip will provide us with a starting point. That missile will still be unaccounted for, and maybe this will buy us enough time to locate it, and the perpetrators, before it can be used.

"Mr. Carpenter, your team should continue trying to develop an event point. I don't like sending a warning back through time. We've never done it before, and I don't like the precedent, but I don't see another viable option unless you can provide us with a target."

"Mr. Director, I believe going back without more time to develop an event point is a mistake." Carpenter replied. "My analysts have only had a few hours, and there's much more we can learn. Time is still on our side."

"My decision is made," Patterson said.

"Understood, sir," Carpenter said, clearly unhappy with the response.

I nodded, mind still whirling as I tried to come up with a way to figure this out in the next six hours.

32

After the decision by Patterson, the meeting ended. There was no point in continuing to discuss and theorize. Carpenter and his team had very few hours to come up with a perpetrator or perpetrators, or I was going to take a trip with nothing more than a data file for the Director's review.

He'd concluded the meeting by giving Carpenter directions to have one of his team put together a succinct briefing for his past self to deliver to the President. I guess it made sense. Deliver a warning and save the President. The threat wasn't eliminated, but POTUS wouldn't die.

My initial reaction had been to argue against the plan. I was remembering his response when I asked about warning the authorities of the terrorist plot against the school. He'd explained why that was a bad idea. At first, I'd thought the same of this but quickly realized the situations were very different.

If the President was saved, the information that did so would be tightly held. As secret as the whole Athena Project itself. No mention on the news cycle and no politicians or pundits making hay out of an assassination that never occurred. But the very idea of a Hellfire missile out there in the hands of unknown conspirators worried me.

What if they had more than one? Or something even more destructive? If this really was coming from the military, there wasn't anything they didn't have access to. That was a sobering thought.

So I go back and deliver the warning to the Director. He, in turn, contacts the President, who changes his schedule. The plan to assassinate him doesn't go into motion. But was it reasonable to believe that the people behind the plot would just say "oh well", and forget the whole thing? Not very likely.

This was obviously a well thought out, meticulously orchestrated decapitation of the US Government. These were serious people with extensive power and resources at their disposal. Those types of individuals did not just roll over and give up because of a setback.

Sure, they'd be nervous when they found out POTUS changed his plans at the last minute. But they wouldn't know why. The White House would have to come up with an explanation as there were so many members of the press involved. But if there's one thing an administration's press secretary can do, it's shovel bullshit until it's over your head. Some semi-plausible excuse would be given, and there wouldn't be any reason for the reporters to look further.

So, the plotters would get together. Maybe not right away, if they were smart and cautious, which I was sure they were. Perhaps in a few weeks, if the President was careful to not give anything away. Then they'd feel secure enough to meet and begin planning their next attempt.

And that was what concerned me. The use of a Hellfire missile told me they weren't concerned about collateral damage. A lot of people in addition to POTUS and the Speaker of the House had been killed. It wasn't exactly a surgical strike weapon, despite how it might be referred to when we used it against an enemy.

If they were willing to cause the deaths of a large number of other people, and that plan didn't play out, why wouldn't they be willing to escalate? There are many weapons with a much greater potential for destruction in the military arsenal. A Hellfire missile really is a small attack in the scheme of things. What if the next attempt was a 1,500-pound bomb right on top of the oval office? Or a thermobaric bomb that would take out the entire building and then some?

But why the hell were they going about it like this? As I kept running things over in my head, I came back to my theory that this was a false flag. Someone other than the US military trying to make it look like this was an operation coming out of the Pentagon. But why? Who stood to gain from killing the President and the Speaker of the House, and placing suspicion squarely on the military?

I'd been wandering around as these thoughts swirled through my head. I hadn't had a destination and was mildly surprised to find myself on the lower level, standing outside Ray's training area. Thinking I should check in and make sure my weapons had been cleaned and stowed, I cracked the door open and stepped through.

Ray was in his small office, working on his computer when I stuck my head in. He looked up, a quizzical expression on his face.

"Just checking on my weapons," I said by way of explanation.

"Cleaned and in their locker," he said. "Got an event point?"

I shook my head, leaning against the door jam. He watched me for a few seconds before closing the lid on his laptop and standing up.

"Come with me," he said, pushing past and heading for the pistol range.

"What?" I asked, falling in behind him.

"You got something you're trying to figure out," he said over his shoulder. "Think on it too hard and you'll never get anywhere. Get a gun in your hand and ventilate some targets. Focus your body on something and give your head a chance to work."

Five minutes later we each had paper targets set up at 25 yards. They were hanging from motorized tracks that would let us retract them, check our shooting, and send a fresh one back downrange with the press of a couple of buttons. It was a nice system and beat the hell out of tromping back and forth after every twenty or so rounds.

"Loser buys the beer," Ray said.

Still looking directly at me, standing with his side to the target, he raised his right arm and fired a single round from his pistol. We both turned to look.

"Fuck me," I said when I saw a neat hole inside the ten ring. "How the hell did you do that?"

"Twenty years of five thousand rounds a month," he grinned. "I knew where the target was, just had to be sure my arm cooperated with what I'd seen."

"Shit," I mumbled, raising my pistol and aiming carefully.

I fired three quick shots, two of them barely inside the ten ring, one of them falling out into the much larger eight ring.

"You're an asshole," I said under my breath.

"Yep."

Ray popped off five quick shots, and I cursed again when five more holes appeared almost dead center in the ten ring. I was pretty sure I could lay a silver dollar on the target, and it would cover all the holes.

We kept shooting for a while, only stopping after I'd gone through 300 rounds. If my targets had been a person, they'd have certainly been dead, even if some of my shots would have hit a shoulder or stomach or arm.

Ray, on the other hand, never had a single round drift outside the ten ring. Fucker.

Cleaning up our brass and dumping it in a bucket, I followed him to a large bench at the side of the room. It was immaculately clean and organized, holding a variety of items needed for cleaning firearms. We sat down, broke the pistols apart and began working on them.

"Want to talk about it?" Ray asked as he ran a brass bristled brush through the barrel of his pistol.

I did, so I told him everything. He listened attentively without interrupting, continuing to clean and oil his weapon as I spoke. He finished before I did, loading the pistol and slipping it into a holster inside the waistband of his cargo pants. Adjusting his shirt to hide the gun, he leaned back and listened to the rest of my story.

"Hmmm," he said when I was done.

Opening a drawer in the bench, he retrieved a pack of cigarettes, lighter and battered metal ashtray. I thought I did a good job of hiding my displeasure but guess I failed.

"Don't be a pussy," he said as he lit up.

I flipped him off, then scooted a few feet away as he blew a plume of smoke in my direction and smiled.

"OK, so I think you're asking the right questions," he said, growing serious again. "Who has something to gain? What jumps out at me is this. Everyone's up in arms about POTUS getting taken out. That's fine. To be expected, in fact. But what about the Speaker?"

"What about him? I don't even know who it is?"

"Yeah," he mused. "They don't let you see any news or get on the internet. That's normal. Until you've been around a while and they trust you."

"What's your point?"

"The Speaker and the President are from opposite ends of the spectrum, even if they are in the same political party. The Speaker is a retired Navy Admiral and very pro-military. The President tolerates the military at best. Kind of treats them like a necessary evil. He's cut the defense budget more than at any point in history."

"So?"

"So, if it's the military behind this, I don't see them taking out the Speaker, too. Maybe a rogue General might get a burr up his ass to wax POTUS, but not the Speaker."

"Alright," I said, getting even more confused. "You're saying this has to be a foreign power?"

"No, that's not what I'm saying. You asked a question. Who would benefit? Let me rephrase it for you. Who would benefit from taking out the anti-military President, and the pro-military Speaker of the House? And blame it on the military?"

"I have no idea," I said. "That's why I'm asking the question."

"OK, so you have no idea of the current state of political affairs in this country. Safe to say?"

I nodded, staring at him.

"Let me back up. Do you know the Presidential line of succession? Who takes over if the President is dead?"

"The Vice President," I said. "Everyone knows that."

"Yeah, but what about after that? So the Prez is assassinated. The VP moves up. But who moves into the VP's office?"

I shrugged my shoulders. I'd been more interested in the hot little redhead that sat a row in front of me in high school civics class. I'd gotten a D for the semester, but I'd also gotten her to go out with me. All things considered, it had been a good semester.

"The VP nominates someone, and they have to be approved by Congress. But the Speaker's party controls both the House and Senate, and he's enormously popular. More popular by far than either the President or VP. Probably going to run for President next year, and will most likely win by a landslide.

"So, let's play this out. POTUS is killed. The VP moves up. If he nominates anyone other than the Speaker, it'll probably never make it through Congress. He's a savvy political animal, so he knows this. But the VP is even more anti-military than the President, and wouldn't want the Speaker and his pro-military views anywhere near his new administration. Certainly not with an election looming.

"Now, take the Speaker out of the equation. That opens up the pool of candidates. There's plenty of Senators and Representatives that would love to slash the defense budget even more in favor of programs that keep getting them elected. So the VP takes the oath of office, moves in to the White House, and nominates a pet Senator as his replacement.

"Can't be someone too controversial, or it'll never make it through both houses of Congress. But I'm sure he can find someone who will say all the right things, and has the right voting record. Once that happens, we've got a new President and VP who gut the military based on evidence from the assassination.

"And who can argue? Hell, if I'm right, there's already been a few high ranking officers who've been selected to be the scapegoats. Wouldn't surprise me if there's not some manufactured evidence already in the VP's possession, just waiting for the right moment to be delivered to the FBI."

I was stunned. Didn't know what to say. Sitting there, I started going back over the scenario Ray had just laid out. I didn't know anything about current politics or who the players were, not much political news in prison, so I had to assume he knew what he was talking about.

Dirk Patton

"Or I'm full of shit and a rogue General got pissed off and sent a missile up POTUS' ass," Ray grinned.

"Jesus Christ," I breathed. "Are you serious? Really?"

"Hey, look, I don't know. I'm just answering the question you asked; *who has something to gain?* I'm just a dumb Delta trooper. What the fuck do I know about politics?"

"I don't understand? Say it is the VP behind this. What does he have to gain by dismantling the military?"

"Power. Pure and simple."

"But if the military gets cut too deeply, we're vulnerable. There're lots of countries in the world that would dance a jig on our graves without a strong deterrent."

"We're still a nuclear power," Ray sighed. "We've got enough bombs to wipe out the human race. Several times over, if need be. But if you're someone with an ultimate goal of seizing total power over the US, the first step is to eliminate the possibility of the military spoiling your plans. With a drastically reduced force, held tightly under control by pet Generals and Admirals, there's no one other than citizens to stand against a tyrant."

I sat and thought about what he was saying, still struggling to put all the pieces together in my head.

"Let's say you're right. If so, how does the VP convince anyone in the military to go along with a plot to assassinate the President?"

"Who says it's the military?" Ray asked, sounding too much like Mr. Miyagi. "The CIA has armed drones at their disposal. I know that first hand. Supposed to be under Air Force control with the CIA defining the missions, but that's just what they tell the public. Fucking Agency has had armed drones operating overseas for years. Under their full control. How hard you think it would be for them to bring one stateside?"

I sat quiet for a few minutes.

"It all fits," I finally said. "And if you're right about the politics, it fits really well. I need to talk to Director Patterson."

I stood, ready to head for the Director's office. Seeing the expression on Ray's face, I paused.

"What?"

"Just thinking," he said, lighting another cigarette. "If I'm right, and I'm not saying I am, this ain't just the VP. Something like this takes a lot of people to pull off. People that will do whatever is necessary to keep from being exposed. After all, they get caught, it's a fast trip to the firing squad."

"You're not saying the Director is involved, are you?"

I moved closer to him, despite the smoke, and involuntarily looked around to make sure we were alone.

"Nope. Just saying I'd be very careful who I talked to if I was you."

33

The time until Patterson's deadline went by slowly. Agonizingly so. I was more than a little distressed after my conversation with Ray. But after thinking about the conspiracy theory he'd laid out, and the warning he'd given me, I decided to keep it to myself. After all, it was just a theory without a shred of evidence to back it up. Sure, it sounded good, but even if someone believed it, it couldn't be proven. At least not by me.

With half an hour left to the deadline, I was called into another meeting with the Director, Agent Johnson and Carpenter. I hadn't seen Johnson since the last meeting, which was unusual, but suspected he'd been spending a lot of time with Patterson. They probably had to figure out the best way for me to carry a warning back in time.

"Mr. Carpenter, any status update?" Patterson asked as soon as we were all seated around the table.

"No, sir. We've gathered a mountain of data and are still parsing through it, but nothing to point us at a specific perpetrator or group of perpetrators. We have made no progress in breaking in to the Pentagon servers. They just completed a system-wide hardening project, facilitated by the NSA. While we're confident we can get in, it will take more time than we have."

"Very well. Continue with those efforts, but we shall proceed with sending the asset back with a warning. Do you have the brief I requested?"

"Yes, sir. But again, I must protest sending him back so soon. There is still twenty-four hours available to us. We should use as much of it as possible before utilizing the asset."

"Noted. However, we will proceed as I stated," Patterson said.

"Mr. Director, I must vigorously protest," Carpenter began before being cut off by a sharp look from Patterson.

"Mr. Carpenter, my decision is final. Get on board, or I will have you replaced. This matter is not open to further discussion."

"My apologies, sir," Carpenter said, eyes downcast.

He slid a small flash drive across the table. Patterson picked it up and slid it into a pocket.

"Mr. Whitman," the Director turned to face me. "I am going to record a personal message, to myself, and load it onto this flash drive. Once that is done, we will send you back. Your destination will be a Project Athena safe house, thirty-six hours distant. Upon your arrival, you will deliver the flash drive to the agent on site and instruct him to transmit the data to me immediately. Is that understood?"

"Why a safe house? Why not here?" I was suspicious, but that was probably Ray's theories making me look for conspiracies where there were none.

"Because there is a potential risk that you will be here. The you from thirty-six hours ago," he said.

I gave him a blank look.

"Ah, forgive me. In your particular circumstance, there was no need to brief you on this issue. Two versions of the same object cannot occupy the same space and time, simultaneously. If you were to encounter yourself, the results could be catastrophic."

"Excuse me?" I said. "What the hell do you mean?"

"I'm talking about theoretical physics. What I mean is, up until now, there was no chance of you going back and encountering your past self as you never leave this facility. As far as the theory, which we've never been willing to test, if you were to encounter yourself in the past there is a high, *theoretical* probability that an extremely violent reaction would occur, potentially destroying this facility. Dr. Anholts is convinced there would be an explosion of a magnitude on par with a thermonuclear warhead."

"Let's trust her and not find out," I said, reminded how we were playing with things man was never meant to do.

"Quite," he answered, standing to indicate the meeting was over. "If you'll accompany me, I'll have the flash drive ready in only a few minutes."

He breezed out of the room without saying anything to Carpenter or Johnson. I rushed to keep up with him, a moment later hearing Agent Johnson's heavy footsteps as he followed.

We went straight to the Director's office, waiting in the hall for him to record whatever message he wanted to send to his past self. Johnson was quiet as we stood there, and I was nervous. I didn't understand why. Maybe Ray's crazy ideas, or maybe because as I continued to think about them, they didn't sound so crazy.

"So, I'm going to a safe house?" I asked after a few minutes of silence.

"Yes."

"Who's going to be there?" I asked.

"An experienced agent named Kirkpatrick. Just do what the Director said and hand him the drive. Tell him to transmit it to the Director. Then you've got a thirty-six-hour pass. Sleep. Get drunk. Whatever, as long as you stay in the safe house."

"Where's the safe house?" I asked.

"You don't need to know that," Johnson said, giving me a sideways look.

"Really? You don't trust me? Where the hell am I going to go and what am I going to do? I was just curious."

I was also lying. A thirty-six-hour break with nothing to do? There was plenty I could do in that amount of time. First and foremost, I hadn't been laid in about eleven years. There was some serious back-up going on. If I couldn't find a willing woman in thirty-six hours, I would have to seriously consider relinquishing my man-card.

"This is the price for your life, Mr. Whitman. I understand it may feel like a prison sometimes. At some point in the future the Director and I may decide to loosen the reins, but for now, this is the way it is."

I nodded and didn't say anything else. Stood there and waited for Patterson. It wasn't a long wait, the Director's door opening a few minutes later. He held the small drive out for me to take. I put it in my pocket.

"Are you ready, Mr. Whitman?"

"Yes, sir."

"Good. I'm going to ops. Agent Johnson will escort you to transport."

With that, he pushed past and disappeared around a corner. Johnson tilted his head, and I led the way to the transport chamber. We went through the same routine with the Marines, then were granted access.

"Remember," Johnson said, stepping close and clapping a big paw on my shoulder. "You're not allowed to leave the safe house. Agent Kirkpatrick knows this and will stop you if you try. You don't want to spend your free time in restraints."

"Fuck you, Johnson," I smiled what I hoped was a dangerous looking smile.

He was unfazed, squeezing my arm hard enough to hurt before moving back. Turning, I stepped onto the waiting dais and watched him leave as the glass door rolled shut. Johnson appeared on the other side of the windows, in the ops center, a few moments later.

"Ready, Mr. Whitman?"

One of the technicians spoke over the intercom. I nodded and gave a thumbs up, noting a faint tingling on the surface of my skin. There was a blink, and I was suddenly standing in a starkly appointed living room. Several feet away, a barrel-chested man with shockingly red hair stared at me in surprise.

I looked around, then down, noticing I was standing on a large circle of heavy plastic that covered the carpet. Landing pad? It made sense. They apparently had the spot precisely located, and the target I'd arrived on was most likely there so no one in the safe house would accidentally be standing at the same place I arrived. I had no idea what the impact of that would be and didn't want to find out.

The man quickly got over his surprise, lifting an iPad and tapping a couple of buttons.

His eyes flicked from my face to the screen, then back. He was verifying who I was.

"Hello, Mr. Whitman. I'm Agent Kirkpatrick," he said after satisfying himself that I matched the photo on the tablet. "Why are you here?"

I reached into my pocket and retrieved the flash drive, holding it out and taking a step towards him.

"Director Patterson sent me back. This is to be transmitted to him immediately," I said.

"Very unusual," Kirkpatrick said after looking at the object in my hand for several moments. "What is it?"

"It's a message for the Director," I said, a little surprised that I was being questioned by a babysitter for a safe house.

After another long pause, he came forward and took the drive from me. Turning it in his hand, he examined it like he'd never seen one before. Eventually, he nodded, turning away and taking a seat at a small table with a laptop resting on it. He plugged the drive into a USB port, inserted a pair of ear buds connected to the computer and clicked the mouse three times.

The screen was angled away from me, and I couldn't see what was displayed. While he worked on the computer, I took the opportunity to walk around and get an idea of the layout of the house. One of Ray's lessons had rubbed off on me.

It was a small, single story home with low ceilings. There was a cramped kitchen and small dining room adjacent to the living room I'd arrived in. Opposite, a narrow hall led to three doors, each of them closed. I suspected two bedrooms and a single bath.

There was a heavy looking door in the front wall of the main living area, a large set of windows to its side. The door was equipped with two deadbolts and a stout, iron rod ran at an angle from the floor to the midpoint of the unhinged edge. It might be battered down, but it would take a concerted effort and enough time for the occupants to be ready to defend themselves.

The windows were covered with heavy curtains, no sunlight visible around the edges of the fabric. This seemed odd, and I took a moment to do the math in my head. No, it should be daytime. Well, I paused, that depended on exactly where on the globe this house was located.

I glanced over my shoulder to make sure Kirkpatrick was still absorbed with the laptop. He wasn't paying any attention to me, so I stepped to the drapes and pulled one to the side. Steel shutters completely sealed the opening. It could have been high noon outside, and no light would have made it through. With a sigh, I let the curtain fall back in place. There was a soft step behind me, and I turned to see Kirkpatrick aiming a pistol at my head.

At any point in my previous life, I would have frozen in place after coming face to face with the muzzle of a weapon. But this was one of many scenarios that Ray had drilled me on, tirelessly. He'd brought in the former Israeli Defense Force commando that taught unarmed combat, and together they'd beaten the crap out of me. Over and over, as they taught me how to deal with an armed assailant.

During the training, I'd thought several times how unnecessary it was. It had taken quite a while for the concept of me not having a weapon in my hand to fully sink in. That happened once I began to gain a degree of competence in responding to exactly this kind of situation.

Now, the instant I saw the weapon, I reacted. Lunging forward and to the side, I thrust a hand up and locked onto his wrist. The weapon fired, but I was already safely below it, continuing the movement. Maintaining my grip, I swiveled and whipped my left leg around, sweeping Kirkpatrick's feet out from under him.

He crashed to the floor, and I rolled with him. The pistol fired again, and I applied leverage to bend his arm as I began punching him in the side of the face as hard and fast as I could. He struggled, finally dropping the weapon when a bone in his wrist snapped.

His other arm was pinned beneath me, and I hit him two more times before twisting around and wrapping my right arm around his throat. Squeezing for all I was worth, I held on as he tried to buck me off. When that didn't work, he flailed at me, desperately trying to free himself from the pressure of my hold. But I'd cut off his air and most of the blood supply to his brain, and he was weakening fast.

I maintained the hold until he went still, carefully relaxing my grip in case he was faking. He wasn't. He was out, or dead. I didn't much care which at the moment. Releasing the man, I pressed two fingers against his neck and felt a pulse. He was still alive.

Rolling him onto his front, I looked for and found the pair of handcuffs I'd expected to be holstered at the small of his back. Pulling his arms behind him, I slapped them on his wrists and left him lying facedown. Checking his pockets, I removed two sets of keys, his FBI ID case and his wallet. Looking around, I spotted the pistol, an FBI issue Glock, and scooped it up. Two spare magazines were on his belt, and I grabbed those as well.

Standing over him, breathing hard, I stuck the pistol into my waistband and a spare magazine in each hip pocket. I glanced at his badge and ID before shoving it in a pocket, then checked the wallet. Drivers license, half a dozen credit cards and twenty-two dollars in cash. Now, what the fuck was going on?

I moved to the table and looked at the laptop screen. He'd been watching a video on the flash drive, and it was still paused where he'd stopped it. I didn't understand why I was looking at Agent Johnson's face instead of Patterson's.

34

I unplugged the earbuds, placed my hand on the mouse, rewound the clip and let it play. Agent Johnson stared into the camera, leaning close and speaking in a low, steady voice. I didn't recognize the location visible in the background, but I'd not been in well over half of the spaces in the oil rig. It could have been anywhere.

"Agent Kirkpatrick. If you are viewing this file, the asset, Mr. Whitman, has become a liability. He will have arrived at your assigned location and told you to transmit the contents of this flash drive to Director Patterson. If this were the drive he believes it to be, it would contain a virus designed to seize control of the Athena Project's computers and cause irreparable damage.

"Mr. Whitman is to be immediately terminated. He must not be allowed to communicate with anyone. Once he is down, contact Mr. Carpenter on the secure circuit. I shall be unavailable for the foreseeable future. Do NOT speak with anyone other than him, personally. Terminate Mr. Whitman immediately."

The video automatically paused as it reached the end of the recording. To say I was stunned would have been an understatement. I sat there, frozen, staring at the screen. After nearly a minute, I reached out with a trembling hand and started the short video over. Watched it a second time. Then a third.

"Son of a bitch," I said aloud. "Son of a fucking bitch!"

Ray was right. There was a fucking conspiracy, and Agent Johnson was part of it! But how had his recording gotten onto this drive? I'd personally witnessed Carpenter hand it to Patterson, who had kept it in his possession until he handed it directly to me. Johnson never touched it.

Was Carpenter in on this? Was the Johnson recording already there? No. I shook my head. That would have been too great of a risk. What if Patterson had viewed the file and seen it? So how had Johnson pulled it off?

The physical contact in the transport room! Like any good pickpocket, Agent Johnson had distracted me with a hand on my shoulder and arm while he substituted the drive. That had to be it. Unless Patterson was involved as well and Johnson was just the face giving the orders.

I rolled that around in my head for a bit but didn't like it. No. If Patterson didn't want a warning sent back, he had all the authority in the world to just stay silent. He wouldn't need to have me taken out. But what the hell were the conspirators thinking?

Thirty-six hours from now, if they'd succeeded, my corpse would have appeared in the transport room. That would set off alarm bells and start a frenzied investigation. I was supposed to be in a project safe house.

So, they weren't worried about a dead asset coming back. But how could they hide my body from Patterson? There didn't seem to be anything that happened within the facility that he wasn't aware of. Unless he wasn't going to be alive to ask questions!

The thought spurred me to action. I yanked the drive out of the USB port and stood up. That's as far as I got. I had no idea what to do next. Standing there, I thought about everything that had happened since I'd arrived. Remembering the order for Kirkpatrick to contact Carpenter, I sat back down and began clicking through the laptop.

I didn't know what I was looking for but had seen a couple of people using their iPads to make video calls. Maybe there was some program on the computer that would allow me to call Director Patterson. After five minutes I gave up. There was nothing on the device that hadn't come with Windows.

That gave me another idea, and I opened the internet browser. Things had changed a lot since before I'd gone to prison, but at least there was still a way to review browsing history. It took a few false starts, but I finally pulled up a screen with a very long list of websites that Kirkpatrick had visited.

"You're a naughty boy," I said to the unconscious agent.

I scrolled through literally hundreds of links to sites with titles like *Rock Hard Studs*, *Muscle Butts* and *He Likes Them Big*. Nothing but gay porn. Closing the browser, I slammed the lid in frustration and stood up. Maybe a phone.

I walked over to Kirkpatrick and checked all his pockets. I'd already done this once and didn't think I'd missed anything as large as a cell phone, but it was worth checking again. Finding nothing, I straightened and stared down at him. He was wearing slacks and a dress shirt with a tie. Where was his jacket?

Looking around, I didn't see it. Heading down the hall, I paused to open a small closet.

Empty. I searched the first bedroom I came to which held nothing more than a twin sized bed and a cheap, particle board dresser. The dresser had a set of sheets for the bed and a single towel and washcloth.

Next was the bathroom, and as soon as I opened the door, I could see everything and tell it was empty. As I was pulling the door shut, I glanced up at the mirror over the sink and stopped. A dark blue suit coat was hanging on a small hook on the inside of the door.

Reaching around, I grabbed it and carried it back to the table with the laptop. A type of cell phone I'd never seen before was in an inside pocket. It had an exposed screen with a small keyboard beneath it. The display lit up when I pushed a button, and I cursed. It was asking for a passcode.

Moving to the unconscious agent, I knelt and shook his shoulder, shouting his name. He didn't respond, and I didn't like the way his body felt so loose. Rolling him onto his side, I checked his neck and didn't find a pulse. Placing my hand over his nose and mouth, I couldn't detect any air movement. Fuck!

What now? I had no idea how to contact Patterson. And other than him, who the hell was going to believe my crazy story? They'd lock me away in a rubber room after shooting me full of Thorazine. Anger getting the best of me, I threw the locked phone against the wall where it shattered into half a dozen pieces.

Breathing hard, I fought to get myself under control. Slowly I succeeded, then walked over to a sofa and sat down. I had to think this through. Figure out what to do and how to accomplish it. Should I find a way to contact the Secret Service and warn them? Would they even listen? How many crank calls and threats against the President did they receive on an average day? I was willing to bet it was at least one.

No, that wouldn't be worth the effort. Without the warning coming from a trusted source, like Patterson, it would just get filed away and ignored. What about the FBI? No, I immediately thought. I knew Johnson was dirty and had no way of knowing who else was. If I called, or walked in, and told my story, he'd get a call. And tell them I was a terrorist or a rogue agent, and I'd wind up in a dank, dark cell. Or worse.

What about the media? I immediately dismissed the idea. No reporter, at least no reputable reporter that would be listened to, would run with my wild story unless it could be confirmed by another source. Shit! What options did that leave?

None, I acknowledged. I didn't even know where the Athena Project facility was located. If I did, I'd try to reach the coast closest to the rig. Steal a boat, if necessary. But I had no clue where to go. The California coast? The Gulf of Mexico? About all I was sure I knew was that it wasn't in the Alaskan oil fields. I'd been outside a lot and it had been way too warm. While I suspected it was located in US territorial waters, that didn't help. The country has a hell of a lot of coastline.

That left one option, I grudgingly admitted to myself. I had to go to DC. Somewhere close to the restaurant would be a man with a laser designator, painting the target for the Hellfire missile. If I could find him and stop him, the attack would be prevented. At worst, they might still fire the missile. But without a laser to home in on, the chances of it missing were fairly good.

With a plan, I realized that I had a time crunch. I'd been sent back thirty-six hours. Twelve hours had elapsed in real time before I was transported. That meant I had arrived twenty-four hours before the event. Over twenty minutes had already gone by. I noted after checking my watch. I pushed a couple of buttons and set a countdown clock running. Twenty-three hours and thirty-eight minutes remaining until the President and the Speaker of the House were assassinated.

35

The first step was to figure out where the hell I was. Hopefully, I was in North America. Examining the front door, I checked the brace and saw that it was locked into a bracket integrated into the door's surface. A key hole was set a few inches above the rod. Flipping through one of the rings I'd removed from the dead agent, I found a small, brass key that looked like it would fit.

It did, turning easily. There was a click and the brace shifted slightly as it was released. Removing it, I placed it on the floor beneath the windows and reached for the first deadbolt. Before I disengaged it, I remembered the review of my assault on the terrorists with Ray. The peephole I'd overlooked.

There wasn't one in this door, but a device that looked like a small tablet was mounted to the surface at eye level. I tapped it, and the screen came on, displaying an image of the other side. My breath caught when I saw a black and white police cruiser sitting at the curb on the far side of a neatly mown lawn. As I watched, two cops stepped out, looked around and began walking towards the driveway.

What the hell? Then I remembered. Kirkpatrick had fired two shots while we were fighting. One gunshot might go unnoticed, or passed off as something else. But two, in fairly quick succession, will probably spur someone to pick up the phone and call the police.

Looking around, I dashed to the body of the dead FBI agent. Grabbing it by the ankles, I dragged it across the floor into the kitchen, then raced back to the front door. I unlocked the two deadbolts and pulled the door open.

Stepping out into bright sunshine, I held his FBI ID badge at arm's length in front of me, my thumb carefully covering the photo. The two uniformed cops froze, both of them placing their hands on their weapons. Fortunately, they hadn't drawn them. Yet.

"FBI," I said in a loud, confident voice.

I pulled the door closed behind me and took two steps towards the driveway where they stood, spaced well apart. The older, and probably senior, of the two squinted at the ID but didn't relax.

"Is there something I can help you with?" I asked, slapping the case closed and shoving it in my hip pocket.

"You live here?" The older cop asked.

My eyes were adjusting to the change in light, and I was able to see his name plate. Tompkins. I also saw all the hash marks along the lower sleeve of his uniform shirt. This guy had been doing the job for a long time and wasn't going to be easy to bullshit. Remembering my training with the con-man, I decided how to handle him.

"That's not something I can discuss. Tompkins, is it?"

My tone wasn't friendly. I sounded like a condescending asshole. Probably about like a local cop expected a Fed to sound.

"What can you discuss? Sir?"

The sir was laced with heavy sarcasm.

"You need to get back in your car and move on, Officer Tompkins. You're drawing unwanted attention to this house."

I knew I'd sold my role when he grimaced and removed his hand from the pistol holstered on his belt. His partner noticed and visibly relaxed, moving his hand as well.

"We had a report of gunfire. Everything OK inside?"

We all looked towards the street as another cruiser pulled to a stop, nose to nose with their police car. Two more cops got out and walked up the driveway, the older of the two moving to stand next to Tompkins.

"Didn't hear a sound," I said. "And this is turning into a fucking parade. It's time for you to be on your way. Or do I need to have my Agent in Charge call your Chief of Police?"

"Maybe we need to come inside and take a look around," the newly arrived cop standing next to Tompkins said.

He had two chevrons on his upper sleeve and even more hash marks on his lower sleeve. Had probably encountered Feds before and didn't mind trying to make their lives a little difficult.

"Federal property," I said, taking a step towards them. "Good luck getting a federal judge to sign a warrant. Now, last chance. Do I need to call my AIC? Have him lodge a formal complaint? You got time to deal with that bullshit? Is it worth it to stand here and compromise this house further, trying to bust my balls?"

I was winging it. Had no idea if the threat would intimidate them. Truthfully, I was borrowing from a cheap, made for TV movie I'd seen many years ago. Don't even remember who was in it or what it was really about. But I did remember a scene where there was a standoff between the FBI and some local cops. I'd just quoted the lines the actor playing a Fed had delivered. Well, quoted as best I could remember them.

When I saw their body language, I realized it had worked. Their backs stiffened, and Tompkins turned his head and spat on the driveway.

"You Feds are fuckin' assholes," he growled. "Anyone ever tell you that?"

"All the time," I said. "Especially the really bad guys that you fuckin' locals can't handle by yourselves."

Yes, I was pushing my luck. But one of the things the con-man had drilled into me was that if you're going to play a part, play it to the hilt. Don't deviate from the character whose shoes you've stepped into. If you do, people will recognize you're a fake.

"Go write a jaywalking ticket or something," I said, pasting a shit eating grin on my face as I raised my right hand and made a shooing motion in their direction.

"Fuck you," Tompkins said, turning and heading for the street.

As he walked past the shiny Suburban parked in the driveway, he rubbed the side of his body along the sheet metal. Something hanging from his duty belt left a long scratch in the paint, the length of the two passenger side doors.

"Oh, look at that," he said, standing on the sidewalk. "Someone scratched your fancy ride."

"No worries. It's on camera. I'll just review it and have the Justice Department send a bill to whoever did it."

I was still grinning, pointing up at a spot over my head. I had no idea if there was really a camera there or not. But neither did they. The look on Tompkins' face was worth the gamble.

They all piled back into their cars, leaving a minute later with lots of tire screeching. I watched until they were out of sight before going back in and locking the door behind me. As soon as I was safely inside, I bent at the waist and began shaking as I struggled to not start hyperventilating. Fuck me. That was a rush. Just not the kind I like.

As nerve wracking as the encounter had been, it had given me an important piece of information. The marked police cruisers had told me where I was. Covina, California. I was in the Los Angeles metro area.

Now that I knew where I was, how the hell did I make it all the way across the country in twenty-three hours? I wasn't sure but was reasonably confident it was close to three thousand miles to DC. No way was I driving it. That only left one viable option. Fly.

But how? I had no money for a ticket, and even if I did, I had no ID. I might have bluffed the cops with Kirkpatrick's badge, but no way would I get through airport security with an ID that didn't have my picture on it. Besides, I was pretty sure the cops had run the plates on the Suburban when they'd first pulled up. They already knew it was an FBI vehicle before they got out of their car. I'd just given them what they expected to find.

The wallet with the driver's license, Amex card, and cash that Johnson had given me before I went after the terrorists had been taken when I'd returned to real time. For this mission, it hadn't been given back to me. Nothing had been provided, other than the flash drive that Johnson swapped before I left. So, how does one get all the way across the continental US, quickly, without cash or ID? I was stumped.

Frustration began to set in, and I fought against the desire to fall into despair. That wouldn't help. I needed to be thinking. There had to be an option that I just hadn't thought of.

Pacing, I tried to think. The only thing I could come up with was somehow getting on a plane. OK, if that's the only way to get there in time, how do I make it work? Could I use one of Kirkpatrick's credit cards to buy a ticket and bluff my way past security?

I brought out his badge case and flipped it open. Looked at the photo on his ID. Fucking Richie Cunningham on steroids stared back at me. Other than white skin, he and I couldn't have looked more different. Even the laziest, most incompetent TSA screener would notice the discrepancy. I started to toss the ID aside, but thought better of it at the last moment and shoved it back in my pocket.

If I just had the wallet from the last time I'd traveled back, I'd be able to charter a private plane that could get me to DC without any security checkpoints to worry about. That thought brought my pacing to an abrupt stop. A private charter. But how did I pay for it?

Opening Kirkpatrick's wallet, I went through it again. A driver's license with a slip of paper tucked in behind it. Four numbers were written on it in a bold hand. I stared at it a moment but had no idea what they meant. Then there were three Visa cards, two Master Cards and one from American Express that was issued to the Department of Justice. His name was stamped below.

Could I charter a plane with one of these? Or would the body be found before I landed? If it was, it wouldn't take long for the FBI to check his credit card records as part of their investigation. And the charter would pop up. I'd probably land in DC to find about a hundred FBI agents waiting for me, guns drawn. There'd be no talking my way out of that, and they wouldn't be in the mood to listen to a story about me trying to stop the assassination of the President. Goddamn it!

Using the dead man's cards wasn't an option. So, how did I come up with enough cash with basically no time? I thought about the Suburban in the driveway. I knew there were chop shops that wouldn't hesitate to take even an FBI vehicle, and that thing was probably worth several grand. But I had no idea how to go about finding the right one.

I used to know a guy who lived in Newport Beach. We served in Iraq together and had been pretty good friends. Maybe if I found him... shit, he wouldn't know me from Adam. My new face wasn't the one he had fought next to, and he'd never believe who I was in time. If he was even still in the LA area.

Sinking onto the sofa, I blew out a sigh of resignation. Time was running out. Fast. And without any resources at my disposal, there wasn't anything I could do. That only left an option I'd already discarded. Call the Secret Service and warn them.

I fully expected that warning to be an exercise in futility, but it was all I had left available to me. Standing, I headed for the kitchen, intending to look for a landline phone. Halfway there, I froze in my tracks. The last time I'd used a phone in a kitchen, I'd been in Julie's apartment. Julie!

Would she help? Could she help? Did she have the money or a credit card that she'd be willing to use to charter a plane? She'd helped me before, going above and beyond without even being asked.

It was worth a shot. I acknowledged to myself. I still remembered her address. I could be there soon. Pulling out the rings I'd taken off Kirkpatrick's body, I was happy to see one of them held a GM key. Now, at least there was a chance. If Julie said no, I'd find a phone, and fall back on my last resort and call the Secret Service.

36

It took fifteen minutes to find the GPS locator beacon wired into the Suburban, and another five to remove it without damaging something that would disable the vehicle. I had no idea how long I had before Kirkpatrick's body was discovered. Once that happened, it would take the Feds about half a second to start wondering where his vehicle was and start looking for it. The last thing I needed was for them to zero in on its location and descend in force.

Tracker removed, I started the engine and examined the large navigation screen built in to the dash. It took several aborted attempts before I figured out how to input a destination address. Once I had Julie's apartment building spotted, a pleasant female voice came over the Suburban's speakers, telling me to start driving south on the street in front of the house.

The big Chevy drove well. Plenty of power, and it handled better than a vehicle its size should have. Probably some special modifications just for the FBI. As I turned off the residential street and onto a major arterial road, I pressed hard on the accelerator, and the SUV surged ahead with a muted roar of power.

Glancing at my watch, I wasn't happy to see I now had less than twenty-three hours remaining. I pushed harder on the gas, weaving through slower moving traffic. I wasn't worried about a traffic cop stopping me. The Suburban, even though it had regular California plates, just screamed *FEDERAL*. They might fall in behind long enough to run the tags, then as soon as they saw FBI pop up they'd say something disparaging and let me pass.

Traffic was bad. Way worse than I remembered it being the few times I'd visited the LA area. Following the GPS directions, I wheeled onto an onramp for the southbound lanes of the 605 freeway that would take me to Downey. I had to slam on the brakes, cursing at the long line of cars waiting to merge. Far ahead, a traffic light controlled entry onto the freeway, only allowing one vehicle to proceed every ten seconds or so.

I started to pound on the steering wheel in frustration, looking up as I mumbled a string of words that would make a nun come after me with a ruler. Head tilted back, I saw a compact bank of red and blue LED lights that could be swiveled down, so they were visible through the windshield. Cop lights! Of course, an FBI vehicle would be equipped with them.

Lowering the foot-long bar into place, the lights came on automatically. They began strobing, alternating between the two colors every second. With lights, there comes a siren, and I found a discreet switch on the center console. Flipping it on, a wailing began from the front of the Suburban.

The driver of the car in front of me looked in his mirror, a second later cutting the wheel and moving slightly to the right. This left enough room for me to swing left and go around him. Staying left, I put the two driver side tires over the curb and in the dirt and gunned the engine. The heavy SUV shot forward, and I raced past the long line of waiting cars.

Bouncing back onto the pavement, I roared onto the congested freeway. Traffic was moving slow, probably no more than 35 or 40. With the lights flashing and siren blaring, I bulled my way across eight lanes and into the mostly empty carpool lane. Pressing hard on the accelerator, I pushed my speed to 100.

The drivers ahead saw me coming in their mirrors and squeezed to the right as far as the tightly packed traffic allowed. I blasted past them on the left, nearly scraping the side of the Suburban on the concrete barrier that separated me from the northbound lanes. One driver, apparently too involved in the conversation she was having on the cell phone pressed to her ear didn't move over.

Roaring up behind, I hit the brakes to match her slower pace, the huge grill only inches from the back bumper of the little Prius. She didn't react, just kept driving along at the same speed. I could see her in the Toyota's side mirror, staring straight ahead as she talked.

Honking the horn, I screamed at the windshield. I knew she couldn't hear me, but it made me feel better. Somehow, after being able to ignore the siren, the sound of the horn got her attention. She looked in her mirror in surprise, and for some unimaginable reason hit the brakes.

The Suburban covered the distance between us in an instant, impacting the Prius' rear bumper with a crunch and violently shoving the much lighter car forward. Now I could see panic on her face, and the brake lights came on again. She was stopping! I didn't have time for this, and sure didn't want her calling the Highway Patrol and having them show up and start asking questions.

Moving far left, I cringed when the exterior driver side mirror impacted the center barrier and was ripped off. Feeding in more power, I squeezed the nose of the big SUV between the Prius and the barrier, then floored the gas. Shooting forward, the Toyota was shoved to the right, colliding with a car in the next lane.

Horns were blaring, and I was sure curses were being shouted, but I didn't care. Keeping the throttle wide open I surged ahead, leaving the wreck I'd just caused in my wake. This wasn't good, but what choice did I have? The clock was ticking, and once it ran out, there would never be another opportunity to stop the assassination.

I glanced in the rearview mirror before going around a curve in the freeway. Dust from vehicles spinning out obscured my view of the crash, and I spent a moment hoping I hadn't seriously injured anyone. Then I thought about all the calls that were being placed to 9-1-1.

I'd been unremarkable before I caused the crash. Just an anonymous law enforcement vehicle driving on the freeway with lights and siren. Nothing unusual or worth taking note of. But now, I'd rammed another driver and sent her spinning into traffic. And kept on going. I was drawing attention. How long before a CHP helicopter was overhead, looking for me?

Checking the navigation screen, I was happy to see that my exit was less than two miles ahead. A few seconds later the computerized voice told me it was in one mile. Traffic was still heavy, but it had opened up after everything behind me came to a stop because of the wreck.

I easily worked my way to the right, cutting off a large tour bus before screaming down the off ramp. Turning right, I raced along a wide boulevard, flashing past cars like they were standing still. A minute later I slowed in surprise when I saw the Downey Motor Inn coming up on the right. The same motel Julie and I had hidden in.

Knowing I was close, and wanting to lower my profile a little, I turned the siren off and retracted the light bar. I kept my foot off the gas until I had slowed to the posted speed limit, then turned right when the navigation system spoke. A couple more turns and I could see Julie's apartment building, two blocks ahead.

Two black Suburbans, identical to the one I was driving, were pulling in to the parking lot. I steered to an open spot at the curb and came to a stop. What the hell? Had the FBI found Kirkpatrick and figured out where I was going? Gotten here ahead of me?

I didn't understand what I was seeing when the back door of the lead vehicle opened and a man in a suit stepped out and looked around. Another similarly dressed man from the other SUV joined him and after a moment, he briefly leaned in the open door.

Julie was immediately recognizable when she stepped out. Her long, blonde hair glowed in the California sunshine. And she was dressed exactly how she had been the last time I'd seen her. Shorts and an oversized, Army issue T-shirt.

The two men escorted her across the lot, one leading the way while the other brought up the rear. I watched them until they disappeared through an arch that led to a small courtyard in the center of the building. Then it struck me. This was the FBI, bringing her home after interrogating her.

I shook my head, knowing I'd been sent back in time, but still struggling to deal with the concept that I was witnessing something I'd been told about several hours ago. For a minute I tried to figure out where in the timeline I was in relation to the last time I was here, but about all I succeeded in doing was giving myself a headache.

Less than five minutes later, the two FBI agents walked back out of the building and climbed into the waiting vehicles which drove away as soon as their doors were closed. I watched them leave the area, then waited a few minutes, carefully examining every vehicle parked on the street or in the complex's lot.

I didn't see any that gave me concern but decided it might be a good idea to make a quick tour of the immediate area. Circling the block, I drove slow and checked out the cars and paid close attention to a couple of pedestrians. Nothing was sounding any alarm bells, and the clock was still ticking. Time to see Julie.

Parking a few blocks away on a quiet residential street, I jumped out and locked the Suburban with the button on the key. Standing there, I took a good look at the damage to its bodywork from scraping along the center barrier and ramming into the Prius. It was bad, and it was very noticeable. Too noticeable.

There was no way I could keep driving around in this thing. By now the Highway Patrol would be at the scene of the crash. They'd have a description of the hulking Suburban from the Prius driver and probably dozens of witnesses. They'd see the black paint left behind on both her car and the concrete median wall. There was almost assuredly a radio broadcast that had already been sent out, letting all the other cops know to be looking for a vehicle that matched the description of the one I'd just stepped out of.

Not happy that I'd compromised my only form of transportation, I turned and started down the sidewalk. I'd only gone a few yards when a thought occurred to me. Turning around, I headed for the back of the Suburban, unlocking it remotely with the key fob as I approached. Reaching the back, I raised the gate and released a spring loaded piece of vinyl that was stretched from the back of the rear seat to the inside of the back door. It was designed to conceal whatever cargo was being carried from view through the large, rear window.

Beneath it, a large, gunmetal grey box covered all of the considerable floor space. Towards the rear, in the center, a combination lock protruded from the smooth surface. It was a large knob with four dials. Each one had numbers from 0 through 9 etched into its surface.

Smiling, I opened Kirkpatrick's wallet and dug out the piece of paper from behind his license. The four digits that I hadn't been able to figure out before made sense now. Leaning in, I rolled the dials until they displayed the same numbers. The knob turned easily, and I felt the locking pins release.

Raising the lid, I was slightly surprised at the sheer amount of firepower contained in the vault. Three pistols, one with a sound suppressor screwed onto the end, with two spare magazines each. Two short-barreled assault rifles. A long barreled rifle with a high power scope and bipod attached. Sniper rifle. Along the side, neatly cradled in foam cutouts were half a dozen flash-bang grenades, used for temporarily disorienting subjects in a building during an assault.

A plain, black plastic case was cradled in the padding, a tamper evident strip of tape securing it in place. Curious, I ripped the tape off and lifted the box. It was about the size of a small, paperback book. Opening it, I stared in surprise at two, loaded syringes. Each had a label affixed that read *M99*.

While I had no idea what M99 was, I suspected this was the stuff they'd knocked me out with the other night. It had acted almost instantly, and I'd been out for well over a day. Closing the case, I slipped it into a side pocket.

The inside of the lid had a large cargo net stretched across its entire surface, divided into multiple pockets. Body armor and two, long windbreakers were tightly secured in place. Pulling the netting open, I checked the jackets. One of them was blue and had "FBI" prominently emblazoned in giant yellow letters on the back. The other was black with no identifying marks.

Looking around to make sure I wasn't being watched, I took one of the short rifles and slung it over my shoulders. Positioning it on my back, it would be completely concealed by a jacket. I quickly shrugged into the black one, slightly surprised that it fit reasonably well. It had multiple, deep pockets sewn into the lining and the hem hung to mid thigh.

I filled the interior pockets with the FBI jacket wadded into a ball and loaded rifle magazines. I then added two pistols, one of them the one with the suppressor, two extra mags for each, and a pair of flash-bangs. The only thing that wasn't here that I could have wished for was some cash. No matter, at least I was better armed. Now, it was time to see if Julie could help.

Julie opened the door when I knocked, holding it in one hand as she stood in the entrance. She put her other hand on her hip and glared at me.

"I need your help," I said, starting to step forward and coming to an abrupt halt when she didn't move to allow me to walk in to her home.

"Really?" She squinted at me. "You've got some balls; I'll say that for you. Do you know those assholes Tased me? Put me in cuffs and took me to a dark, musty house and questioned me like I was some sort of criminal?"

"I'm really sorry about that," I said. "For what it's worth, they Tased me too. And drugged me. They weren't too happy about you being involved. But there is something really bad that's going to happen, and I need your help to try and stop it."

"Here we go again," she scoffed. "Let me guess. More terrorists. What this time? A shopping mall? The airport?"

"Can we discuss this inside?" I asked, looking around to see if there was anyone within earshot.

She stood there for nearly a minute, unmoving. Looking into my eyes. Finally, she heaved a big sigh and stepped back. I walked into the apartment, and she closed and locked the door behind me.

"Thank you," I said, turning to face her.

"Don't thank me," she said. "I haven't done anything. Now, are you going to tell me what's going on or just keep standing there looking at my tits?"

The wave of heat began at my collar and quickly spread up and across my face. I must have turned a nice shade of red because after a moment she burst out laughing.

"You really are something else," she said, pushing past me and taking a seat on the sofa. "Sit your ass down and tell me so I can kick you out and get on with my life."

I sat on the opposite end of the couch, turning slightly sideways to face her. She was completely turned, her legs crossed with both feet under her ass. How the hell do women sit like that? I'd be in traction if I tried it.

"In slightly over..." I paused to check my watch. "Twenty-two hours, the President and Speaker of the House are going to be assassinated. I'm trying to get to Washington DC and stop it."

"And I suppose you're the only one who can?"

I nodded, not breaking eye contact.

"OK, buddy. That's enough. Time for you to go," she said, standing and heading for the door.

"Wait! Please," I said, resisting the impulse to get to my feet and stop her. "I'm telling you the truth, just like I was before. If I had any other option, I wouldn't be here."

She had made it to the door and paused to look at me. Her hand was on the deadbolt lever, ready to unlock it.

"You know, just because I'm a blonde doesn't mean I'm stupid. Or gullible. You're working for the FBI. The same guys that snatched me up and made sure I'd keep my mouth shut before they'd release me. Get them to help!"

"The FBI is involved in the plot," I said, trying to come across as level-headed and sincere. "Well, probably not the entire FBI. But the part of it that I'm involved with tried to kill me an hour ago to stop me from intervening."

It was quiet in the apartment, and I could hear her breathing as she stood looking at me, processing what I'd just said. Trying to decide if I was a loon or not.

"How?" She finally broke the silence.

"How, what?"

"How did they try to kill you?" She said, an exasperated tone in her voice.

"I was at a safe house. The agent assigned to me pulled a gun and tried to shoot me in the head."

"How did you survive?"

"I'm better trained, I guess," I said, shrugging my shoulders.

"You know, I appreciate modesty in a guy. In fact, after some of the egomaniacal assholes I've gone out with, I find it kind of attractive. But you're not applying for a date. If you want me to keep listening, you'd better start giving up all the details. I already stuck my neck out once for you, and damn near got it chopped off!"

She turned the deadbolt, unlocking it, and tugged the door open.

"So. Spit it out, or get out. I don't much care which one you do."

I sighed, nodding my head.

"OK," I said. "Close the door and I'll tell you."

She watched me closely for a bit, then pushed the door shut hard enough to rattle the window next to it. Re-engaging the lock, she walked stiffly back to the sofa and resumed her seat.

"Yes, I work for the FBI, but I'm not an agent. I was recruited for a special, secret project. Our job is to detect impending attacks on America, like the school the terrorists were going after, and identify the perpetrators. Once we know who, and where they are, I'm sent in to stop them before they can execute their plan.

"We recently developed intel that there is a plot by government officials to assassinate the President and the Speaker. I was at a safe house, here in the LA area. I thought I was getting ready to deliver a warning so the Secret Service could be alerted. Turns out I was betrayed by my FBI handler. The guy you talked to on the phone.

"I was carrying a data file that contained the intel we had collected. It was proof of the assassination plot. Somehow, Agent Johnson intercepted the flash drive and substituted one that contained orders for the agent guarding the safe house to terminate me. He tried. We fought. He's dead.

"Now, I'm on my own. The FBI wants me dead, or at least the part of the FBI that's involved in my project. All I can do is get to DC and try to stop the assassins. But I've got no money and no ID. No way to get there in time."

I told her as much of the truth as I could. At this point, I didn't give a shit about revealing the classified time travel machine, but I needed her to believe I was sane. If I started talking about supercolliders and Black Holes and jumping around between the past and present, she'd bounce me out the door in a hot second.

"Why don't you just call the Secret Service?" She asked.

"They don't know who I am, and there's nothing I can prove to them," I said, shaking my head. "I already thought about that. They must get hundreds, if not thousands, of tips and threats against the President every year. I'd just be one more nut in the peanut gallery."

She nodded, and I could see the wheels turning behind her eyes.

"Let's just say I believe you," she began. "I'm not saying I do, but if I did, what is it you need me to do?"

"The only way I can get to DC in time to intervene is if I fly," I said, hope causing me to speak faster. "But I can't go commercial. No money for a ticket and no ID to get through security. There's another way, though. Private charter. There're no security checks, and they could get me there as fast as the airlines."

"You need money?"

"I do," I nodded. "If I'm successful, I'll make sure you get paid back. Every penny. If I'm not, I'll probably be dead."

"And I'd be out of luck in getting paid back," she smiled to let me know it was a joke.

"Pretty much," I grinned.

"I must say, you're original," she said. "I wouldn't have been surprised if you'd told me I needed to sleep with you to save the world."

Despite myself, I blushed again. But, I smiled at her too.

"If you think that will help…" I grinned, taking a chance.

Her cracking a small joke was a good sign. Some part of my story had gotten through to her. Instead of kicking me out she was making light of the situation. But I had to be careful. That could change in a heartbeat if I said or did something wrong.

"Don't hold your breath," she grinned back at me, before standing and starting to pace.

"Can you prove any of what you've told me?" She asked.

I started to shake my head, then remembered the flash drive in my pocket. Reaching in, I brought it out and held it up for her to see.

"You have a laptop?"

She just looked at me for a long beat, probably surprised that I was actually producing something to back up my fantastic story. If she only knew how fantastic it really was.

Stepping closer, she took the drive from me and headed down the hall towards the bedroom. I couldn't help but admire the way she looked in the shorts as she walked away from me.

"Quit looking at my ass," she said over her shoulder.

38

"Why can't you take this to the Secret Service?" Julie asked after watching the video of Johnson ordering my murder.

"He doesn't mention anything about the President. And what do you think they're going to do with it? Contact the FBI. I have no idea who I can trust. If they speak to the wrong person, I'm dead and so is any chance to stop the assassins."

"Who's this Director he mentions?" Julie asked.

"The director of the project," I said. "And I don't have any way to contact him. I've only ever worked directly through Agent Johnson."

"There has to be a way to get someone to believe you," she said, unplugging the flash drive from her computer and handing it to me.

"I wish there was," I said. "And I'd be willing to try if I thought they'd believe me. Or knew I wasn't walking into the hands of one of the conspirators. I can't take the chance."

She was quiet for a bit, chewing on her lower lip in thought. Despite the situation, I couldn't help but watch. Fascinated. Mind starting to drift to more pleasurable things I could do with her besides talking about assassination plots. Then she pulled out a cigarette and lit up, killing the fantasy that was taking shape in my head.

"Look," I said, forcing myself to focus on the issue at hand. "I'm sorry to be here involving you in this. Time is running out. If you're not going to help, I've got to figure something else out before it's too late."

"I am trying to help," she said, eyes flashing. "You men. You always think the solution is to charge in headfirst. Guns blazing. Just like my husband. Guess what his favorite expression was."

"No idea."

I shrugged, growing more impatient by the moment.

"Kill them all and let God sort them out," she said.

"Sometimes, when every option has been explored, that is the only solution," I said gently, making up my mind. "OK, then. I'm going to be on my way. I'll figure something else out. I'm sorry I've caused you so much trouble."

I stood and headed for the door. Had no idea what I was going to do. Didn't even have a starting point. All I did know was that I was still alive and kicking, and as long as that was the case, there was a chance. Reaching the door, I unlocked it and started to turn the knob.

"Wait," Julie said.

I turned as she stubbed the cigarette out, stood and walked over, coming to a stop in front of me. She stared into my eyes, and I could tell she was trying to come to grips with a decision.

"I'll help you," she finally said. "But if you've lied to me, or are using me, so help me God I will cut your balls off and make you eat them."

"Yes, ma'am," I grinned, fairly certain she was capable of carrying out the threat.

"What do we do?" She asked.

"You have the money? This is going to be expensive."

"I've got all the money from the Survivor Benefits the Army pays me for my husband's death. I was saving up to buy a house. How much do you think we'll need?"

"No idea," I said, releasing the knob and locking the door again. "But a last minute charter all the way across the country isn't going to be cheap. If I had to guess, at least ten or fifteen thousand."

She nodded and moved back to the table, sitting down in front of her laptop. I watched her click a few times, type something in and read the results, then click some more. I walked over and stood behind her. She was looking at a website for a private charter company.

"Here we go," she said. "They operate out of John Wayne Airport in Orange County."

"Is that close?" I asked, not very familiar with the area.

"Not really, but close enough," she said, filling out a booking form.

"Hold on," I said, watching what she was doing. "Two passengers? You're not coming with me!"

"Then you're not going," she said, clicking the submit button. "My money. That means I get to go if I want to. Besides, you might need me again. Just like the other night."

A large wheel was spinning on the screen as her request was worked on by the charter company's website. I thought about arguing with her intention to come along but realized I didn't have much of a leg to stand on. If she wanted to join me, I couldn't stop her.

"Jesus Christ," she breathed when the screen displayed the results. "$21,000! Seriously?"

She quickly cleared the results and redid the booking form. The wheel spun again, then popped up with the same amount.

"Is there an in-flight meal with that?" I asked.

It took a moment to sink in, then she began laughing.

"There'd better be Wolfgang Puck in the galley, a massage from George Clooney and an all expense paid shopping trip to Tiffany's," she chuckled. "But at least it will get us there in time. Departs John Wayne at nine PM. Lands at Reagan International at five-thirty in the morning, DC time."

"You have that much?" I asked

I needed to know but was afraid to ask. Didn't want to cause her to rethink the huge amount of cash she was about to spend on nothing more than my word, and a short video on a flash drive.

She nodded and stood, heading for her bedroom again. This time, she didn't yell at me for watching her walk away. When she came back, she had a purse. Digging in it, she removed a wallet and flipped through until coming up with a debit card.

"This is almost every penny I have to my name," she said without looking at me. "You'd better be right. If I don't get this back, you're going to owe me for the rest of your life."

I didn't say anything. Knew she wasn't looking for reassurances. She was just voicing the fear she was feeling over draining her bank account.

With a sigh, she input the numbers off the card, filled in a couple of other fields and moved the mouse cursor to the *PAY* button. She held it there for a moment, not moving. Stared at the screen. I tried to imagine the thoughts going through her head.

"Fuck it," she said and clicked the button.

The wheel churned again for a long time, finally going away and displaying a new screen. It said the transaction was being processed.

"What does that mean?" I asked.

"I have no idea," she said, peering at the laptop. "Maybe it's because of the amount. I've never spent more than five hundred dollars on this card. Maybe the bank is freaking out."

We both jumped when a phone began ringing. Julie smiled in embarrassment and dug the device out of her purse. She answered it and listened for a few moments, then proceeded to provide some personal information. Apparently she passed the first test.

"Yes, that is an authorized transaction," she said into the phone. "Twenty-one thousand to Imperial Air Charters. Correct."

She listened for a few more seconds, thanked the person on the line, whom I assumed was from her bank, then broke the connection.

"Good to go?" I asked.

"Yes. I was right. The bank freaked. They were calling to make sure it was really me."

"What about the tickets, or whatever? Do we need to take something with us?"

"Hope not. I don't have a printer."

She clicked around the charter company's website for a minute, then leaned in to read something that was too small for me to see from where I stood. Opening her email, she waited for it to connect and download all her new messages. At the top of the list, I could see one with a bold header that was from the charter.

Julie opened it and read it quickly, then picked up her phone and tapped an icon. An email app opened, and a moment later she was looking at the same message.

"We're good," she said, closing the app and putting the phone back in her purse. "There's a barcode in the email, and as long as we've got that for them to scan, everything's cool. Now, we've got two hours to get to the airport, and I'm going to take a shower and change clothes before we leave. Sit tight and stay out of trouble."

She didn't wait for me to say anything, just jumped to her feet and hurried down the hall. I wandered over and plopped my ass onto the sofa, turning when I saw movement in the hall. It was Julie, going into the bathroom with a towel and pile of clothes in her arms. The door closed, the lock clicking a moment later. I guess trusting me enough to spend $21,000 on a private jet didn't mean she trusted me enough to take a shower with the door unlocked. Smart girl.

39

Julie was ready faster than I expected. Fifteen minutes later she walked into the living room, freshly showered. Her hair was braided, falling down her back. She wore dark green cargo pants and a black T-shirt. Tossing a small overnight bag on the table, she sat down next to me on the couch and dropped a pair of well worn, desert boots on the floor.

I remained sitting, watching her pull on a pair of thick socks, getting a closer look at her ankles. She'd removed the gold chain from the one with the combat medic tattoo. On the opposite, just above the small round bone on the outside near her foot, was another tattoo. This one was of a grinning skull in front of a pair of crossed arrows. A knife pierced the top, a snake coiling around the hilt. Her husband had been a Green Beret, and she'd honored him with the ink.

As she laced her boots, I questioned myself for having waited. While she was in the shower, I had seriously considered stealing her phone and leaving without her. With it, I'd be able to get on the plane. But I didn't know her well enough to begin to guess what she'd do if she came out and I was gone. The tickets were purchased in her name. I didn't think it would be difficult for her to call the charter company and tell them to hold the jet until she could arrive and kick my ass.

She was a headstrong woman, of that there was no doubt. There was a lot of iron in her. Had to be. You didn't do the job in a war-zone that she'd done if there wasn't. And then to lose a spouse? I had to admit that I admired her. Respected that she'd been through hell and seemed to have come out on the other side relatively intact. That, or she was a hell of an actress. Nah. No one's that good.

"Ready," she said, standing and stomping her feet to settle them into the boots.

I stood and took my jacket off. Her eyes momentarily narrowed when she saw the weapons I was carrying.

"Do you have a small duffel or something?"

I didn't want to spend a five-and-a-half-hour flight with the rifle and pistols digging into my back and sides. I also didn't want to run the risk of the flight crew catching a glimpse of my small arsenal and deciding to warn the authorities at the arriving airport.

"Just the big suitcase you saw," she said. "I haven't exactly had time to move in. Do you want it?"

"Can we bring it on the plane?"

"I think so. Their website said there was room for normal luggage."

I nodded, and she waved for me to follow her into the bedroom. The bag was lying on the bed, half the contents strewn across the mattress. Julie looked at it and eyed the weapons, magazines, and flash-bangs I was unloading onto the top of the dresser. She rushed out of the room, returning a moment later with the small overnight bag she'd already packed.

She lifted the top of the large suitcase and dumped the remainder of its contents onto the bed. Clothes and shoes spilled out, then a large vibrator landed on the pile and rolled off onto the floor. I couldn't help but look at it, trying to suppress a grin.

"What?" She challenged as she opened the overnight bag and dumped its contents into the empty suitcase.

"Nothing," I said.

"Say a word," she said. "I fucking dare you."

She didn't sound like she was kidding, and I wasn't brave enough to test her. Instead, I watched as she arranged the clothes she was taking with her, then picked up the rifle. It was a short barreled version of a standard Army issue M4. With obviously practiced hands, she made sure it was unloaded before placing it in the bag.

Adding some clothes for padding, she found spots for all of the spare magazines and the two grenades. I'd kept one of the pistols. It was stuck in the waistband of my pants at the small of my back. Tossing the jacket into the bag, I made sure the weapon was well covered by my shirt.

Julie picked up the other pistol, again handling it with a familiarity that only came from years of being around weapons on a daily basis. Satisfied there was a round in the chamber and a fully loaded magazine, she slipped it into a large pocket on the right leg of her cargo pants. They were tight enough around her narrow waist that its weight, while slightly noticeable, didn't drag them down.

"What?" She asked when she noticed me looking at her pants.

"You know you're committing a felony in California just by concealing that in your pocket.

And DC has even more strict gun laws. Tagging along is one thing, but you're putting yourself in a bad position."

"I'm a big girl," she said.

She stuffed more clothes into the bag to keep everything tightly packed before closing the lid and spinning a combination lock to secure it.

"And," she turned to face me. "If I'm about to walk into a situation where people might be shooting at me, I want to be able to shoot back."

I nodded, not about to argue. Stepping forward, I lifted the suitcase off the bed and set it on the floor. Extending the handle, I pulled it along behind me as I followed her back into the living room.

"Are we ready?" She asked, taking a quick look around as she slung her purse over her shoulder.

I nodded and led the way, suitcase dragging along behind. Releasing the deadbolt, I opened the door and came face to face with two men wearing suits. I stopped so sharply that Julie ran into the suitcase before she realized something was wrong.

One of the men had his arm raised, preparing to knock, looking as surprised as I was. Our eyes locked and a heartbeat later I saw a look of recognition in his. FBI! Had to be.

He dropped his arm and started to step back, his hand moving towards where a weapon would be holstered on his belt. His partner was a little slower on the uptake, glancing at him before moving. I stood frozen for another heartbeat, spurred to action as his other hand came around to sweep his suit coat clear.

His hand was inches from the butt of a pistol when I dropped the suitcase handle and lunged. I bulled into the first guy, knocking his arm aside and shoving him against the railing that protected from a three story drop. The partner was moving now, and I spun, delivering a strike to his solar plexus with my elbow.

He folded, and I raised my knee into his face hard enough to lift him a couple of inches into the air. His body went limp, and he fell to the side. The other agent had scrambled away, still trying to bring his weapon into use, but was frozen when I looked at him. He had a pistol in his hand, pointed straight down as he stared into the apartment.

I risked a glance over my shoulder, more than a little surprised to see Julie with a pistol leveled at the man's face. She held it in both hands at arms length, knees slightly flexed and shoulders forward. Her finger was on the trigger, and the gun was rock steady in her grip.

"Hand me your weapon, butt first," I said to him, making sure I was clear of her line of fire.

After a moment of hesitation, he slowly raised his arm across his body and extended the gun in my direction. I took it from his hand and stepped back, aiming it at him.

"Inside," I said.

"This is not a good idea, Mr. Whitman," he said, not moving.

"Neither is not doing what I tell you," I growled. "Now, get inside that fucking apartment before I completely lose my patience."

For a bit, I thought he was going to be a problem. But, when there are two weapons pointed at your head, and both are held by people who are keeping space open and look like they know what they're doing, you don't have a lot of options.

Carefully, he straightened and slowly moved forward, stepping across the threshold. Julie slipped sideways, keeping room between them as he advanced, the muzzle of her pistol never wavering.

"On the sofa. Hands in plain sight at all times," I said, remaining outside and hoping a neighbor hadn't seen what was happening.

Once he was seated, his hands on his knees, I glanced at his partner. The man was still out, lying on the concrete walkway. A small pool of blood had spread out around his head. Probably from a broken nose.

Keeping the new pistol tight against my body, aimed at the unconscious agent, I reached out with my free hand and removed his weapon. Sticking it in my waistband, I grabbed his belt and dragged him inside, dumping him on the carpet underneath the front window.

Circling behind Julie, who was keeping the two men covered, I went into the kitchen. I was looking for something I could fill with water to rinse the blood off the walkway. But there wasn't anything. Like she'd said, she hadn't had time to move in yet.

"Anything in the bathroom I can put water in? Blood outside I need to clean up."

"Shampoo bottle in the shower," Julie said. "Dump it out and use it."

I did, and a few minutes later there was no longer an obvious blood stain right in front of her door. Now it was just a slightly soapy wet spot with an indeterminate dark splotch in the middle. It would be noticed if someone walked by, but it would be dismissed.

Closing the door, I knelt over the unconscious agent and searched him. Wallet, keys, cell phone, handcuffs, a folding knife and an FBI badge case. I flipped it open and looked at the ID card. Special Agent Reginald Hart. Piling the items on the table, I stepped to the side of the guy on the sofa.

"On your feet," I said, waving him up with my hands.

He sighed and stood. Reaching out, I grabbed his shoulder and turned his body until he was facing away from me. Running my hands over him, I found the exact same things I'd taken from Agent Hart, plus a snub nosed revolver in an ankle holster. Pushing him back onto the couch, I added all of his possessions to the pile on the table, noticing my watch as I worked. We only had slightly more than an hour before our flight left.

But then I wasn't terribly worried. This was a charter, not a commercial flight. There was no point in them leaving without us. Still, we needed to be moving.

"You know who I am," I said to the conscious agent, opening his badge case to look at his ID. "Special Agent Arnold Cooper."

"I know who you are, and I know what you did," he snarled at me.

I closed the case and tossed it onto the table.

"What did I do?" I asked.

"You murdered Kirkpatrick," he hissed. "He was a friend of mine. Wife. Two kids. And you killed him."

"Yes, I did," I said. "After he tried to shoot me in the head on orders from Agent Johnson."

"Bullshit!" He spat. "I've heard about you. About the cops you killed in Arizona. You never should have been brought in to the project."

"Would you believe me if I showed you a video of Johnson ordering my termination?" I asked, brief hope flaring that maybe I could use the FBI to help.

"So what? If he did, I'm sure he had a good reason. Maybe you did something else I don't know about. You're dead, asshole. You're fucking dead! You don't kill an FBI agent and get to walk around like nothing happened. One day you're going to turn around, and I'll be standing there. And I'm going to put a bullet in your goddamn head!"

I sighed and picked the two pairs of cuffs off the table.

"Stand up," I said. "And keep your mouth shut and you just might live long enough to try and kill me."

He stood, eyes boring into mine. I twirled my finger in the air, telling him to turn around. When he did, I pulled his hands behind his back, put the cuffs on and pushed him back onto the sofa. Next, I cuffed his unconscious partner, then walked into the bedroom.

Sweeping all of Julie's clothes onto the floor, I stripped the sheet off the mattress and used a knife I'd taken from one of them to cut it into long strips. Once I had them ready, I went back out and picked up one of the kitchen chairs from around the table and moved it to the middle of the living room. Pointing at it, I stepped back as Agent Cooper slowly stood and moved to take a seat.

"Think about something," I said as I worked with the strips of sheet. "If I'm who you think I am, why are you still alive? Why is your partner alive? Why am I tying you up when it would be much simpler to just cut your throats?"

"Who knows why a fucking psycho does something," Cooper said.

"Whatever. Just remember something. You'll survive this because I don't want to kill you. No matter what you think, I'm not some bloodthirsty madman. So, unless you're in on the whole conspiracy with Johnson, you'll come out of this OK."

"You're fucking crazy," he hissed. "That fucking machine has scrambled your brain. Or were you always fucked up like this?"

At that point I wrapped a strip of fabric around his head, covering his mouth. That ended the conversation. His hands were cuffed behind his back, and he was completely secured to the metal frame of the chair. Each ankle was tied to a leg, and a thick strip went around his chest, holding him tight in the seat.

With the gag in place, I grasped the back of the chair and pulled, tilting it back to rest on the floor. I didn't want him to start bouncing around and come crashing over. He just might succeed in making enough noise to alert the downstairs neighbor that something was wrong.

Five minutes later his partner was in another chair, secured in the same manner. I'd worried about gagging him at first, afraid he wouldn't be able to breathe through a broken nose and would suffocate. But the blow with my knee had missed his nose. There was a long split in the skin of his forehead. That was where the blood had come from.

Agent Cooper watched every move I made, glaring at me with hate filled eyes. I couldn't say that I blamed him. If our roles were reversed, all I'd be thinking about would be getting my hands around the throat of the guy who had tied me up.

Once they were secure, I had Julie open the suitcase. I paid attention this time and memorized the combination. The three guns I'd taken off the agents went in, and I was starting to close the lid when Julie stopped me. She snatched her laptop off the table and put it in, too.

A quick trip to the bathroom to make sure I looked presentable enough to board a chartered jet, and we were ready to go. Leaving the apartment, Julie locked the door with her key, then lead the way to an aging VW Jetta in the rear parking lot. The suitcase went in the trunk, and I slipped into the passenger seat as she got behind the wheel and started the engine.

40

I sat there looking at Julie, waiting for her to put the car in gear and start driving. But she just sat there, hands tightly gripping the wheel as she stared through the dirty windshield. She was breathing fast, trying to get herself under control.

"I just screwed myself," she whispered. "Those were FBI agents!"

I didn't know what to say. She was right. If things were normal. But there was nothing about this that was normal. A time traveling ex-con trying to foil an assassination plot that involved the Vice President of the United States and at least one FBI agent. God only knew who else was involved.

"And you haven't told me everything," Julie said accusingly, turning to face me. "What was he talking about? You killed two cops in Arizona? And what machine has messed with your head?"

"You're right," I said with a sigh. "I haven't told you everything. Some of it would just be too hard to believe."

"Harder to believe than the fact that I've just ruined my life helping a man I don't even know? Emptied my bank account. Pointed a gun at an FBI agent while you tied him up. What the hell was I thinking?"

"You were thinking that I'm telling the truth," I said gently. "And I am. Just because there're some things I haven't told you doesn't mean I'm lying. If I don't get to DC and stop this, the President and the Speaker of the House will be dead this time tomorrow. And the people behind the conspiracy will be in control of the country. That's the truth."

"I don't know if I can believe you," she said after a long stretch of silence. "I did. Or I wanted to, maybe. But the deeper I get, the more it feels like there's more going on here that you're hiding from me."

I leaned my head back on the car seat and blew out a quiet sigh of frustration. She was smart and intuitive. There was no denying that. And she also had enough strength of character to stop helping me as quickly as she'd started if she felt I was playing some sort of game. The truth was, without her help, I wasn't going to be able to pull this off.

"Look," I began. "Nothing I haven't told you has anything to do with why you're helping me. I understand you don't trust me at the moment. Don't blame you. But we're running out of time. I'll tell you everything once we're on the plane. We'll have plenty of time to talk."

She stared at me so long I grew uncomfortable and wanted to look away. That's probably what she was waiting for. To see if I couldn't look her in the eye. So, I forced myself to endure the scrutiny, sitting still and remaining quiet. Finally, she broke eye contact, savagely yanked the transmission into drive and roared out of the parking spot.

The drive to the airport took most of an hour. And it was quiet. Neither of us spoke. I didn't think Julie was mad at me or pouting. I suspected she was thinking. Trying to figure out how she'd gotten in so deep, so fast. But isn't that the way it always is? It takes one decision and minutes of action to get yourself into a mess that will take years to put behind you.

Exiting the freeway, she followed large signs to the airport entrance. A smaller road peeled off from the heavy traffic, heading for the charter terminal. We pulled into a half full lot, and Julie whipped the VW into a parking spot near the walkway to the building's entrance.

"I'm not going," she said after turning the engine off. "You can take my suitcase, and I'll go in with you so they can scan the barcode on my phone. After that, we're done."

"What are you going to do?"

I was surprised. Of all the possibilities I'd mulled over during the drive to the airport, this wasn't one of them.

"I don't know," she said. "Maybe head for my brother's house in Oregon."

"Julie, I think you should come with me," I said, turning my upper body so I could look directly at her.

"Why? So you can lie to me some more?"

"I haven't lied to you! I haven't told you the whole truth, but I haven't lied."

"A lie by omission is still a lie," she said in a sad voice.

"And I've said I'll tell you everything. Most of it, you aren't going to believe anyway. That's why I didn't tell you before. Well, that and it's classified. But I'm going to tell you as soon as we're on that plane and have time.

"I know I have no right to ask, but please trust me. I am going to stop the assassination, and then I'm going to deal with Agent Johnson. You will get reimbursed every penny you've put out, and your name will be cleared. I promise. All you have to do is trust me."

I watched her closely as I spoke, hoping my words would get through.

"Why do you want me to come along so badly?" She asked suspiciously.

"Because it's not safe for you to stay behind. They're looking for me. And when those two agents we left tied up get free, they're going to be looking for you, too. And it will be men working for Agent Johnson. They aren't interested in the truth or anything other than following their orders.

"You know what orders he issued to deal with me. Do you really think he's going to let you live? The safest place for you for the next twenty hours is right next to me. Then it will all be over, and you can go back to your life."

She turned and looked at me for a long moment. Thinking. Deciding what to believe and what to do. Faster than I expected, she removed the keys from the ignition and popped her door open.

"We've got a plane to catch," she said, resignation clear in her voice.

I hopped out and dashed to the trunk. Julie already had it open, and I lifted the suitcase out and placed it on the ground. She locked the car, and after we made sure our pistols were well concealed, we walked across the sidewalk and into the terminal.

Imperial Charters was a large outfit with professionally dressed staff working the check-in counter. Julie and I walked up, and she identified herself. Within minutes, the bar code on her phone had been scanned, the suitcase had been taken to be placed in the luggage compartment, and we were escorted through a set of doors into a large hangar.

A gleaming Gulfstream, medium range jet reflected the overhead lighting. As we approached, I saw an employee load the suitcase in the plane's belly. He closed the hatch and locked it in place.

The cabin door was open, a set of stairs integrated into the jet extending to the hangar floor. A tall, trim man wearing a pilot's uniform stood on a narrow landing at the top of the steps, waiting for us.

"Mr. and Mrs. Broussard. Welcome!"

I was momentarily taken aback at the greeting.

"I'm your pilot, Captain Henderson. My copilot, Ms. Torrel, is in the cockpit finishing the pre-flight checklist. We'll be ready to go in just a few minutes."

He had descended to the floor and shook hands with each of us as he spoke.

"Thank you, Captain," Julie said, somehow managing to give him one of her thousand watt smiles.

I followed her up and into the plane. We turned right, and I couldn't help but stop in amazement. Plush carpeting. Burled walnut trim. Gold fixtures and accents. And half a dozen, well-spaced leather seats that looked big enough to hold two people each. This was nothing like I remembered air travel being.

There was a bang as the pilot retracted the stairs and secured the door, then he appeared briefly to tell us where the bathroom was. There wasn't a flight attendant, and I suspected that was an expensive option that Julie hadn't selected. When the pilot disappeared into the cockpit, I sank into one of the seats. It was the most comfortable chair I'd ever sat in.

Julie stepped into the small galley, returning a moment later with a bottle of Jack Daniels and two, cut crystal tumblers. She poured a healthy slug into each as there was the gentle bump of a tractor pushing the jet out of the hangar. Handing me a glass, she leaned back and fastened her seatbelt.

"Start talking," she said, downing half the amber liquid in one swallow.

I took a sip, resisting the urge to cough when the fiery whiskey hit my throat. The engines started as we came to a stop. There were a couple of bumps as the tractor was unhooked from the front landing gear, then the pilot throttled up slightly, and we began rolling.

He came on the intercom and reminded us to fasten our seatbelts and thanked us for choosing Imperial Charters. We bounced along and waited for a couple of Delta and one Alaska commercial airliners to take off. Then the engines howled, and we began rushing down the runway. Much faster than I expected, we left the ground. I looked out the window at the lights of Orange County and began speaking.

41

"You are either the most accomplished liar I've ever met, or that's a story that should be made into a movie," Julie said when I finished.

She was a good listener. Attentive, even when refilling our glasses. She hadn't interrupted, and let me talk until it was all out there. And I'd held nothing back. My brother. Bringing the drugs across and killing the two cops before they could kill me and my entire family. My trial and imprisonment. My execution or my faked execution to be accurate. The Athena Project. My plastic surgery. The training I had gone through. All of it.

"Do you understand why I didn't tell you before?"

"I understand, but that doesn't mean I'm happy about it," she said. "That's if I believe you. I may not be a genius or have a college education, but it just sounds too much like science fiction."

"It did to me, too. At first," I acknowledged.

We both looked up when the cockpit door opened. It was the pilot coming to check on us.

"Can I get you folks anything?" He asked with a big, friendly smile.

"Do you have internet access?" Julie asked.

"Yes, ma'am. Onboard Wi-Fi. No password needed," he beamed.

I was starting to wonder if he was a pilot or a salesman, but after making sure we had everything we needed he disappeared back into the front of the plane. Julie had taken her phone out and was busily tapping away. Draining the last of my drink, I placed the empty glass on the table between us and got up to check the galley for food.

There was a small fridge, and after a moment, I figured out how to release the catch that secured the door while the aircraft was in flight. Two large platters of vacuum wrapped dinners rested on the middle shelf. Taking them out, I read the contents of the first one. Roasted chicken breast with gravy, new potatoes and baby carrots and a dinner roll. Hoping for something different, I checked the other. It was the same.

There were heating instructions printed on a label stuck to the outside, and I got the first one going in the microwave. As it heated, I poked around until I found plates, forks, knives and napkins.

"Hungry?" I called to Julie after sticking my head around the bulkhead that separated the cabin from the galley.

"Yes," she said without looking up from her phone.

As the food continued to warm, I thought about the conversation we'd just had. Well, it hadn't been much of a conversation. It was mostly me telling the story of the past decade or so of my life.

Did she believe me? Hell, could she believe me? Was what I said really any less fantastical than if I'd told her I was from an alien civilization, here to save the world? A soft beep from the microwave interrupted my thoughts.

I removed the first tray and put the second one in, starting it heating. Unwrapping the steaming food, I transferred it to what I was almost certain was expensive China. The flatware was solid and heavy, and I was willing to bet it was sterling silver. Only the best for the charter air traveler, I guess.

Soon the second tray was done, and I quickly had the food on another plate and carried both back into the cabin. Julie was staring at her phone, occasionally swiping the screen with her fingertip as she read something. I put the plates on the table, went back to the galley and returned with two bottles of water. As much as I'd have enjoyed another drink, I needed to be clear-headed when we arrived in DC.

Sitting, I began eating in silence, letting Julie do whatever it was she was doing. She knew the food was there and would eat when she was ready. I, on the other hand, was famished. Every bite vanished quickly, and I sat back and drank most of one of the waters.

Julie put her phone away and stood up. Stepping around the table, she leaned over me and lifted her hands, pausing with them only inches from my face.

"May I?" She asked before touching me.

"What are you doing?"

"I want to see something," she said.

I looked at her for a moment before shrugging.

"Go ahead."

She began examining my head and face. Gently probed with her fingers and leaned close for a better look at the skin behind my ears and under my jaw. She moved hair aside and inspected my scalp, then pressed on the bridge and tip of my nose. As she checked me over, I caught a whiff of a subtle perfume and barely resisted the urge to reach up and wrap her in my arms.

"Well, at least that part of your story is true," she said, returning to her seat and picking up her fork. "You've definitely had extensive plastic surgery."

"You should see me when I don't shave," I grinned. "I look like Patches the Poodle."

Despite everything, she smiled. I decided it was time for me to shut up. There wasn't anything else I could say to prove I was telling the truth. It was up to her to think about what I'd told her and make up her own mind. I'd truthfully answer any questions she asked, but other than that there wasn't anything else I could do.

"You were better looking before your face was changed," she said.

"What?"

"I looked you up on the internet. Figured there would be plenty of stories about a cop killer who was executed. There were. Found your real name, too. Robert."

I blushed, not wanting her to know how much I liked hearing my real name. Or how much I liked hearing her say it.

"But what I found was a very different version of events than what you told me."

I started to open my mouth to protest, staying quiet when she held her hand up for me to stop.

"I believe you," she said, looking me in the eye. "Lord help me, I don't know why, but I believe you. As wild and crazy as your story sounds, I do. Honestly, I'm struggling with the whole time travel thing, but the rest of it rings true. Especially after some of the things I've seen."

"Thank you," I said. "And I'm sorry I didn't tell you sooner."

"Actually, I'm not sure I blame you," she said. "If you'd told me any of this right off the bat, I'd probably have dismissed you as a crank."

She put the last bite of food in her mouth and chewed slowly. Wiping her lips with the linen napkin, she sat back and took a sip of water. We sat there looking at each other for a while, the silence stretching out but not growing uncomfortable. Finally, I checked my watch and cleared my throat.

"Three hours to DC. We'd better get some rest. I don't think we'll have time for a nap once we're on the ground."

Julie nodded and took our plates to the galley. Back in the cabin, she poked around and found blankets and pillows. Tossing one of each into my lap, she sat down and belted herself in. A large button on the side of her chair activated a motor that lowered the head and raised the feet until it turned into a bed. She punched the pillow before putting it under her head, then spread the blanket over her body.

"Goodnight, Robert," she said, eyes already closed.

I sat there watching her for several minutes. Wanted to go lean over and gently kiss her. Thank her for being the only person in the world I could count on. Gently brush the hair off her face and tell her just how special she was.

I settled for pushing the button on my chair and rolling over to get some rest.

42

My eyes flew open when someone shook my shoulder. Turning my head, I saw Julie leaning over me, a worried expression on her face.

"Something's wrong," she said.

Those two words dumped about a gallon of adrenaline into my system. Throwing the blanket off, I sat up without bothering to use the button to return the bed to a chair configuration.

"What?" I whispered.

"I don't know," she mumbled, still leaning close to me. "I woke up when the pilot opened the cockpit door. He was checking on us. Saw me open my eyes and immediately slammed the door and locked it."

"That could be nothing," I said, hoping she was just jumpy.

"You didn't see his face when he saw I was awake," she said. "He was worried. Not frightened, but he wasn't the same smiling guy he's been."

"What could be wrong?" I asked, a bad feeling descending over me as an idea popped into my head. "You still have internet access?"

Julie grabbed her purse and got her phone. She tapped a couple of times and squinted at the small screen.

"Yes," she said a moment later.

"Check your bank account."

"Why?" She asked.

"Just do it," I said. "See if everything looks normal."

It didn't take long for her to look up with fear in her eyes.

"It's locked," she said. "I can't get in. That's never happened before."

"FBI," I said. "They either found those two agents or they got free. They checked your bank records and found the transaction for the flight. Froze your account and called the charter company. The pilot probably just got a call, checking on his safety and letting him know he had two fugitives on board."

"What do we do?" She asked.

I checked my watch. Forty minutes to DC, if that's where we were still going. For all I knew, the FBI had told him to divert to a different location. Either way, there were going to be men with guns waiting for us when we landed. The only question was whether they'd be there to arrest us, or kill us.

I didn't voice these thoughts to Julie. We needed to get control of the pilot. There was really no other option. Had to find out where we were going.

"We have to take control," I said.

"Can you fly? I can't," she said, looking at me like I was crazy.

"I mean we have to get control of the pilot."

"How? The cockpit door is locked, and I don't think we can break through."

I looked around the cabin, an idea taking shape when I spotted an intercom for communicating with the flight deck.

"Call the cockpit on that," I nodded at the small panel. "Tell them I'm sick. No, not sick, having a heart attack. Really sell it."

"Will that work?"

"Got a better idea?" I asked.

After a moment, she shook her head and stood up. I reached behind me and drew the pistol, hiding it beneath the blanket as I stretched out on the bed facing the cockpit. Grabbing a bottle of water off the table, I used it to dampen my face and hair as if I were sweating heavily. Meeting Julie's eyes, I nodded.

She did a masterful job of acting. With terror and panic in her voice, she pleaded with the pilot for help. He didn't want to leave the cockpit, and this confirmed for me that our suspicions were correct. Normally he'd break his neck to get to the side of an ill passenger as quickly as possible.

After almost two minutes of frantic pleading by Julie, the cockpit door cracked open. I moaned loudly, peering through squinted eyes. The pilot was still on the flight deck, the door only a foot open as he looked into the cabin. I groaned, pulling my knees up and acting as if I was writhing in pain.

"Please, help him!"

Julie had heard the door open, and now she stood behind me and yelled at the pilot. She kept it up, sinking to her knees and rubbing her hands across my face and chest like a distraught wife. Finally, the pilot started to move. Slowly, the door swung the rest of the way open, and he stepped through.

He approached cautiously, and I was glad to see the cockpit door remained open. Beyond him, the co-pilot leaned to the side with her head turned, watching. I'd have to be very careful that she didn't have an opportunity to jump up and close the door.

Finally, he reached the edge of the bed and knelt down. Julie had maintained her role, begging for help and pleading with me to be OK. When the pilot began to reach out to touch me, she grabbed his wrists and held them tightly.

His body blocking the co-pilot's view, I brought the gun out and pressed the muzzle against his chest. His eyes opened wide, and his mouth fell open in surprise.

"Make a sound and you're dead," I whispered, waiting to make sure he was going to comply. "Where did they tell you to go?"

"Who? What are you talking about?" He asked in a shaking voice.

"The FBI. Last time I'm going to ask nicely. What did they tell you to do?"

He swallowed a couple of times, sweat popping out on his face.

"Andrews Air Force Base," he stammered.

Shit! If we landed on an Air Force Base, Julie and I would never be seen again.

"How far are we?" I asked.

"Maybe half an hour."

"OK, listen very closely," I said. "I don't want to hurt you or your co-pilot. But I will if you don't do exactly as I say. Do you understand?"

He just stared back at me, frozen in fear.

"Tom? Everything OK?" The co-pilot called from the cockpit.

"Careful," I whispered.

He swallowed hard, again, and took a deep breath.

"He's not doing so good," he shouted.

"Where can we divert?" I whispered.

"I don't know," he stammered, and I ground the muzzle of the pistol against his chest.

"You'd better think of something. Now," I said. "We're not going to an Air Force Base!"

"Fredericksburg, Virginia," he said after a moment of panicked thought.

"Stand up slowly and don't try to run," I said. "You can't move faster than I can shoot."

He jerked his head up and down in a nod, and slowly stood on trembling legs.

"Now back up," I said, shifting and getting my feet on the floor.

He was between the open cockpit door and me, and I carefully stood, hoping I was screened from the co-pilot's view.

"Back to the cockpit."

I followed tight against his back as we covered the short distance. Julie stayed right behind me. Reaching the open door, I stopped the pilot with a firm hand on his shoulder.

"Got him?" I mumbled over my shoulder.

"Yes," Julie answered quietly, and from the corner of my eye, I could see her gun come up and aim at the pilot.

Quickly stepping around him, I moved through the door and pressed the muzzle against the back of the co-pilot's neck. She went rigid and let out a tiny squeal of fright.

"There's a pilot available right outside the door," I said in my most menacing tone. "Do as I say, and you'll live. Otherwise, I'll shoot you and let him take over."

"Tell me what you want," she said. "Just please don't shoot, mister. I've got a daughter I want to see again."

"Do what I tell you and don't try anything foolish and you will," I said, not liking myself very much at the moment. "Fredericksburg, Virginia. Change course, and put us down there."

"OK," she said. "No problem, but I have to call them on the radio."

"No!"

I tapped her on the neck with the muzzle, stopping her before she could reach the transmit button. The FBI already knew what plane we were on. If that plane called in a destination change, they'd know immediately and would be in hot pursuit.

"Where can we land that you don't need to call ahead? And don't fuck with me. My dad was a retired pilot. I know there are smaller airports that don't have towers. You can just sit down without any notice."

"I need to look at the GPS," she said. "I'm not from here. I don't know the area."

"Carefully," I warned.

I watched closely as she began searching for a general aviation airport that wasn't staffed by the FAA. It took a few minutes, then she tapped an entry on the screen.

"Gore, Virginia," she said. "No tower. Runway is long enough for us to land safely. We can be on the ground in ten minutes."

"Do it," I said to the co-pilot, then to Julie, "Take him and you two buckle up."

She herded the pilot away as the jet banked and began to descend. I bent my knees to absorb some slight turbulence.

"I'm going to stay right here," I said to the co-pilot. "Just in case you get any ideas about trying something, like braking hard when we land or suddenly turning, I'm going to keep the muzzle of this gun pressed against the back of your neck.

"And don't forget my partner back there. She's buckled in. You might knock me over, but if you do she'll get you. Stay cool, do what I'm asking, and you'll walk away from this with a great story to tell."

"I'm no hero. I just want this over with."

"Smart lady," I said.

I watched the gauges as she flew, finally spotting the altimeter. We were descending rapidly for a landing. I just hoped there was time once we were on the ground to get out of the area before the FBI showed up.

"When we get a little closer, I have to dial in that frequency and press the transmit button on the radio," the co-pilot said, pointing at the screen. "Unmanned airport. That's how I get the runway lights to come on."

I did actually know this, remembering listening to my dad and his pilot buddies telling stories when I was little. I told her that was fine, and a minute later she did. There was a several-second delay, then a lighted runway appeared in the darkness ahead of us.

She landed the plane so gently I barely felt the bump as the landing gear touched the tarmac. Braking cautiously, she slowed the jet and steered onto a taxiway. Following it, she brought us to a stop near a terminal building not much larger than a convenience store.

"Shut down and move back into the cabin," I ordered.

She threw several switches and the engines quickly spooled down to silence. She removed her headphones and started to unbuckle her flight harness, but I stopped her.

"Power it all the way down. No need to be emitting any signals," I said.

She pressed some more buttons and the instruments all went dark, one of them whining down the musical scale as it came to a stop. Harness off, I stepped back to give her room. I pointed at the door, and she opened it, the stairs automatically unfolding and deploying to the ground.

"Can you watch them?" I asked Julie.

"Yes, but why? What are you doing?"

"Going to find something to restrain them so they don't call the cops the second we leave."

I descended the steps, moving away from the jet. It was warm and humid in Virginia, the fresh air invigorating. I looked around, but the airport was dark. Shut down for the night. No one was around and other than frogs and insects singing in the surrounding forest, it was quiet.

Gaining entry into one of the two hangars was simple. Once inside, I looked around until I found what I needed. Gathering up some medium weight chains and a few padlocks with keys sticking out of them, I returned to the plane and climbed aboard. Julie had the two pilots seated in the main cabin, and I quickly secured each of them to their seats and snapped padlocks in place.

"I'm sorry about this," I said, making sure they couldn't slip the chains, and there wasn't enough slack to allow them to reach anything that could be used to call for help or break free. "Someone will be along in a few hours. You'll be fine until then."

"You're not going to kill us."

The co-pilot made it a statement, not a question. I paused, looking at the relieved expression on her face.

"Don't know what the FBI told you about me, but whatever it was probably isn't true," I said. "I don't kill people that aren't trying to hurt me or someone else. Thanks for the flight. I'll be sure to leave a good review and use your company again."

I don't know why I said that. Probably just needed a little relief after the tension of forcing them to land the plane. I guess we all did as both of them began laughing in nervous giggles. Behind me, I heard Julie snort. Turning, I lead the way out of the aircraft and into the night.

43

Once outside, I raised the stairs and secured the cabin door before retrieving the suitcase from the luggage hold. Lifting it out, I gently placed it on the ground and paused, tilting my head up towards the dark sky. Something, barely audible, was making noise on the horizon. I listened for a moment, then fear coursed through me when I remembered the briefing I'd received from Carpenter about the assassination.

The analysts believed the Hellfire missile that had killed the President had been fired from a helicopter. And I was pretty sure the faint sound I was hearing was the sound of a rotor. Could they have more than one missile? Would they be willing to use it to stop me and sound the alarm that there was someone out there with a Hellfire in their possession? I didn't want to find out the hard way.

"Run!" I hissed to Julie.

Snatching the suitcase off the ground, I sprinted away from the parked jet. Julie was on my heels, and I was gratified to see that she hadn't wasted time wanting to know why I was panicking. We were halfway to the hangar where I'd found the chains and locks when there was a whooshing sound behind us. Then we were picked up and propelled through the air by a massive explosion.

The force of the blast wave was tremendous. I tumbled through the air, my brains nearly scrambled. Falling to the tarmac, I rolled until striking the base of the hangar wall. Somehow I'd managed to hold onto the suitcase, and it slammed into my head when I came to an abrupt stop.

I don't know how long I lay there, aware the chartered jet was burning furiously, unable to make my body start moving again. Sounds were muted from the pummeling my eardrums had received, and I hoped they hadn't been ruptured by the violence of the explosion.

Suddenly, full awareness and control returned, and I realized I was in danger of being cooked by the raging fire. The heat was blistering, the air around me so hot that it hurt to take a breath. Sitting up, I looked around for Julie. She was twenty feet away, apparently still stunned or unconscious as she lay against the hangar wall.

Scrambling to my feet, I rushed towards her. The side of my body facing the jet felt as if it were being roasted and I ducked and turned my face away as I ran. There was a large secondary

36

explosion from the devastated aircraft, and I was nearly flattened again.

Reaching Julie, I slowed long enough to grab her wrist. I knew enough to not move someone who's been injured. Understood that she could have suffered a neck or spine injury from the initial blast, and that moving her could make the damage worse. But if I didn't get us clear of the fire, we were both going to be burned to death. I didn't even consider not moving her.

Holding tight to her wrist with one hand, and the suitcase with the other, I dragged her unconscious form behind me as I headed for the corner of the hangar. Making the turn, the tall, metal structure shielded us from the searing heat and the air instantly cooled. Still moving, I pulled her to the midpoint of the wall, putting the majority of the large building between us and the inferno.

Dropping the suitcase, I came to a stop and leaned over Julie. It was pitch black in the shelter of the hangar, and I couldn't see anything. Carefully, I reached out and touched her body. Gently, I moved my hands over her limbs, afraid at any moment I'd feel a deformity that would mean a broken bone.

Both legs felt fine, and I fumbled around until I was able to check her arms. Also good. I began working my way down her torso from her shoulders, tentatively pressing lightly on her ribs, then placed my hand flat on her abdomen. If she had any damaged organs, I might be able to tell by feel.

But that would mean she was bleeding internally, and there wasn't anything I could do to help. I snatched my hands away in surprise when she suddenly spoke from the darkness.

"If you grab my tits, I'm going to kick your ass," she said, then slowly sat up with a groan.

I helped her, a small amount of reflected firelight allowing me to see a grimace of pain on her face. We needed to get away from here. The explosion and fire would almost certainly have been noticed, and emergency crews were probably already on the way. We didn't have much time. But what about the helicopter?

Was it hanging around, waiting to finish us off? Was it possible they had a third missile? Hell, they'd obviously had a second one. There was no reason to think they couldn't have a third. But maybe they wouldn't want to stick around and risk being seen.

This wasn't exactly a third world battlefield or even the empty Arizona desert. We were only a couple of hours' drive from the nation's capital, and they'd just blown up a jet sitting at an airport. The response was going to be massive. No, I was pretty sure they'd probably already gotten the hell out of the area. And that's exactly what we needed to do.

"Can you stand?" I asked. "We need to get out of here before the cops and fire department start showing up."

"I'm OK," Julie said, extending her hands for me to help her up.

I grasped them and pulled slowly, not wanting her to get to her feet too fast. Despite the caution, she swayed dangerously, and I grabbed her shoulders to steady her and keep her from crashing back onto the ground.

"I'm fine," she said a few moments later.

I relaxed my grip but didn't move my hands. If she wasn't fine, I didn't want her falling. But she was apparently good to go. Reaching up, she took my hands in hers and removed them from her shoulders.

"Really, I'm OK," she said. "How are we going to get out of here?"

"Have to find a car," I said, bending and grabbing the suitcase.

One of the wheels on the bottom had been torn off, and it wouldn't roll along behind me. Slapping the handle into place, I picked it up and headed for the far side of the hangar with Julie right behind me.

The building separated the tarmac from a small parking lot. It was empty. Coming to a stop, I turned a slow circle, surveying the area. Not a single vehicle to be found.

"What now?" Julie asked, then squeezed my arm and pointed to the left.

Headlights were approaching. Fast. Grabbing her hand, I led the way to a thick hedgerow that bordered the side of the parking lot. It was only about five feet tall, and we had to duck behind the dense foliage to conceal ourselves from the new arrival.

I peered over the top, watching as a Ford Explorer turned into the parking lot with a squeal of tires. It screeched to a stop, and a man jumped out and ran a few steps towards the tarmac before coming to a halt and staring at the burning aircraft.

"Hear that?" Julie whispered.

A moment later, I did. Sirens. Faint, but growing closer by the second. Any moment, cops and firemen were going to descend on the scene, and the chances of staying undetected were very slim. Besides, we were on the clock and didn't have time to hide. We needed to move.

"Stay here," I whispered.

Leaving the suitcase with Julie, I ran around the end of the hedge and came up behind the man. He'd left the driver's door of the Explorer open, the dome light illuminating the interior. As I passed the vehicle, I glanced inside to make sure he was alone. Glad to see he was, I drew the pistol and stopped ten feet behind him.

"I need your vehicle," I said in a loud voice.

His head snapped around in surprise, his eyes going wide when he saw the weapon in my hand.

"Take it," he raised his hands in a protective gesture. "Just don't hurt me!"

"FBI," I said, holding out one of the ID's I'd taken off the two agents at Julie's apartment. "This is an urgent matter of national security. I need you to get in and drive me out of here. Now. Let's go!"

His mouth was still open in shock as he stood immobile, staring at the badge case. The sirens were growing louder, and it was only a matter of seconds before they would be close enough to see us.

"Now!"

I shouted at him and pointed the pistol directly at his face. He gulped, then nodded and began walking forward. I stepped back, keeping some space between us, shouting for Julie to get in the Explorer. She came at a run, raising the back gate and tossing the suitcase in. The man had paused when he saw her appear out of the dark, but I barked at him and guided him to the rear passenger door.

"I thought you wanted me to drive," he said in a shaking voice.

"Get in," I said, noticing Julie running towards the burning plane.

"What are you doing?" I shouted at her.

"My purse," she yelled back, throwing her arm up to shield her face from the blistering heat.

She ran to the corner of the hangar and scooped the bag off the ground where it had wound up after the explosion. Racing to where I stood, she headed for the front passenger seat.

"No," I said. "In back, behind the driver's seat. Keep your eye on him while I drive."

She ran around the back and jumped in, pistol in her left hand so it was as far away from the man as she could get it in case he decided to try and disarm her. I jumped behind the wheel, the sirens now so loud I didn't understand why I couldn't see the approaching vehicles.

Slapping the Explorer into gear, I cut the wheel and hit the gas. We screamed through a tight turn and approached the road. To the left I caught a glimpse of red and blue strobes through thick trees. Turning right, I shut off the lights, so there were no taillights to give us away, and floored the SUV's accelerator.

We roared into the darkness. A couple of seconds later, bright headlights and flashing emergency beacons appeared in the mirror. They were close enough for the Ford to be visible, but I was fairly confident all eyes were on the flaming wreckage of the jet.

I nearly turned us over when a sharp curve suddenly appeared. Driving fast at night, without lights, is a dangerous endeavor. Somehow, I got the vehicle under control without killing us. Glancing in the mirror I could see the glow of the fire over the tops of the trees that lined the road, but we were out of a direct line of sight to the airport.

Turning the lights on, I slowed and took a deep breath. Ahead, a narrow ribbon of asphalt disappeared into the darkness, dense forest pressing in on both sides of the road. Soon another curve came up. This time, I was able to see it, slowing enough to negotiate the turn without any dramatics.

"What's going on? Who the hell are you people?" The guy in the back seat asked.

"FBI," I said in a strong, authoritative voice. "I apologize for frightening you, but this is an emergency."

"Fine," he said. "Pull over and let me out. The car's yours. Take it. I don't want nothin' to do with whatever's going on!"

"What's your name?" I asked, meeting his eyes in the mirror.

"Trip. Trip Cummins," he said after a pause.

"Well, Mr. Cummins, I'm afraid you're going to have to come with us for the moment. That was our plane that blew up. We're trying to stop some terrorists who are planning to attack Washington, and we may need your help."

"My help? Look, mister. I'm just the assistant administrator of a hospital. Was on my way to work when I saw the fire. I can't help you."

"Yes, you can," I said. "And the first thing I need is for you to tell me how to get to DC from here."

"You're FBI, and you don't know how to get to DC?" He asked in disbelief.

"I've been there," I said. "But I'm assigned to the west coast and always fly in. I have no idea where I am other than west of the city. Now, which road do I need to take?"

He was quiet for so long I thought I was going to have to ask again. Finally, he heaved a big breath and gave me directions to a highway. We made a series of turns, each new road slightly wider than the last, then came to US Highway 50.

"Go east," he said. "This'll take us right into DC."

I glanced down at the dash before turning, not happy to see the gas gauge flirting with the E. Ahead, a large truck stop lit up the whole side of the road, and I headed for it. Pulling in, I bypassed several idling big rigs and stopped at a row of pumps designated for passenger cars.

Turning the engine off, I twisted around and looked at our unwilling passenger.

"I need your credit card, Mr. Cummins," I said.

"What? Are you kidding me? You don't have a credit card or any money to buy gas? What kind of FBI agent are you?"

"I do have a card, as well as cash. But I don't want to use my card and don't want to go inside to pay with cash."

I tried to put the right condescending tone in my voice. The tone of a federal agent talking to a citizen.

"Here," Julie said.

We both turned to see her holding a hundred-dollar bill out towards him. His eyebrows went up in surprise, but he didn't reach for it.

"Take it," she said. "Gas can't cost more than fifty bucks to fill this thing up. Consider the rest a nice profit for your inconvenience."

After a long stretch of silence, he leaned to one side and pulled his wallet out of a back pocket. Taking the cash, he slipped it inside before handing me a Visa card. I stepped out and swiped the card, then filled the Ford's tank. I made sure to retrieve the receipt and handed it and the card back when I was behind the wheel again.

"I've helped you out. Stay on 50 and it'll take you straight into DC. Why don't you just let me out here?"

"Mr. Cummins, I wish I could," I said, starting the engine and shifting into drive. "But I can't have you calling anyone."

"You're not FBI," he said, a note of certainty and resignation clear as he spoke. "Don't want to use your card and don't want to go inside where a security camera would get your picture. What the hell's going on? You going to kill me?"

"If I was going to do that, I'd have done it back at the airport," I said, pulling out onto the road. "Now, relax and enjoy the ride. This will all be over in a few hours, and you'll be on your way, safe and sound."

Merging onto the highway, I began driving east. The horizon had been lightening for a while, and as I crested the onramp, the sun peeked above the low, forested hills. It was dazzlingly bright, and I wished for a pair of sunglasses as I drove in the heavy traffic heading towards the capital.

I looked at my watch once I was comfortably in the middle lane and moving with the flow of morning commuters. -13:27:11 until the President was assassinated.

44

The drive into DC took every bit of three hours. Traffic was bad. Worse than bad. Frequently we'd come to a complete stop for minutes at a time. When the flow resumed we'd cover several miles, never seeing anything to explain why. And the closer we came to the capital, the more often it happened.

I'm not patient by nature, and the stop and go of the congested highway was almost more than I could take. But, we finally made it. Once we crossed the beltway, the large freeway that circles DC, traffic improved slightly. We would only slow to five miles an hour instead of coming to a full stop.

With all the time spent crawling along, I'd taken the opportunity to figure out the navigation built into the Ford's dash. I'd used it to pinpoint the restaurant where the attack would occur. Gratefully exiting the highway, I worked across the madness of the surface streets that is DC. Finally, I turned a corner, and two blocks ahead was the building.

I had been worried about being able to cruise the area slowly enough to check it out without being noticed by the Secret Service teams, who were almost certainly already in place. But I didn't need to be concerned. Traffic was clogged with far too many cars. The area was defined by bars, restaurants and nightclubs, and it seemed every one of them had a double parked box truck in front, making a delivery.

It took nearly twenty minutes to cover the two blocks, and I was able to scope out the entire street. Low buildings built tight against each other. Lots of rooftops and plenty of narrow alleys. Too many places for a ground team to set up. I needed to walk the area to get a better feel for it.

I remembered what laser designators looked like from my time in Iraq. I'd seen a few of the Special Ops guys heading out on missions, frequently toting one along. They're not big, but they aren't exactly compact, either. They won't fit in your pocket. More likely, whoever was going to paint the target for the missile launch would have a large backpack or duffel with the device inside.

The bag to carry it wouldn't necessarily pique anyone's interest. That wouldn't happen until it was taken out and set up. Then, anyone who saw it would be looking, wondering what the hell the person using it was doing. That eliminated the possibility of it being deployed at ground level. Too great of a chance of discovery.

Assuming that Carpenter was right and wasn't involved with Johnson and flat out lying, the three Secret Service counter-sniper teams were in the clear. They would be the guys with the best, concealed view of the front of the restaurant, but I was going to take it on faith they hadn't been co-opted by the conspirators. With that in mind, all that was left was a window or door in a building that had line of sight to the target.

Not too close, however, I reminded myself. The ground team would want to be out of the blast radius of the warhead. These weren't radical jihadists that were willing to sacrifice themselves for the furtherance of their cause. These were Americans, probably military or military trained, and they would want to walk away in one piece.

So I was looking for a building with a rear or side exit, and the location for the laser had to be far enough away to ensure a high probability of survival for the ground team. That meant on the opposite side of the street. And it eliminated the two buildings directly across from the restaurant. Both had taken heavy damage, and the crew manning the laser would have discounted them right off.

Dirk Patton

What I needed to do was walk the street. Get a feel for the angles. Get a good look at each of the buildings. I'd been shown a detailed map that included the location of the three Secret Service teams, and I wanted to be sure to identify those as well. While not impossible, I was willing to bet those locations were avoided due to the risk of detection.

Traffic finally opened up, and I cut off a minivan with Kansas plates as I changed lanes. Ahead and to the right I'd spotted a Hilton hotel, and we needed a place to work out of. I also needed to do something with our passenger.

Bypassing the valet stand, I turned into the underground parking, drove down a short ramp and found an open spot near the elevator to the registration desk. I would have liked to go farther into the bowels of the structure, but a security gate blocked the way. Probably needed the key card for your room to get it to open.

"What's happening?" Cummins asked fearfully.

Poor bastard probably thought I was taking him somewhere that I could put a bullet in his head and dump the body without being noticed. I turned off the engine and looked into the back seat, meeting his eyes.

"Relax," I smiled, hoping I wasn't overdoing it. "Nothing is going to happen to you, but I need one more thing. Do this, and I hand your keys back and thank you for your help. All I ask is that you agree to not tell anyone about this. Like I said, it's a national security matter, and we can't have it being discussed."

"I don't know anything, so you don't have to worry about me," he said, hope flaring in his eyes. "What do you want me to do?"

"You and I are going upstairs to registration. You rent a room in your name, with your credit card. Once you have the key, we go up to the room to check it and make sure the key works. If it doesn't, it will need to be you that asks for a replacement. If it's all good, we come back down here. I hand you the car keys, you give me the room key, and she and I are gone. You drive away. And, agree to keep your mouth shut."

"That's it?" he asked, not trying to hide his disbelief.

"That's it," I smiled and nodded, pulling out some of the cash liberated from the two FBI agents I'd left in Julie's apartment. "Here's three hundred bucks. That should more than cover the cost of the room, and hopefully, compensate you for the inconvenience."

He stared at me for a long pause, turning to look at Julie. She met his eyes, nodded and smiled. And, in what I thought was a masterful touch, tucked her pistol away so that he no longer felt he was being held at gunpoint.

"I want to ask what the hell's going on, but it's probably better that I don't know. Isn't it?"

"Yes, Mr. Cummins. It is. Now, will you help us with this final thing? Please?"

"What the hell," he said after a moments thought. "Why not?"

I motioned for Julie to stay in the car and climbed out, waiting for him to join me. We rode the elevator up, stepping out into the lobby. A large sign with an arrow pointed the way to registration, and we walked in the indicated direction. When we were a hundred feet from the large desk, I placed my hand on his arm to stop him.

"Mr. Cummins, I understand this is all very odd. It is for me too. I just wanted to convey the Bureau's thanks for your assistance. Because of your help, I have a chance to stop a terrorist attack and root out a traitor in our midst."

I'd been thinking and decided I needed to give him a little bit of a patriotic push, and an acceptable explanation for why I needed him to use his credit card.

"So that's why…"

I made a production of shushing him, giving him a look that said I'd just revealed inside information. He nodded and smiled, straightened his back and marched up to the registration counter.

As I watched him approach the young woman standing behind it and ask for a room, I could tell by his body language that he'd bought in to my ruse. Another lesson from the con-man instructor. Give people a reason to want to help you. I'd treated him well, been polite, and now I'd let him get a peek behind the curtain. He'd responded exactly the way the instructor had described.

A couple of minutes later he walked back over to where I was waiting, plastic key card in his hand. He held it up and smiled as he approached.

"No problems?"

I lowered my voice and looked around, playing my role to the hilt. He saw what I was doing and mimed my actions by speaking quietly and checking around himself.

"Not at all. Room 1223. Let's go check it out."

He was fully committed now, leading the way to the elevator and pushing the up button. It took a while for one of the two doors to slide open, and we had to step back to allow a pair of harried looking parents with four children to exit. The mother had a fistful of tourist brochures, and when I looked at her, my heart skipped a beat.

It was Monica. A little older and a little thicker after having more kids. Her hair was cut differently, but there was no mistaking her. And she was still a beauty. I looked for Manny, her son from a relationship before she and I had met, but didn't see him. Doing the math, I realized he was probably old enough by now to either be working or in college. Or the Army. Too old to join his young siblings on a tour of Washington DC.

Monica saw me looking and smiled a greeting, then had to turn away when one of the boys pushed his little sister against the elevator door. She scolded him in rapid fire Spanish before smiling and kissing him on the forehead and scooping the little girl into her arms. Her husband herded the other children past, a boy of about 10 or 11 sulking and staring at an iPhone. He was dragging behind, on purpose. Monica turned to him as she followed her husband into the lobby.

"Roberto, keep up," she smiled and reached out to wrap her free arm around his shoulders.

I was rooted in place, staring at the woman I had loved and the boy who was already nearly as tall as her. She pulled him close and together they hurried to catch up with the rest of the family.

Roberto? Could it be? He was the right age. And as I watched, I noticed his skin was several shades lighter than his mother's, and his hair wasn't as thick as either of the adults. I glanced at her husband, who was obviously of Latin descent. He was a darker bronze than Monica. I'm not a geneticist, but...

"You OK? Look like you just saw a ghost," Cummins said, tugging on my arm to pull me into the waiting elevator.

Without taking my eyes off of Monica and Roberto, I followed Cummins into the car. Just before the door shut, I saw her move next to her husband and playfully bump his hip with hers.

He looked at her, smiled and leaned close. The last thing I saw before the doors slid shut was their lips meeting in a kiss.

It took me a moment to get over the impact of seeing Monica and a boy who I'd already convinced myself had to be my son. Finally, I shook my head and turned to see Cummins watching me intently.

"Fine," I said. "That family just reminded me of something."

I probably should have kept chattering as we rode up. Thanked him again for his assistance. Praised his sense of duty to America. That's what the con-man would have done. But I was too unsettled after seeing Monica.

The elevator dinged to announce we had arrived at the twelfth floor, and I forced myself to focus on the moment. Stepping out, I looked around and let Cummins lead the way to the room. I stood close behind him, reaching into my jacket pocket, as he inserted the key card.

The lock beeped and a small light changed from red to green. He withdrew the card, turned the handle and pushed inside. I was right behind him, withdrawing one of the syringes labeled M99 that I'd found in the back of the FBI Suburban. Lifting it, I stuck the hard plastic needle cover in my mouth, bit down and pulled it free.

Taking one quick step, I reached around Cummins and placed my hand on his forehead, pulling his head tight against my shoulder. He tensed and reached for my hand, but the needle was already in the side of his exposed neck. I pressed the plunger home and withdrew it.

His arms went limp, hands falling to his side. Two seconds later his entire body collapsed against me, and I dropped the syringe and lifted him into my arms. He wasn't a big man, but he wasn't light either. Heading for the sofa, I glanced around and saw that we were in a two-bedroom suite. Changing directions, I carried him into one of the bedrooms and gently placed him on the bed.

I spent a few minutes making sure his neck was straight, and his airway wasn't compressed. I removed his shoes and placed them on the floor next to the bed and started to cover him with the sheet, but paused. Could the M99 drug make him sick?

To be safe, I rolled him onto his side so if he did throw up he wouldn't inhale and drown in his own vomit. Pulling the sheet to his shoulders,

I closed the bedroom door behind me and headed downstairs to get Julie.

45

"What the hell was that all about? Going back for your purse." I asked when we were in the room.

I hadn't wanted to discuss anything in front of Cummins, and to her credit, Julie had picked up on this and stayed silent. Now, we had a few things to go over before I took a walk.

"My purse."

She looked at me like that explained everything. I stared back at her and shrugged my shoulders.

"My wallet, ID, credit cards, cash, phone. Everything was in there," she said, shaking her head like I was a dullard.

"Your phone," I said, realizing the mistake we had made. "Give it to me!"

She reached in her purse and pulled it out, pressing a button and staring at the screen.

"Sorry, it's dead," she said, holding it up for me to see. "I don't remember the last time I charged it, and looking things up on the internet while we were on the plane must have drained it."

I took it from her hand and tapped the screen a couple of times with my finger. It stayed dark. Turning it over, I popped the cover off the back and removed the battery before pulling the SIM card.

"What are you doing?"

"This is the FBI. They froze your account and tracked us to that airstrip in the middle of nowhere. If they can do that, they can locate your phone. It's a good thing for us that the battery did die, or we might not have made it here."

The look on her face told me she understood exactly the error we'd made. Only sheer luck had kept us from driving around Virginia and DC with a phone constantly transmitting our location. Well, as a friend of mine used to say, I'd rather be lucky than good.

I put the pieces of the phone next to a large, flat screen TV. Opening the suitcase, I began unloading weapons and placing them on a small, round table near the windows that had a partial view of the distant Capitol building. Once the bag was empty, I took off my jacket and removed all of the other items I'd taken from the FBI.

While I did this, Julie opened the door to the bedroom where I'd put Cummins. The first question she'd asked when I went downstairs to get her was what I'd done with him. Now, she was checking on him, disappearing into the room for a couple of minutes. When she came back out, she met my eyes and nodded that he was OK.

"So, what do we do now?" She asked, looking at the array of weapons on the table.

"I want to take a walk," I said. "Get a good feel for that street and try to figure out where the ground team is set up."

"You should look at it on Google Earth, first," she said.

I looked at her blankly. Had no idea what the hell she was talking about.

"Google Earth? Satellite photos of the entire planet?" She spoke as if by phrasing it as a question I'd suddenly know what she was talking about.

"I told you where I've been for more than a decade," I said. "I wasn't making that up, and I really have no clue what the hell you're talking about."

"Sorry," she said, walking over to the suitcase and picking up her laptop.

She messed with it for a bit, getting up and looking at the paper the front desk clerk had given to Cummins when he checked in. Reading something off it and typing it in, she sat back with a smile a few minutes later and patted the sofa cushion next to her. I sat down and looked at an amazingly crisp overhead image of a street lined with buildings.

"Is that real time?" I asked, amazed.

"No. I don't know if there's any way to tell when the pictures were taken, but Google runs cars all over the place with big camera setups on the roof. Their goal is to photograph every street. Don't know how close they are to completing that, but I've yet to see a large city that didn't have every single road already imaged."

I leaned close and peered at the screen. Thinking, I was able to remember the three rooftops where the Secret Service was stationed. I pointed them out, and Julie clicked her mouse and marked each one with what looked like an upside-down red teardrop.

"OK, I've already eliminated these two buildings."

I tapped the screen to indicate the ones directly across from the restaurant. A moment later, two more teardrops decorated the image.

"Has to be a location with direct line of sight to the restaurant. Right?" She asked.

"Yes," I said.

"And the missile impacted the center of the front wall?"

I nodded.

"OK. Let's try something to speed this up."

Julie clicked a bunch of times, opening menus and selecting options faster than I could keep up. Soon she had a blue dot placed at the base of the center of the front wall of the target. Still clicking, she drew a straight line directly across the street from the point she'd created.

"So, we eliminate these two buildings," she began. "We can also eliminate anything on the same side of the street. That leaves..."

She used the mouse cursor to begin dragging the end of the line farthest from the dot. Moving it up and down the street, she identified five buildings. Everything else was at an impossible angle to the target.

Of the five possibilities, two were structures that had already been tagged as having Secret Service on the roof. Of the remaining three, one was a restaurant, one was a boutique coffee house, and the final was an office building.

"It almost has to be the office building," I said. "The restaurant and coffee shop are too public. Can you turn on that view that lets me see the front of the building?"

"Street view," she reminded me, clicking and pulling the image around until we had a clear shot of the entire front of the structure.

A door at the midpoint of the building. On either side, half a dozen windows. Most of them had the name of the business occupying the suite stenciled on the glass that faced the street. Twelve windows. Nine of them were obviously occupied, but just because the other three weren't labeled didn't mean they weren't in use.

Julie zoomed and began making notes on a pad of hotel stationery. She wrote down the name of each business, then opened a new browser window. In the search box, which I noticed was Google, she typed in the name of the business at the top of her list. Within seconds, we had results, and she scanned them quickly.

Realizing I was out of my depth, I sat back and let her work. She spent almost twenty minutes researching the businesses, then did a final search based on the street address of the building. She clicked on a couple of links, scribbled some more notes, then sat back with the pad in her hand.

"Alright," she said, flipping back to the first page. "An independent insurance agent. Copyright attorney. Two different personal injury lawyers. Credit repair company. Residential alarm systems sales office. That's what's to the right of the entrance.

"To the left is a small publishing company. A public relations firm, but it looks like it's a one-man show. And a CPA. That leaves three offices unaccounted for."

"You're thinking it's one of the empty ones?" I asked, glad to have another head working on this.

"Maybe," she said, lifting her hand and waggling it back and forth. "I looked up the building itself. It's owned by a corporation named New Look Ventures. They're incorporated in Delaware. I tried to follow the ownership back to an individual or individuals, but it's a maze of shell companies. I'm sure there's a way to unravel it, but that's beyond my abilities."

"You said maybe," I prompted.

"Right. Sorry. So here's what's interesting. New Look Ventures purchased the building one month ago. And they paid a premium for it, even though none of these tenants are the type that write a big rent check each month."

"How much?"

"Fourteen million," she said.

"Sorry," I shook my head. "I haven't exactly been following the commercial real estate market. Is that a lot these days?"

"In this economy? With low rent tenants? That alone is a red flag. But check this out. The restaurant, two doors down, which is a much larger building, was bought two and half years ago for less than three million!"

That got my attention. I may have never been more than an Army grunt, a roofer, and an inmate, but I was still smart enough to recognize the smell of the US Government. Basically, unlimited funds when they really wanted to buy something. No one else was dumb enough to overpay for a piece of property by a factor of seven. It was damning, but not quite a smoking gun.

"How long did the previous owner have the building?" I asked.

Julie leaned over the keyboard and typed and clicked some more.

"Thirteen years," she said. "A private individual was the sole owner. Josiah Holmgren."

"Out of the blue, he gets a fourteen million dollar check for a property that's probably worth two million at best," I said. "Anyway to tell if he was trying to sell, or if the buyer came to him with an unsolicited offer?"

Julie shook her head and leaned back, lifting the notepad again.

"I'm sure there is, but I'm not the one to try and figure that out. I'm an office manager for a large real estate company in LA. That's the only reason I know how to look for this stuff. Probably the agents in the office could find out, but I don't have a clue where to start.

"But, here's the final thing I found. You'd think, if you just paid a shitload of money for a building that's one-quarter unoccupied, you'd be trying like hell to lease out the empty offices.

Right? Well, not here. If the owner has them listed, they would have come up when I searched the street address. But nothing other than the property records and a listing of the businesses that are operating at that location."

I sat there and turned over what she was telling me. On the surface, it sure looked suspicious. And what was a fourteen-million-dollar expenditure if it resulted in the death of the President and the Speaker of the House? To the people that operated at that level of government, it was nothing. A pittance in exchange for gaining control of the White House.

"Is there a phone number listed for the owner?" I asked when an idea popped into my head.

Julie clicked a few times before shaking her head.

"No, not the owner. Just the law firm that handled the transaction. I pulled up their website, and they look like a really big deal here in Washington. Their home page has a photo of the senior partner standing next to the President on a golf course."

"Give me their number," I said, stepping over to the hotel phone.

I dialed as Julie read it off the screen. It rang once before being answered by a woman with a melt you in your tracks sultry voice with a slight British undertone. When I could put my brain back in gear, I identified myself as the first fictitious name that popped into my head and explained I was interested in leasing space in one of their client's buildings. I provided the address and was asked to please hold.

While I listened to sappy music, I tried to dispel the image of a naked goddess that the receptionist's voice had conjured up in my head. I had little doubt that was exactly why she had been hired.

It was almost five minutes later before she came back on the line and told me that she had checked with the attorney for that particular client and there were not any offices available at this time. Before I could say a word, she thanked me for calling and disconnected.

"Well?" Julie asked with raised eyebrows when I hung up the phone.

"Nothing definitive," I said. "But there's supposedly no space available."

"Could be true," she said. "One of the other tenants could have rented out the empty offices as their business grew. Probably cheaper than relocating to a larger space."

"OK," I said, thinking. "Or she didn't do anything other than put me on hold long enough to make it seem like she asked someone. Or, our theory is right. Time to take a walk."

"Give me a minute," Julie said. "I haven't been to the bathroom since we left LA."

"I should go alone…" I stopped when she glared at me.

"Are we really going to have this conversation? You're the one that talked me into coming with you. Now that I'm here, I'm not going to sit in a hotel room. It's just a walk.

"Besides, you said you think the Secret Service will already be in place. That means they're checking out everyone that passes through the area. A couple, walking to the coffee house, will attract a whole lot less attention than you by yourself."

"I'll wait," I sighed.

She smiled and disappeared into the unoccupied bedroom after grabbing some items out of the suitcase. I didn't want to tell her, but I was damn glad she had come with me. She was very smart, but also much more thoughtful than I am. Where I would charge in before thinking, she considered all the angles.

Sitting there waiting, I let my mind drift to Monica. I'd managed to push thoughts of her aside while we worked on the problem of where to find the ground team, but with a few minutes alone, the image of her roared back into my head.

And Roberto? Had I gotten her pregnant? Was he my son? If he was, did he even know who his father was? Did he know he'd been sired by a convicted cop killer and drug runner? I hoped she'd never told him the truth. No kid needed to have that weighing them down. Growing up is hard enough without having a father on death row.

Monica looked happy. Happy with her clutch of kids, and with her husband. The man that could have been me. Should have been me. If only...

I stopped myself right there. There was no point in dwelling on the past. Even though I did have access to a time machine, I couldn't go back that far and change things. But, what if I could? Dr. Anholts had been hinting it might be possible. Did I have the right to go back and undo the happy family I'd just seen? Not that if I changed things any of them would ever know, but where did it stop?

What if I could go back twelve years and fix my mistakes? Not go to prison. What's to guarantee that Monica and I would ever be more than friends? Sure, we were heading for more, but how much of that was due to the emotions resulting from the events that transformed my life?

Without me, she'd found someone she obviously loved. Had children with him. Built a life. Apparently a life good enough that they could bring their kids to the nation's capital for an educational vacation. If I messed with the past, those other kids would never be born. The husband, whoever he was, would never meet and marry her. How many ripples across the timeline that couldn't be predicted would that create?

Even if it was possible, I couldn't take that away from her. And I couldn't risk the impact on the present and future. No matter how much I wanted to.

"Are you OK?"

I snapped out of my musings and looked up to see Julie standing in the bedroom doorway. She had changed out of the cargo pants and boots into a lightweight skirt and skin tight, white tank top. Low-heeled sandals were on her feet. Her blonde hair was loose, framing her freshly scrubbed face and falling around her shoulders. I couldn't help the big smile.

"You look terrific," I said without even thinking. It just came out.

I was surprised when she blushed slightly and looked away. She fussed with her purse for a moment before turning back to face me, smiling. I stood, unable to take my eyes off of her.

"I'm great," I said, answering the earlier question. "Shall we go?"

I extended my arm and a moment later she stepped forward and slipped her hand through the bend, resting it on the inside of my forearm. Together, we walked out and headed for street level.

We strolled down the sidewalk, avoiding a couple of homeless men who hit us up for change. I'd thought about passing out some more of the FBI agents' cash but was afraid that if I did, word would get around, and we'd get mobbed by more desperate people looking for money. That would make us stand out, and I couldn't have that happen.

It wasn't that far to the target, and we covered the distance on foot in about a quarter of the time it had taken to drive it earlier. We stuck to the side of the street opposite the buildings I wanted to get a closer look at. Julie kept her hand on my arm, her body close to mine as we walked.

I didn't know if she was playing her role as part of a couple, or not. Perhaps she was enjoying the physical contact as much as I was. Either way, it was exactly how we needed to appear to anyone who might notice us.

We slowed to a stop in front of the restaurant where the President was going to be killed. To any observers, we were reading a small menu posted in an enclosed display case mounted to the exterior wall. Julie was directly in line with it, but I had a clear view of the interior through the heavy, plate glass windows that fronted the street.

Four men wearing dark suits were moving about the dining floor. They were carefully checking over every inch of the room. Two additional, dressed more casually in slacks and polo shirts, were slowly sweeping across the interior with some sort of electronic equipment.

I refocused my eyes to use the glass as a mirror rather than look through it. Turning slightly, I leaned my head close to Julie as if I were talking to her. But instead of whispering something in her ear, I was adjusting the angle of my view to see the roofs of the buildings across the street.

There was a flicker of movement at the parapet on one of them. One that I knew would be the location of a counter-sniper team. Looking back inside, I watched one of the men reach to his earpiece a moment before he turned to look in our direction.

My head was still close to Julie's, and I leaned the final couple of inches and kissed the side of her neck. She stiffened at the intimate contact but didn't pull away.

"They're watching us," I whispered, brushing her ear with my lips. "Smile and laugh like I said something you liked."

There was a momentary pause, then she smiled brightly and turned to look up at me. Withdrawing her hand from my arm, she placed it on the back of my head and pulled me down until our lips met. It may have started as a theatrical kiss for the benefit of the Secret Service, but it immediately became more. And lasted longer than it should have.

I wanted to wrap her in my arms and crush her body against mine. Fortunately, there was still a tiny part of my mind that remembered what we were doing and why. Breaking the kiss, I looked into her eyes for a long moment before smiling at her and straightening up.

Careful to not look into the restaurant again, I turned to continue down the street. Julie put her hand back on my arm and pressed against my side. From the corner of my eye, I could see the man inside the restaurant still watching. Making a production of the gestures, I pointed across the street at the coffee house, then the crosswalk at the next intersection.

Julie nodded and leaned her head on my shoulder. We started walking, strolling like two lovers without a care in the world. After a couple of yards, I heard the restaurant door behind us open. I wanted to turn and look but resisted the urge. I was supposed to be completely absorbed in the beautiful woman on my arm, not worrying about anything else.

We took our time reaching the intersection, pausing for Julie to look in the window of a small shop. A dress that was fabulous on a mannequin caught her eye. She stared at it for a few moments before heaving a sigh.

"Maybe we shouldn't have done this," she said quietly when we reached the end of the block and had to wait for the signal to change so we could cross.

"What?"

I was hoping she wasn't talking about the kiss. Then I mentally kicked myself for getting distracted from the task at hand.

"Walking the area with the Secret Service watching. I keep forgetting you haven't kept up with current technology. They're probably already running our picture through facial recognition software. How many flags is that going to raise?"

Dirk Patton

I thought about what she said for a few moments. Facial recognition had been around before I went to prison, but it was slow and laborious. Now? I knew computer technology had advanced exponentially. They probably already knew who we were.

"I think we're OK," I said. "The part of the FBI that is hunting us doesn't want anyone else to get their hands on us. They aren't going to put any alerts out there. You'll come up as who you are, and I'll come up as a long haul truck driver from Dallas."

"You're sure?"

"No, but it's too late to worry about it now," I said. "If they find something to make them take an interest in us, we're boxed in and on foot. All we can do is what we came here for and hope for the best."

"Don't you think the FBI is already here? Looking for us? They have to know you're trying to stop them."

The light changed, and we stepped into the intersection after I glanced both ways to make sure some idiot wasn't running the red signal. Crossing, we turned onto the far sidewalk, and I moved Julie to my right so I could get a good look at the front of each building we passed.

"I've been thinking about that. There can only be so many agents involved in the conspiracy. Things like this, well, you don't exactly invite every Tom, Dick and Harry to participate. There will be a select few. They've probably known each other for years, or maybe even decades.

"That's great for operational security, but it sucks when you need resources in different parts of the country at a moment's notice. So, you have a good point. There will be some of the people involved in the plot here looking for us, but I think we got here faster than they anticipated. At the moment, they don't even know if we made it off that jet."

We had passed several of the buildings, and a close up and personal look reinforced the opinion I'd reached after looking at the street on Google. Arriving at the coffee house, I held the door for Julie, and we were greeted by the wonderful aroma of roasted beans being brewed.

Three women were hard at work behind the counter, one of them operating the register while the other two busily made the drinks ordered by a short line of customers. We stepped up behind a man of no more than 25, wearing an expensive suit, and waited our turn. He had a phone pressed to his ear, talking a mile a minute. After briefly listening to the conversation, it was clear he worked for a politician from Minnesota.

When it was his turn, he ordered without even looking at the woman behind the register and tossed a five-dollar bill at her before walking away. The look on her face said it all as she picked up the money, put it in the drawer and dropped twenty cents of change into a tip jar.

I had read the menu and already knew what I wanted, but after we stepped up, Julie kept staring at it. My order placed, the woman looked expectantly at her. Waiting. After a bit I prompted her.

"Know what you want?" I asked.

"Trying to decide," she said.

"Didn't take you this long to decide to come with me."

I was teasing and earned myself a sharp elbow in the ribs. She finally ordered I paid with some of my purloined cash, and we moved to a quiet corner to wait for our drinks.

"You don't think they've already counted the bodies on that plane?" Julie asked in a quiet mumble to keep our conversation private.

"That thing was a blast furnace. Jet fuel burns at something like 6,000 degrees. More than hot enough to completely consume a human body. Maybe the fire department got there in time to knock down the flames, but I don't think so. I'll be surprised if there's enough evidence for them to determine if we were on board or not."

"Fine. But what about the helicopter that fired the missile? They probably had night vision. Don't you think they would have seen us?" She asked.

I thought about that for a minute. Replayed the whole scene in my head.

"Maybe not," I said. "We were running for the hangar when it fired. From the far side of the jet. We should have been screened from the helicopter's view at the time. And once that plane went up, it would have washed out the electronics. If they'd stuck around, they would have eventually seen us when we took the Explorer, but I'm pretty sure they got the hell of the area when that missile struck."

Our drinks were ready, and I walked over to pick them up. The young man was still on his phone, stepping forward directly into my path to collect his, which had been sitting waiting for him for almost a minute. I bumped into him, jostling his arm and causing him to nearly drop the phone.

"Watch out, asshole," he barked without even looking at me.

The impulse to twist his little pin head right off his shoulders surged through me, my hands curling into fists. Julie must have recognized the signs as she quickly moved up and grabbed my arm, distracting me. I looked down at her face, the message clear in her eyes. We could not afford to make a scene. Nodding, I smiled my thanks at her and stepped back until Poindexter walked away, still completely oblivious to just how close to a serious beating he had come.

"He's a dick," the young woman who had made our coffees said when I picked them up. "Keep hoping someone is going to kick his ass."

"He has no idea how close he just came," Julie smiled.

She smiled back, and we headed for the door, drinks in hand. Exiting onto the street, we turned left, towards the hotel. And the building we were interested in.

It was near the end of the block, and when we got there, I wanted to turn to check the angle on the front of the restaurant. But I didn't want to be obvious about it.

"When we reach the building, stop and mess with your shoe like something's wrong," I said to Julie. "I want to turn around and look at the target."

We sipped our coffee as we strolled, now holding hands. Julie was on my right, closer to the street. As we approached the suspect building, I took note of the three windows that didn't have any stenciling on the glass. Two of them had blinds tightly drawn, but the third had them rolled open slightly.

When we were in front of the third window, Julie came to a sudden stop and leaned down to examine her right shoe. She had held onto my hand, and I'd continued to walk so that when I suddenly came up against resistance, it looked perfectly natural for me to turn to my right. Directly facing the restaurant, across and down the block.

I released her hand and stood there, like a man waiting patiently for his companion to repair a problem with her wardrobe. My head was tilted slightly down as if I were watching her, but my eyes were cut up as I stared at the target. Line of sight was perfect. Distance was good.

Not too far, but far enough to be clear of the blast radius.

"Good?" Julie asked, still fussing with a strap on her sandal.

"Good," I said.

She straightened, reached out and took my hand, moving close to me again. As we moved past, I cut my eyes to the left without turning. The bottom edge of the window was a foot above the top of my head. That gave the location an elevated view of the street. More importantly, it gave the ground team enough height to not have to worry about the laser being blocked by a car parked at the curb. This had to be it.

At least I was pretty sure this was the right spot. The team was hidden from view, which I knew had to be the case. Carpenter's analysts had reviewed archived satellite images and hadn't been able to find them. The on-site, Secret Service teams hadn't seen them. There was no question that they had to be concealed inside a building, and this one was the best candidate. By far.

Moving beyond the far edge of the structure, a narrow alley ran between it and the adjacent building. It was just wide enough for a truck to pass. I wanted to head down it, look for a rear entrance, but couldn't come up with a way to do so without raising a big, red flag.

Julie had seen my head turn, slowing with me as I took as much time as reasonable to stare down the alley. We'd talked about rear entrances, so she must have guessed what I was thinking.

"The floor plans will be available online," she said, exerting light pressure on my arm to get me moving faster. "I'll be able to pull them up when we get back to the hotel."

Again, I was very thankful she was with me. We'd spent enough time in the area. Any more, and it wouldn't be surprising if a Secret Service agent stopped us to ask questions. Questions we wouldn't be able to answer satisfactorily. Recon was complete. Now, it was time to get the hell out of sight for a few hours.

We held hands for the entire walk back to the hotel. I finally released Julie's when I opened and held the door to enter the lobby. Despite myself, I scanned the entire area, looking for Monica. I was hoping to get a glimpse of her, and Roberto, but was glad when I didn't. The last thing I needed was to get distracted, thinking about what could have been.

Julie was quiet on the elevator ride to our floor, following me down the hall and into the room. I had learned that she wasn't a talker. She didn't feel the need to fill every silence with inane babel. But this was quiet even for her.

"We should check on our guest," Julie said, leading the way to the second bedroom.

Cummins was still sleeping soundly. Quietly closing the door, I walked towards the table where her laptop was, ready to look at floor plans for the building. We had just over eight hours until the missile was fired, and I wanted to be ready. Memorize the layout and prepare to go in and take out the ground team before they could paint the target. But Julie didn't head for the computer. Turning, I saw her standing in the middle of the living room floor.

"Something wrong?" I asked.

"No," she said, shaking her head and taking a couple of steps closer. "I was just thinking we should talk about that kiss outside the restaurant."

"Look. About that," I stammered. "I'm sorry. I kind of got carried away. That wasn't cool on my part, and..."

I stopped, surprised, when she rushed forward and threw her arms around my neck, pulling me down into a deep kiss. It lasted much longer than the first one, and this time, I didn't stop myself from pulling her tight against me. We stood there for nearly a minute, making out like two horny teenagers, grinding our bodies against each other.

When I finally came up for air, she leaned her head against my chest and wrapped her arms tightly around my waist. Giving me a squeeze, she took my hand and stepped away to arm's length. Smiling, she tugged, and I followed her into the bedroom.

An hour or so later, we lay naked in each others' arms. Sweat dampened sheets were twisted around us, not covering any part of her spectacular body. We were both breathing hard from some of the most athletic lovemaking I'd ever experienced. Now, her head was pillowed on my chest, and her leg was thrown across mine. My arm was under her, hand slowly tracing the curve of her exposed hip.

"That's the first time since my husband," she said in a far off voice.

I wasn't sure if I should say anything to that. Was she feeling guilty, or relieved? After a moment, I realized I should say something.

"Thank you," is what I came up with, instantly regretting it and trying to fix it. "I mean, I'm glad it was me. Well, that's not what I mean. I'm... well... fuck! I'm sorry. That's a pretty profound thing, and I wanted to say something nice. Sorry. I'll just say I'm touched and shut the hell up."

Julie had lifted her head to look at me half way through my fumbling speech. When I finished, she looked into my eyes for a moment and began laughing.

"That's why you were the first," she smiled, snuggling her head back in place. "You really are a good guy. I could tell that two minutes after the first time we met. Well, maybe longer than that. Maybe after you quit aiming a rifle at my head."

She chuckled and lifted her hand, tracing her fingertips across my chest and stomach. I shivered at the sheer pleasure of her touch. Turning my head, I kissed her sweaty brow, leaving my lips pressed against her face.

"First time for me in eleven years," I said in a far off voice.

"I could tell. You damn near bent me in half," she teased, flicking my nipple hard enough to send a jolt all the way to my feet.

"I'd say I'm sorry, but I told you I won't lie to you," I said, earning another nipple flick.

"So, what happens now?" She asked after a long silence.

"I stop the assassination, then go after Johnson," I said. "Once that's cleared up, I get you reimbursed, and the director has the horsepower to clear your name of any wrongdoing."

"That's good," she said. "But not what I meant."

"Oh."

"Not exactly the right answer to the naked woman who just screwed your brains out," she said.

Her tone was light, but I could tell I'd hurt her a little bit.

"Sorry," I said. "It's been a while since I had anyone interested in me. I'm not exactly saying the right things."

"Just be honest, and I'll deal with your stupidity," she chuckled.

I laughed with her, squeezing her tightly against me. Thinking about how to answer her question.

"Remember I told you about having to return forward in time?"

She nodded.

"That's going to happen tonight. I'll just disappear from wherever I am. I'll be back in the project facility, and I don't even know where that is. It's on an oil rig, or a modified oil rig, somewhere in the ocean. That's all I know.

"They don't let me have a phone or computer or any way to communicate with anyone. For that matter, up until now there wasn't anyone for me to communicate with. I don't know if I'll ever see you again."

"Do you want to?" She sat up and crossed her legs, looking down at me.

"Is this where I'm supposed to be completely honest?" I asked.

She gave me a warning look before reaching down and firmly grasping my balls in her hand.

"It would be in your best interest to answer truthfully," she smiled.

"Yes, I want to see you again," I said in a firm voice.

"Well, then, we're just going to have to figure something out. I'm not going to be the girl that you banged in a hotel room and forgot about."

"No chance of that happening," I said, reaching up and pulling her down on top of me.

We spent another hour in the bed, exploring and enjoying each other. I think both of us had some demons to exorcise, and I can't speak for her, but for the first time in years, I felt some faint hope for the future. But, first things first.

Finally, we were spent and after a few more minutes of holding each other tightly, we got up. I stepped into the bath and cranked on the water in the shower. Julie joined me, and we soaped each other up. Rinsed off, I stepped out and found two robes hanging from a hook on the back of the door. Handing hers over, I paused when a thought struck me.

"Can I ask a question? And I don't mean it to be offensive, just something that occurred to me?"

"You can ask," Julie said, an expression on her face I hadn't seen before.

"Birth control," I said. "If you haven't been, um, active since your... Um, well..."

"Isn't it a little late to be asking?"

"I'm sorry," I said, feeling like an ass. I'd hurt her again.

"No need to worry," she said, opening the robe she had just donned and exposing her nude body. She pointed at a scar on her lower, left abdomen. "See that? Hysterectomy. Courtesy of some shrapnel from an Al Qaeda IED. I can't have children."

I stared at the jagged, white line on her otherwise flawless skin. Not only had I asked a jerkoff kind of question right after having sex with a woman, but I'd stumbled into an area that was probably very sensitive for her.

"I'm really sorry," I said, hanging my head and pulling my robe's belt tight. "That was a pretty shitty thing to ask."

She looked at me for a bit, then walked to where I was standing without bothering to close her robe. Pressing against me, she slipped her arms around my waist and buried her face against my chest. My arms automatically went inside her robe, holding her bare skin.

"You really are kind of awkward, aren't you?" Her voice was muffled. "It's OK. It was a really touchy subject for me for a while. I felt... I don't know. Incomplete? Less of a woman? Whatever. I've dealt with it. Cried my eyes out. Got drunk and raged at the world. Purged it from my system. I only hope I'm right when I think your question was innocent, and you weren't going into a panic thinking the crazy bitch you just screwed is going to get knocked up and ruin your life."

"Wasn't thinking that at all," I said, laying my cheek on top of her head. "I just have a bad habit of saying the first thing that pops into my head. It was more of a... well, logistical question."

"Logistical?" She stepped back and looked up at me. "My God, you're not awkward. You're a dork! I slept with a dork!"

She began laughing, pulling away as I reached for her and dashing into the living room. I followed, grinning at this amazing woman.

"OK, dork. We need to do some work," she said, closing her robe and cinching the belt tightly.

I joined her on the couch, our hips touching. She began working the laptop and in a few moments had found a diagram of the building on the DC building commission's website. She downloaded the file and opened it, both of us leaning close for a better look.

48

It was a warm evening as I made my way down the alley. I had circled around to the next street behind the building I'd identified as the probable location of the ground team. Following the path I'd mapped out on Google Earth, I had slipped into darkness and come to a stop, listening and watching.

After a few minutes of seeing and hearing nothing, I opened the cheap duffel Julie had purchased in the hotel gift shop. It held my weapons, and the FBI logo jacket I'd taken from the Suburban in California. Slinging the rifle in front of my body, I pulled the jacket on and filled the inside pockets with magazines and the two flash-bang grenades.

Initially, I'd thought about wearing the all black jacket, but Julie had convinced me to wear the other one. Her point, which I acknowledged was valid, was that I was going to be prowling around in close proximity to the President of the United States. Secret Service had snipers on the rooftops. If they so much as got a glimpse of one of my weapons, they'd probably put a bullet in me and ask questions later.

Maybe, if I was wearing an FBI jacket, they wouldn't be quite as quick to shoot. Maybe. But that maybe was what had swayed me. I didn't want to get shot. I just wanted to get this over with, get back to real time and deal with Johnson, then find a way to see Julie again.

Rolling the thin, fabric duffel into a tube, I stuck it in the back of my waistband. Once the ground team was down, I needed to slip out of the area quickly and quietly. Wearing a jacket with FBI on the back in foot-high, yellow letters, with a rifle in my hands, wouldn't exactly be stealthy.

Julie and I had gotten into the first real fight of our budding relationship before I'd left the hotel. She'd wanted to come with me. Said I needed someone to watch my back. I'd flatly refused. I had trained for this, she hadn't. It was that simple. Plus, I didn't want to risk losing her to a stray round once the bullets began flying.

She'd argued that she knew how to handle and use a weapon. The Army had trained her well so she could defend herself on the battlefield if necessary. And I agreed that she seemed to be more than competent with a pistol. But she didn't know how to clear a building and mount an assault on a superior force. For that matter, I didn't know if she'd be able to pull the trigger on a man who wasn't actively trying to harm one of us. I knew I could. And would.

So, I'd won the argument. And to my great surprise, she didn't sulk. Didn't stop talking to me or give me a cold shoulder to let me know how unhappy she was. Maybe it was the maturity one gains from being in and near combat, or maybe it was just who she was. Either way, it was another thing in a growing list of things I was finding irresistible about her.

We'd shared a long, passionate kiss on my way out of the hotel room door. Her eyes were damp as our lips parted, and I wondered if she was thinking about the last time she sent her husband off to war. Fortunately, I'm a fast learner and didn't pose that particular question.

Now, I was creeping along in a dark alley in the nation's capital, trying to prevent an assassination that would change the power structure of the country, and possibly even the world. Pausing, I shook my head. I didn't need to be thinking about what would happen if I failed. Failure wasn't an option I could consider as it would almost certainly assure both mine and Julie's deaths.

Refocusing, I took a minute to wait and listen. Traffic sounds. A jet descending for a landing at Reagan. Boisterous voices from the nightclub a few doors down the block. Closer, a rustling from within a large, metal dumpster. A rat, I guessed, starting to move again.

Reaching a cross alley, I hugged the wall and approached the rear door of the building. It was the only way in or out other than the door facing the street. The plans Julie had downloaded were detailed drawings submitted for a remodel a few years ago by the previous owner. I suspected they were still accurate as there was no reason for the new owner to have changed anything. All they needed was an empty office with a view of the target.

The door was a layered slab of steel with a high-security lock. A metal plate covered the gap between the door and jam where the deadbolt was located, preventing a burglar from cutting it with a thin saw blade and gaining easy access. Even if it hadn't been there, I wouldn't have tried to gain entry that way. Too much noise.

A security seal, to indicate the building had been cleared, spanned the door jam above the lock. It was some sort of translucent, high strength plastic with an adhesive backing. The Secret Service seal was printed on the surface, along with ominous warnings against disturbing the device. A small, red LED embedded near the top edge glowed softly. Half a dozen different federal laws against tampering with the unit were cited.

Looking closely, I could see wires and a couple of small circuit boards embedded into the material. In the bottom right corner was a small lock for disarming and opening the seal. I wasn't positive, but I was willing to bet this was both an audible alarm as well as a transmitter. Damaging, or removing it, would probably sound a siren and a signal would be sent to alert the Secret Service.

I paused for a moment, thinking. If the seal was intact, how had the bad guys gotten inside? And how would they get out without triggering an alert? Assuming I was correct about their location, of course. But then if the FBI was involved in this, why was it so difficult to imagine the Secret Service was as well? How hard would it be for the agent responsible for securing the door to let a couple of guys slip inside before he attached the seal? I was too far down this path to start second guessing myself. It was time to find out if I was right.

Dropping to a knee, I checked both directions of the alley and saw nothing moving. I inserted two thin pieces of spring steel I'd cut out of one of Julie's bras into the alarm's keyhole. Part of my training had been how to pick a lock, and while I hadn't gotten what I'd call good, I'd at least learned enough to do it.

Now, I worked as quietly as I could. The first piece of metal was used to manipulate the lock's tumblers and fool them into falling into place the same way a key would. This was the hard part, and it was all by feel.

Several times I thought I had it, but the cylinder wouldn't turn. Keeping at it, it was more than ten minutes later when I felt the last one drop. Holding my breath, I used both hands to rotate the lock. I exhaled a quiet sigh of relief when the seal emitted a soft beep, and the LED changed from red to green. Grasping the edges, I pulled firmly, detaching it from the door and jam. Now all I had to do was pick the deadbolt.

Five more minutes and I had the door unlocked. Slipping the picks into a pocket, I took a moment to stand and release the kinks in my legs from kneeling for nearly twenty minutes. I glanced at my watch while I stretched. 83 minutes. Plenty of time. As long as I didn't run into any problems.

For example, the building itself might very well be alarmed. I pull the door open, and a siren starts wailing. The Secret Service would converge in a hot second. But then, would that be so bad? They would be thorough and clear the building, finding the ground team.

Yes, that would count as a success. The President and Speaker would be saved. But I'd lose the opportunity to gather any intelligence from the men operating the laser. I wanted, needed, to know as much about the conspirators as I could. The more information I had when I returned to real time, the better.

Grimacing, expecting the worst, I carefully turned the knob and pulled the door open a few inches, waiting for an alarm. And waited some more. Gave it a full minute in case there was an entry delay built in so someone arriving could reach a panel and deactivate the system. Nothing.

After a full minute, I pulled the door open far enough to slip through. I closed it gently behind me, locking the knob. I didn't want one of the homeless who populated the area to find an unsecured door and decide they'd found the perfect place to spend the night.

The hallway was dark and musty, smelling of mildew and other things I couldn't identify. Not unusual in an older building in a part of the country as humid as DC. Hell, it was a swamp that was drained when the founding fathers decided to make it the capital. Draining the land didn't do anything to help with the brutal humidity that descended on the area in the spring and summer.

I stayed still, suppressed pistol gripped tightly in my hands. The safety was off, and my finger was indexed along the side of the receiver. I could move it and fire in the blink of an eye, but by keeping it outside the trigger guard, I mitigated the possibility of an accidental discharge. Standing still, I gave my eyes time to adjust as I listened to the sounds of the building.

Quiet. Absolutely quiet. But that didn't tell me anything. A disciplined team wouldn't be making any noise. The last thing they would do is make a sound or show a light and give away that someone was in a location they weren't supposed to be.

Padding silently down the carpeted corridor, I reached the lobby quickly. Two halls extended from either side, six office suites located in each direction. I knew where everything was from studying the floor plan, and I turned right. Passed two rented offices and came to the first empty room.

The door was closed, and I stopped short of it, looking it over. Nothing unusual or out of place. Cautiously, I moved close and pressed my ear against the surface and listened. Gave it a couple of minutes. Muted traffic sounds from the street in front, but nothing to indicate the presence of occupants.

Ignoring it for the moment, I moved on to check the rest of the doors. I didn't want to be farting around trying to get in, and there be a roomful of bad guys just down the hall. Before I entered any of the offices, I wanted to at least look and listen first.

The two remaining suites that were unrented were just as quiet as the first I'd checked. OK, I didn't expect this to be simple. Starting with the one farthest down the hall, I gently tried the knob. I was surprised when it turned easily in my hand. Pistol up, aimed at the slowly widening gap, I pushed the door and stepped in. Empty.

Quietly pulling it closed, I moved to the next suite. Same results. The tension was ratcheting up, and I was sweating as I approached the final door. Standing to the side, just like Ray had taught me, I tried the knob. It didn't turn. Confident I'd found the ground team, I stepped back and rammed my foot into the door just below the knob.

The wooden jam splintered as the door burst into the office. I followed it, pistol up and scanning in tandem with my eyes as I searched for a target. I had come in fast and now pulled to a stop in the middle of the space. Empty. Shit!

All that was left was to check the occupied offices. Maybe I'd been wrong to assume that just because it was rented, the ground team wouldn't use it in favor of a vacant one. Rushing into the hall, I kicked in the first door I came to.

Time for slow and stealthy was past. I'd made too much noise breaking in to the final vacant suite. If the team was in the building, they knew someone was searching. Speed was my friend now. Find them while they were still panicked and put them down.

The rented office I'd just crashed into was empty. Well, not empty of furnishings, but there wasn't a two-man team with a laser designator waiting for me. Sweating heavily, I worked my way through all of the suites. None of them held anything that shouldn't be there. Son of a bitch, where were they?

I checked a communal copy room. The bathrooms. Janitor's storage and a couple of closets without finding anyone or anything. I'd been wrong. This wasn't the location. But where then? There was nowhere else. A laser designator is about the size of a cinder block and has to sit on a tripod because of its weight. There was no way to do that out in the open without immediately being spotted by the Secret Service.

Wandering into one of the offices, I looked across the street at the target restaurant. People were arriving, singly and in pairs. Two Secret Service agents were already bracketing the doors. One of them ran a handheld metal-detecting wand over each person while his partner opened and looked through purses, bags, and briefcases.

I checked my watch. 58 minutes. This was probably the press and minor dignitaries, arriving early, hoping for a good table as close to the President as possible. I doubted they'd have any luck. Someone had probably already laid out a seating chart, and the Secret Service would make sure no one deviated from the plan.

When I looked back up, my blood froze when I saw the man that stepped out of the back of a Lincoln Town Car. I knew that face. He straightened his jacket and turned to help someone out of the back, extending his hand.

When she stood, I instantly recognized her, without even seeing her face. Monica slipped her hand through her husband's arm.

After being quickly checked by the agents, they were admitted to the restaurant.

49

I stood there, gaping at the restaurant. What the hell was Monica doing here? I hadn't really given it any thought when I'd first seen her in the hotel lobby. Chance encounters happen, and I suppose I'd passed it off as just that. But walking into a restaurant where the President was about to have dinner?

Her husband? Could he be some kind of politician? A lobbyist maybe? Then I reset my thinking. Maybe Monica was here because of what she had become. When I'd known her, she was a lead cashier at a Walmart. But a lot can happen in eleven years.

Realizing it didn't matter, I shook my head to clear it. Right now, I needed to get out of the building and figure out where the ground team was. I started to take a step before pausing. Unless there wasn't a ground team. The thought hit me like a slap of cold water.

Carpenter's analysts had believed that the missile had been fired from a helicopter, most likely from over Anacostia Park. I didn't know where that was but remembered him saying it was only a couple of miles away. But, they'd arrived at that conclusion based on the assumption that whoever had done this was worried about operating an aircraft over DC.

What if they weren't worried about it at all? What if they had enough power, and co-conspirators in the right positions of authority, that the investigation could be steered in whatever direction they wanted? If that was the case, fly a Reaper drone overhead, lock on with its targeting systems and fire the missile. There wouldn't be the need for anyone on the ground.

If I was right, there was no way I could stop it. But maybe I could cause enough of an incident that the Secret Service would cancel the President's appearance. Some gunfire a few minutes before he was scheduled to arrive should do the trick. I checked my watch. 53 minutes.

But that was the time remaining until the missile struck! I didn't have any idea what time the President actually arrived. It could be any minute!

I was reaching to open the blinds, intending to use the rifle to start shooting at the empty building across the street, when a sound caused me to spin and raise my pistol. I didn't see anything but was sure I'd heard a soft footstep from the hall. Creeping forward, I cautiously approached the door, pausing at the threshold to listen. Didn't hear anything.

Taking a deep breath, I tightly gripped a small flashlight in my off hand. Stacking my gun hand on top so that the muzzle and beam would be pointed in the same direction, I rolled around the jam as I thumbed the button on the butt of the light. A man froze when I illuminated his face. My face.

"Wait! It's me," he shouted, extending a flattened palm in my direction. He held a suppressed pistol in his other hand, not quite pointed at me. "We don't have much time, and you need to listen."

"What the hell?"

"I'm you," he said. "I just arrived."

"Bullshit," I said.

"No. It isn't. I'm really you, and I'm trying to un-fuck this whole mess, so shut up and listen. Johnson is here, and Julie is about to die! He traced her laptop when she started using it. I don't know how, but he did, and in a very few minutes he's going to put a bullet in her head."

"Then why the hell are you talking to me and not saving her?" I asked, still unconvinced.

Dirk Patton

"Because one of us has to save the President, dumbass! Thirty hours after the VP is sworn in, he announces to the nation that he has evidence the military was behind the assassination and is preparing to seize control of the government. The fucker asks the UN to intervene. They're going to do it! They're going to put foreign soldiers on US soil and disarm our troops!"

"I don't believe you," I said. "I was about to stop the assassination. Start shooting at that empty building across the street."

"You can't stop it," he said, shaking his head.

"There's no way the Secret Service lets the President come to that restaurant after there was gunfire in the area," I said, steadying the pistol on his face. My face.

"Unless the agent in charge, and key members of the detail are part of the plot. You start shooting, and they descend on this building. Bottle you up and keep it quiet until POTUS is inside. Then it's too late."

"No way," I said.

"Listen! You slept with Julie a few hours ago. She told you that you were the first since her husband. You said she was the first in eleven years. She took shrapnel from an IED. Can't have kids because of the injury. If I'm not you, how the hell do I know that?"

As he'd spoken, my head swam. There was no way anyone else could know that. I stared for a moment, then slightly lowered the pistol and started to step farther into the hall.

"You have to hurry! Now! Quit fucking around and go save Julie! I know which agents to target, and I'm going to take them out and stop the assassination."

"Wait," I said, bringing the weapon back up and on target. "If I'm here, how can you be here? And know what you know? It just happened a few hours ago, and I would have had to return to real time between then and now, and I haven't!"

"We have to stop this, and you have to trust me. Save Julie! You need to go. There's no time!"

I didn't know what to believe. How was it possible for him to know what he knew if he wasn't me? But how could it be me? There wasn't a *me* in the future to be sent back. I was still here.

Still, how did he know the intimate details of a private conversation between Julie and me? We'd been alone. Unless someone was listening. Could the room be bugged? Had they tracked us somehow and slipped a microphone inside while we were scouting the restaurant?

"Monica," I said.

"What?"

"Tell me about Monica."

He stared at me for a beat. In the beam of the flashlight, I could see him hesitate. Confused. Trying to come up with a response. I pulled the trigger.

The suppressed pistol spat out a round that punched through his forehead. His head snapped back an instant before his body crumpled to the floor. Stepping forward, breathing hard, I approached cautiously.

If I was wrong, I'd just fucked myself. Killed my future self. But if this had been me, he would have instantly known what I meant when I spoke Monica's name. There wouldn't have been any confusion or hesitation.

Reaching the corpse, I looked down at the face. My face. With a neat, red hole in it. My lifeless eyes staring up at nothing. Leaning down,

I ran my hands over his clothing, retrieving a wallet and a badge case.

I had a pretty good idea who this was, and when I flipped through the two items it was confirmed. The wallet held a Texas commercial driver's license in the name of JR Whitman. But the badge case identified the same person as FBI Special Agent Michael Bering. I'd just killed the undercover agent my new face had been copied from.

He had to be one of Johnson's boys. In on the conspiracy. And if he was here, they knew too much. Had to have the hotel room bugged. There was no other way he knew the things Julie and I had said to each other. If he was here, Johnson might not be far behind. Maybe that was the one truthful thing he'd said.

Shoving his wallet in my back pocket and the FBI ID into my jacket, I rushed back into the first office suite. Ripping the blinds down, I looked for a way to open the window, but it was a solid, fixed pane of glass.

Pausing in thought, I ran back out, grabbed the arm of the man I'd killed and dragged the body into the office. Looking down at my face, another thought occurred to me, and I leaned back and aimed the pistol. When I had it lined up at a sharp angle, I pulled the trigger.

The bullet entered on the side of his left cheek bone, tearing across and obliterating the nose and leaving a gaping hole when it exited through the right eye socket. Maybe I was being paranoid, but I didn't like the idea of leaving my face lying around at a crime scene. Now his own mother wouldn't recognize the ragged mass of pulp.

Stepping back a few feet, I raised the rifle to my shoulder. Aiming at the window, and the building across the street. Flipping the fire selector to full auto with my thumb, I pulled and held the trigger.

The M4 was loud in the enclosed space, quickly spitting out all thirty rounds in the magazine. The glass shattered and I could see puffs of dust where the bullets blasted small craters into the stone façade of my target building. I changed mags and fired another thirty rounds out into the night.

Dropping the expended magazine, I loaded a fresh one and bent over the corpse. Put the rifle's pistol grip in its hand and bent the index finger onto the trigger. With my finger over his, I squeezed and fired a long burst into the walls and ceiling of the room.

Releasing my grip on the dead man's hand, his arm flopped to the floor, and the rifle clattered next to it. Now, when the forensics team checked his hand for burned powder, gunshot residue, they'd find exactly what they were looking for. Confirmation he was the one doing the shooting.

I could already hear sirens and voices shouting from outside as I pounded down the hall. Unscrewing the suppressor from the end of the pistol as I ran, I slipped it into my jacket and pulled out the FBI ID case. I didn't think I could get out of the area before cops and Secret Service converged, but I had a perfectly good FBI badge and ID, with my face on it.

Reaching the back door, I burst through and skidded to a stop when several flashlights blinded me. Voices were screaming, telling me to stop and get on the ground. Fortunately, I'd had the foresight to stick the pistol in my waistband, so they didn't see a suspect waving a weapon around and immediately open fire.

"FBI!" I shouted, extending my arm and holding the ID high in the air. "One shooter down inside, but there's another in the area. Did you see him?"

"On the ground!" A voice commanded from behind one of the lights.

"I'm FBI you fucking idiot," I screamed back, waving the badge case. "Did you see the other shooter or not?"

It was quiet for a beat.

"Keep your hands in sight!"

A shadow moved in front of one of the lights and carefully approached. A man, dressed in black body armor, Kevlar helmet, and goggles, cautiously walked up and took the badge case from my hand. He clicked on a small light and examined it for several seconds, looking up to compare my face. Tilting it to the side, he checked for a holographic image that all but ensured it was genuine, then handed it back.

"He's legit," he shouted, and all but one of the lights went dark.

"Secret Service," he said as three men rushed past me into the building, rifles at their shoulders. "What are you doing here? And how did you get past our seal?"

"Been tracking a couple of white supremacists for a few days. Followed them here. Seal was already off when I went in. They must have picked it before I arrived. Got one of them, but the other ran when the shooting started. You should have seen him."

I was making it up as I went along. Pulling the story out of my ass. But it was a good one. Explained the gunfire, and placed a second shooter loose somewhere in the area.

The man raised his hand and activated a small radio.

"Emergency scrub Ramrod! Repeat. Emergency scrub Ramrod!"

"What's that?" I asked, already knowing the answer.

"POTUS was scheduled to have dinner at a restaurant just down the block," he said, looking up when the three agents who had gone into the building appeared at the door.

"One down, boss," one of them reported. "M4 next to his hand. Shot in the head."

"Me," I said, confessing to shooting the man. "Now I need to find this other asshole. Could use help. My backup is still five minutes away."

He nodded, placing another call on the radio before bringing his team into a tight circle. I kept pulling ideas out of thin air, coming up with a description of a man who didn't exist. Maintaining the persona of a federal agent taking control of a situation, I sent them off in three different directions. I took the fourth, which just happened to be the way back to the hotel.

One of the agents was detailed to remain at the building, securing the scene. He moved through the door, taking up station in the lobby. The rest of us split up, heading in our assigned directions.

50

I moved through the alley as more and more sirens sounded all around the area. Initially, I'd planned to remove the FBI jacket and try to blend in, but rethought that idea. There were about to be a few hundred cops and federal agents descend on a several block area of the city.

And thanks to my story, every single one of them would be looking for a white male about the same age as me. Since every pair of eyes would zero in on adult males with white skin, I decided to maintain the role of an FBI agent participating in the search. And it was a good thing I did.

As I emerged from the end of the alley, a DC Metro police car swerved to the curb in front of me, spotlight momentarily freezing me. They saw the jacket and ID I held up, waved at me and roared away. Turning, I set off for the hotel at a fast walk.

All up and down the street, police cars were pulling to a stop, roof lights flashing. The cops driving them jumped out and began checking each pedestrian that was in their immediate area. I mimed what they were doing as I walked, carefully looking at each person I passed.

Halfway to the hotel, I came to a sudden stop when I recognized a face that shouldn't be there.

"What are you doing here?" I asked, stepping close to Ray.

Alarm bells were going off in my head. What the hell was he doing here? Was he in on it too? Had I made a mistake talking to him and trusting him? Had he been sent along as backup, to kill me?

My hand moved to the pistol, but his shot out and gripped my shoulder. He pressed with his thumb, my arm immediately going numb and failing to respond to the command from my brain to draw the weapon.

"Relax," he said. "Carpenter sent me. I'm here trying to intercept Johnson. He killed the director and got off the rig."

"Get your fucking hand off me," I said, trying to twist away.

He pressed harder and a bolt of white hot lightning shot through my shoulder and into the back of my head. I gasped in pain, reaching for the pistol with my other hand. Ray shifted his grip to my neck and pushed on another spot. Now I was completely paralyzed, unable to do anything other than stand there and breathe.

"I'm not your enemy," he said in a calm voice. "I'm here for Johnson. Carpenter tracked him after he fled the rig. He's here in DC. In this area, but I haven't been able to locate him."

"I know where he is," I said, surprised I was able to speak.

"Where?"

"My hotel room. He's going to kill the woman I'm with."

"Then let's go get the cocksucker," Ray said, releasing his hold.

All feeling instantly returned, as well as control over my body.

"You've got to teach me how to do that," I said, deciding to accept him at face value.

I resumed my fast walk to the hotel and Ray fell in beside me. More police screamed by, slowing to check us out before continuing on when I raised the ID.

"What did you do?" he asked.

"Stopped the assassination," I said. "They're looking for a white supremacist who's supposed to be running around with a rifle. Best I could do."

"What assassination?" He asked.

I came to a stop in the middle of the sidewalk before realizing that in his timeline the attack hadn't happened yet. And wouldn't.

"The reason I'm back here," I said, walking again. "Too long to explain."

Ray nodded, and we covered the rest of the distance to the hotel in silence. At the entrance, I pushed through a small crowd of guests and employees who had gathered outside to see what was going on down the block. Several of them stared at the FBI jacket, but I ignored them and walked into the lobby.

Running to the elevator, I held my ID out and told a small group of businessmen to wait for the next car. We stepped inside, and I pushed the button for the twelfth floor. As soon as the doors slid shut, I drew my pistol and screwed the silencer back on. Ray produced a suppressed pistol from beneath his shirt, dropping an extra long magazine to check the load. Satisfied, he slapped it home and looked at me.

"We drop him on sight," he said.

"No argument here."

We stepped to either side as the elevator arrived at 12. It dinged, and the doors slid open. Our pistols were already up, each of us aiming at an angle into the hall, the sides of the elevator protecting our bodies in case anyone started shooting at us. The hall was empty.

Ray nodded, and I stepped through first. He followed, flowing around the corner and covering our backs. I led the way down the hall, stopping short of the door to the room Julie was in.

"Just like we practiced," he mumbled near my ear.

I had stopped on the handle side of the door. If it suddenly opened, the person inside the room wouldn't be able to see me without sticking their head all the way through the opening and looking to the side.

Fumbling in my pocket, I found the room key. Extending my arm, I slowly inserted it into the slot on the lock and pulled it back out. There was a soft beep, the tiny LED changed to green, and a click sounded as the bolt released. Turning the handle, I rolled around the jam and slammed the door open with my shoulder.

I came in fast, dropping low as I entered, pistol in both hands extended in front of my body. Scanning left, like Ray had taught me. He came in on my heels and broke to the right. The living area was empty, and both bedroom doors were closed.

Ray glanced at me and raised his eyebrow in a question. I pointed at the door to the room I'd put the unconscious man in and we padded across the thick carpeting and stacked up to the side. We repeated the entry we'd performed at the main door, and I came to an abrupt halt when I saw the body on the bed.

It was Cummins, right where I'd left him. But there hadn't been blood staining the white pillow the last time I'd checked on him. And there hadn't been a bullet hole in the back of his head.

Ray was signing for me to provide cover while he cleared the bathroom, but I ran out of the room. Ran straight to the other bedroom door, turning the knob and bursting through. I dropped the pistol and dashed forward, falling to my knees at the edge of the bed.

Julie lay on her back, blood stained hair fanned across a pillow. Her face was swollen and bruised from a beating. Her big, blue eyes stared lifelessly at the ceiling.

51

"Send me back!"

I began shouting the instant I arrived on the dais. It had been an excruciating wait for the return to real time, hiding in the hotel room. I'd spent several hours with Julie's body cradled in my arms. Working through the anger and emotion. Trying to get it under control so I could operate effectively when I had the opportunity.

Ray had assured me he would get the room cleaned up, removing any evidence of the presence of any persons other than Julie and Cummins. There was nothing we could do with their bodies, and if I couldn't change past events, they would have to be left for houseckeeping to discover.

I wasn't happy. Not at all. Wasn't thinking clearly. Thankfully, Ray had sat me down and calmed me. Or at least focused me. Got me ready for the task ahead.

Pounding on the curved glass in impatience, I squeezed through and sprinted for the door as soon as it began opening. The two Marine guards looked at me in surprise as I raced past them, heading for the control room.

Bursting in, I ran to where Dr. Anholts and Carpenter stood. Both of them stared at me, taken aback at my entrance.

"Send me back to DC! Now!" I screamed at them.

"What happened?" Carpenter asked.

"Johnson killed someone I have to save," I said, trying to calm myself. "I stopped the assassination but lost some people. I can go back, save them, and get Johnson."

"What assassination?" Carpenter asked.

"The President," I shouted. "Sorry. It's on my chip, but we don't have time. You've got to send me back."

"We need you to save the director," Dr. Anholts said. "Agent Johnson killed him before leaving. Ray went after him, but we haven't heard from him."

"I just left Ray," I said in a rush. "He didn't find Johnson. Our only chance is to go back, and I'll stop him."

"Wait. Slow down," Carpenter said, holding both hands up. "The director is the priority."

"Bullshit!"

I snarled and moved forward. Carpenter saw the expression on my face and took a step back.

"Mr. Whitman. Please," Dr. Anholts stepped between us and looked me in the eye. "You're not thinking clearly. If we send you back to a point where you can save the director, you can stop Agent Johnson before he leaves the facility. If he never leaves the facility, he can't harm the people you're trying to save."

I stared at her, processing what she'd said. Letting out a long breath, I nodded my head when I realized she was right. If Johnson never left the rig, he couldn't hurt Julie.

"OK, fine. Let's go," I said, impatient.

"You should watch the recording," Carpenter said, stepping closer now that I didn't seem to want to rip his throat out. "See what happened so you know what you're walking into."

After a moment, I nodded in agreement. Impulsiveness and lack of preparation had gotten me into enough messes in my life. Maybe it was time to start acting like an adult.

I followed Dr. Anholts and Carpenter to the conference room. Nervous energy made me want to pace while he queued up the surveillance video, but I forced myself to take a seat.

Sitting there, all I could think about was Julie. The last kiss we'd shared before I set out to stop the murder of the President. Then another thought occurred to me that chilled me to the bone.

"There are cameras everywhere in the facility. Right?"

"Yes," Carpenter answered. "With the exception of the director's private quarters, the entire facility is under constant surveillance."

"Johnson would know this?"

Carpenter stopped tapping keys on his laptop as he and Dr. Anholts turned to look at me.

"Of course," she said. "What's your point?"

"Think about it," I said. "He kills the director, knowing it will be captured on video. Knowing he's sitting in a facility that houses a time machine. Whatever he is, he isn't stupid. Do you really think he doesn't expect me to come back and stop him? Why would he make it so easy for us?"

They sat there staring at me. Thinking about what I'd just said.

"I must confess I've had similar concerns," Dr. Anholts said. "And I've known Agent Johnson for a long time. This is completely out of character for him."

"Doctor, you've seen the footage," Carpenter said, exasperation clear in his tone. "There's no other explanation."

She glared at him for a time before looking down at her lap.

"Show me the video," I said after a minute of silence.

Carpenter turned back to his laptop and finished loading the file. A moment later an image of the corridor outside the director's office and quarters appeared on the large screen at the front of the room. I watched as Johnson, looking as dapper as ever, approached the office door and knocked.

He paused for a moment, then opened it and stepped through. The video jumped to a shot from inside Patterson's office. The office was empty, and Johnson crossed the small space and went through another door.

"He went into the director's quarters," Carpenter explained. "No camera in there so we can't see what happened."

"No audio?" I asked.

"No. It's in the budget for next year, but the system hasn't been upgraded yet."

The video was still rolling. According to the time stamp in the lower right corner, it was only one and half minutes before Johnson reappeared in the director's office and passed back out into the hall. The view kept jumping as multiple camera feeds were spliced together, tracking him as he headed directly to the helipad where a helicopter waited for him.

It was painted red and black with the logo for Texaco prominently showing on the sides. The engine was apparently already running. The rotor slowly turned as he walked directly to the aircraft and climbed aboard. The rotor sped up, and it quickly departed. Carpenter hit a button, closing the file.

"After he left, we tracked the helicopter to an airport where Johnson boarded an FBI jet and flew to Washington DC."

"How long after this was the director found?" I asked.

"His assistant went looking for him when he missed a scheduled conference call with the Department of Defense. She found him eleven minutes later. The director was shot in the back of the head at close range. Johnson must have used a silencer as no one heard the shot."

"Anyone else in or out of his office or quarters?"

"No," Carpenter shook his head. "Half an hour after he was found, we had reviewed the tapes, and I asked Ray to go after him."

"Why Ray? Why not just call the Department of Justice? They could have been waiting to scoop him up when he landed."

"One of Director Patterson's standing orders is that we, in his words, wash our own laundry. It is appropriate, considering the sensitive nature of the Athena Project. We can't afford to have investigators looking into what happens here in the facility."

I nodded, understanding. But it still bothered me that Johnson had apparently been so careless. He'd made no effort to cover his tracks. Knew very well that his actions would be discovered, and I would be sent back to stop him from killing the director. Then why did he do it? How did he think he was going to get away with it?

"Agent Johnson is a very dangerous man," Carpenter said. "Perhaps he thinks you couldn't stop him even if you did come back. I've heard stories. He was a Marine. A MARSOC Marine, assigned to one of the Raider battalions. From what I've heard, he is a grade A badass. When you get back there, you have to put him down immediately, the instant you see him. You cannot hesitate."

I looked at Carpenter. What he said was right. I couldn't give Johnson the opportunity to defend himself or fight back. But the whole thing still bothered me. Even more so now that I'd learned he was a Marine. And not just a normal Jarhead, but a Raider. You don't get there if you're not the best of the best.

And one thing I knew about the guys that wound up in Special Forces. Regardless of whether they were a Marine, SEAL or Green Beret, they were duty bound to a fault. Despite popular fiction, they didn't go off and join conspiracies to overthrow the government. At least not the operators I'd met.

Of course, they're still human, and there's always exceptions. But I'd never gotten that vibe from Johnson. He could be annoying. Rigid. Certainly had a stick up his ass. Probably chewed on ground glass for breakfast. If not for the video I'd carried back, where he ordered my death, I'm not sure I would be convinced.

"We have a distance point calculated for you to arrive five minutes before Agent Johnson enters the director's office," Dr. Anholts said. "We're ready whenever you are."

"When is that?" I asked, still struggling to reconcile the events in my head.

"Nearly twenty-three hours ago," Dr. Anholts said, checking her iPad.

"If I go back twenty-three hours," I said, trying to work out the timelines in my head. "That means that by the point I come back to real time, I'll have lost the window to save Julie."

Dr. Anholts began rapidly tapping keys on her iPad. The screen at the front of the room flared to life and I was looking at a vivid image of the inside of the hotel room in DC. Ray was sitting on the couch in the living room, looking at me. She tapped some more keys, and the view began running backwards at a very fast rate.

"I'm streaming directly from your data chip, Mr. Whitman," she explained. "How much farther back do I need to go?"

I thought about it for a minute, trying to fix the images that were flashing on the screen to some point in the timeline.

"Try twelve hours," I said.

She tapped some more, and the rewind stopped. There was a blink, and I watched as I fired a bullet into the side of my face. Well, not my face, but the face of the FBI agent that had tried to convince me he was another version of myself.

"Oh," Dr. Anholts exclaimed, turning a shade of white that didn't look good.

She froze the image after the camera swung away from the corpse and took a long, slow drink from a bottle of water.

"How?" I asked, realizing something was wrong. "How did you record that? I was wearing this FBI jacket that I put on in the past. It can't have cameras."

She looked at me, obviously trying to come up with an answer. Finally, she looked down at the table before speaking.

"We haven't been completely honest with you," she began.

"Doctor," Carpenter interrupted, the warning clear in his tone.

"Shhh," she said. "He has the right to know. Mr. Whitman, the reason for the surgery to your eyes wasn't to change their color. That can be done with contacts. It was to implant an interface that allows your data chip to record everything you see."

"What? Are you serious?" I was surprised, but not as much as I would have been before coming to work for these people.

"Yes, I'm afraid so. Cameras are too unreliable. Lenses can be damaged, or covered at a crucial moment. And what if the asset changes clothes? We would lose the ability to record what happens."

"Jesus Christ," I breathed.

I was upset but recognized I didn't have the luxury to worry about something that had already happened. There would be plenty of time to address this little topic once I saved Julie.

"Fine, we'll deal with this later. Right now, we need to figure this out."

"Of course," Dr. Anholts said, sounding relieved. She resumed rewinding the video, stopping at an extreme close up of Julie's face. The moment I'd kissed her as I left the hotel room. "This point is eleven hours and forty-five minutes before you returned to real time. You've been back thirty-one minutes. Twelve hours and sixteen minutes elapsed."

"And if I go back twenty-three hours to save the director when I come back to real time that would only leave a forty-four-minute window for me to stop Julie's killer. Maybe less. I don't know the precise moment when she was murdered. This was the last time I saw her alive. I can't save them both!"

"Yes, you can!" Carpenter interjected. "When you stop Agent Johnson, you save the woman!"

"If he's the one who killed her," I said.

"Who else?" Carpenter asked.

I shook my head, unable to answer the question.

"Will you save the director and put an end to this?" Dr. Anholts asked after a short silence.

"No." I shook my head. "I won't take the chance with Julie's life. She's an innocent. Didn't go looking to be involved in this. I know the director didn't deserve to die, but if there's even a chance that Agent Johnson didn't kill her, I can't risk her life on going back so far I lose the opportunity to save her."

Dr. Anholts exchanged a look with Carpenter. After a moment, he nodded and turned back to me.

"Very well, Mr. Whitman. We will send you back thirteen hours to DC. But you must be very careful and not come into direct contact with that version of yourself. The results could be disastrous."

I arrived in a battleship grey, steel corridor. What the fuck? Looking around, I nearly screamed in rage. They had lied to me! Tricked me. Instead of sending me to save Julie, I was standing outside of Patterson's office.

They had pushed the issue. Made the decision for me. Now, I didn't have a choice. Had to fully accept that Johnson was the killer. I couldn't let him live. If I did, there was too great of a risk that Julie would die in a few hours. Goddamn it!

With no options, I took a deep breath and forced myself to calm down and think about what I had to do. Setting my watch for a five-minute countdown, I opened the door without knocking and stepped into the director's office. It was empty, and I headed for the entrance to his private quarters, pausing when I heard his voice. It sounded like he was speaking on the phone.

Everything about this was still bothering me. The pieces of the puzzle fit together, especially with the video ordering Kirkpatrick to terminate me. Regardless, it felt more like someone had forced some of the jigsaw together with a mallet.

I paused before proceeding to the director's quarters, reviewing everything I knew and thought I knew. All of the evidence pointed at Johnson as part of the conspiracy. I remembered the mantra Carpenter had kept repeating before I'd been told I was being sent back to save Julie.

"He's a very deadly man. Don't give him an opportunity. You have to take him out the instant he walks through the door, or your chances go way down. If he gets his hands on you or reaches a weapon, you are dead. And that means the director will die as well as the woman in DC."

He had reiterated the point as if I wasn't smart enough to understand it the first time. Part of me, the ego I'd developed as my training progressed, wanted to dismiss his concerns. I'd trained for this. I could take him.

Then I reminded myself that I'd only been doing this for six months, whereas Johnson had years of experience under his belt. Sure, I'd been in the Army. But I'd been an infantry soldier. Walk long distances and know how to shoot a rifle. That was pretty much the extent of the training invested in a run of the mill foot soldier.

I'd learned a lot since arriving at the project facility, but when I thought about things honestly, Carpenter was right. I didn't stand a chance against a seasoned warrior. I'd been reminded of that most recently on the sidewalk in DC when Ray had disabled me with only his thumb. If he could do that with a single finger, what could he, or Johnson, do if they really wanted to inflict damage?

The door to Patterson's quarters was ajar, and I pushed it open, stepping through. He was seated on a leather sofa, a cup of coffee on a table at his side, speaking on a phone. When he saw me, his eyebrows went up for just an instant.

"I need to call you back," he said into the phone and disconnected the call.

"Mr. Whitman. What has happened?"

"Sir?"

I had expected to be met with anger or indignation that I had entered his private space, uninvited. Instead, he was behaving as if this were a normal occurrence.

"Here you are, standing in my private quarters, dressed in an FBI jacket with a weapon in your waistband. Not a difficult deduction on my part to surmise you have been sent back for some reason."

He picked up his coffee and took a small sip, watching me over the rim of the cup. I almost blushed under his scrutiny. The man was sharp as a tack. He'd taken one look at me, and despite the surprise of my unannounced entry, had the fortitude to analyze the situation. And arrive at an accurate assessment.

"Your guess is right. I've been sent back. You will be murdered in," I checked my watch. "Two minutes and forty-three seconds."

"And will you be the one pulling the trigger, Mr. Whitman?"

"No, sir. Agent Johnson. There is a conspiracy involving him to assassinate the President. He's already ordered my death, and killed the woman who helped me in California."

"Ms. Broussard?" He asked eyebrows arching in surprise.

"Yes, sir," I nodded. "In a couple of minutes, he's going to walk in here and shoot you in the back of the head. Then he boards a helicopter and flies to DC where he kills Julie. I'm here to stop him."

"I see," he said, taking another sip of coffee. "And I suppose you've seen evidence to prove Agent Johnson's guilt?"

"Yes, sir. I have a flash drive, the one you gave me to take back to Agent Kirkpatrick. There's a video on it of Agent Johnson ordering him to terminate me. There's also the facility's security footage of him walking in here, then leaving a couple of minutes later. No one else enters or leaves until your assistant finds your body eleven minutes later. Pretty damning evidence."

"I would agree," he said, taking another sip of coffee.

Why was he so fucking relaxed? Didn't he understand what I was telling him? That someone was about to walk through his door and try to kill him. I checked my watch again. Fifty-three seconds until Johnson arrived.

"Mr. Whitman, I believe you are sincere and have seen compelling evidence of Agent Johnson's guilt. However, I'm going to ask that you trust me. Here's what I'd like you to do. Step into the bathroom, out of sight. Have your weapon ready. When he comes in, I trust that you will shoot him if he attempts to harm me in any way. If he does not attack me, please restrain yourself and do nothing."

I stood there looking at him for a long pause. Wondering if he knew more than he was letting on. He had to realize he was playing games with his life.

Checking my watch again, I looked back up and met Patterson's unwavering stare. Thirty seconds. Deciding to trust him, I moved quickly across the room and into a spacious bath. The light was off, and I moved the door until it was half closed.

I was completely concealed in the darkness, the pistol in my right hand. Raising it, I aimed at the door from the office into the quarters. The farthest point away from where I stood was no more than twenty feet. I was confident I could drill a round into Johnson's head the instant he started to draw a weapon.

Right on time there was a muted knock from the direction of the office. Patterson shouted permission to enter, and I heard the clank of the steel door open, a moment later a thud as it was closed.

"In here," Patterson called.

A moment later, Agent Johnson appeared and stepped into the living area. It took every ounce of restraint I possessed to not shoot him the instant my sights lined up on his head.

"What can I do for you, Agent Johnson," Patterson asked, still sipping the damn coffee.

"Just checking in before I leave for Washington," he said. "Any last minute instructions?"

"No, I think we've covered everything quite well. Our Department Of Justice liaison will meet you when you arrive and provide some more insight on the meeting."

"Good. I'm looking forward to it. Well, I should be off. The helo is waiting."

Johnson turned and headed for the door. I didn't understand what was going on. Why hadn't he tried to shoot the director?

"Oh, one more thing," Patterson said as Johnson was passing through the door on his way out.

"Sir?" He asked, turning.

"If you would be so kind, can you delay your flight for a few minutes? I'd like you to go out to the helicopter and tell the pilot to stand by, then come back. Take your time doing it."

"What's going on, Ian?" Johnson asked, eyes darting around the space.

"I need you to trust me," Patterson said. "Now, please go speak with the pilot. Come back in, shall we say, fifteen minutes?"

Johnson squinted his eyes, staring hard at Patterson. After a few seconds, he nodded his head, looked around the room again and left. When the outer door clanged shut behind him, I lowered my pistol and stepped out of the bathroom.

"How did you know?" I asked.

"I've known Agent Johnson for almost twenty-five years," Patterson said. "I was his battalion commander in the Marines. As far as I'm concerned, there was never a question."

"Then who killed you?" I asked.

"I suspect we'll find out shortly," he said calmly. "Now, if you'll return to the bathroom and exhibit some patience, I'm sure the guilty party will be along shortly."

I nodded, despair setting in. It wasn't Johnson. That meant I'd failed to save Julie. She was going to die because Dr. Anholts and Carpenter had lied to me and sent me to the wrong point in time! Anger surged, and I thought about what I was going to do to them for their betrayal.

First, I needed to put a stop to this. Maybe, when the murderer revealed himself, I could get enough information to send a warning to Julie. There was still time for that. Turning, I resumed my post behind the bathroom door. And waited. Checking my watch, I saw that the time for the assistant to walk in was almost there.

It wasn't long before there was a clang as the office door from the corridor opened again. There was a thud as the outer door closed, then a shadow passed across the opening from the quarters into the office. I was surprised when the director's assistant walked in with a suppressed pistol in her hand.

"You fucking bitch," I said, stepping into the room.

The pistol was gripped in both my hands, sights steady on her. She had frozen, looking up in surprise when I came into view. The pistol in her right hand was still pointed at the floor. If it so much as twitched, I was going to blow her fucking head off.

My finger began to tighten on the trigger as I tried to decide if there was any reason not to put her down like a rabid dog.

"I see your surprise," Patterson interjected, looking at her from where he sat on the sofa. "That's the problem with playing with time. You think this is the first time you've done this. Sneaking in here to kill me and set up Agent Johnson. But, it's not. It might be the second. Or possibly the twentieth. You see, the more we're learning about how time actually works, the more possibilities we're discovering."

"Why did you kill her?" I shouted, ignoring Patterson's babbling.

"I don't know what you're talking about," she said. "I was on my way back from the range and remembered I needed to discuss something with the director."

"With a suppressed pistol in your hand?" I scoffed. "Give me a break. You know who killed her. Or will kill her. Beat her first, then put a bullet in her head and leave her for me to find in that hotel room. Why? Trying to make her tell where I was?"

"She can't answer that question, Mr. Whitman. For her, it hasn't happened yet. But she can tell us what her orders are and who's giving them."

Patterson stood, careful to stay well clear of my line of fire. He came to stand near me, a large pistol held loosely in his hand. Where the hell had he been hiding that?

"I know who's giving the orders," I said. "It's Carpenter."

The assistant's eyes widened slightly, for just an instant, confirming I was correct.

"I'm well aware of Mr. Carpenter's betrayal," Patterson said. "I've left him alone, hoping to use him to lead me to the real architects of the conspiracy. Unfortunately, it seems as if I've underestimated them and they decided I was an impediment to their plans."

"What about Johnson?" I asked. "Why do they want me to kill him?"

There was a clang as the outer door opened and closed. A moment later, Agent Johnson appeared at the entrance to the director's quarters, immediately drawing his weapon when he saw our little tableau.

"Please take Ms. Silas into custody," Patterson said. "And when she is properly secured, detain Mr. Carpenter."

Johnson gave me an odd look before stepping forward and removing the pistol from the assistant's hand. He slipped it into a suit coat pocket and produced a pair of handcuffs, slapping them onto her wrists after pulling her arms behind her back.

"Everything else OK here?" He asked Patterson but kept his eyes on me.

"Quite," the director smiled. "I'm explaining some things to Mr. Whitman."

I lowered my weapon as Johnson led the assistant away. Patterson turned back to me and continued where he'd left off.

"They knew that once I was killed, Johnson wouldn't rest until he'd found the truth. And he can be a formidable enemy. One they wouldn't want on their trail. So they decided to remove both of us from the board. Kill me and pin it on Johnson. And it worked. At least in one iteration of the timeline.

"Apparently the people involved underestimated the import of trying to use time. They got too clever for their own good. Carpenter is too well versed to fall into the trap of thinking he could control events. I imagine he was given orders without any latitude and has attempted to carry them out."

"He's the one that kept telling me to shoot Agent Johnson the instant I saw him," I said. "He was insistent on it. I thought he was just trying to help me."

"Hardly," Patterson snorted. "He was trying to salvage the plan before it completely unraveled. If you had listened and done as he said, which you nearly did, Agent Johnson would be dead. And so would you. There would be no one to save the President."

"But why?" I asked, not understanding. "I've already stopped the assassination."

"No," Patterson said. "You *will* stop the assassination. If that had already happened, I wouldn't be aware of it. And I'll take you at your word that you were, or will be, successful. But coming back here in an attempt to kill Johnson? That would prevent actions you are yet to take. At least in this timeline."

"I don't understand," I said. "I did stop the assassination. I remember doing it!"

"There's an area of theoretical physics that explains this. Dr. Anholts and I have had many late night discussions on the topic, and I must confess they were quite stimulating. Intellectually, that is. To explain, time is multi-dimensional. Sometimes. At any given point, we each have to make decisions that will affect our path forward.

"When a point that is significant to an individual's timeline is reached, multiple branches of time are created. Like a tree. No one can explain why or how it is triggered, but we've been able to prove it and start studying the phenomenon. When this happens, it creates an instability in time. This, in effect, is lateral time. Multiple scenarios occurring in tandem, with only one of them eventually winning out."

"This is really beyond me."

I was struggling to remain patient. Patterson recognized this and gave me a small smile.

"I'll try to simplify. While you are standing here, there is another timeline unfolding in which you are endeavoring to stop the assassination. Normally, you wouldn't exist at the same time as past events. But when you are sent back, a new, artificial timeline is created. Now, spacetime is trying to resolve which branch of your time will become reality.

"Because you have not yet stopped the assassination in the parallel dimension, there is the possibility that what you do in this one will result in the other ceasing to exist, allowing the events to go unchanged. You will be completely unaware of this. At least consciously. Unconsciously, there's a part of your mind that we are yet to identify that is aware. This is where the feeling of déjà vu comes from. Or so we believe."

My head was reeling. Trying to follow what he was telling me was so far beyond my ability to comprehend that I was quickly growing frustrated.

"You're telling me that what happens here can erase what I've already done?"

"You haven't done it. Yet. That's part of the greater risk of sending a person back in time that we're still trying to understand. But to answer your question, if you were to die in this timeline, all others would collapse and vanish. No matter what you did in them. Death is the one constant that can't be changed.

"So perhaps I underestimated Mr. Carpenter. As I consider the possible outcomes, his ploy was actually rather brilliant. If you had walked in here and been unreasonable, unwilling to listen to me and follow my instructions, or if you had tried to harm Agent Johnson, I would have shot you. If you had succeeded in killing Agent Johnson, I would have shot you. Either outcome, the result is the same. You're dead, the alternate timeline is dissolved, and the assassination cannot be stopped."

He held up the pistol in his hand to demonstrate his point. I looked down and watched as he returned it to a holster hidden beneath his suit coat.

"Hold on," I said, reaching in my pocket. "What about the video of Johnson ordering my death? How do you explain that?"

"Easily faked by an expert like Mr. Carpenter," Patterson said, taking the flash drive out of my hand. "And with the sophisticated equipment available to him here, he could produce a product that would put Hollywood to shame. Nevertheless, I'll have it checked."

I nodded, feeling foolish for having been sucked in.

53

Touching my arm to get my attention, Patterson pointed at an armchair next to the sofa as he sat down. I returned the pistol to my waistband and sat where he indicated.

"Now, how do we contact you and Ms. Broussard?"

"We can contact them? I thought they were in another timeline."

"Another timeline, yes. Not another planet. Yes, we can contact them. The timelines can momentarily merge. Communicating across them is not dangerous, other than the possibility of setting events into motion that would be better left alone."

I nodded. Checked my watch and tried to figure out where Julie and I were at this particular point.

"We should have just arrived at a hotel in DC," I said, relatively sure I was correct.

"Excellent. Name of the hotel and room number?"

"Wait. If I warn myself, that self, I'll be trying to protect her and not stopping the attack."

"There is that distinct possibility, Mr. Whitman. That is why it is vital that you impress on that version of yourself the importance of stopping the conspirators."

I nodded and told him the name of the hotel and where it was located. Picking up a handset from the table next to the sofa, he instructed whoever answered it to connect him to the Hilton. Moments later his call was answered, and he asked for the room number I'd given him, then handed the phone to me.

I listened to the phone in 1223 ring a dozen times, but it wasn't answered. Just kept on ringing.

"I don't understand," I said. "We should be in the room. We arrived, did some research on her laptop for close to an hour. I know the phone works because I used it to check on a vacant office in the building I believed the assassins were in. Then we took a walk to recon the street. But we shouldn't have left yet."

"Did you receive any calls on the room phone? Perhaps its ringer had been turned off."

"No. Just the one outgoing call I made," I said. "Try it again. Maybe I'm on the phone right now, and it doesn't have call waiting."

Patterson placed the call, confirming with the person that answered at the hotel that 1223 was in fact registered to a Mr. Trip Cummins. Satisfied he was trying to reach the correct room, he asked to be connected. This time, he didn't bother to hand the phone over, just listened for nearly a minute. I could faintly hear the repeated, unanswered rings.

"Are you sure of the timing, Mr. Whitman?"

"Maybe," I said. "Truthfully, I'm a little turned around at the moment."

"We need to speak with Dr. Anholts."

Patterson dialed an extension and told the person on the other end to locate the Doctor and have her immediately meet him in the conference room. Hanging up, he jumped to his feet and headed for the door.

"Follow me!"

We moved quickly through the corridors, and I was surprised when I had to concentrate to keep up with Patterson. He didn't appear to be someone who could cover a lot of ground quickly, but I guess once a Marine, always a Marine.

Dr. Anholts was waiting at the door to the conference room when we arrived. The director ushered her inside and closed the door behind us. Sitting, he explained what the situation was. She listened attentively, frequently looking over at me as he talked.

"Is there a problem, Mr. Whitman?" She asked when Patterson finished.

"I'm sorry?"

"The expression on your face indicates anger, and based on the intensity with which you are looking at me, I can only assume it is focused in my direction."

Patterson turned to look at me, both of them waiting for an answer.

"You lied to me," I said, figuring it was best to just get it out in the open.

"Excuse me?" She looked offended.

"You were supposed to send me back to DC to save Julie. Told me that's what you were doing. But you sent me here."

Dirk Patton

"You cannot blame Dr. Anholts for something she hasn't done," Patterson defended her.

"Yes, I can," I grumbled. "Because to me, she's already done it."

"I'm sure there must have been compelling circumstances," she said. "I cannot speak to those as I have yet to experience the events that would have prompted me to be less than honest with you."

"Like lying to me about the data chip? How it really records what I'm doing in the past?"

There was silence for a moment as they both stared at me. Finally, Patterson spoke up.

"Mr. Whitman, you are justified in your anger. We have deceived you. Either directly, or by omission of certain facts. That was my decision, and one I'm coming to regret. If Dr. Anholts made a decision and it was necessary for her to lie to you to ensure your cooperation, perhaps you should consider the ramifications if she hadn't.

"But for now, if you want to save Ms. Broussard, we need to move on from this and work together. Time is fleeting, and our efforts could be better spent in preventing her death."

Sometimes the man was infuriating. Especially when he was right. Shelving the topic for another day, I nodded my head. Dr. Anholts gave me a small smile, then set to work on her iPad. Once again, the screen in the room flared to life, and I was looking at an image that had been captured from my own eyes.

"What point am I looking for?" She asked.

"Go backwards until I tell you," I said.

She started a high-speed rewind, and I found it surprisingly easy to identify the events that were happening despite how rapidly images were changing. I saw the inside of the building where I'd fired the M4. A second later Julie's face flashed past, the moment I'd kissed her as I was leaving to stop the assassination.

Several more images as the video continued in reverse. There was half a second that her naked body appeared on the screen, then I was looking at street scenes from our recon of the target. It unwound quickly, and I glimpsed the interior of the hotel's elevator doors.

"Stop," I said, Dr. Anholts freezing the image. "Go back slow from here."

She did as I asked, the video unwinding until we had a view of the interior of the hotel room's living area. Julie's laptop was in front of me, her hands visible on the keyboard and a photo from Google Earth displayed on the monitor.

"Right there," I said. "If I'm remembering right, that point should correspond to right now."

Dr. Anholts opened a new window and after checking a complicated time stamp on the video from my chip, input the data into a form and clicked a button marked *calculate*.

It took the tablet a few moments to complete the request. When it displayed the results, they meant nothing to me. Appeared to be a jumble of numbers with no apparent purpose. But they meant something to Dr. Anholts.

"Close, Mr. Whitman. You're only off by eleven minutes."

She adjusted the playback of my data chip, coming to a stop on a scene nearly identical to the one we'd just looked at. She let it play at normal speed this time, Julie working the laptop as I occasionally reached forward and tapped a spot on the display.

"I've synchronized the playback with our real time," she said. "This is what you were doing, coordinated with now."

"So we're in the room," I said. "We should hear the phone if it rings."

Patterson had already stood and retrieved a phone from a small table against the far wall. Once the call was placed, he set it to speaker mode and placed it on the conference table. It began ringing. And continued to ring. On the screen, Julie and I continued to look at the laptop.

"Damn it!" I said, slamming my hand on the table's surface and causing Dr. Anholts to jump. "What do we do?"

The director reached out and disconnected the call.

"Did Ms. Broussard have a cell phone with her?" He asked.

"Its battery was dead," I said, looking up at the screen. "That's it in pieces. There in the background next to the TV."

We all stared at the screen for a moment.

"Call the hotel back and tell them it's an emergency," I said to Patterson. "Get them to send someone up to the room to check the phone.

Or have them take me a phone number so I can call you."

"Possibly," the director said. "Were you in a frame of mind to allow anyone into the room? To call a number that someone unknown brings to you?"

"No," I said, then had an idea. "Have them bring a number to me and tell me it's an emergency and that I need to call Monica. That will get my attention."

Patterson looked at me for a short pause before picking up the phone and calling the Hilton again. This time, he asked to speak to the manager, telling the operator it was an emergency. He was quickly speaking again, explaining he was the father of the man in room 1223, and there was a family emergency. He asked that a phone number and message be delivered right away, then asked if he could hold until there was confirmation that the guest had been contacted.

We sat in silence, waiting. The director had the phone held to his ear, and I could hear faint strains of hold music. While we sat there, the door opened, and Agent Johnson walked in.

"I'm on hold," Patterson said to him.

"Ms. Silas and Mr. Carpenter are in holding, sir. Dr. Willhoit has administered the specified dosages for interrogation, we're just waiting for it to reach full effectiveness. I should have some initial answers for you within the hour."

"Thank you," Patterson said, and Johnson disappeared without another word.

"Yes, I'm still here," he said into the phone.

It was only a few seconds after Johnson left the room. The director listened briefly before speaking again.

"You're certain?" There was another pause as he listened. "Thank you for your cooperation. If you would, please leave a message for that guest to call Monica the instant he returns, I would be most grateful."

Patterson broke the connection and placed the phone on the table in front of him.

"There was no answer at the door," he said. "The manager opened it and looked inside, but there was no one in the main room. He did not enter or check the bedrooms, but said he shouted loudly to announce his presence."

Dr. Anholts leaned over her iPad and worked furiously for nearly a minute, sitting back when the results of her calculations appeared.

"The only explanation is something has happened to alter that timeline," she said. "The calculations, as well as Mr. Whitman's memory, are correct. He should be in the hotel room."

"Send me," I said. "There's still time."

"You're already back, Mr. Whitman," Patterson said.

"So what? Why can't you send me back another couple of hours, to DC?"

The director turned and looked at Dr. Anholts for support. She looked bemused for a moment as she thought.

"That might be possible," she said after a bit more reflection. "But it could also be incredibly dangerous. This wouldn't be a simple straight line back, it would also be a lateral shift across timelines. We've never considered the possibilities. Or impacts."

"But it's possible?" I asked, trying to contain my hope.

"That's not what I said. I said it *might* be" she answered.

"Then let's find out!"

"There isn't even a theory to support this! If there was, I'd probably be the one to develop it. And theories aren't created sitting around a table, hoping a wild idea will work. It takes calculations. Observations of behaviors. So many things we do not have time for. What you have is an idea. A wish, born of desperation."

"Look, Doc. If we don't do something, two innocent people are going to die. There's a man I basically kidnapped and used to get into DC, then there's Julie Broussard. They are both there because of me. I'm not willing to sit back and do nothing while someone puts a bullet in each of their heads. Unless you have a better idea, I need you to figure out how to make this work in the next couple of hours."

I held her eyes with mine until she looked away. Shifting my gaze to Patterson, I saw surprise in his eyes.

"What?" I challenged.

"You are not who your past mistakes would seem to indicate," he said.

"Surprise," I said, sarcastically. "Now, can we make this work, or not?"

"Dr. Anholts?" He asked, turning to look at her.

"There are so many things that could go wrong," she said, evading providing an answer.

"Is there a risk of an explosion like I was told would happen if I came into contact with my past self?"

"No, I don't believe so," she said after thinking for a minute. "Not as long as you're aware of that danger and take steps to prevent it from happening."

"Then what's the risk?"

"The risk would most likely be to you, Mr. Whitman. I can't predict the forces that will act on your body and mind from a lateral transport. You could be torn apart. You could die a slow, painful death like the early test animals. You could cause a rift and slingshot to an unknown time or location. And these are just the possibilities that spring to mind."

"I'm willing to take the chance," I said. "I don't see another option."

I said the last to Patterson. He had sat perfectly still, listening to the discussion. Now he appeared to be weighing the options.

"Doctor, can you make the machine do this?" He turned and looked at her.

"Sir, I'm not sure you understand..." She stopped when he held up a hand.

"Yes or no, Doctor. Risks to Mr. Whitman aside, can you do this?"

She stared at the table for a long time. Chewed her lip. Took a drink from her bottle of water.

"Yes," she finally said. "I can do it."

The world around me blinked, then I was standing in one of the empty office suites in the building across from the restaurant. I turned my head, but when it stopped, the world kept going. The room around me whirled, picking up speed. Staggering sideways, I reached out, but there was nothing to support me. Crashing to the floor, I lay there and slowly curled into a ball.

I've been drunk and had the bed spins so bad I wanted to die. I've been whirled on amusement park rides until I threw up. I've been on a C-130 flying through the edge of a Typhoon over the Sea of Japan. Turbulence so bad we were bouncing up and down several hundred feet at a time. For over an hour.

None of it compared to this. Not even close. It didn't matter what position I tried to take, or whether my eyes were open or not. The world was nothing more than a whirlpool of colors and shapes, spinning faster and faster as it sucked me down into the vortex. So this was what the other assets had been talking about.

The only good thing was that when it stopped, it stopped. Suddenly. Without warning, everything snapped into sharp focus. Blessed, stationary focus. Slowly I climbed to me feet, amazed to not find the floor and myself covered in vomit.

I checked my watch. I'd only been down for three minutes. Three minutes! How had the people who'd been affected for an hour ever agreed to endure this a second time?

If things had worked according to plan, I had arrived before Julie and I took a walk to recon the street. If we were even here. I was concerned that we hadn't been in the room when Patterson sent the hotel manager to check, but wasn't able to come up with an idea for a better time or place to arrive.

Right now, I needed to confirm I was when and where I was supposed to be. Pulling out the cell phone Patterson had provided, I pressed the redial button. The Hilton's number was already in memory.

My call was answered quickly, and I confirmed that Mr. Trip Cummins was a guest at the hotel. The operator connected me to the room, but after twenty rings the phone remained unanswered. I hadn't really expected it to be that easy.

So I was in the right place at the right time. Where the hell were Julie and I? My head still had problems wrapping around referring to myself in the third person, but I was starting to get used to it. A little.

Stepping to the window, I opened the blinds a few inches and looked out at the street. A few pedestrians strolled by and there were two large, black Suburbans parked at the curb in front of the restaurant. Secret Service. They'd been there when we'd walked by before.

Moving back and forth, I looked up and down the street, hoping to catch a glimpse of us. Nothing. Where the hell were we and what was happening? Did I head for the hotel? Try to get inside and break into the room? All that stopped me from that course of action were Dr. Anholts' repeated warnings about the danger of coming into contact with myself.

So, I stood where I was and waited. Trying to decide what to do. Where to even start looking. Checking my watch, I was surprised to see that over an hour had passed. In frustration, I decided to run the risk of a foray into the Hilton when a woman with long, blonde hair caught my eye.

She was slowly approaching on the far sidewalk, holding hands with a tall man. Even though they were too far away for me to pick out their features, I instantly knew it was us. Breathing a sigh of relief, I kept watching as they approached, caught completely by surprise when Julie lifted her face and kissed him, me, on the cheek.

That hadn't happened!

I, or that me, looked down and kissed her back, then they resumed their walk towards the restaurant.

This version of us had already become intimate! That was all that made sense. And they'd probably been rolling around in the sheets, or maybe even the shower, and hadn't heard the phone or the manager opening the door and checking on them.

What the hell? Why were things different, and what had accelerated the timeline? Initiated the intimate part of our relationship. In my version, it had been the kiss outside the restaurant as part of our disguise. What had happened differently here to make it happen earlier?

Continuing to observe, I forced myself to remember that it didn't matter. What did matter was that I warn Julie and myself. That's all I had to do. Then I could go sit in a bar or a movie and wait for time to expire and transport me back to my real time.

I'd wait until they were on this side of the street. I knew they'd pause directly in front of the window I was standing in, wanting a good look at the angles to the restaurant. While they were stopped, I'd go out the front door and let them see me. Keep some distance between us, but be sure they both understood the mortal danger Julie was in.

It seemed to take forever for them to appear in front of my window. Julie came to a stop, bending to check her sandal. The other me turned to face her, and the restaurant. I left the window and headed to intercept them.

Opening the office door, I stepped into the hallway and turned towards the building entrance. I came to a stop when I saw two men in dark suits, standing in the lobby. One of them held a clipboard in his hand, looking something over, but the other one spotted me and nudged his partner. He looked up, and they both turned to face me. Fuck! Secret Service doing a sweep of the building!

So far, I hadn't done anything to warrant undue scrutiny from them. Fighting the impulse to run, I casually pulled the office door closed behind me and began walking towards them. I intended to just stroll on past and out the front like I didn't have a care in the world.

"Sir. Secret Service. We need to speak with you," one of them said as I approached.

He held up a badge case, and his partner took a step away, opening some space between them. I didn't like the look of that. You open space between you and your partner when you're expecting trouble.

I had showered and changed clothes before being transported here. Hadn't wanted to take the time, but Patterson convinced me I smelled like a gym room locker and needed to be presentable. I was now dressed in slacks and a polo shirt, a light jacket covering the pistol holstered on my belt. I hadn't said anything about the FBI ID I'd taken off my doppelgänger, and it was in my hip pocket. Thank God I'd thought to keep it with me.

"FBI," I said, approaching them. "ID in my back pocket."

I warned them before reaching behind me. Their eyes followed my every movement, locking in on the badge and ID card when I held it up. After a brief inspection, I saw both of them relax.

"What are you doing here?" The older of the pair asked.

"Tracking a white supremacists and his shithead brother," I said, falling back on the last story I'd spun. "What about you? Counterfeiters in the building?"

I could tell they didn't like that question. They were part of the Presidential detail. Maybe not the guys who walked next to the big man, but they were still several rungs in the pecking order above the guys that dealt with financial crimes.

"Advance team for POTUS," he answered, voice tight. "Tell me about these guys you're looking for."

"Couple of asshole, skinheads," I said, anxious to get away from them. "Got away from us in Virginia. Found a piece of paper with a business name at this address in their house. Business is gone. Office is cleaned out. That's what I was checking."

I hoped it sounded good. I also wasn't concerned if it raised enough of a red flag for the President's dinner to be canceled. The more senior of the two reached into his shirt pocket and removed a business card, handing it to me.

"Can you email what you've got on them? Need to do a threat analysis."

"Sure. No problem," I said. "Gotta run, fellas. More leads to track down."

I didn't wait for them to say anything else, just took off. Walked across the lobby and out the front door. Looked around, hoping to spot Julie and myself, but we were nowhere to be seen. Turning to my left, I headed for the hotel.

55

I covered the remaining distance to the hotel in just a few minutes. Stayed on the sidewalk on the opposite side of the street, keeping a close eye out for Julie and myself. Actually, I was looking more for her than me. With thick, blonde hair that glowed in the morning sunlight, she'd be the easier of the two to spot. But I never saw either of us.

Stopping in front of a flower shop that faced the hotel, I looked across the street, thinking. Decided to try contacting myself by phone, again. Same results as last time. Either they hadn't gone back, or they'd already found something else to occupy themselves. Lucky bastard, I thought, before realizing I was talking about myself. Hell, this was getting confusing.

Standing there, I tried to think of where they could have gone. Couldn't come up with any ideas. Thought about the best way to approach myself. Ensure I believed me when I was able to warn me. I knew I'd be suspicious, just like when I'd encountered the fake me in the empty building. Sure, he'd known some details about a conversation...

My thoughts came to an abrupt halt. How had he known those details? Only one way I could think of. He'd gone into the room and planted a microphone. It was time to do something. Continuing to stand on the sidewalk with my thumb up my ass wasn't accomplishing a thing. I needed to make contact and get Julie to a safe place.

I glanced both ways. The street was clogged with traffic. Bumper to bumper, occasionally moving a few feet before coming to a full stop again. Stepping off the curb, I slalomed my way through the idling cars. Crossing the center stripe, a horn blared to my right as I stepped in front of a shiny Lexus.

Jumping slightly from the sudden noise right next to me, I looked around, thinking I'd stepped in front of a car that was starting to move. That wasn't the case, and there hadn't been a reason for the horn. The car in front hadn't budged, and it didn't look like it was going to in the immediate future. I shot a glance at the driver of the Lexus, who had honked, a woman wearing a business suit and shouting into a phone held to her ear.

"Bitch," I muttered to myself.

Glancing around to make sure I wasn't about to get run down by a distracted driver, I froze when I saw a face behind the wheel of a car in the next lane. It was a plain, white Chevy sedan and was stuck three positions back from the Lexus. The face was mine.

I was alone in the car. Where the hell was Julie? There was no reason for her to not be with me. Our eyes locked and even from a distance, I saw recognition and an instant of panic on his face. This wasn't me!

The instant I realized this was the FBI agent I'd killed, or would kill, when he tried to make me believe he was me, all the pieces fell into place. He was the cleanup man. He'd managed to find us and get into the hotel room and bug it. Waited for me to leave to stop the assassination before he'd moved in.

He would have no idea how much I'd told Julie or the unconscious man in the other bedroom. Cummins had been shot without another thought. But maybe he could find out if I'd told Julie anything. And if she'd told anyone else. So he'd worked her over, trying to make her talk. I'd be very surprised if she'd said a word.

Time had been short, so he'd killed her whether he got any answers or not. Then he'd come after me. He'd been listening, so he knew where I was going. Followed along, tried to lure me into the open so he could make an easy kill and not have to get into a fight that could draw attention. That was the last thing he would have wanted.

If the Secret Service got a hint of a gunfight anywhere in the area, they'd scrub the President's plans. Just like they'd done when I fired the rifle and told them there was a shooter loose in the area. Only this guy didn't want that. He wanted everything nice and calm so POTUS would roll up and go inside. So that Hellfire missile could be launched to take him out.

But I'd been the fly in the ointment. He'd almost had me. Made me drop my guard at first with the details he'd provided as if he had been me and experienced them firsthand.

If chance hadn't put Monica in the same hotel I'd been in, it would have worked, too. His plan had been smart, but you can't prepare for something as unexpected as the presence of a woman I hadn't seen in over a decade.

All of these thoughts flashed through my mind in the blink of an eye. So did my decision. I had to stop him now. Drawing my pistol, I leveled it and moved to the side, so I had a clean line of sight on the windshield in front of my, his, face. The instant the sights came on target, I pulled the trigger three times.

The bullets punched through the glass, but I couldn't tell if I'd hit him or not. As I'd fired the first round, I was pretty sure he'd ducked beneath the dash. Moving forward, I ignored the frightened screams that started up from the cars on either side of me. Doors began to open as people exited their vehicles and ran away.

Rushing forward, I kept the pistol trained on the windshield as I approached. His head didn't pop up, and no return fire came my way. Had I gotten lucky and put him down with one of the shots? Slowing as I reached the front bumper of the Chevy, I craned my neck, trying to see into the front seat.

It looked empty, but he could have squeezed onto the floor, weapon in hand as he waited for me to show myself at the side window. Circling, I angled in. With my finger tight on the trigger, I darted my head forward and cursed when I saw the car was empty.

The passenger door was ajar, and I raised the pistol and scanned for my target. I didn't see him, but if he was staying low and moving through the now abandoned vehicles that filled the street, he'd be hidden from me.

Dashing around the back of the Chevy, I knelt and put my face close to the pavement. I had open sight lines as I looked under the surrounding cars and trucks. In every direction I checked, feet were running. All except for one pair. Someone was duck walking, staying low and moving slower than the panicked civilians.

I didn't have a clean shot. Jumping to my feet, I leapt over the hood of a car that had rolled forward and come to rest against the truck in front of it when the driver bailed out. Weaving between the cars, I headed for where I'd seen the feet and legs.

Before I could reach a spot that gave me a shot, I heard sirens approaching. Shit. There had probably been about a hundred people that dialed 9-1-1 as soon as I started firing the pistol. The cops would be here soon. And probably the Secret Service agents that were just down the block. This had to end quickly.

Movement to the left caught my eye, and I ducked as two shots sounded. I heard the impact of the bullets on sheet metal as they slammed into a car next to me. I looked for a target for some return fire, but he had already disappeared.

Moving laterally, I stepped into a narrow gap between the vehicles parked at the curb in front of the Hilton and the first lane of traffic. More movement, and I whipped the pistol around and started to pull the trigger when I saw him running, gun in hand. A panicked woman with a small child in her arms ran directly between us and I barely managed to stop my finger from completing the pull. If I had, I'd probably have hit her, the child, or both.

That moment of cover gave him time to vanish down the entrance ramp to the hotel's underground parking structure. Stepping around an idling Town Car, I sprinted after him. I needed to catch up and put a bullet in his head before he got lost in the maze of the garage. There would be blind corners. Vehicles to hide behind, under or in. I would probably be unable to locate him before the cops flooded in.

I should have slowed and exercised caution before charging around a blind corner. Every bit of training I'd received told me I was making a mistake, but I didn't have time to be careful. Urgency to not lose my target's trail drove me as I rounded the turn and started down the ramp that descended beneath the street.

He was waiting at the bottom, where it flattened out for the first level below grade. Tucked up tight against a concrete wall, pistol braced as he waited for me to appear. He fired three times. The first two rounds missed, but the third caught my left arm.

It didn't hurt, and I only knew I'd been shot because of the impact. It was a dull blow; kind of like being punched by a fist. It hit me hard enough to twist my upper body and cause me to tumble to the ground. Rolling, I slammed to a stop against the curb and brought the pistol around, seeking a target.

He was gone again. Goddamn it! I tried to ignore what was becoming a burning pain in my arm. I could feel blood running, inside my jacket. Had time to hope the bullet hadn't hit anything big that would cause me to bleed out before I could kill him. Then dismissed it from my mind. Getting to my feet, I started running again.

As I reached the first sub-level, the sirens grew louder and sounded as if they were almost on top of me. I had no idea how the cops were getting into the area. The street was completely blocked with abandoned cars. Maybe they were driving on the sidewalks.

Putting aside pointless thoughts, I tried to look in every direction, swinging the pistol around to stay in sync with my eyes. I was holding it one handed now, my left arm refusing to cooperate any longer. It hung limply at my side, flopping against me as I ran. I could feel blood running across my hand and dripping off my fingers.

I hesitated when it dawned on me I was leaving a trail for the police to follow. I had to do something to stop the bleeding, or at least cover my tracks. There was no doubt they'd be coming into the garage, looking for me, and I needed more time to find this asshole. If I could stop leaving a trail, maybe I could buy myself a few more minutes before I was run to ground by the cops.

Quickly, I pulled the jacket off and dropped it on the floor. Unbuckling my belt, I ripped it out of the loops on my pants, holster flying away to skid beneath a parked car. Looking down in the dim lighting, I could see a small hole in the front of my upper arm, a larger one where the round exited in back. At least the bullet wasn't in me.

Threading the end of the belt through the buckle, I slipped my arm into the loop and positioned the thick leather directly over the wounds. Grasping the end of the makeshift tourniquet, I took a deep breath and pulled hard. It tightened onto the holes, compressing into the surrounding tissue. The pain nearly caused me to pass out, a wave of heat and nausea immediately washing over me.

Cursing a blue streak, I pushed through and secured the buckle. Grabbing the jacket, I shook it a couple of times to clean as much blood from it as I could, then put it back on. I wasn't exactly presentable, and my arm throbbed like a son of a bitch, but blood no longer ran down across my hand to leave a trail even Helen Keller could have followed.

Pistol up, I started running. I was confident he hadn't stopped on the first level. It was small, only a couple of dozen spots for arriving guests to park and ride the elevator up to register. Then, with a room key in hand, they could come back down and drive through the security gate into the main area of the garage.

Slipping past the gate, I jogged down the curving ramp that led to the second sub-level. Lighting was weak, the dark grey concrete walls, ceiling, and floor doing nothing to reflect it and help me see. Rounding the bottom of the turn, I stopped and held the pistol at arm's length as I reached level floor.

The garage was large, nearly a hundred cars in the narrow spaces lined out on the floor. Shadows ruled, filling every corner and the gaps between the parked vehicles. It seemed pitch black beneath them, the light unable to reach. He could be anywhere.

Hidden in a corner. Concealed behind one of the massive, concrete support columns that marched away from my position in a long, perfectly aligned row. Or in the darkness beneath any one of the cars. And that's if he hadn't kept running, going deeper underground to the third or fourth sub-level.

I checked my watch. Less than an hour remaining before I was returned to real time. When and wherever that would be. If I understood things correctly, I now had *two* real times.

But that didn't matter. I was already hearing voices echoing down the ramp from the first level. Cops. They were coming, and I was out of time. A dog barked a moment later, lending wings to my feet. Sending me sprinting across the open space towards a door that was marked *FIRE STAIRS*.

If they sent a dog down the ramp, I'd be taken down in seconds. Maybe I could get a shot off and stop it before it slammed into me, but I didn't like the odds. Compared to a human, dogs are small targets when they're charging at you. Small and low to the ground. And damn fast. Besides, I have a big soft spot for dogs. No, I needed to get out of here. Now.

56

Slamming through the metal door without pausing, I shoved the pistol into my waistband at the small of my back and pounded up the steps. The stairwell was a dangerous choke point, nothing more than a narrow set of poured concrete steps inside towering slabs of the same material. The air was musty, smelling of mold and mildew and the treads were covered with a thick layer of dust.

Dust that captured and held a clear footprint with every step I took. Just like the marks that had been left by someone else who had climbed this same flight of stairs. They'd left clean spots behind, and they'd been running. Taking two steps at a time. Had I just gotten lucky and inadvertently taken the same route the man I was chasing had used?

Running hard, I quickly reached the first sub-level landing. I bypassed the metal door that exited into the garage, knowing there would be a whole army of cops on the other side. Pushing on, I came to a stop at the lobby level door. This was as high as the stairs went.

There was a dim, overhead light and I took a moment to check myself. My slacks and jacket were dark, and though the wetness of the blood was visible, it wasn't obvious what it was. But my polo shirt was tan, and it was stained a bright shade of red over most of the front.

Working one handed, I struggled with the jacket's zipper. Finally getting it started, I yanked it up, concealing the bloody shirt. I was out of options and had to step into the lobby where there would almost certainly be cops. Maybe, if I didn't immediately attract their attention, I could slip into the elevator and head up to the room.

Holding a deep breath, I gently pushed on the crash bar that controlled the lock. There was a soft click as it disengaged, then I cracked the door open and looked into the lobby. The stairs had come up into a small alcove, and after a moment, I realized I was around a corner, behind the elevators. Hidden from the main lobby.

Exhaling, I moved through and let the door quietly close behind me. To my left were the restrooms and the end of the short hall. To my right, ten yards away, the corridor bent to the left. That's where the elevators were.

Moving as if I belonged, and wasn't aware of the disturbance on the street in front, I stepped around the corner and pressed the up arrow to call the elevator. While I waited, I looked around the lobby. Nearly fifty people, staff and guests, were gathered just inside the glass entrance doors, trying to see what was happening outside. There weren't any cops in the lobby, and no one was even looking in my direction.

The car arrived, it's presence announced by a soft bell. I hustled inside the instant the doors opened, pressing the button for 12. Trying to appear as normal as possible, in case someone I hadn't noted was watching, I resisted the nearly overwhelming impulse to pound on the close button.

Finally, the damn doors slid shut, and I tilted my head back and let out a sigh as the car started ascending. I panicked, placing my hand on the butt of the pistol at my back when it stoppcd on 5. It was only a maid with an armload of towels. She smiled at me, stepped into the elevator and pressed the button for 6.

The wait for the doors to close, the car to ascend one floor and let her exit, then continue on to my floor seemed interminable. Excruciatingly slow. I was sweating heavily by the time it came to a stop on 12.

I waited, looking into the elevator alcove before stepping out. It was offset from the main hallway that led to the rooms, and when I saw it was clear, I stepped out of the car. Behind me, the doors slid shut, and there was a soft hum as it headed for another floor.

Edging to the mouth of the alcove, I peered up into a large, convex mirror on the far wall of the hallway that let people see around the corner. Probably there so a maid pushing a heavy housekeeping cart didn't accidentally run into a guest coming out into the corridor.

To my left, the direction opposite the location of the room, one of those carts was sitting outside an open door. To my right it was clear. Stepping out, I began heading for 1223 but came to a stop halfway there.

What if he was already in the room? I'd left the room key with Ray, and had no way to get in quietly. I had intended to knock, hoping Julie and I were back. But what if I knocked? He looks through the peephole and sees me. Puts a few rounds through the door. I'm toast, and Julie will die.

Thinking, I turned and looked at the housekeeping cart. Changing directions, I strode down the hallway as I pulled the FBI ID case out of my pocket.

A maid was vacuuming the carpet in the room where the cart was parked. The door was propped open while she worked and I stepped through the entrance, ID held in front of me. She was startled by my sudden appearance, hand flying to her chest in surprise as she stepped away from the vacuum cleaner. I nodded at it, and she reached out and turned it off.

"FBI," I said, wiggling the badge case to make sure she looked at it. "I need your master key. This is an emergency."

She stood rooted in place, staring at me in shock. I didn't have time for this shit.

"Now," I said, emphasizing the word with a shake of the ID.

"I cannot," she stammered in a heavy, eastern European accent. "I lose my job."

"No, you won't," I said, taking a step closer to her. "But if you don't cooperate, you'll be on the next plane back to the Ukraine, or wherever the hell it is you're from!"

Fear replaced the shock. She might not have been from the Ukraine. I had no idea. But I'd taken a chance and had hit a home run. She quickly grabbed a key card on a long lanyard from around her neck and held it out to me.

"Thank you," I said, putting the ID away and taking it. "Close the door and stay here."

"You not send me back?" She asked, hands clasped in front of her in a pleading gesture.

"Not if you stay in the room and don't tell anyone. One hour. Understand?"

"Yes. One hour. Thank you! I happy to help FBI!"

I stepped back into the hall, grabbed the cart and shoved it through the door into the room with her. Kicking the stop out of the way, I held the door with my shoulder and paused.

"One hour," I reminded her.

She nodded emphatically, and I let the door swing shut. Turning, I headed for the room, transferring the key card to my nearly useless hand. Drawing the pistol, I held it pressed against my body with my good arm as I screwed a suppressor onto the end.

Reaching the door marked 1223, I paused and listened. Didn't hear anything other than the muted sounds of a TV from across the hall. Careful to stay out of viewing range of the peephole, I moved forward and pressed my ear to the door.

The hotel was higher end, the guest room doors heavy and solid. I could make out a voice from within, but not well enough to tell male from female. I couldn't even tell if I was hearing a live voice or the TV.

Grimacing in pain, I forced my left arm up and used my right hand to quietly insert the maid's master key into the lock. Visualizing what I would do, I pulled it out and swiveled. The lock beeped, and I used the elbow of my right arm to slam the handle down an instant before my shoulder rammed the door open.

The pistol was in my hand, coming up as I rushed through and fell to the side, placing a short wall that created a bar area between me and the main living area. Behind, the door sighed and clicked as it closed, and the lock engaged.

I'd gotten half a second of a look as I'd come in, seeing Julie's body lying on the floor. Unconscious or dead. There had been a shout of surprise when I'd burst into the room, but no gunfire came my way. Now it was quiet, and I popped my head up for a look. And saw myself, pointing a pistol at another myself, who was pointing his own back at the first me. Fuck, this was getting even more confusing.

"What the hell?" The left me said, glancing back and forth between the right me and me.

"What happened to her?" I asked, aiming at a point halfway between the two of them.

"He knocked her out," the right me said. "Who the hell are you?"

"I'm me. I mean you," I said. "I'm here to stop one of you from killing her."

Both of them glanced at me before turning back to face each other and resuming the standoff.

"He's lying," left me said. "We got back from a walk, and I went to the bathroom. When I came out, she was on the floor, and he jumped me."

Each of them were disheveled with various marks on their faces. Clear indication that at least that story was true.

"Tell me about Monica," I said, expecting the same ploy from the other night to tell me who was real and who wasn't.

"My old girlfriend?" Right me asked, confusion on his face.

I shifted my aim to left me, ready to take up the slack in the trigger and put a round in his head. When I saw his expression, I stopped.

"*My* old girlfriend," left me said, correcting the other me. "What about her?"

What the hell? How was this possible? If one of these was really me, he should clearly remember seeing Monica in the lobby with her family. That had to have already happened. Unless that was the difference in this timeline! Dr. Anholts had said the only explanation for us not being in the hotel room was that something must have altered the timeline. Shit! What now?

"One of you is here to stop the assassination of the President," I said, shifting the muzzle of my weapon back to the halfway point. "The other is here to clean up anyone who might know anything. You kill Julie and try to kill me."

I left the thought of, "maybe I just kill both of you", unspoken.

They both looked at me before turning back to each other. What the hell did I do? I needed something that only I could possibly know. Something that would have never been put into a file during my trial. Nothing that could have been noted since I'd been scooped up by the Athena Project. And that was the problem.

I'd been forced to spend a lot of time with a Psychiatrist before they were willing to turn me loose in the past with a weapon. At first, I'd resisted talking to the shrink about anything. But over time, he'd gotten through, and I'd gradually opened up. After six months of multiple sessions per week, I wasn't sure I had any secrets left.

But would the impostor have bothered to study my file? He couldn't have possibly anticipated this scenario. Studied and prepared for it.

"So, what are we going to do, Chief?" Right me asked.

I shifted aim and shot him in the head. I've never called anyone "Chief" in my life, and it's one of those little things that grates on me when someone uses it like he just had. There's no way that was me.

"Fuck me," left me, alive me, breathed as he lowered his pistol. "What took you so fucking long to figure it out?"

"Piss off," I said to myself. "And be glad I didn't trust my gut. I thought you were him."

I stepped around the corner, intending to head for Julie. He shouted and held his hand up to stop me.

"No closer," he said. "Remember the warnings."

I nodded and had to stand there and watch as he knelt over Julie to check on her.

"Is she OK," I asked, impatient.

"Yeah, I think so," he said. "What about you?"

He was looking at the wetness on my slacks and jacket.

"Fucker shot me," I said. "No worries. I'm back to real time in twenty minutes."

"Is she safe?" He asked.

"Goddamn it! No!" I said when I realized I still remembered Julie being killed. "It wasn't him. Who the hell was it?"

He shook his head, looking back down and brushing a stray strand of hair off Julie's face.

"What was that about Monica?" He asked.

"Oh. Guess you should know. Don't know which one of us is going to remember this."

I talked quickly, relaying the events of the timeline as I remembered them. I could see the sadness, my sadness, in his eyes as I finished the story.

"I'm guessing that her not being here was the change to the timeline Dr. Anholts talked about. That's how I tripped him up when he was pretending to be me. So. What do we do? I've got just over ten minutes left."

He looked around the room, thinking. I saw the idea occur to him, and a moment later he lifted Julie onto the sofa.

"You take her with you," he said. "She'll be safe that way."

"Will that work? Can she go through with me?"

"Remember the question I, we, asked Dr. Anholts when we were first learning about the project?" He asked.

"Right," I smiled. "I remember. The one they hadn't thought of, and it kind of tweaked her that I did. She found out someone could come forward without being harmed because there's no Black Hole involved in returning to real time."

He nodded and smiled back at me.

"You'd better be holding her," he said. "If she's touching anything other than you, she might not go."

I nodded, accepting the logic. He leaned down and kissed Julie gently on the forehead. Despite myself, a surge of jealousy passed through me. How stupid is that? Jealous of myself!

When he stepped away, I slowly came forward. We were careful to never come within more than ten feet of each other. Reaching Julie, I knelt by her form and checked my watch. Seven minutes.

"How is it you're here, by the way?" He asked as we waited.

"Dr. Anholts. Who else?" I grinned. "Parallel, but different, timelines. She sent me back and sideways. And by the way, going sideways makes us sick. Lasted a few minutes and it was bad."

He nodded, staring at me.

"I'm thinking maybe things are pretty good here," he said after a minute, nodding at Julie. "Maybe don't want to be trying to go back and change things."

"Agreed," I said, thinking about the irony of agreeing with my own thoughts.

We didn't have anything else to say to each other. To ourselves. Whatever. The remaining time passed in silence. When there was 90 seconds remaining on my watch, I bent and worked my good shoulder under Julie. Wrapping my arm around her body, I rolled it up against my neck and carefully stood.

She wasn't big, or particularly heavy, but in my weakened condition, I swayed and nearly fell. The other me automatically began to step forward to steady me. I stopped him with a shout, his hands only a couple of feet from me.

When he realized what had almost happened, he leapt backwards to open space between us. I nodded and stood there swaying. Waiting for time to expire.

Then there was the blink, and I was standing on the dais in the facility. With Julie draped over my shoulder.

"Mr. Whitman, you'd better have a very good explanation," Patterson's voice said over the intercom.

58

Julie laughed at the hat when I tried it on. I'd try on a thousand more to keep hearing that sound. We had just arrived at the airport in Nassau, the Bahamas, on a well-earned vacation. Our flight had been early, and we had some time to kill before the shuttle from the resort where we were booked was scheduled to pick us up. Removing the hat, I winced at the sharp pain in my left arm as I returned it to the rack in the small gift shop.

"OK?" She asked, the smile on her face immediately changing to concern.

"Fine. Just a little twinge."

I slipped my good arm around her waist and hugged her against me as we browsed the goods on display. Three weeks had passed since we had stopped the assassination of the President and Speaker of the House. And it had hardly been an uneventful time. Well, not for us, but in the larger world.

I'd arrived back in the first real time with Julie on my shoulder. My arm had been treated, and she'd been examined by the medical staff and declared fit, other than a mild concussion. Then it was time to return to *real*, real time. The whole concept still made my head hurt when I tried to work out the logistics.

After a protracted discussion with Patterson, I'd been allowed to take Julie with me. I guess he'd gotten the message that after all I'd gone through to save her, I wasn't about to let her out of my sight. Not for a while, at least.

So, we'd made the final jump. Fortunately, this one was a straight line forward, and the director was expecting both of us when we arrived. My data chip was downloaded, then Julie and I were sent off to clean up and get some much needed rest. Rest hadn't been a priority for either of us. Not until we'd worn each other out on my lumpy mattress.

We spent the next couple of weeks getting to know each other. She had been assigned private quarters but never spent a night in them. We seemed to be attached at the hip. I introduced her to Ray, and she gave him a funny look.

"What?" He asked.

"I don't know," she said. "It's just that there's something familiar about you. Can't put my finger on it."

After the timeline change as a result of me saving Julie, the events where Ray and I discovered her body didn't happen. I didn't even remember them, horrified when they were finally shown to me. But not as horrified as Julie. She didn't sleep for two nights.

I attended multiple meetings with Patterson, Agent Johnson, and Dr. Anholts. A young woman named Forman, Carpenter's replacement, also attended. Julie was excluded. It was explained to me that the director had not yet decided how to deal with her.

She'd been allowed to call her brother, her only living family, letting him know she was doing well and was involved in a sensitive project which would make her unreachable for a few weeks. I didn't ask, but from the tone of the call, it didn't sound like this concerned him. It didn't seem as if they were particularly close.

Nearly three weeks after returning, Julie and I were strolling on the helipad. I was getting some fresh air as she puffed on a cigarette. My nagging was paying off as she was down to less than half a pack a day, and swore she was determined to quit.

There was a warm breeze across the deck. Sunlight diffused through her windblown hair.

Focused on her, I jumped when Agent Johnson's voice spoke from right behind me.

"Good morning," he said.

"Hi," I grumbled, chagrined that he'd been able to walk right up without me noticing.

"Agent Johnson! Good morning," Julie said with a bright smile.

They had become instant friends. I didn't get it. Didn't make sense to me, but it did to them. And when he was in her presence, a little bit of the façade slipped. I was getting more and more glimpses of the real man under the hardened exterior shell. I guess I wasn't the only one whose best was brought out by her.

"I've been remiss," he said to me as he lit a cigar. "I haven't thanked you."

"Thanked me?"

"For not shooting me in the head the instant I walked into the director's quarters," he said.

"Don't make me regret it," I grinned.

He gave me a look that could freeze iron, a moment later his face cracking open into a broad smile. Then he laughed. An actual laugh!

Seconds later it was gone. I wasn't sure it had happened.

"I'm actually here to discuss something with Ms. Broussard," he said. "And the director would like for you to join him in his office."

"That OK?" I asked Julie.

She leaned forward and kissed me before shooing me on my way. I nodded at Johnson and headed for the door to the interior.

Patterson was sitting at his desk when I walked in after knocking and waiting for him to grant permission to enter. I had dusted off my military manners, learned from when I was in the Army and had begun interacting with him as if he was a superior officer. Our relationship had improved dramatically.

"You wanted to see me, sir?" I asked, standing in front of his desk.

"Take a seat, Mr. Whitman."

When I was comfortable, he closed his laptop and leaned back in his chair. Looking at me, he took a deep breath and started talking.

"I believe we have finally unraveled all of the machinations of the conspirators. I thought you might be interested in the details," he said.

"Very much so, sir." I sat up a little straighter.

"The conspiracy was more widespread than originally thought. The Vice President and the Deputy Director of the CIA were the two highest ranking officials involved. Beneath them were thirty-two other individuals, ranging from FBI agents to CIA officers and three Secret Service agents.

"This cabal, for lack of a better word, has been plotting for some time. You won't recall, due to your personal circumstances, but the Vice President ran against the President for their Party's nomination. And lost. But not by much. That's how he wound up on the President's ticket and was elected.

"Apparently, he wasn't satisfied with waiting for the President to serve out his term. He recruited an old college friend and convinced the President to appoint the man to the position of Deputy Director of the CIA. Only the Director of the CIA need be approved by Congress. The DD requires no such approval and is selected at the discretion of the President.

"With a high level, co-conspirator in place, the VP had access to information and intelligence that allowed them to target persons in government service who were susceptible to recruitment. Some did so out of greed for power or money, others were blackmailed. And there were a few, such as FBI Agent Bering whom your features are copied from, who were resentful of how their career had played out. Were ready to jump at any opportunity to prove a mistake had been made in regards to the assessment of their capabilities."

"He was pissed that he was driving a truck?" I interrupted.

"Basically, yes. He had been an underperforming agent for some time. Repeated reprimands for tardiness, insubordination, sloppy work, things of that sort. This assignment was given to him, against my wishes by the way, as a last opportunity before being dismissed from the Bureau."

Patterson paused and reached forward, picking up a coffee cup and taking a sip. Leaning back, he held it in front of him as he continued.

"Suffice it to say, without detailing every individuals' motivations, that the VP and DD did a good job of selecting the right people. Once their network was in place, the plan to eliminate both the Speaker and the President was put into motion."

"I've never understood their thinking, sir," I interrupted again. "Wouldn't it have been simpler to have a sniper take them out? It seems that would be much less complicated than what they did."

"On the surface, I would agree with that assessment. However, the probability of successfully assassinating *both* the President and the Speaker of the House in this manner is incredibly low. Perhaps one, but not both. They are rarely together in public. In fact, this was the first time in the current President's time in office that it has happened.

"That removes opportunity. Plus, a successful sniper kill is not as simple as the movies make it appear. Yes, there are men, and women, who can do it. But the margin of error is so slim that the attempt is very high risk. And assume that it is successful. If the President is killed first, the Speaker will immediately be taken to a secure location, and his protective detail will be on high alert for months to come, making it exponentially more difficult to reach him.

"And the inverse of that is also true. If the Speaker is killed, security around the President will be trebled. Public appearances will be very limited, if not eliminated. So, to answer your question, they chose the most viable option to achieve their goal."

"Which was?" I asked.

"Agent Bering let it slip when he was attempting to convince you that he was you," Patterson said, taking a sip. "Seizure of power by the VP. Produce evidence of an attempted coup by the military. Arrest every officer above the rank of Lieutenant Colonel, and make an emergency request to the UN for peacekeeper troops. The ultimate goal was to put new senior officers in command. Officers loyal to the new President. Once that was done, he would remove the UN and use the military to fully seize control of the country. Eliminate Congress and the Supreme Court. That would only leave the Executive Branch, and he would have unchecked power. Permanent power, as long as the military remained loyal."

"Bering had those details?" I asked, surprised.

"Apparently. He was a true believer. He was actually responsible for recruiting nearly a third of the conspirators. With his assignment of driving a truck, he traveled all over the United States. With no one watching or paying attention to what he did while on the road, he would meet with people identified by the VP and DD, in person. Feel them out and report back. Once the

VP signed off, he would go back and sit down with the targeted recruit.

"At that point, he'd have an envelope full of cash, or a promise of promotion and expanded power. Or, in a few cases, evidence of the individual's indiscretions. Indiscretions severe enough to ensure they would cooperate to avoid exposure."

"What kind of indiscretions?" I was completely caught up in the story.

"In two cases, the men involved preferred their sexual partners to be young. Very young. There were also instances of homosexual activity that the targeted individuals did not want to become public."

"I don't need to know more," I said, holding my hand up and shaking my head.

"Quite," Patterson said.

"But how did they pull off the assassination? There wasn't a laser designator anywhere on that street within range of the restaurant. I'm guessing a drone?"

"No, not even the VP and DD could pull that off. They had two Hellfire missiles that had been purchased from an Army Master Sergeant at Fort Hood. One of them was used to destroy the jet you were on. Fired from a CIA operated helicopter. It was intended to be the fallback if something went wrong at the restaurant. But, they panicked as you began to close in and decided to use it to take you out. Fortunately, they failed.

"So they fired from a helicopter? Over Anacostia Park?" I asked, surprised.

"No. That's what Mr. Carpenter suggested. Trying to divert investigative resources away from how it was really done. Hellfire missiles can also be fired from static, ground-based launchers. One was assembled inside a warehouse, three miles from the target. Strike coordinates were programmed in to get it into the immediate area once fired.

"On the ground, in front of the restaurant, a Secret Service vehicle was parked at the curb. Part of the President's protective detail. A new generation laser designator was hidden in the rear bumper, painting the target. As the missile entered the area, it detected the reflected laser energy and homed in. In the investigation after the assassination, it was not discovered due to the heavy damage sustained by the vehicle."

I pictured the footage I'd first seen when it happened. Remembered seeing Secret Service

Suburbans burned and twisted, lying on the opposite side of the street from where the missile had detonated. I shook my head, impressed, despite myself, with the meticulous planning this must have required.

"You mentioned Carpenter. How was he recruited? And your assistant?"

"Money. Pure greed. Mr. Carpenter was paid nearly two million dollars into an offshore account over the past 18 months. Ms. Silas received just over half a million dollars in the same manner."

"What happened to the VP and the DD and the rest of the people involved?"

"The VP suffered a massive coronary and died in his sleep last night. The DD was killed in a plane crash in Iraq where he was touring CIA facilities at the same time. Even now, the military is gearing up to go after the insurgents suspected of firing the missile that brought his plane down.

"The others are meeting similar fates. Undercover FBI Agent Bering is currently preparing for a vacation in the Bahamas after his truck was stolen and skidded off the road, bursting into flames. The thief was burned in the fire, which was quite intense as I understand it, and a piece of the wreckage damaged his skull so severely that not even dental records could be used to identify the body. DNA tests were unsuccessful. No record was found on file matching the individual."

"Something else," I said. "That flash drive I gave you. The one with Johnson ordering my death. What did you find out?"

"Masterfully faked, as I suspected. When it's broken down and analyzed, there are some artifacts that give it away, but it was a first rate counterfeit. Mr. Carpenter really outdid himself with that one. Agent Johnson was not amused when he viewed it."

"I imagine not," I said. "But I thought you recorded a message to yourself on that drive. How did it get switched?

"It didn't. Mr. Carpenter at work again. When he put the brief together on the flash drive, at my request, he included the false recording of Agent Johnson ordering your death. He also placed a simple virus on the drive. It was on a timer, so I wouldn't see it when I recorded my message. It activated when the agent in the safe house inserted the drive into his laptop. It erased everything except the faked video of Agent Johnson."

"About that agent..."

"He was part of the conspiracy. Even though Mr. Carpenter could have accomplished the same thing with a simple message from himself, he wanted to muddy the waters and implicate Agent Johnson. And it nearly worked."

I nodded, thinking about how close I'd come to shooting the man.

"There's something else that's been bothering me. How did Agent Bering find us in DC? And he knew details of private conversations we had in the hotel room."

"Through a fellow conspirator in the CIA, he had access to a very specialized tracking and surveillance system. When Ms. Broussard turned on her laptop and connected it to the internet, he was able to find her. I am not well versed in how a specific computer out of billions is detected and located, but the system works very well. It also allows the user to break in to the targeted computer, undetected. When we found Agent Bering's laptop, it was still connected to Ms. Broussard's. And the built-in camera and microphone had been activated. He was able to see anything within the camera's field of view and hear every conversation that occurred."

"That is incredibly frightening," I said, once again amazed at how far technology had progressed in the decade I was in prison.

"Yes. Yes, it is. Especially in the hands of people with bad intentions."

I chose to let that one slide. Now wasn't the time to get into a philosophical discussion about the surveillance tools available to big brother. Then I reminded myself that I was part of big brother now.

"What about Julie's killer?" I asked. "I thought Bering had done it. But even after I put him down, I still remembered her being murdered."

"We've been unable to identify the suspect," Patterson said, watching me closely.

"So there's still someone out there who's involved in the conspiracy?"

"Possibly," he acknowledged. "Unfortunately, since that timeline was collapsed when you saved her, there is no way for us to investigate."

I sat thinking about that for a moment. Worried for Julie's safety.

"Monica Torres. What was she doing in DC?" I changed the subject.

"Wouldn't it be best to leave her in the past, where she belongs?" Patterson asked.

"That's not why I'm asking," I said, shaking my head. "I'm just trying to understand the freak circumstance that put her and me at the same place and time."

Patterson stared at me over his coffee cup for nearly a minute before finally answering.

"She is Monica Hernandez, now. Married to a newly elected Representative from Arizona, Miguel Hernandez. He's in the same political party as the President and was invited to attend the dinner as an inducement to help push through a new piece of legislation that won't go over well in his home state. I'm not a big believer in coincidences, Mr. Whitman, but that's exactly what this was."

I nodded, thinking about that chance encounter. An encounter that had wound up saving my life because Bering had no idea she was in town and I'd seen her. Even if he had, he couldn't have known the thoughts in my head.

"There was a boy with her. The right age. She called him Roberto. Is he...?"

"Your son?"

Patterson finished the question for me. I met his eyes and nodded.

"Do you really want me to find out?" He asked, eyebrows raised questioningly.

"Let me think about it," I said after a long pause. "Was anyone else from the project involved?"

"No. With the assistance of the FBI and Secret Service, we have aggressively investigated every member of the project team over the past three weeks. Myself included. No other improprieties were found."

"Did they investigate me?"

"Not for the same reason," he said. "With Agent Johnson's prompting, the investigation that was already underway into the judge, sheriff's office and prosecutor, where you were convicted, was expanded."

"And?"

"It is not final, but as of this morning, the US Attorney is preparing to begin handing down indictments. There is no question that you shot the two deputies, but as more evidence comes to light, the consensus is that you should not have been charged, much less convicted. At most, you were guilty of self-defense."

Dirk Patton

I was stunned. This had been a pipe dream for the past decade or more. Hell, it was every convict's dream. But it never came true.

"You mean…" I couldn't put my thoughts into words.

"After speaking with the Attorney General and the President this morning, I expect you will be receiving a Presidential pardon sometime within the next few months. Posthumously, of course."

"What?"

"You're dead, Mr. Tracy," he said, using my real name for the first time. "Executed by the state of Arizona. You no longer have your face or even your fingerprints. But your name will be cleared. Eventually. Once the legal process plays out."

"I can't go back?" I asked, head spinning.

"Not as Robert Tracy, no. That man is dead."

"What are you telling me? I have to stay here? You're going to force me to work for you? Threaten to kill me again, like when I first arrived?"

"No, Mr. Whitman. In retrospect, that was a mistake on my part. You are not a prisoner.

Not any longer, as far as I'm concerned. I'm telling you that you are free to go. Do whatever you wish. As long as you don't do it as Robert Tracy. And remember that you are bound by the National Secrets Act and can never talk about this project. If you do..."

I sat staring at him, mouth hanging open.

"But, I'm hoping you will choose to stay with the project. You are still the only asset we have, and I believe you can see the value of the work we do."

I continued to just sit there. Unable to speak.

"If you do, you are already an FBI Agent. Mr. Bering. You would fully assume the identity and the pay and benefits of a veteran employee of the Bureau. You could come and go as you pleased, as long as you were available and ready when we needed you. In fact, the project will provide you with a modest home in the Houston area, which is only a short helicopter ride away. You will not have to live in the facility any longer."

"You're serious," I said, finally able to put a coherent thought into words.

"Very, Agent Bering," he smiled. "We need your help. Without you, Project Athena is nothing more than an incredibly expensive line item in a black budget."

We stared at each other for a few moments, the silence stretching out.

"You don't need to answer this minute," Patterson finally said. "You need to finish healing before you're medically cleared to return to duty, anyway. Take some time off and complete your recuperation. I'm sure Ms. Broussard would be a lovely companion while you're convalescing in the Bahamas."

"Bahamas?"

Patterson smiled and leaned forward, sliding a thick, manila envelope across his desk.

"Passports for you both. Airfare, first class of course, and details on the resort where a suite is reserved in your name, Agent Bering. And some cash and a credit card, compliments of the President of the United States. Take Ms. Broussard and think about my offer."

I had walked out of the director's office so stunned I didn't know what to do. The vacation was nice, but the thought that I was going to be exonerated would take a while to fully sink in.

And I had a job offer to think about, and soon learned that Julie did as well.

Agent Johnson had asked her to join the analyst team as a research assistant. Not very glamorous, but it paid well and brought the only civilian in the world who was aware of the Athena Project into the fold. Both of us had already decided to accept the offers on the table.

"Oh, wait," I said to Julie.

It was getting close to time to catch the resort shuttle, and we'd left the gift shop without purchasing anything. On the way out, I'd seen something that reminded me I'd forgotten to pack a specific item. Running back inside, I grabbed a blinder, like air travelers wear over their eyes to block out light and get some sleep on a long flight.

All too clearly, I remembered sitting with Dr. Anholts as she sped through the footage from my implanted data chip. The one that recorded everything I saw. Seeing the momentary flash of Julie's bare flesh.

I cared too much about her to have footage of our escapades recorded and available for government review. Paying for the blinder, I rushed back to where she waited for me.

"Seriously? What's with you and either complete darkness or wearing a blindfold? I'm starting to think there's something wrong with me that you don't want to see me naked. Or are you imagining someone else when you're with me?"

"Absolutely nothing wrong with you," I smiled, tucking the blinders into my pack. "And you are, without a doubt, the center of my attention when I'm with you. I promise."

"Then what is it? Why the blinders?"

"You really don't want to know," I smiled, kissed her and led the way to the curb to board the bus.

59

"Are you still secure?"

"Yes. The director had a full review and vetting of all staff. I came out smelling like a rose."

The two men were seated in a booth at the back of a dark restaurant. It was mid-afternoon, and the lunch crowd had already departed. It was too early for dinner and, other than a tired waitress, they had the place to themselves.

"That's good," the older of the two said. "But there are concerns about your performance."

"Fuck your concerns," the younger man growled, taking the last sip of a beer. "I came out of this clean. I'm still in place. How many others can say that?"

"You didn't follow your instructions."

"There was no point. If I'd killed him by the time I located him, it could have drawn attention to me. It was too late. He'd already taken actions that stopped the plan. Maybe if I'd been given better information in a timelier manner, I could have intervened."

They fell silent as the waitress walked up. She removed their empty glasses from the table and left a check when they declined to order more drinks.

"That nuance is the only reason you're still walking around," the older man said, placing cash on the table to cover the check. "However, there are additional concerns about the woman."

"What concerns?"

"In your debrief, you mentioned that she commented you seemed familiar when she met you."

"So what? She can't remember something that didn't happen."

"But that's the concern. What if she does? We're dealing with a new frontier, Mr. Cox. There are too many unknowns when it comes to Time. Can you say for certain she won't wake up one morning and remember you were the one who tortured and interrogated her? Who pressed a gun to her head and pulled the trigger?"

"No, I guess I can't. But who would believe her? Where would the proof be?"

"The Director would not need proof. He understands that memories of events that can't possibly have occurred are actually memories of parallel timelines. Timelines that collapsed. And the asset will as well. By your own report, he is becoming a formidable force."

"Nothing I can't handle when the time comes."

"Perhaps," the older man mused. "Regardless, the decision has been made. The young lady will be eliminated. Your position and access inside the Athena Project is too valuable to risk. Especially now. Events are already in motion for the next phase of the plan. We cannot allow her to remember why she felt she knew you."

"Are those my orders?" Ray asked.

"No. We have another agent in place of whom you're unaware. That individual will solve the problem, Mr. Cox."

DATE DUE